TIDEWATER

Antoinette
Stockenberg

St. Martin's Paperbacks

TIDEWATER

Copyright © 2001 by Antoinette Stockenberg.

ISBN: 0-312-97730-1

Printed in the United States of America

St. Martin's Paperbacks edition / June 2001

St. Martin's Paperbacks are published by St. Martin's Press, 175 Fifth Avenue, New York, N.Y. 10010.

10 9 8 7 6 5 4 3 2 1

For Steve Axelrod—
Thank you, sir, again and still.

TIDEWATER

Prologue

ABIGAIL. IT SEEMED like such a good name at the time.

"Source of joy," that's what the word meant according to the baby-name booklet that Sarann had picked up at the checkout register of her grocery store. Four months later and with no man at her side, Sarann had cradled her seven-pound, two-ounce Abigail and marveled at just how much joy she was holding. That was twelve long years ago.

It seemed like such a good name at the time.

Chapter 1

THE BLACK NIGHT and pounding rain were doing little to improve Sarann's mood. She was rattled to the point of fear.

When had she last filled the tank?

It had to be over a month ago, and yet here she was, still rolling along on three-quarters full. Obviously she must have stopped recently at a gas station—but when? Where? The effort to remember consumed her: she drove straight through a red light and got pulled over immediately by a cop.

Where had he come from? Sarann didn't know the answer to that one, either. Her hand was shaking as she handed him her license and registration through the partly rolled-down window.

"I'm sorry, Officer, really," she said, wincing under the lash of driving rain. "I was totally preoccupied. I never saw the light."

"Is *that* the reason," the cop muttered.

He beamed a small flashlight on her Massachusetts license and the now-damp registration. It was clear that he resented being forced out of the dry warmth of his car for the sole purpose of ticketing someone else's absent-minded stupidity. If Sarann had been rushing to an emergency room, maybe, or returning home from a wake . . . but all she was doing was driving home on a tank of gas that seemed too full. It would be pointless to try to explain.

"It's my gas tank. I don't understand it; it never seems to go empty anymore," she said, powerless to stop the stream of her babble. "I can't remember when I last filled up. I'll have to, to, you know, start using American Express, start

keeping records of, you know, everything I do—you know?
Start taking notes and things like that?"

The ponchoed officer gave her an appraising look, then
went off with her documents back to his squad car, presumably to fetch his Breathalyzer.

Good grief, Sarann, get a grip. The only thing worse than
going crazy was announcing out loud that she was doing it.

She drummed her fingertips nervously on the leather-
bound steering wheel of her Mercedes while she waited. The
sound was louder than the pound of the rain, louder than the
beat of her heart. The message in it was earsplittingly clear:
shutup shutup shutup shutup!

The officer returned.

"You can go, Mrs. Bonniface," he said, handing her back
her license. "Please drive carefully. The roads are slick. You
could easily get in an accident on a wild night like this." He
nodded a dismissal and then beat a retreat through the pouring rain.

It was an about-face. Apparently he had figured out who
she was: the wife of one of the most well-regarded men in
Farnham, certainly the most generous, a man beloved by all.
Sarann had been married to Rodger Bonniface for nearly a
year and she had known him for five years before that, but
every day she learned a little more about the depth of affection—and influence—that he enjoyed around town.

Or maybe the officer was just being nice. Sarann slipped
her license into a glove-soft wallet and tossed the registration
on the passenger seat.

And then she reconsidered. Better to put it back where it
belonged, in the glove compartment, right now, while she
was thinking of it, before she forgot. The way her mother
had once begun to forget. First the little things. Then the big.

*Who are you? Who said you could be here? Get out right
now, you, or I'll call the cops. Get out! Out!*

Sarann could still hear her mother's voice, shrill and terrified; could still see her mother's eyes, round and green and blank with paranoia. The day that her mother hadn't recognized her had been the single most shocking of Sarann's life. For years now, and probably until the day she died, Sarann's mood would plunge whenever she herself forgot the most trivial thing—the name of a movie she'd just seen, or the outfit she'd worn to work on the preceding day.

Or the last time she'd topped off the tank.

Sarann pulled into the flow of traffic with ridiculous caution. The patrolman could well be watching her, after all— unless, of course, she was just being paranoid.

Rain hammered the roof of her wagon and swept over the windshield in sheets as she continued on her way in a slow crawl home. Puddles of water pooling on the shoulder rose up in high arcs as she drove through them, anxious to show up before Rodger became worried.

Her husband had seen firsthand how forgetful she'd been lately and was doing his best to reassure her that her state of distraction was perfectly normal. His most recent try had been at breakfast.

"You're about to open your own shop, for Pete's sake," he had said as he cracked the fat end of an egg with a spoon. "There are a million things to do, contractors to oversee, more antiques to acquire—what did you expect? Of course stuff is slipping past you. You can't remember every little thing."

"The store won't be ready to move into for weeks," she had pointed out. "I'm not all *that* busy yet."

There was a silence—far too long for Sarann to feel comfortable with it.

"Well, then," Rodger had said in a softer, more tentative voice, "maybe you should look somewhere else for the reason you're so distracted. Could the reason be Abby?"

The name was a hot coal on a raw nerve. "Abby? Why Abby?"

It was such a dumb question. The man wasn't deaf; obviously he had been hearing the recent arguments between her daughter and her.

Rodger had shrugged offhandedly as he scooped the oozy egg with a monogrammed spoon into a porcelain bowl. "She's growing up, your little girl; it's bound to be hard for you to let go. That's natural, Sarann," he had said, looking up with a quick, sympathetic smile. "You've raised her yourself. You two have always been a team. You've done—you're doing—a great job. But Abby's twelve now, and feeling her way."

Sarann had responded with a vehemence that surprised even her. "She's not just feeling her way, Rodger; she's roaring like a freight train toward a washed-out bridge!"

"It's only a phase, Sarann," he had reassured her, and then he had come around to her side of the table and had wrapped his arms around her in a show of support. "She's at an age when knowing about her father is important to her. You can't really blame Abby," he had said. "If you're going to blame anyone, blame the teacher who dreamed up the family-tree project. Personally, I've never been a fan of assignments like that; they can be unnerving for certain parents. Family skeletons aren't always six feet under, after all."

He had kissed Sarann's cheek in sympathy and added, "It's hard on a kid when a parent dies before the child is old enough to remember him. Sooner or later Abby will have picked your brain all she can, and then she'll stop. Trust me. It's only a phase."

Instead of being grateful to him, Sarann had shouted, "Don't tell *me* what phase Abby's in, Rodger; I'm her *mother*!"

And then she'd wrenched free of him, grabbed her purse and jacket, and left him standing flabbergasted on the quarry-tiled floor of their two-hundred-year-old kitchen.

That was this morning, and although Sarann had called

her husband at the Academy later in the day and apologized, she was still feeling guilty. He had been trying to help. She had behaved like a shit.

She glanced at the low-lit clock on the dashboard: seven fifteen. So much for the chicken with citrus sauce. The fixings for Rodger's favorite dinner were sitting uncooked in two brown bags behind her.

She drove down dark and winding River Street, then pulled onto the graveled drive of the wine-red, gambrel-roofed house, known all around as Tidewater, that Rodger had lived in all of his life. Lights were on both upstairs and down, pouring their soft glow through multipaned windows onto fat-budded rhododenrons and leafing summersweet that lined the stone foundation.

Sarann glanced up at her daughter's bedroom. *She's at that damned computer again*, she realized with a sinking heart. Her daughter's obsession with the Internet had become a source of constant bickering between them. Sarann wanted to allow Abby enough access to be stimulating but not too much to be addictive. It was a tricky balancing act.

The light was on in Rodger's study downstairs. He was either slogging through a pile of papers or he was on the phone, managing some crisis or other. Sarann didn't envy her husband his position as headmaster of Faxton Academy. It entailed a ridiculous amount of stress and pressure, more so because he was grandson to the academy's founder: he couldn't walk away if the going got tough, or accept a better offer at another boarding school.

Probably the only thing more stressful than managing kids with Attention Deficit Disorder was managing privileged kids with ADD: Rodger was always meeting with their high-powered parents, who were themselves impatient, demanding, and used to getting their way. After working in the headmaster's office for several years, Sarann had seen first-hand how well Rodger was able to keep his cool. Still, the stress factor at the exclusive academy—either despite its small size or because of it—was sky-high.

Poor Rodger. She wasn't making his life any easier.

"Sorry, sorry, sorry," she said to her husband at the door, handing the grocery bags into his outstretched arms. "I stopped to check on the shop. The contractor was still there and he had a lot of questions. I would have called—"

"But you left your cell phone on the kitchen counter," Rodger said with a wry smile on his handsome face. He set the bags carefully on a marble-topped table that sat in the hall, then pushed his reading glasses over the top of his receding hair and arched his back, easing out the fatigue.

"I was worried about you," he admitted as she hung up her rain-spattered jacket. "I think you ought to have a second cell phone, this one just for the car."

"Oh, one is enough—really," Sarann said. *I won't forget it again. I won't.*

Wanting to move past the painful issue of her breakfast tantrum, she hugged her husband and said, "You're right, I think; it *is* Abby." On tiptoe, she gave him a kiss on his cheek. "She's driving me cr—up a wall lately, and I'm taking it out on you. I'm sorry."

Rodger kissed the top of her rain-dampened hair affectionately and said, "Nothing to be sorry for. I never should have put in my two cents."

"But I *want* you to put in your two cents! We're both her parents now, you as well as me—I. And think of all the kids that have passed through your doors. Who knows more about children than you do?"

He answered quietly, "Just about any real father."

He hadn't had children of his own during his first marriage, but it was still hard for Sarann to believe he felt so humbled by the fact. "Ohh, you know that's not true," she said, reassuring him. They had been trying to have children for nine months now, which wasn't very long; it would only be a matter of time.

She ran her fingertips across his cheek, already stubbly with the day's growth. She preferred him this way—slightly rumpled, without his tie, a man instead of a headmaster. He seemed more approachable. It made it easier for her to accept the astonishing fact that she was his wife now, and not merely the assistant to his secretary.

Sarann had a sudden, vivid flashback to the night of his proposal. She had been working late, determined not to drop the ball while she filled in for his ailing secretary. Rodger had offered to take Sarann to a late supper, but she had declined because Abby was alone at home and waiting for her.

Despite having worked at the academy for four years, Sarann had been uneasy about spurning her employer's friendly offer. But far from taking it personally, Rodger had shrugged and said, "If we were married, Abby wouldn't be alone and on her own right now."

Sarann had no answer to that except . . . yes. After a whirlwind engagement, they were married in a beautiful, tasteful ceremony. She was grateful to Rodger for her new life.

She shook herself free of the memory. "You must be starved," she said, taking up one of the grocery bags.

Rodger picked up the other and followed her into the kitchen. "Actually, I figured Abby might be hungry, so I heated up the stew from last night for us."

"Oh, good."

"But she didn't come down. She said she would later."

"What? Rodger! You have to put your foot down with her. She can't just—"

"Yes, she can, Sarann," he said, shrugging. "I won't go ordering her around," he added as he took out a bag of oranges. "She has to come of her own free will."

"Baloney! She'll come to dinner when she's called, period. Damn it, I wish you'd take my side just *once* when-ever—"

She was doing it again, picking a fight again. She reined herself in and changed the subject altogether. In a more off-hand tone she said, "Any good mail?" and picked up the stack on the counter.

Rodger, in a mild snit of his own now, said, "I've taken all of my mail out; the rest is yours. Well, I've got work to do." He left her to put away the groceries herself.

Sighing, Sarann began flipping through the hefty pile, sur-prised again at how a marriage to someone of stature could instantly quadruple her mail. The day's haul included *Art and Antiques, Colonial Homes*, a dozen upscale catalogues, ap-peals from three or four charities, an equal number of VISA applications, an invitation to a lecture on historic architecture, another one to dinner—and a bill that she'd just paid, re-turned for lack of postage.

She stared at the envelope, to which she clearly remem-bered attaching a peel-away stamp. It would take a fireman's hose to get one of those things off.

I did stamp this envelope. I did.
Didn't I?

Sarann felt a familiar rush of heat to her cheeks. She laid the envelope carefully back on the pile and, just as deliber-ately, finished emptying the second bag of groceries. After that she turned a low fire under the pot of stew still on the stove, and whispered in a shaking voice to no one in partic-ular, "She will come when she is called."

Abigail Johnson Bonniface sat hunched like an elf owl in front of her computer, searching through cyberspace for only God knew what.

Standing in the doorway of her daughter's room, Sarann had to make an effort to control her rising irritation as she said, "It was rude not to come down after your father heated up supper especially for you."

"Oh, please," Abby said without turning around. "Speaking of rude, don't you ever knock anymore?"

Sarann gritted her teeth and said, "Fair enough. I'll knock from now on. But it would be a lot easier to be nice to you if you were nice to others."

"When am I not nice?"

"Right now. By not looking at me when you speak to me."

She saw her daughter's shoulders rise and then fall on an aggrieved exhale.

Bracing herself on the arms of her swivel chair, Abby spun it slowly around to face her mother. Intelligence and anger flashed from heavily lashed blue eyes.

"Tell me who my father is."

Here we go again. "I've told you, Abby. Many, many times. A man named Nick McElwyn."

"Then why was our name Johnson instead of McElwyn until you got married last year? Why were you using your maiden name all my life?"

"I've told you that, too: lots of women had begun to keep their own names by the time you were born."

"Then why did you all of a sudden decide to take the name Bonniface when you got married this time?"

"Because your stepfather isn't like your birth father. Rodger wanted us to share his name."

"So my real father was ashamed of us, is that what you're trying to say?"

Surprised to find herself in new, dark territory, Sarann said carefully, "Your father just . . . never insisted the way Rodger did. And I'm a different person now than I was then."

Like a cat who smells fear, Abby pressed on with the hunt. "Why don't we have more pictures of my birth father?

Only one tiny photograph of some people sitting around a couch. And it's overexposed. It sucks."

"Oh, Abby. I've explained it to you so many times. There was a fire in the apartment we lived in, and my shoebox of photos was burned."

The fire had been a grease fire, and Abby had slept peacefully in her crib through the whole thing, but never mind; at least there'd been a fire. As for a so-called photo collection, there'd never been one of those. There'd only been the one snapshot, which Sarann had kept tucked in her wallet for years. The only reason she had shown it to Abby at all was because it *was* so overexposed.

Sarann locked gazes with her bright, calculating offspring and felt suddenly vulnerable. And more than a little frightened. She added in a tiptoe voice, "Doesn't it matter to you at all that we have a thousand pictures of you and me together?"

Sensing weakness, Abby lashed out. "You don't know who my father is, do you. You don't have a *clue*."

"Abby!" The swipe of her paw was so swift, so deep, that for a minute Sarann had to think whether she should know or not. But yes, she did know. Nick McElwyn, an up-and-coming attorney, had been run over as he dashed across the street against the light, in the rain, at twilight. It was a terrible, terrible tragedy, and he was dead. That was Sarann's story, and by God, she was sticking to it. She took a step backward and began to turn, ready to run.

Too late. Abby pounced.

"You're lying! You've been lying to me, like, all my *life*. You never married my father. How could you, if you don't even know who he *is*?"

Sarann was forced to defend the indefensible. She turned back to her daughter and tried to look bored. Impatient. Indignant. She failed in all three and fell back on the tired old refrain: "I've told you: Your father is Nick McElwyn."

"Then why can't I find him anywhere? I wrote to city hall in Norfield, and they don't have any death record for a Nick McElwyn."

"You *wrote* to them!"

"E-mailed," Abby said with a lift of her chin. "They e-mailed back that they don't have a record of death. So you lied. And by the way, I haven't tracked down a record of marriage, either."

"I can't believe you went behind my back," said Sarann, stunned. She closed the door behind her in an effort to muffle the coming brawl.

"Admit it, Mom! I'm a one-night stand."

"No. I told you."

"Oh, you *told* me!" Abby said. Her voice was high, loud, and clear. "You haven't told me *anything*. Where did he die? What street corner? What kind of car ran him down? What hospital did they take him to? What cemetery is he buried in—and *don't* try telling me you scattered his ashes at sea. I'm not a little girl anymore."

She *was* a little girl, going on forty. There was such betrayal, such fury, such disillusionment in her eyes that Sarann had to look away. Where was the darling girl who'd always adored her?

Sarann stared blankly at a red paisley pillow, bought for the shop, that she had recently decided would be perfect for the overstuffed chair of her daughter's room. During that brief space of time, her resolve faltered. "When you're older," she said, "you'll understand."

That's all it took.

"I *knew* it!" cried Abby, jumping up in shrill, panicky triumph. "I *am* a one-night stand!"

Exactly that. In the single most collossal indiscretion of her life, Sarann had managed to get high, get laid, and get pregnant, all in the space of a single torrid encounter with a stranger. She carried a list of excuses for her reckless behavior that was as long as her arm. She was eighteen, inexperienced, a casualty of booby-trapped brownies. He was not much older, damnably good-looking, damnably charming, damnably carefree. They were a volatile mix, and they had exploded. And Sarann had been forging through life with a limp ever since.

Her resolve returned; it was a habit by now, not easily abandoned. "You are *not* a one-night stand, Abby."

"I'll never believe you! Never! And I'll never forgive you for having me!" Abby sprinted to the bed, threw herself across it, and burst into tears.

It was bitterly ironic: Sarann had friends who were trying for years to get pregnant, presumably so that they could raise children like Abby who would one day make their lives misery. Sarann, no slouch, had managed to get the job done in a few short hours.

How could she possibly be a good example to a daughter who knew the truth behind her conception? "I would never hurt you, Abby," Sarann said, sitting on the side of the bed. "Never. I'd sooner cut off my arm. Please believe me."

Abby lifted her head in a teary-eyed look of contempt. Without a word, she got herself back under control, sat down in her computer chair, and swiveled it around to face the screen again.

Her mother was dismissed.

Chapter 2

SUNDAY WAS DEFINITELY Abigail's favorite day of the week. It was the only day she had the house to herself for a while. On Sunday her stepdad often went to his office at the school because that's when it was quietest, and on Sunday her mom went to check on her new shop because that's when the contractors weren't working on it. People needed some peace and quiet so they could think; Abigail understood that very well.

That's why on Sundays she searched for her father.

Of course, she didn't have a driver's license and couldn't go searching by car, so she had to let her fingers do the walking—on the keyboard of her computer. After two months, she had a set routine. The first thing she did was go down to the kitchen to make some tea. (After experimenting with all different kinds, she found that two bags of Lipton made her think the best. With three spoons of sugar and lots of milk, it actually tasted pretty good.)

After that, Abigail took her cup of tea—and Molly, of course, draped over her shoulder—upstairs to her room. Then she plopped Molly on top of the warm computer monitor, where the old orange cat was always willing to stay, and she latched the rickety, thin door to her room. At the beginning, she used to prop an armchair up against the door, but, wouldn't you know, her mother caught her at it and wanted to know what Abigail was hiding, and that's really what started the whole long war between them.

Because it *was* war. You couldn't call it anything else, not when your own mother wouldn't tell you who your own father was. Nick McElwyn, a lawyer? It was so lame. At least her mother could have made up a more interesting career for him.

If he was a lawyer before he died, then why weren't they rich when Abigail was growing up? A lawyer would have life insurance, even if he was just starting out, Abigail was almost positive. Why did she and her mother always live in tiny apartments and take buses, and when they did get a car, why was it rusty and always breaking down?

A lawyer wouldn't do that to his family, leave them without life insurance. And if he really got run over—*obviously* they would sue someone and get tons of money from that. So, as far as Abigail was concerned, Nick McElwyn couldn't have been a lawyer, although it wouldn't hurt to check.

And she was almost positive that Nick McElwyn wasn't dead, either. So far, every Nick McElwyn that she'd found searching public records on the Internet was older than the guy in the photograph would be, thirteen years later.

Abigail picked up the framed eight-by-ten photograph, blown up from her mother's wallet-sized one, of the man who was supposed to be her father. She studied the picture closely, but there was nothing in it she hadn't already memorized: the tacky furniture, the beer cans on the end tables, the empty plates on the coffee table, the three guys and two girls in jeans and tee shirts, all sitting around and laughing about something. They looked like they were having a really, really good time. One of the girls had her head thrown back and her mouth was wide open and *huge*, she was laughing so loud. You could see her fillings.

Abigail's mother was the one who took the picture, which was too bad, because Abigail was sure that if she could just see her mother's face, she'd know for sure which guy was her real father. As it was, all she had was her mother's word that it was the man on the hassock, his face turned partly toward the camera, his features washed out by the flash. They were nice features, what Abigail could make of them. He wasn't gross-looking or anything. He had an okay nose, kind of heavy eyebrows, and who knew about his chin—his shoulder was covering it. He wasn't smiling, so she couldn't even tell if he had teeth. But anyway, he and Abigail didn't seem very much alike.

In her heart, Abigail was convinced that her father was actually one of the other two guys, the one at the end of the couch. He looked so cool. He was the only one wearing a turtleneck—black—and he had a really great smile and there was just something about the way he was leaning back on the couch and looking at the camera. Could he maybe be looking at Sarann Johnson instead? One thing Abigail knew: she was never going to get a straight answer from her mother.

Which is why it had to be war.

Abigail sighed and stood the framed photo on its stand again, and took a sip of tea. In the "search" box on her computer screen, she typed "Massachusetts Bar Association."

Sarann was in her empty shop on Main Street, holding color strips up against the walls, when one of the competition popped in.

"Come across the street; I want you to see this," said Gloria Dijon, flamboyant owner of Glorious Stuff. She plucked the paint strips out of Sarann's hand, tossed them on the cardtable, and began dragging Sarann from her shop.

Their friendship, such as it was, was new. Sarann had never been taken under anyone's wing before, but since Gloria had the wingspan of a bald eagle, Sarann wasn't sure it would be wise to resist. Besides, secretly she admired Gloria's breezy confidence. The woman had gone through four husbands and a dozen careers in her fifty-six years, but did she have an inferiority complex about any of it?

Not in the least. Her motto was, what doesn't kill you makes you stronger. She didn't care at all what other people thought (which was just as well, because everyone thought she was at least a dozen apples short of a bushel). What Gloria Dijon did care about was whether or not she was listening to her Inner Voice.

Earlier that day at a flea market in Vermont, Gloria's Inner Voice had told her to plunk down a lot of cold hard cash on a carousel frog.

"A carousel . . . frog? Won't it have limited appeal?" asked Sarann as she and Gloria stood gazing at the waist-high, carved wooden creature, which was dressed in a lavender shirt and checkered knickers and wearing a sailor's cap. "Aren't carousel figures usually, you know—horses?"

Gloria flipped her dyed blond curls over her shoulder and said, "That's what makes him valuable. Besides, look at his face. Who could resist a face like that? What a cute, cute, *cutie* you are," she said to the creature, bending over it. She planted a palm on each of its cheeks and kissed it on its mouth with a noisy smack.

Smiling, Sarann folded her arms and said, "He's not gonna turn into a prince, Gloria, no matter how hard you try."

"Tell me something I don't know," said the older woman, straightening up with a little groan. "I keep marrying frogs who keep turning out to be frogs."

Gloria was financially well off, Sarann knew, so it was a safe bet that there would never be a shortage of frogs lining up to be kissed by her.

Sarann glanced around the shop, crammed to its exposed beams with whatever had caught Gloria's eye—from a pink leatherette sofa to King Kong ephemera—and said, "I believe the frog will feel right at home here."

"I think so. Let's put him in the window. Give me a hand, would you?"

After a struggle, they managed to get the unwieldy creature nicely snugged down on a patch of Astroturf alongside a pair of flamingos under an inflatable palm tree. The resulting tableau wasn't quite tacky enough to be called camp; it mostly just seemed weird. In any case, it wasn't terribly New England, which was why people came to the quaint, seafaring town of Farhnam in the first place—because Farnham had dozens of shops filled with charming regional antiques like armoires and seamen's chests and nautical lamps that could be wired for electricity and mounted on someone's front porch in Kansas City.

On the other hand, only at Glorious Stuff could one find King Kong earrings and beanbag chairs and a nightstand made out of 7UP cans.

"Y'know, Sarann, if you see anything here that you'd like for your own shop, just point; I'll let you have it at cost."

"Oh, no, really; I couldn't."

For so many reasons. Sarann could just see the look on Rodger's face if he ever found out that he was bankrolling inflatable palm trees. She may as well establish a porno shop.

A clock—in the shape of a clown clutching a bowling bowl that had a dial on it—struck five and Sarann said, "I'd better get going. I have to stop off at the drugstore before it closes."

"I guess I'll take off, too; business is dead today," said Gloria, slapping the dust from her long denim skirt. "It's too nice out; the tourists are all on the river, taking in the wildlife. By the way, I'll be in New Jersey visiting my daughter for a few days, so . . . I'll see you at the fundraiser next Saturday, yes?"

"Fundraiser?" Sarann blinked and fought back a familiar tightening in her stomach. "What fundraiser?"

"The charity auction for the garden club?"

"That's next Saturday?"

"When did you think it was?"

"Not then," Sarann said. "Whenever it's supposed to be, I wrote it down on my calendar when what's-her-name— Ginny, that's it!—asked me to donate something." She frowned, then shook her head. "I know I got it right. I double-checked the date after I hung up."

"You should have triple-checked it, then," said Gloria with typical bluntness. "It's next Saturday."

"No, please. Don't say that," Sarann begged. "You're wrong; you must be wrong!"

That provoked a crisp response from her friend. "I'm never wrong, Sarann. Not to mention I just got off the phone with Vivian; we're going together. I was about to ask if you wanted to come with us—but apparently you plan to go some other day," she added dryly.

"I'm sorry; obviously you're right. I must have marked it down on the wrong Saturday. A stupid mistake."

"People make them."

"Me, more than others," Sarann said, distressed.

"Take gingko biloba. I do."

"Yes . . . gingko . . . it's worth a try."

"Now—where did I leave my keys?"

Rodger Bonniface got kicked out of his office by his secretary—the same woman who had worked for his father for eleven years—on the grounds that she wouldn't be able to get anything done if he was going to be hanging around and interrupting her every two minutes. She had come in specifically to catch up on her filing, and she was mightily annoyed that her boss had chosen to occupy the same space at the same time.

"Out! Out! Out!" she said, shooing him from the office as if he were a stray cat begging at the back door.

At loose ends, Rodger drove home with every intention of forcing himself to work there. He went upstairs to change and was surprised to find his stepdaughter rummaging through the shelves at the back of the closet, too engrossed to hear his approach.

"Abby?"

The sound of her stepfather's voice behind her sent the girl dropping awkwardly down from the chair and staggering back into his arms. He steadied her and said, "What're you looking for?"

She whirled from his grasp. Wide-eyed, she said, "I don't know."

"You don't know?"

"Ballpoints!"

"In here?"

"Well . . . I couldn't find any in my room! Mom is always borrowing them from me!"

Rodger cocked his head at her. "Okay, Abby, what's going on?"

"Nothing! Nothing's going on."

His brows drew together in disappointed skepticism. "You can tell me, honey," he said quietly. "I'm sure you know that."

Her look turned wary. "It's . . . complicated," she mumbled, letting her gaze fall to the needlepoint rug at their feet. "I'd rather not say." She slipped her hands into the hip pockets of her jeans and outlined an amber rose with the toe of her sneaker.

Her stepfather nodded but said nothing. The girl remained quiet as well. "And yet," he remarked at last, "I think I'm entitled to know why you're going through my things."

Her head shot up. "Not *your* things, Dad," she said quickly. "I told you!"

"Okay, your mother's things, then. Abby, we're a family now. That means that what affects one of us affects all of us. You get that, don't you?"

Instead of answering, Abigail looked away from him and out the west window, where light from the setting sun slid through the opened Indian shutters, highlighting her rich black hair. When she turned back to face her stepfather, her eyes had tears in them.

"She's keeping something secret from me," Abigail said
in a subdued voice. "I don't know what it is." Without re-
moving her hands from her pockets, she lifted one shoulder
in a gesture of girlish helplessness.

"Ah. A secret. That's not good." Rodger removed his
glasses and began to clean them with a handkerchief from
his hip pocket. "Would you like me to try to find out for
you?"

Abby snorted and looked back down at the rug. "As *if*."

"We're talking about your birth father, I assume?"

"What else?"

"Fine. I'll sit down and have a serious talk with your
mother tonight about him. I promise."

Abigail threw up her hands and let them flap onto her
hips in a sudden, melodramatic gesture of despair. "Don't
you get it? She's not going to tell you, either! It's, like, an
awesome waste of time!"

Rodger grinned and said, "Hey, at least it'll be my time
we're be wasting and not yours. Homework all done?"

"Homework? That's a farce. It took about three minutes,"
she said over her shoulder as she turned to leave the room.

"Let me pull some strings," he called after her. "I think I
can get you into Harvard next fall."

That got her to stop in the hall and turn around, grinning
widely. "I'd accept the offer, except all the guys there are
geeks."

Her stepfather laughed and said, "Watchit, kid; I'm from
Hah-vad."

"Welll— . . ."

"Seriously? You think I'm a geek?"

"No, I was only teasing," she said, suddenly looking uncomfortable. "Anyway—I have to call Heather. See ya."

She left her stepfather standing alone in the doorway.
Smiling a little ruefully, he hooked his wire-rimmed glasses
over his ears as he stepped back into the room. On his way

to the bathroom, he caught a glimpse of himself in the mirror as he passed by the armoire. Backing up, he took a hard look at himself. With a frown he dabbed at his graying temples and smoothed a hand over his receding hair.

His scowl turned to sudden outrage when he saw, in the reflection of the mirror, an orange-and-white cat hop up onto the George II wing chair behind him and stretch luxuriously in obvious preparation for a nap there.

"Forget it!" he snapped. He scooped up the offending feline with one hand and half hurled her out of the chair.

Chapter 3

DINNER WAS A strained affair.

Sarann, Rodger, and Abby sat, as they always did, at the drop-leaf table in the cozy space that once had been a keeping room. Candles flickered, as they always did, in the draft that wound its way through all twelve rooms of the old Colonial. And Molly begged, as she always did, for anything that smelled like meat, fish, or angel food cake.

But spirits and conversation were at an all-time low. Sarann was too disheartened to say very much, afraid that she'd trip herself up in some new memory lapse—afraid, for that matter, that she might say, "Pass the camera," when she really meant "the salt."

Abby said nothing at all, at least to her mother. When she wanted something, she either pointedly asked her stepfather for it or she made a production of rising from her chair, going to the side of the table that had what she needed, and carrying it back to her place. It was hurtful behavior; but then, Abby was feeling hurt.

It was only after Sarann left the table and was settled with her stationery catalogues in the front sitting room that she heard her daughter in low conversation with Rodger back in the kitchen. Sarann couldn't make out what they were saying above the sound of dishes being loaded into the dishwasher, but she felt uneasy, even embarrassed. It was obvious that they were talking about her.

Eventually Rodger walked in carrying tea things on a tray. At the same time, Sarann heard Abby stomping noisily up the back stairs, apparently to make the point that she couldn't stand the sight of her mother and thank God there was another way to her room than through the sitting room.

"She never reads with us in the evening anymore," Sarann said, not without irony, as she laid her catalogues aside to accept the porcelain cup and saucer that Rodger handed her. "I miss that."

He smiled and said, "I predict that you're going to be no fun at all at her wedding."

Sarann wrinkled her nose at the thought—and at the pungent aroma of green tea wafting up to her. "This stuff tastes so . . . bleh. Too bad it's good for us."

"I have yet to find something that both tastes good and is good at the same time," her husband said as he set the antique butler's tray on its stand.

"Wait a minute. On second thought . . ." He walked back to Sarann and bent down to steal a kiss, running his tongue lightly over her lower lip. He smiled, then stole another. "I stand corrected."

"That's so sweet," she said, gratified by his gesture. After the bruising silent treatment she'd just received, Sarann needed that kiss of approval.

Rodger settled with the *Gloucester Daily Times* in a tufted leather wing chair opposite the smaller armchair that became Sarann's favorite after she and her daughter moved in. Although Rodger liked to play classical music softly after dinner while he read, tonight, for some reason, he did not. It was quiet, except for the occasional ruffling of his paper and the rubouts of Sarann's eraser on her sketch pad as she experimented with different layouts of the business cards that she was about to order.

Business cards! She loved the mere sound of the words. Sarann Johnson Bonniface was going to own and operate her very own business. After a lifetime of waitressing and low-paying office work, Sarann was going to be her own boss. It was a dream come true, and it was almost enough to make her forget that she was dreaming on the edge of a canyon.

"Sarann?"

She looked up from her agreeable task with a half-vacant smile. "Mm?"

"We need to talk. It's time. We need to talk about Abby's father."

It was a sudden kick in the shin, and it left Sarann angry and smarting.

"*Why?*" It was the first thing to pop into her head, shorthand for, "What the hell has her father got to do with you and me?"

"Abigail asked me to intercede for her, and I am," Rodger said quietly. "I think that she hasn't been able to articulate her feelings very well."

"Are you kidding? She can communicate her feelings brilliantly—with or without words, as you've just seen."

He wasn't listening. "This can't go on, this running battle of wills. You two are going to end up permanently estranged. And frankly, the atmosphere's too tense for me. I like a calmer household than this. That's why I'm stepping in and—"

"Who're you, her guardian angel?" Sarann said, slicing off the rest of his speech. She knew that Rodger hated being interrupted, but she felt a reluctance bordering on revulsion at the thought of discussing her past with him.

He's dead. Nick McElwyn is dead. That's my story, and I'm sticking to it.

"Sarann, I'm Abigail's father now. You said yourself that you wanted me to take sides more often."

"*Mine*, not hers!" she blurted. Fair or not, it was how she felt.

Sidestepping her resentment, Rodger said, "Abby's convinced that her birth father is alive; you know that."

"Which is ridiculous. Who—whom—are you going to believe, me or a twelve-year-old?"

"Why are you being so defensive? All I was trying to say

is that the girl needs more information about him. She can't come to terms with his death, simply because she's never been able to know about his life."

"She knows as much as I do, Rodger."

Since Sarann knew next to nothing about Abby's father, the statement was more or less true. It was a humiliating burden that she had to carry with her every day of her life, like a big giant STUPID sign hanging around her neck. And every time that she gazed at her engaging, bright, and head-strong daughter—the one who looked nothing like her at all—Sarann felt just a little more stupid.

She snapped out of her quick trance of remorse in time to see that Rodger was watching her closely.

"You've never said much about Nick, Sarann. I suppose, because I haven't wanted to ask."

"And I appreciate that," she said quickly. "It was a painful time in my life." That much was bitterly true.

Hoping to snap the thread of his conversation, she added, "I haven't asked you about Hilary for the same reason. Sudden deaths are awful to deal with; the pain never really goes away."

His brow twitched, and immediately Sarann felt a stab of guilt for bringing up the subject. His wife had fallen from a third-floor window while shaking out a rug—one of those absurd but still tragic deaths that instantly becomes part of the family legend, much more so than death by cancer or stroke or even a car crash.

Rodger retreated into a cloud of thoughtful silence, and Sarann went back to her business cards.

"Where was he from, did you say?"

Damn. She looked up. "Norfield."

"That's a low-rent town. He must've been fairly rough around the edges."

"I was born in Worcester," she said, bristling. "We *matched.*"

Rodger seemed taken aback by her indignation. "I didn't mean any offense, Sarann," he said with a querulous look. "Are you all right?"

"Yes, I'm . . . oh, God," she murmured on a sigh. "I'm sorry, Rodger. I don't know what's come over me lately."

"You look weary."

"But I feel fine, physically."

"Physically, yes."

Don't say it, she said, leaning her head back on her chair and closing her eyes. *Don't say I'm crazy.* She became so seized by the fear that he was about to drop the hint that she came up with a little lie and gently placed it on top of the big one, simply to appease him. "Actually, I feel an awful headache coming on. I think I'll go to bed."

"So early? Maybe you should take a nice, long bath instead. I'll be up soon to check on you." He gave her a warm, reassuring smile.

She got up from her chair and put her tea things next to his on the tray.

Rodger held out his hand for hers and Sarann allowed him to take it. He kissed her fingertips. "Let's not argue, darling," he said softly. "Life's too short."

She feigned a smile. "We're not arguing; we're having a spirited difference of opinion." It's what Rodger's over-educated sister-in-law would have said.

He laughed and was about to answer when a loud crash came from upstairs. "Good grief, now what?"

Sarann raced upstairs to find Abby setting a chair next to the French armoire that dominated the north wall of the master bedroom. "What was *that* all about?" she asked her daughter.

Rodger was right behind her. "Abby, you know you're not supposed to chase Molly through the house; something could get broken."

Abashed, the girl mumbled, "Okay, I won't," and shot her

stepfather an odd look before she sidled out of the room.

Sarann gave her husband a puzzled glance but didn't actually ask the question.

"Kids," he replied with a shrug, and he went back downstairs to his books and papers.

Abigail waited until she heard the water stop running into the tub, and then she waited another couple of minutes, just to be sure. She was sitting like a statue in front of her math assignment. (It was finished, but she wanted to look as if she was doing something constructive.) Molly jumped onto her lap and tried to curl up there, but she must have realized that Abigail was in a mood, because she decided not to stay and jumped back down again.

Molly was right. Abigail's heart was pounding a mile a minute. The envelope that she'd found on the shelf in her mother's closet was still under her sweatshirt, tucked into her bra—the corner of it, was, anyway—and she could feel it crinkle against her skin every time she moved. She could feel its shape exactly, a rectangle of fire against her skin.

A letter. A letter in an envelope that had come back with a label slapped over the address marked NOT DELIVERABLE. A letter, written in her mother's own handwriting.

Abigail could so easily have missed it. It had been flattened between the shelf and some boxes of canceled checks. You had to be really looking to find it. At first she'd thought it had just dropped there by accident. But after thinking about it . . . no. The letter had been saved and hidden on purpose; it was important. It burned against her skin with importance.

Abigail had her bases covered. If anyone knocked, she'd instantly drop the letter into an open manila envelope that she had taped to the back of her desk. But she wasn't worried, not really. Her mom was in the tub and her stepdad was on her side. With the door behind her closed tightly and her sneaker jammed under it, Abigail at last withdrew the letter from her bra. Her hands were tingling as she pulled out the single folded pale-blue sheet from its air-mail envelope. She tucked her hair behind her ears, took a deep breath, and read:

Dear Ben . . .

Ben?
Who was Ben? Crushed with disappointment, Abigail picked up the envelope and looked at the address again. The return address, yes, Franklin, Massachusetts, where her mother had once lived. But the NOT DELIVERABLE label covered the name and most of the address. The country underneath it was probably Germany; the last four letters still showed, and they were M-A-N-Y.

Could she peel the label back from the name? Just a little? No one would notice a little thing like that. With her fingernail she did the deed. Last two letters: Y-N.

Ohmigod. A light bulb went on over her head that was bright enough to grow corn; Abigail was furious that she had allowed herself to be so easily duped. She peeled the label back farther, recklessly now; she owed no scruples to a mother who was so sneaky.

Uh-huh. As she figured: C-*E*-L-W-Y-N. She could safely assume that the first letter of the last name was a capital M. So: Ben McElwyn. Ben McElwyn. On the hassock or in the black turtleneck, whichever. Now she knew why she hadn't been able to find any records of him.

Because Mom gave me the wrong stupid first name.
She went back to the letter and read it through.

Dear Ben,
I was thinking of you recently, and when I called
Gerry, she told me that you'd left college and enlisted!
I have to admit, I was surprised. You don't seem like

the soldier type to me. Can you really take orders—get up, get dressed, march, turn, salute, eat, sleep—just because someone tells you to? I remember you said that you always wanted to be as free as a kite. At the time, I thought you meant the bird. Were you really talking about the thing on a string?

I'm sorry; I shouldn't tease. But it was so much fun that day that I'm doing it still. You were a blast to be with. I know it was the brownies, but I've never laughed so hard in my life. Funny; that was five months ago, but it seems like yesterday. And yet a lot— a lot—has happened since then. For both of us, I guess. I know what I told you on the phone later, but things have changed, Ben. I really would like to talk to you. But you're in Germany, which at least isn't dangerous anymore, but it's still overseas, and we can't exactly meet at your campus coffee shop, can we, even if I could get off work.

This is a garbled letter, I know. I feel frustrated and a little bit scared. I'm not even sure I should be saying that, but it's true. I just wish I could talk to you. Will you be coming home anytime soon? Gerry didn't know. I haven't seen her since that day I met you, but she sounds really busy with school. She's a good student and a hard worker; we're all impressed that she made it out of the neighborhood. I'll be surprised if she doesn't run for office someday.

I'm sorry for what I said on the phone.

Yours truly,
Sarann Johnson

And that was it. Abigail snatched up the envelope, looking for a second page, a long postscript, a few more facts. But there was nothing, only the one onionskin sheet with its sad and mysterious message.

Right off the bat, Abigail had questions. Brownies, for one. Brownies didn't make you laugh unless they had something illegal in them. Her mother had lectured her practically since she was born about not drinking or taking drugs. Where did she get off eating pot-laced brownies?

She picked up the framed photograph of the laughing group and studied the plates closely, looking for brownie leftovers.

As if.

Another question. When did her so-called father have time to finish college and go to law school if he ended up in the army?

Another: what exactly had her mother said to him on the phone, and why was she so sorry about it?

Another and the most important question of all: did her mother ever get in touch with Ben McElwyn again? Was it possible, actually possible, that Abby had been right and she *was* a one-night stand?

She zeroed in on the guy sitting on the hassock. If her mother had lied about the correct name, she certainly could be lying about the correct man.

Let it be the one on the couch, Abigail prayed. *Please.* She touched her fingertips to her full lips, and then to the face of the cool-looking guy in the black turtleneck.

She reread the letter and was well on her way to memorizing it when she heard a knock on the door of her bedroom.

Yikes! Abigail threw the letter into a desk drawer and said with panic-stricken annoyance, "*What.*"

"May I come in?" her mother asked. She sounded as if she was trying not to sound sarcastic.

"If you must."

Of course the door wouldn't open; a sneaker was jammed under it. Abigail had to unwedge it, and when she turned to go back to her desk, she realized that she had left the envelope with its torn-away label just sitting there on display.

Her mother, standing behind her and wrapped in a bathrobe, saw the envelope, too.

Chapter 4

SARANN HAD BEEN in the tub for less than two minutes before it occurred to her that the noise they'd heard was Abby knocking the chair over as she rifled through the closet.

It was inevitable that Abby would find the letter; the only safe place for something that dangerous was in a sealed chamber at a toxic dump. As she crossed the hall to her daughter's room, Sarann wondered whether she hadn't left the letter on the closet shelf deliberately, knowing that sooner or later someone would find it. She was like the killer who scrawls in lipstick across a mirror, STOP ME.

Before I lie again. Standing in Abby's room, seeing her child's cool glare and compressed lips, Sarann knew two things: the lie was over, and the harm would go on.

She said quietly, "May I have that, please?"

With unnerving calm, Abby handed over the envelope.

"And the letter that belongs inside?"

Still scathingly nonchalant, Abby opened the top drawer of her desk and retrieved the letter. She held it by her thumb and her forefinger, as if it were evidence in a homicide case.

It was. The death of innocence.

"Do you want to talk about this, Abby?" Sarann asked, slipping the letter and the envelope into the pocket of her robe. Part of her mind was already thinking ahead to Rodger. More harm coming.

In any case, she wasn't prepared for the first words out of her daughter's mouth.

"You smoked *pot*."

"I . . . didn't smoke it; I ate it. But I didn't know it at the time."

"Grownups look really stupid stoned."

"I'm glad I wasn't in the photograph, then."

"Why did you keep it?"

"It was the only one I had of your father."

"If he is my father."

"He is."

"Where is he now?"

"I don't know."

"Is he dead?"

"I don't know."

"Did you ever get in touch with him after that letter came back?"

Sarann shook her head.

"Why not?"

"I don't know."

"Why did you tell me his name was Nick? Oh, never mind, it's obvious: to make it harder for me to find him."

Sarann's response to that was a shrug.

Abby sighed. "At least," she said on a weary exhale, "tell me he's the one on the couch."

Her mother did a double take. "Why on earth would I do that?"

"No reason," Abby said dully. Her face became eerily blank, as if someone inside her head were running around pulling down all the shades. "Well, this has been a lot of fun," she said at last. "We haven't played twenty questions since I was little."

"Oh, Abby, I can't explain this in twenty answers— maybe not in twenty thousand answers. This is big. Huge. I know it is. We need time to talk it out, to feel our way. We might have to see a counselor together. I know I've done a terrible thing, hiding your . . . your—"

"Origins?" Abby offered, still uncannily composed. "Why didn't you just tell me that you found me under a cabbage leaf? All in all, I'd prefer that lie to your lie. A lawyer killed in a traffic accident. Hel-*lo*."

Cry, scream, throw something at me. Sarann could see her daughter retreating farther inside herself with every passing sentence. She reached out, trying to catch hold of the girl before it was too late.

"Look . . . honey . . . why don't I get dressed," she said in a pleading voice, "and you and I will go out somewhere, and I can try to explain." She had her hand on the doorknob, ready to sprint across the hall and change. "We'll stay at an inn in Gloucester; it'll be kind of a girls' night out—"

"I have school tomorrow."

"I'll write a note."

"Fat lot of good *those* do," Abby said with a pointed glance at the pocket of her mother's robe.

"It'll be like before, when it was just you and me," Sarann insisted, ignoring the relentless sarcasm.

Abby's wonderful, luminous blue eyes seemed to look right through her. "And we'll tell Dad what, exactly?"

Sarann blinked. "Dad?"

Rodger. Sarann had blocked him completely out of her thoughts; only one dad was front and center in her mind just then. "You're right. That's a problem," she said faintly.

Sarann felt the doorknob twist under her hand and had to swallow a yelp of fear. On the other side of the door stood the new dad, the willing dad, the wealthy dad, the one who had the power to give Abby a life she'd never known before—a life the child deserved.

"Problem? What's a problem?" he asked, nudging the door from the other side.

God in heaven; he heard. Instinctively Sarann jammed her fist over the letter in her bathrobe pocket. Stepping back to let him pass, she wracked her brain for a plausible lie to tell. But it had been a long week; she was plumb out of them. She merely stood there, a boxer in chenille who's taken a

near-knockout punch in the second round and can't deal with
the thought of still eight more to follow.

It was her opponent and not some referee who went and
mercifully rang the bell. Abby explained to her stepfather,
"We were talking about how hard it is to rent a video when
it's number one. With *Last Stop* it's been, like, totally hope-
less."

Sarann turned to her daughter with grudging admiration.
"Right, so let's make sure we reserve it next weekend instead
of just walking into the video store cold."

Rodger seemed to buy it. He shrugged and said to Sarann,
"I was surprised to see a tub full of water and no one in it.
Should I just pull the plug?"

"No . . . um . . . or, yeah . . . I . . ." She was watching
Abby, watching for signs. Was the girl about to explode and
tell all?

Apparently not. In a suddenly bored and dismissive voice
she said, "Well, if you two are done discussing the plumb-
ing . . ."

"Yes, yes, sorry; go back to your homework," Sarann
urged. "Come on, Rodger; let's leave her to it."

A virtuoso performance, Sarann thought, as she and
Rodger returned to their bedroom together. And more than a
little scary. No one that age was entitled to so many wits in
a situation like theirs.

As soon as they had the bedroom door closed behind
them, Rodger said to his wife, "Okay, I'll bite. How did you
manage to smooth things over with her?"

"Oh . . . you know how preteens are," Sarann said over
her shoulder on her way into the bathroom. "Their hormones
ebb and flow."

She yanked the plug in the clawfoot tub, then turned and
caught her reflection in the small, square mirror of the milk-
painted medicine chest. Her cheeks were still flushed, her

breathing tight. She looked like what she felt: a candidate for a heart attack.

She would have to tell Rodger everything before Abby did it for her—tell him now, tonight—but the confession stuck in her throat like peanut butter. How did you tell your new husband that you've killed someone off who didn't deserve to die and who, incidentally, most likely wasn't dead? How did you tell your new husband that you were a lying fake?

He'll despise me, she realized. *Despise me and pity me and regret his rash decision to marry down. His mother will say "I told you so," and his brother will hardly be able to contain his glee. Abby and I will be out in the street and I won't even have the security of going back to a job at the school. Not when the boss is my ex.*

"Sarann? Is that the water draining?"

"Yes," she answered, walking out into the bedroom. "I didn't feel like a bath, after all. My headache's better."

"Huh. So here I am, half undressed . . . I was planning to read in bed while you soaked," Rodger said. Stripped to his jockeys and tee shirt, he was hanging his slacks in the mirrored armoire.

"You can still read," she mumbled. It would give her time to try to think of a lighthearted way of explaining the obvious: that technically one couldn't be a respectable widow if one had never been respectably married.

She watched as Rodger sized himself up in the armoire's mirror, patting a nonexistent gut. He did look good—lean and sinewy, especially for a guy in his forties. He worked hard at staying fit, and most of the time he seemed pleased with what he saw in the beveled mirrors. Tonight was no exception.

He turned to his wife and smiled. "You have great color; I suppose it's the bath."

Or guilt. Or fear.

Sarann smiled halfheartedly and said, "Thank you, sire."

She had to pass close by him to reach the white ruffled nightgown hanging from a hook on the side of the armoire. He did not move as she untied her robe but instead, hovering behind her, helped her out of it.

She caught her reflection, not as perfect as his by a long shot, in the mirrored doors. She was no prude, but Rodger, of the half-dozen men she had known intimately, seemed somehow to make her feel the most shy about her body. There was just something about his look; she never knew what was going on inside his mind.

She made a point of looking away from both their reflections as she lifted her nightgown from its darkened brass hook.

"Are you interested?" Rodger murmured, dropping the robe across the chair that Abby had used to find the letter that was making Sarann feel anything but.

He nuzzled the damp curls that still clung to the nape of her neck. "You have a good body," he whispered in her ear. "A grown-up body."

"I'm grown up; that must have something to do with it," she said, dipping her head with a self-conscious smile. *Please, please . . . not tonight.*

From behind her, he cupped her breasts and pulled her buttocks into him. He was aroused and ready, all in the blink of an eye.

It boggled her mind. It seemed impossible that she could make love with him with her deadly lie hanging over their bed like the sword of Damocles.

He nipped the curve of her shoulder gently. "Hmmm? So . . . what do you think?"

"What do I think?"

Pretend you want him. You've done it for months; why stop now?

She sighed, a long, shuddering sigh.

He took it as a yes.

In another bedroom down the hall, Abigail Johnson Bonniface was on fire with the possibility of adding one more
surname to the two she possessed. She wasn't sure how it
could be accomplished legally, but she knew that she
wouldn't feel right until she was able to use all three.

There were probably a hundred Ben McElwyns in the
United States, which was a depressing thought; but you had
to start somewhere. She went to the white pages on the Internet, typed in her father's real name, and hit "search."

Look everywhere, she begged her machine. In every state,
and don't come back until you find him. Please please please.

One date and one phone call. That's all her mother knew
about her father. How much could you learn in one crummy
date? Even if they talked all night—which they couldn't if
they were doing it—you still couldn't learn all that much,
like what was his favorite color (Abigail's was yellow) and
his favorite food (hers was pizza) and his favorite song
("Yellow Submarine" for her, what else?). Did he like dogs
or cats? Baseball or football? Rock or classical? (Okay, that
one was easy. Rock.)

Her computer came rushing back with three Ben Mc-
Elwyns. Only three! You'd think his name was Schwieppen-
heimer. Abigail was ecstatic at the discovery that one of the
three, Benjamin L. McElwyn, lived in Connecticut. Connecticut wasn't that far from Massachusetts. They touched!
So the next thing was to search for "Benjamin L. McElwyn"
in the public records. He could be important—a senator or
something—or famous. A rock star! He could be a rock star!

Or not. The guy on the hassock didn't look like a rock
star; the guy in the turtleneck did.

Still, he wasn't a lawyer and he wasn't dead—most likely.
People just didn't die that young. Usually. But if he *had* died

sometime, somewhere, think how tragic that would be. She would dress in black and play sad music and wonder if he had known all the words to "Yellow Submarine," which her stepfather did not.

No. It was too tragic to think about, the real death of her real father. Her eyes welled up with tears. *No.*

She kept on searching.

Chapter 5

Dear Mr. McElwyn,
I'm e-mailing you instead of writing you because I'm
not sure if you're married or not. If you are, then
please write down my name and e-mail address and
delete this as soon as you finish reading it.

What the hell?
Ben McElwyn, hung over after an all-night send-off
for one of his bachelor pals on the force, sagged across
his keyboard and stared, bleary-eyed, at the screen. His
tongue felt like cotton and his mouth tasted like canary
shit; his brain was still soaked in Jack Daniels.

Dear Mr. McElwyn,
I'm e-mailing you instead of writing you because I'm
not sure if you're married or not. If you are, then
please write down my name and my e-mail address
and delete this as soon as you finish reading it.
*   What I want to know is, did you ever date someone*
named Sarann Johnson?

Sarann. Jesus Christ, Sarann.

This would be about thirteen years ago, probably dur-
ing spring break in college. It was in the months before
you would have joined the army and been stationed in
Germany. You and Sarann both knew someone named
Gerry. Sarann Johnson would have been eighteen. She
is 5' 6" and I'm not sure what she weighs now, but

she used to weigh 128 lbs. Her eyes are green and her hair is lightish brown. She wore it cut medium length, not really in what you would call a style. It kind of goes its own way.

Sarann!

She was going to secretarial school when you met her, and she also was working full-time at Jobber's Warehouse. She lived with her mother, who was sick and Sarann was taking care of her. She wanted to get a good-paying job as an executive secretary so that she could earn enough money to go to college, but she never did.

If she sounds like anyone you ever went with, please e-mail me back. Thank you in advance for your time,
                                    Abigail Johnson Bonniface

Ben slumped back in the kitchen chair and stared blankly at the screen. If someone had pointed out that he'd grown an extra ear overnight, he couldn't have been more stunned.

Sarann.

"Hey, sexy—what're you doing up so early?"

It was noon. Ben glanced at the doorway between his bedroom and his kitchen. It was occupied by a tall, nicely turned-out party girl standing buck naked with her arms folded across her killer breasts.

"Hey, babe," he said absently. "What's happenin'?"

"Not much, without you." She was purring now, in heat again. She crouched down a little, her palms on her thighs, and smiled mischievously. "You still wanna play?"

"Uhhh . . . yeah . . . gimme a minute to regroup."

Cherie stuck out her lower lip in a fetching pout and said, "Don't tell me I've worn you out."

He was so worn out it wasn't even funny. Still, it was a sad day in the precinct when he couldn't keep up with a twenty-two-year-old. First the Maalox episode, and now this.

He stared at the screen. What the hell *was* this? A summons; what? He read through the e-mail again.

"Excuse me—sir? You at the kitchen table?" Cherie said, waving her hand prettily at him. "Have you noticed I'm not wearing any clothes?" She turned in a fluid, taunting movement.

"*Oh*, yeah." He smiled at her briefly, then frowned at the screen. Abigail Johnson Bonniface. He didn't remember an Abigail. Not that he necessarily would have.

"Well . . . !" Cherie stomped a bare foot. "What's so important about a computer that it can't wait?" She came over to him and leaned over him from behind, then wrapped her arms around him and began pulling lightly at the hairs on his chest while she flicked her tongue along the curve of his neck.

It was vastly annoying. "Honeybunch, sweetie . . . don't do that, okay?" His mind was a million miles away, lost in the hauntingly simple picture of Sarann Johnson that someone named Abigail had painted for him in cyberspace.

Over his shoulder, Cherie read the e-mail and then let out a low whistle. "That is, like, a weird letter. I mean, it's really weirding me out."

Ben shrugged. "Someone's just trying to find out if I once knew a girl named Sarann, that's all."

"Why? Not because they want you to be an organ donor, that's for sure," she said, tugging at his earlobe with her lips.

He snorted. "My organs are nicely pickled, thank you very much; they should last forever."

"Only one of your organs interests me," Cherie mur-

mured. She slid her hand inside his boxers and grabbed
hold of the organ in question, then began a slow, practiced
stroke designed to make him crazy.

"I've never done it with a disgraced cop before," she
confessed in a sly tone.

"We're all a disgrace," Ben said, feeling his dick lifting
halfheartedly to the challenge. "It goes without saying."

"I mean, with one who's actually been kicked off the
force."

"Yeah, well, that's a little more rare. Appreciate me."

"Ohh, sweetie, I do. You have no idea."

Surprising, how it smarted to have her refer to him that
way. *Kicked off the force.* Ben preferred to believe that
he'd found a reasonable way for someone else to make it
convenient for him to leave. A pleasant bonus was the
fact that he couldn't be labeled a quitter for once.

Cherie began licking and teasing the lobe of his ear
again; she was like a cat on a grooming kick. He turned
and kissed the tip of her perky nose and patted the back
of her blond head. "One more minute," he said, drawing
her hand out from his shorts.

She let out a little hiss of exasperation. "Y'know, a
date could begin to take this personally."

Yeah, he thought, *if you were my date.* But she wasn't.
She was just someone he'd picked up at the party. She
saw him and he saw her and they clicked and they fucked
and very soon she'd be gone. No need for a follow-up
call, no obligation beyond getting her a cab. She knew it,
too, which was why she'd come on to him in the first
place.

Thank you in advance.

Who was Abigail Johnson Bonniface?

It sounded like a sister—but Ben had no recollection
of a sister. A mother, yes, that rang a bell. She was mental, given to hallucinatory episodes, and it was tearing

Sarann apart. Could Sarann have had a sister that she was estranged from, maybe someone who wasn't pulling her share of the caregiving load, and Sarann hated her and had refused even to mention her?

He shook his head. Hard to believe that Sarann could have hated anyone.

Actually, the e-mail sounded fairly businesslike, if not particularly sophisticated. No suppressed urgency, no rising panic, none of that stuff; certainly no overwrought emotion. A lawyer in the family, maybe? A niece?

Niece, schmiece, what Ben wanted to know was, what did the Abigail woman care if he knew Sarann or not? Was she putting together a surprise this-is-your-life package for Sarann's—what would it be?—thirtieth birthday? Well, sweet Abigail could just count him out for help on that one.

Or—and of course it wasn't possible, life didn't happen that way, but it was amusing to toy with the notion, anyway—had Sarann maybe been reminiscing aloud about him, and had Abigail maybe taken it on herself to drag him back into Sarann's life? Aunt Abigail the matchmaker?

Yeah, right. More likely, Sarann—in a bout of pity—had left him her bedroom suite from Sears.

Ben remembered as if it were yesterday the way she had nailed down who he was and what he was about. After they'd left Gerry's place, he had taken her to his hole-in-the-wall apartment near the college campus in Bristol. They had made love twice and, still too consumed with one another to sleep, had fallen into an easy, intimate discussion about Life and Love. He remembered, still, the way she had analyzed his digs in metaphysical terms:

You live in this pit because it's easier to leave a pit. If you fixed it up—bought a rug or some dishes from Kmart or a philodendron from Stop and Shop—you might begin to care. And pretty soon you'd start having people over, because you wouldn't be ashamed. And you'd begin to care about them, too; they'd become your friends. And then where would you be? You'd be like everyone else, that's where. You wouldn't be special anymore. You'd be an ordinary human being with ordinary commitments, not some lone eagle who hovered above everything, swooping down only when he needed refueling.

He had bristled and told her that *she* was there, after all (in fact, she would be his first and only guest). And she had smiled and said, yes, she was a quick little snack for him.

He'd had no comeback to that.

It had just turned dawn; they'd been watching the sun come up over Narragansett Bay. After that they had fallen asleep exhausted in one another's arms, and when he woke up, she was gone, like some faery creature who had let him have his way with her and then had escaped to her sprite world. Ben had found the whole experience so completely unnerving that he now refused to watch the sun come up. It was too much like watching the sun go down: a daily herald to a dark and empty void.

No, he didn't remember any Abigail; but he sure as hell remembered Sarann.

Cherie had given up on him. When he finally returned to the bedroom, he found her sitting cross-legged in the middle of his rumpled bed and working her nails with an emery board. Hopefully she was making them less sharp; but somehow he wasn't willing to bet the ranch on it.

"So tell me this," she said without looking up at him. "Why were you thrown off the force?"

"They didn't like the cut of my jib, I guess." He sat on the side of the bed, wondering when—or whether—to call a cab. He was looking at a set of killer, killer boobs.

She held out her hand in front of her and squinted at

her fingernails in appraisal. "I don't understand what that means, the cut of your jib. Raymond said you got caught with stolen evidence in your car. Is that true?"

"Sadly, yes."

"Did you steal it—the coke?"

"They thought so."

"But I'm the one who's asking you now."

He laughed softly. "Why the hell would I tell *you*," he asked her, "if I didn't tell them?"

Possibly he hit that "you" a little too hard; she was offended, and maybe rightly so.

"You're a prick, you know that?" she said calmly.

"Yeah. I've heard."

She rolled over, picked up the phone and called for a ride.

He shrugged and left the room. The last two reasons he could think of to coax her into staying suddenly didn't seem so killer, after all.

Half an hour later, Ben was scrubbed and shaved and generally disinfected enough to feel half human again. He made a pot of new coffee from old grounds and set one of his landlord's chipped mugs, filled with the truly vile brew, on his landlord's battered kitchen table. He pulled the torn shades all the way down to darken the room and make his computer screen easier to view. And he changed the rickety chair he'd been sitting on earlier for the last one that still had working glue in its joints.

Benjamin Lowell McElwyn was ready to face down Abigail Johnson Bonniface.

He read her e-mail for the twelfth, the fifteenth, the twentieth time, looking for clues and not finding any. Ben McElwyn, streetwise smartass, ex-detective and now private dick—that same Ben McElwyn was like, *totally* clueless, as Cherie would say. He could not imagine why Abigail was trying to find him.

To warn him about an STD? Twelve years later?

He'd given blood and knew he was clean, but that couldn't be it. Sarann wasn't the type to have anything to transmit. He remembered well how she had jumped out of bed to put on her diaphragm at the appropriate time. He remembered thinking, *All ri-i-ght; no need for a rubber.* (He was young and horny and, like, totally clueless even then.)

All in all, he considered that it had been his lucky day, until he woke up and found Sarann gone without so much as a by-your-leave. He remembered well—very well indeed—how he'd felt as, half asleep, he patted the sheet around him and found no Sarann . . . how he'd sat up and looked around in confusion at his one-room pit . . . and checked the bathroom . . . and even pulled aside the shower curtain, for pity's sake.

But she was gone, and she stayed gone. Oh, he'd got drunk once and had called her up, whining the way drunken men do about her fickle heart and her abusive ways, and he had ended up saying some really mean and nasty stuff, the way drunken men do, about her fickle heart and her abusive ways.

She hadn't been swayed by any of it. She said he'd been—talk about mean and nasty—nothing more than an "aberration" in her life. That she was engaged (which, by God, had been news to him) and that her fiancé was a good and decent guy she'd known all her life. That if Ben was half the man her fiancé was, then he'd never—ever— try to contact her again.

When Ben called her, he'd been half a man at best; the other half was afloat in a sea of Jack Daniels. By the time she'd hung up on him, he was nothing more than a tiny air bubble easing up from the bottom of the ocean. Oh, she'd sunk him good during that phone call, all right. Real good. It had taken him two full months to resurface, by which time he'd missed all of his exams. Faced with the prospect of five incompletes, he opted to haul his ass off to the nearest recruiting office. It was easier than getting a real job.

He sat back on the chair, driving it onto its hind legs, and looked around him with a wry smile. Twelve years later, the faces and places had changed, but he was the same. He still lived in a pit. He still regarded women as fast food. And he still had no real friends.

Still, he did now own a possession he prized—a computer, because it made his job easier—and he knew how to use it. He reread Abigail's e-mail one more time, pondering all the lost sunrises in his life. The truth was, he was a mess. His life was a mess. His hopes and dreams and expectations, if he'd ever had any, were a mess, floating aimlessly in that vast darkness between sunrise and sunset.

He wanted it so much to be some other way.

With a knot in his throat and his hand on the mouse, he dragged the cursor over to the "reply" box on his screen. He let it hover there for an interminable time, much longer than his average dark period between sunrise and sunset. And then he moved the cursor sharply to the right and hit "delete."

Take that, Abigail Johnson Bonniface.

Chapter 6

THE NEXT TWO days were hell. Abby withdrew completely from Sarann, and Sarann knew why: the daughter was waiting for the mother to act like an adult.

It was easier said than done. An adult would never have got herself into the mess that Sarann had in the first place, and if she had, she would have cleaned it up simply by telling the truth. Sarann couldn't do it. She wanted too desperately to be up to Rodger's standards. He'd taken a chance on her, and he deserved to have his faith in her justified.

If only she'd come from wealth and breeding! If she had, having a baby out of wedlock would have been seen as a sophisticated, Murphy Brown-kind of thing to do.

But Sarann's background had given her neither the money nor the confidence to pull off single motherhood. She was from the kind of neighborhood where unwed mothers were labeled trailer trash, so after her mother died and Sarann went apartment-hunting with Abby in her arms, she made up a story to the landlords about being a widow.

Whether she had been looking for sympathy (and a break in the rent) or mere social acceptance, she still couldn't say. But the lie felt good, like a pair of old slippers, and by the time Abby was able to ask questions about her daddy, Sarann almost believed her story herself. It took years before she figured out that lying was trashier behavior than having a baby out of wedlock. And by then it was too late.

So now what?

You're going to tell him. As soon as you get home. As soon as you walk through the door. No more excuses.

A brilliant sun burst from among blue clouds and shined

a blessing on her resolve as she emerged from the fabric shop in the mall. *Yes. How hard could it be?* And after she told Rodger, they'd once again—really, for the first time—be able to enjoy true intimacy with one another.

She felt better already, lighter than she had in weeks—despite the heavy bolt of fabric that she had just bought for window treatments for the new shop. It was a struggle to carry her purchase to the far end of the row in the mall where she'd parked her brand-new Mercedes.

As it turned out, her struggle had just begun: when she got there, there was no Mercedes.

The big green Explorer was still parked in the space on one side. The new red Taurus was still parked in the space on the other side. But the dark blue Mercedes that she had so carefully aligned between the two vehicles, that was gone.

Her brand-new car . . . where was it? Hampered by the heavy bolt of cloth, she ran to check the rows in front of and behind the one where she had parked. Nothing. She was in a panic now. Had she remembered to lock it? Maybe yes, maybe no. She couldn't remember if she remembered. But she must not have, or the alarm would have gone off.

Oh, God. Not now, not on top of everything else.

All she could think of was her in-laws' reaction. They'd regard her as a slut *and* a dingbat. Rodger had given her the car as a birthday present—he'd even picked out the color—and though she didn't like dark colors in cars, Sarann was touched and thrilled by his gesture. And now the Mercedes was gone! Stolen! The enormity of it took her breath away.

She hauled herself and her bolt back inside the mall and went straight to the security office. After giving the man in charge a quick rundown, she left his office to call Rodger on her cell phone, tell him the bad news, and ask him to come and get her. How she dreaded it.

She got the answering machine instead and hung up; how did you leave a message like that?

A minute later, Rodger called her back. He sounded out of breath and annoyed. "Why did you hang up? I was out in the garden and nearly broke my neck trying to get to the phone in time."

They had caller ID, of course; she'd forgotten. More embarrassment. All in a rush, she said, "Rodger, something awful's happened. I locked the car, I thought I did, I'm pretty sure I did, but maybe I didn't, and when I came out it was gone. I've told mall security and they're letting the police know, they're on their way over, but I'm so sorry, it was your gift to me, I really thought I locked it . . . I really did. Oh, God, I am *so* sorry."

By the end, her voice was trembling and she was in tears.

Immediately Rodger became gentle with her. "Shh, shh . . . it's not worth getting upset over. There was no mugging, it wasn't a carjacking . . . you weren't hurt. That's all that's important. Where are you? I'll clean up and come for you."

"I'm by the security office at the Midland Mall."

"Good grief, way out there?"

She said sheepishly, "They had a sale."

"All right," he said, sounding resigned. Without a single crack about false economies, he said, "Just sit tight. And don't be upset."

It was like telling the tide not to go out with the moon. Sarann waited on one of the rainbow-colored plastic benches in the mall's playpit where children romped under the watchful eyes of their parents, and in a daze she toted up her inadequacies. Unwed mother, chronic liar, irresponsible property owner—the list seemed doomed to go on.

He never should have entrusted me with such a valuable car; I told him an Escort would've been fine. I told him.

She stared into space, lost in thought. *A used Escort would have been better still. A used and rusting Escort would have been best of all for someone like me.*

Fifteen minutes later, the security officer, a kindly man in his sixties, tracked her down; he had a smile on his face. "You've got your car back, Mrs. Bonniface," he said. "It was parked a few rows away, all secure and locked up. You just forgot where you left it, that's all."

A wave of relief capped with dismay rushed over her. "Oh, thank God—but . . . I parked it where I said I did. I know I did."

The guard nodded sympathetically. "It's confusing, these big malls. This one has three almost identical entrances. You just lost your bearings, that's all."

My wits, you mean. Sarann thanked him and apologized for the trouble she'd caused and then made a second, even more dreaded call to Rodger on his cell phone. This time, her husband was less understanding.

He was turning around, he said, and he would meet her back home. His manner was terse, but it was his sign-off that made Sarann wince. "I'm glad," he muttered, "that Abby's at a sleepover tonight."

And isn't around to see the fiasco. Sarann had thought of that, too.

A field trip scheduled for the next day had provided Abby with the perfect excuse not to stay under the same roof as her mother: the teacher's daughter was having a sleepover for any girls who felt like joining her. Sarann couldn't very well say no to the plan, but she'd had to beat back the fear that Abby was about to run away in search of her father. It was a silly fear, an irrational fear—but still. It had added one more element of uncertainty to Sarann's precarious state of mind lately.

And now this.

By the time that Sarann returned home, all her bright re-solve to come clean with Rodger had evaporated. She was feeling completely demoralized, and the last thing she wanted was to see her brother-in-law's Range Rover parked in the drive.

She hoped, at least, that James's wife was there, too, with their little Maggie. Of everyone in his family, it was Glenys who had made Sarann feel the most welcome. Both women were the same age. Each had a child. Both loved quilts, gardens, antiques, and old movies. And both had a sense of humor that their more serious husbands did not.

But *James*. He was a younger, more ambitious, less patient version of his older brother Rodger, and a bigger snob to boot. Maybe that was because he was not only a younger son, but an adopted one; it always seemed to Sarann that James had something to prove. Then, too, she suspected that he'd had a terrible childhood before he was adopted. That couldn't have helped.

Sarann parked the Mercedes alongside the Range Rover and dragged her heavy bolt of toile, which by now she hated, down the brick path that led to the front door, painted a stately blackish green. Rodger was undoubtedly showing off his garden, which would be aglow on such a golden spring evening, so Sarann didn't bother with the bell but instead fished out her keys.

She fitted the house key in the old lock and tried to turn it, but it wouldn't turn. Puzzled, she took the key out to check that she had the right one and tried it again. No luck. She propped the bolt of fabric in its bag on end next to her; immediately it fell over on a clump of huge white-and-wine Darwin tulips—favorites of Rodger's—and broke most of the stems.

Unbelievable!

Sarann laid the bolt of cloth on the brick path, took a deep breath, and tried the key one more time. It just didn't work. She left the keys hanging from the lock and the fabric where it was and walked around to the garden, but the garden was empty.

From inside she heard tapping on a kitchen window and then the window being raised.

"We're done with the tour; come on in," Glenys said.

She sounded her usual unconcerned self, which meant that Rodger hadn't said anything, and that made Sarann glad. She wasn't in the mood to be the subject of any more odd looks or whispered asides.

"I can't get in the front door," she explained on her way up the back stairs. "My key won't work."

Rodger opened the screen door for her. "What do you mean, the key won't work? Mine worked for me a little while ago."

"It's been that kind of day," said Sarann with a sigh.

He volunteered to try the key himself. "Maybe part of it broke off in the lock. Did you force anything?"

In his house? God forbid.

"No, not at all; I'm too tired for that," she said with a truly limp smile.

He hardly heard her; she could see that he was intrigued by the failed key. Off he went to solve the puzzle.

Glenys said, "Did you get any fabric?"

"Oh, good grief. I left it lying on the front path," Sarann admitted. She remembered the crushed tulips, too. She should have warned her husband about them.

She tried to regain some composure. "Have you had supper yet? I was going to order Chinese for us. You're welcome to stay."

Glenys wrinkled her nose. "We should get back to the sitter. James just stopped by to borrow a book from Rodger."

James popped out of Rodger's downstairs study on cue and said, "Got it. Let's go. Hello, Sarann," he said briefly.

Apologetically, Glenys whispered, "Big hurry. His book tour is just around the corner. Getting a wee bit tense."

"Glenys? Shall we?"

As usual, he somehow made Sarann feel like a chambermaid waiting to do up his room.

Glenys smiled at Sarann and kissed the air beside her

cheek. "Coming, Dr. Bonniface," she said with a sigh.

Leaving the kitchen, they were intercepted by Rodger, holding out Sarann's keys to her. "There's nothing wrong with this key. It works fine," he said with a puzzled look at her. Sarann knew that look—she'd got it often lately—but coming from Rodger, it frightened her.

"It can't possibly work," she said. She felt angry at him for suggesting it in front of the others. "Give it to me." She snatched the ring from his outstretched hand and marched in a huff to the front door, which had been left swung open. Standing in the hall, she very carefully slipped the key into the lock and . . . turned it. Easily. Just the way she always had.

Shit. Shit! The missing stamp, the phantom calendar entry, the misplaced car—none of it bothered her as much as the fact that the key now turned. "This is insane," she said, withdrawing, inserting, and turning it once more.

The second time, her husband and in-laws were there to see her do it. Outraged by the perverse and wicked brass key, Sarann turned to Rodger and blurted, "You switched keys on me!"

"*What*? Are you—?" He checked himself and said calmly, "That is your key. Look at it."

She did, and it was. Her key had a telltale blob of white paint on it, acquired when she fished the ring out of her jeans once in the middle of a painting project.

She said, "Oh." But she wanted to say, "Then you switched locks, goddammit!"

She said, "So it is." But she wanted to say, "Please, please, someone, anyone, tell me I'm not going mad."

James walked out without a word, and Glenys let out a tiny, pained laugh. "Um . . . we'll be on our way, then. Cheerio. Don't forget your fabric, Sarann," she added on her way out.

Sarann had done just that. Swinging the door back open,

she stepped outside to retrieve the bolt. When she came back in with it—after a dismal attempt to fluff up the smashed tulips—she found her husband ensconced in his study.

Sarann stood in the doorway, hugging the bolt, feeling as beaten down as the tulips by the latest events. "I'm sorry about the flowers. And the car."

"But not about the key?" asked Rodger without looking up. He had been studying some papers spread across his exquisite mahogany desk. When he finally did lift his head and face her, it was with an expression of subtle disappointment, as if he'd sniffed a hyacinth that was past its prime. "Well?"

She shrugged. "I don't know what to say about the key. It didn't work when I tried it."

"That's not what I mean. You embarrassed me in front of my brother. I'm surprised at you."

Sarann felt color rush to her cheeks. This was a scolding, pure and simple. "I'm sorry about that," she said. "I don't know why I accused you. No one could possibly take what I said seriously, least of all James."

He wasn't assuaged. "This erratic behavior has got to stop, Sarann," he said cooly. "I know why you're being like this. Do you think I'm blind? Your daughter is barely speaking to you, and it has something to do with Nick McElwyn. Do you plan—ever—to tell me what it is?"

He looked weary of the whole charade and determined to have an end to it. Propping his elbows on the desk, he locked his hands together, tapping his chin with the knuckle of his forefinger as he waited for her answer. His wedding band gleamed dully in the light of the green-shaded lamp with every tiny tap.

Sarann's first, unrelated thought was envy that he could keep his hands looking so elegantly groomed though he worked in a garden; she herself always came out of there with cracked and dirty nails and splits in her fingertips. Her second thought, far more relevant, was that the bands of gold they both wore on their fingers came with obligations, chief among them, to be truthful.

She stood the bolt against the wainscoting of the hall, then came in and sat down. It was difficult not to feel like a student being summoned before the headmaster; she wished she were wearing something more presentable than jeans and a tee shirt from Gloucester emblazoned with a fishing net.

Struggling to maintain an equal footing with the calm and dignified man who sat across the desk from her, she held her head high and looked him straight in the eye. "It's not about Nick," she said. "It's about Ben."

Rodger stiffened and then sat back in his leather desk chair. "Ben? Who the hell is Ben?"

"Ben is Nick . . . Nick was Ben. I made him up—Nick. That's not his name. He's not a lawyer, and he didn't get run down crossing the street. But his last name *is* McElwyn. That part is true."

For the first time in their marriage—for the first time, really, in the more than five years that she'd known him— Rodger looked blown away. He opened his mouth to say something, but nothing came out. He stared at a bookcase, which he seemed to scan, but there was no manual there that he could reference. He frowned and ran a hand through his salt-and-pepper hair and let it remain, rubbing the top of his head as if he'd bumped it on an eave.

"I see," he said at last in a voice that was scarily controlled. "In that case, tell me about . . . Ben, why don't you." He turned and settled his chilling, appraising gaze on her.

Sarann wanted to bow her head and slap on a scarlet letter then and there—anything to soften the cold, hard look she saw in her husband's eyes. "He was a guy I met at a party once."

"How do you mean, 'once'?"

"I mean it just the way it sounds."

"You never married him."

"Noo. I did not."

"So Abigail is—?"

"Yes." Now she did bow her head. *My bastard daughter.*

"Does she know it?"

"What do *you* think?" Sarann said with a flash of impatience. She was dismayed by his teacherly queries and his headmaster's calm.

"I *think*," Rodger said, "that one of you might have said something to me."

Tears sprang suddenly from a stir of emotions that included guilt, shame, and an unexpected dose of resentment. Sarann wiped her eyes hurriedly: Rodger did not like her to cry; he said it gave her an unfair advantage.

After a deep breath to regain control, she said as humbly as she knew how, "Rodger, do you think I haven't wanted to tell you? But if I had, then you would have become part of the lie. You would have become a conspirator. You would have ended up in league with me against Abby."

He didn't look in the least convinced.

"Don't you see?" she pleaded. "I couldn't tell you before I told her. And I haven't, I just haven't, been able to admit it to her before now. I'm not sure I ever would have admitted it, if she hadn't put two and two together herself."

Still he said nothing. Sarann allowed herself one brief sigh and then raced on, in a rush to prevent her daughter from falling into disfavor.

"Abby only just found out. I'm sure she's waiting to see what I do. But in any case," she said with another unexpected surge of resentment, "it wasn't her job to tell you anything. It was mine."

She could see that Rodger didn't like having her point out the proper protocol to him. It was like telling Miss Manners how to set a table, or a governor when he could grant parole.

"I'm sorry, Rodger," she whispered, bringing her confession to a close. "I wish it weren't all true."

Without a word, he stood up and touched all ten fingertips to his desk. She had the absurd suspicion that he was going to give her detention or make her sit in a corner somewhere. There was just something about the way he looked down over the bridge of his nose at her.

She waited, jumpy with apprehension for the punishment she knew would follow. When he didn't say anything but just kept looking at her, she fairly exploded with anticipation.

"*What?*" she cried, gripping the carved arms of her chair. "What are you going to do? Tell me and be done with it! If you want a divorce, then say so. If you want—"

"A divorce?" he asked, frowning at the notion. "Why would I do that? I married you for better or for worse, Sarann. I admit, right now things look worse rather than better; I'd be lying if I said I was anything but shocked by your deceit. But perhaps you can't be blamed. Perhaps you were never taught—"

"Oh, please, Rodger. Of course I was taught. Do you think I was raised by wolves? Do I really seem that clueless to you?"

He said nothing; nothing at all.

So this was going to be her punishment: that there would be no punishment. He was going to take the high road, at the same time implying that anyone *she* knew would have taken the low one by wailing and carrying on.

He was going to be, in short, very decent about it.

She covered her face with her hands and said in a muffled voice, "I'm so sorry. You thought you were getting someone else . . . I'm sorry."

She was filled with so many regrets, but the biggest of all was regret that their marriage, which she had entered into with such high hopes and such good intentions, had been derailed so early in its journey. Sarann was the one who'd thrown the switch that had sent the train careening off its rails; she knew that. She also knew that the daunting job of getting the train back on track would fall mostly to Rodger. It wasn't fair to him, and there wasn't a blessed thing she could do to make it fair.

He broke through her revery by saying gruffly, "What's done is done. We won't speak of it again."

If only life were that easy.

She said softly, "What about Abby? Abby will want to know more about Ben."

Rodger shrugged in agreement. "I'll arrange to get Abby what she needs to know about her birth father. That can be done very discreetly. The one thing I don't want is for you to upset her so much that she becomes foolishly indiscreet with her friends. Since you don't know anything about Ben McElwyn anyway," he said dryly, "I'd appreciate it if you'd avoid the topic altogether with her for a while."

Sarann nodded, although something inside of her rebelled at the way Rodger had taken control. She said with gentle irony, "Is it really so despicable if you're married to a woman with an illegitimate daughter? Couldn't your marrying me be considered almost an act of . . . kindness?"

Rodger sighed and said, "No. Not after I've told everyone what you've told me—that your husband died tragically early. Do you see what a box I'm in? If anyone finds out, I'll come off as either a liar or a credulous fool."

"Oh, damn, I hadn't thought of that," she said, even more distressed now.

Rodger walked over to the west window in time to catch the last of the sunset filtering through the louvered shutters. Without turning around, he said, "Just . . . don't make things any worse than you have, Sarann. You owe me that much. Let me find out about Abby's father. If for some reason he really has died—and stranger things have happened—then there really isn't an issue."

It was a stunning thought. Sarann had spent a dozen years

telling people that Abby's father was dead, but it never occurred to her that it might really be so.

She whispered, "I only want what's best for Abby . . . and for you."

"Yes. Well. We'll have to see, won't we?"

He turned around to face her. She saw fear in his dark eyes, proof that she had screwed up royally. He was headmaster of a private school with a sterling reputation, a school that was founded by his grandfather and presided over by his father, men of unquestioned integrity. But they were then, and he was now. His reputation was on the line, and it was Sarann who had put it there.

"I'm sorry, Rodger," she repeated numbly, following him with her gaze as he headed for the door. After all her rehearsed speeches, it was all she could think to say.

He turned to her and said, "I know you are."

Encouraged by his softer tone, she said, "Should I throw together a couple of omelettes for us? I'm not very hungry."

He smiled ruefully. "No, neither am I. But all right. And then we'll have tea."

Because that's the way his people faced adversity, she knew. They fortified themselves with tea.

Chapter 7

Dear Mr. McElwyn,
It's been two days, and unfortunately I haven't heard
from you in reply to my e-mail. If you're on vacation
I'll understand, but if you're not and are just nervous
about answering me, don't be. I'm not a stalker or
anything. All I'd like is a simple yes or no to my ques-
tion of did you know a girl named Sarann Johnson
twelve years ago?

> *Yours sincerely,*
> *Abigail Johnson Bonniface*

P.S. I'm sending you a copy of this e-mail via snail
mail, just in case for some reason you aren't able to
get online. I'd rather have you answer me by e-mail,
though, and not snail mail. You can e-mail from a
cybercafe or even a library if your computer is on the
fritz. Did you know that?

Not a stalker? The hell she wasn't! She knew where
he lived now, and she was sending him mail. What next?
Carrier pigeon?

What a pain. He moved the cursor over to the delete
button and zapped her into oblivion for the second time.

Dear Mr. McElwyn,
I still haven't heard from you. You must be on vaca-
tion. I've been doing a little research and have dis-
covered that you're a private investigator. That is so
cool. Are skills like that inherited? I would love to do

an interview with you for our school paper. Hopefully
when you get back, you'll get in touch right away.

> *Best wishes,*
> *Abigail*

The e-mail was so filled with scary implications that
Ben choked on his toast, then scalded his tongue when he
tried to wash down the bread with black coffee. He was
a fraction away from being apoplectic. *School paper?*
Lawyers didn't write for school papers, and neither did
matchmaking aunts. Just how old was Abigail, anyway,
and why, dear Jesus, did she care if there was a gene for
investigative skills or not?

Who the hell was she?

Was it *possible*?

His mind went tumbling back to a certain midnight in
a tumbledown apartment overlooking Narragansett Bay.
He'd been lying on his bed with his dick pointing straight
up to the ceiling light, waiting for Sarann to come out of
the bathroom where she'd been doing things with a diaphragm. He remembered how she looked when she
emerged: shy but willing, a feast for him to behold. She
had a great body. It was on the old-fashioned side and
just made for loving, and he remembered thinking that he
was on the verge of having the best night of his life.

He remembered saying, "You all set, then?"

But he could not, for the life of him, remember her
answer.

Not her exact words. They had seemed reassuring at
the time—but then, she could have said, "Oh, sure; I have
a bottle of vinegar in my purse," and he would have been
just as reassured. He didn't really care if she was protected
or not. All he really cared about at that moment was getting her between him and the ceiling light. Everything else
was just words.

He raked his memory, trying to dredge up the exact ones she'd used. *Uh-huh? You bet? Fer sure? Darn tootin'?*

Just how safe were diaphragms, anyway? Did they pop, like rubbers?

Could she have lied? Could she have said nothing at all, and could he have made up a lie in his head for her? Had he been that fucking horny for her?

Could sperm wiggle their way home around that kind of barrier? Were diaphragms just a truly lousy concept in birth control?

Was Abigail Johnson Bonniface somewhere around twelve years old?

Ben was in a sweat now. He shut his computer down and made himself get dressed and drive to city hall and spend the morning in the dusty, dreary basement there, poring over deeds and assigns, trying to track an exspouse's hidden assets, trying to understand how Abigail could possibly think that being a PI was cool.

By the time he walked out it was raining; by the time he got home he was soaked. He had a simple reason for returning to his apartment instead of trying to cozy up to the neighbors of his client's ex-spouse to find out where the bum might be hiding: he needed to change into dry socks. So he peeled off the wet ones and while he was at it, he turned on his computer. Abigail's e-mail glared at him, demanding action.

Delete. Delete delete delete her from his thoughts. Whoever she was, she was an unnecessary intrusion into what he laughingly called his life. He didn't ask for the e-mail. He didn't want the e-mail. He had better things to do than to wonder all day who Abigail Johnson Bonniface was.

He deleted the e-mail, shut the computer down, and went back out to do his job. He got in his car, turned on the ignition, swore, turned off the ignition, went back to his apartment, and turned on the computer.

He had to go back and poke through the computer's trash folder, something he didn't like to do on principal—trash was trash—but he retrieved Abigail's last e-mail and, for whatever reason, hit the reply button. Best not to use her name; best to be simple and to the point.

Who are you?

Sincerely,
Ben McElwyn

Before he could second-guess himself, he hit the send button. Off it went. At least the damn ball was finally out of his court, and he'd be able to get some sleep.

Night came, and he tossed and turned.

Abigail came home from school and went immediately to her computer to check her e-mail. She hadn't been able to get online for nearly twenty hours, and she was almost sick from the frustration of it.

She closed her eyes and crossed her fingers as she waited. *Please, please, please let there be a bmac5 today.*

She opened her eyes and there he was: bmac5. It was a miracle! She opened the e-mail in a state of ecstasy but was instantly crushed to see such a short message. It was practically rude. She'd done everything she could think of to be intriguing but not clingy, and this is all he could come up with? Six words? He probably had his secretary write it for him. It was *so* insulting. She felt like a panhandler who had just had someone throw a crummy nickel in her cup.

Deciding to give him a taste of his own medicine, she composed a response:

I think, your daughter.

Sincerely,
Abigail

She sat back and folded her arms across her chest. How would he like getting *that*?

Should she send it? Really, actually send it? It would teach him *such* a good lesson.

No, she decided, after thinking about it. It was too abrupt. He could have a heart attack or something. Anyway, he hadn't even said if he was the Ben who knew Sarann—although if he wasn't, then he probably wouldn't have answered at all.

Either way, Abigail resolved not to send the e-mail. She would stick with her original plan. First he had to tell her if he knew Sarann. Then, and only then, would Abigail tell him who she was.

A shave-and-a-haircut knock on her door told her that her stepfather was on the other side of it. "Abby?" she heard him say. "You in there?"

"Yes! No!" she said, hitting the send button in her panic. Off went her answer through cyberspace, leaving Abigail too shocked to think. She had enough sense to get rid of Ben McElwyn's e-mail, but that was about it. When her stepfather came in smiling, she was speechless.

The smile faded from his face. "Hey, sweetie, what's wrong? You're all flushed." He went up to her and felt her forehead. "You feel okay?"

"Why wouldn't I feel okay?" she whispered between pants of panic.

"Well, you were on that field trip to Boston. You could've caught something; different germs, you know," he said, smoothing her hair back and tucking it behind her ear.

"Oh, Dad, there's nothing wrong with me," she said, forcing her voice to sound bored.

She didn't like it that he was always so concerned about her. He was always watching every little thing she did. She was used to being on her own, or at least to not having to explain things to anyone but her mom. Now she had two jailers watching over her.

"I just want you to know," her stepfather said, speaking very softly, "that I'm here for you. If you're sick . . . if you're in trouble . . . if you're upset, I'm here for you."

"Okay," she said, wondering where he was going with that. Did he know about Ben McElwyn? He didn't act like he knew. He acted like nothing was wrong. Her mom, too. Everyone was running around the house acting, like, oh-so happy, but Abigail could feel them watching her all the time.

"So . . . how're things going in school?" he said, perusing the bulletin board that hung next to her desk.

"The usual," she said, shrugging. "Mrs. Larkin gives way too much homework and Miss Selby doesn't give any."

He pointed to a photo she'd tacked up of Leonardo DiCaprio in *Titanic* and kind of laughed. "You like him, huh?"

Again she shrugged. "He's okay. That movie is, like, so over with. I should take that down." It made her really, really uncomfortable to talk about boys with her stepfather. What business was it of his, anyway?

He leaned a little closer over her shoulder to look at her computer screen. Her heart felt like it was stuck between her tonsils, and she knew that her cheeks were *totally* beet red. If he asked to see what kind of e-mail she got, she would just die.

"You spend a lot of time at this thing," he teased. "Why don't you read a good book instead?"

"Well, this is good for my reading *and* my writing skills. Even Miss Selby says that."

"So who are your correspondents? Do you still have that pen pal in Dublin?"

"Oh, yes! She's great!"

This was awful! He was getting too interested!

"Hey, what's this?" he asked, picking up the printed-out image she'd brought home from her field trip.

She took advantage of his distraction to shut down her computer as she explained, "Oh, that. I . . . meant to show it to you and Mom. They took digital pictures of us at MIT and then they had this computer program that scans the pictures and adds years to who you are, and that's me at, like, twenty-five. I hope they're wrong," she said with a nervous laugh, although secretly she was fascinated to know that she could look so grown-up.

"My God."

Alarmed, Abigail looked up at her stepfather and said, "What is it? It's my chin, isn't it, you think it's going to be too long for my face."

"No, no—how can you say that?" he muttered.

He studied her picture for so long that Abigail began to squirm in her chair. She stared at the flecks of gray in his hair and then at his hand, which was shaking. Did it always shake like that? She never noticed.

At last he whispered, "You're going to be beautiful."

"Well . . . thanks, I guess." It was a weird compliment, about something that she was eventually going to be, but who knew if she'd ever really look like that? "I mean, it's, like, just some computer, guessing."

He handed her back the sheet with her so-called picture on it and then he smiled and said, "Of course, you're beautiful now, Abby. You'll just be a different kind of beautiful in a dozen more years."

"Oh, Dad," she said, even more uncomfortable with

that compliment than the first one. She dismissed it by saying wryly, "Tommy used to call me Flabby Abby whenever he saw me, so I don't think I'm all *that* beautiful."

"Oh? And who's Tommy? An Academy boy?"

He asked as if he didn't really care one way or the other; but Abigail had seen that look in his eyes before. It was the same one he got when he found out who ripped all the flowers out of the window boxes by his office. She was getting Tommy into trouble—Tommy! The last person in the world!

"He didn't really mean it, Dad; he was just trying to get my attention. I know what he really meant."

"So do I," her stepfather said with another smile. But the look in his eyes didn't change.

She wanted to get him off the subject of Tommy as well, so she said, "Did you want to see me for something?"

His smile got bigger and even more fake. "Yep, as a matter of fact, I did." He picked up the computerized picture of her again and propped it up against the framed photo of Ben McElwyn. "Have you tried to look for any resemblance?" he asked oh-so casually.

"Oh, Dad, why would I do that? He's a guy."

She had studied the two images side by side for hours. There might have been a similarity around the eyes, but even there, Abigail wasn't sure. She was still holding out hope that Ben McElwyn was the guy on the couch.

"So . . . I guess you know the latest about him," her stepfather said.

She snorted. "There isn't much to know, is there."

"Well, that's what I wanted to talk to you about."

He sat back against her desk with his legs in front of the drawers. The desk was jammed against the wall on the other side, so she was trapped between her stepfather and the star of *Titanic*.

Her stepfather sighed and shook his head. He said, "This has come out of the blue—for me as well as for you, I hope you know that; I wasn't keeping anything from you, Abby. Still, like it or not, all we can do now is make the best of a bad situation."

"That's what I'm trying to do," she said without looking at him. She kept her gaze glued to the blank computer monitor, afraid that Ben McElwyn was going to appear on the screen like Conan O'Brien or someone and start telling jokes.

Her stepfather said, "I think you're being really grown-up about this, Abby. It's incredibly mature of you not to go crying to everyone around you that you've been badly treated. I admire you very much for it. Very few people would behave so well in your situation."

She nodded silently in acknowledgment of the compliment, but she was thinking someone could cut through his spiel with a knife. All he cared about was his precious reputation and his precious Academy.

"So, anyway, this is what I propose to do, provided you're in agreement with it: I'll have a professional inquiry done into the facts and history of your birth father—"

"Professional?" she said, gulping. "You mean, like a PI?"

"Yes; a private investigator would be the most thorough and efficient, we think."

But Ben McElwyn *was* a private eye! And *she* was investigating *him*! It would be too confusing—maybe dangerous, you just never knew—to have a third person involved.

She balked. "I don't see why we can't do the investigating ourselves. It wouldn't be that hard." To say the least.

Her stepfather sounded serious as he said, "We don't know anything about this man, Abby. He could be—"

"A serial killer? Do you think so, Dad?"

Her stepfather was not amused. "I *meant*, he could have a wife, a family, a sensitive career. You don't want to hear this, Abby, but he might not want to know that he has a daughter. I'm afraid that there are a lot of men who would resent the sudden responsibility."

Although not him. *He* had welcomed Abigail with open arms, and he seemed to want to make sure that she knew it. She felt guilty even for thinking about another father than the one who was standing so near and trying so hard to be nice.

She sighed and patted her hands together in a nervous gesture. "Can't we just wait a day?" she pleaded. "Can't I think about it?"

"I was fairly sure that you've *been* thinking about it," her stepfather said, shrugging. "That's why I came in to chat."

He seemed very relieved. He skimmed his hand over her hair again and tucked it behind her ear. "But whatever you say, Abby; you're the boss."

Just then they heard the door opening downstairs. Her mother had come home from the shop, so that was good timing; Abigail had no desire to get into a family fight over what to do about Ben McElwyn.

Not until he answered that e-mail.

Chapter 8

"HAS ANYONE SEEN my wallet?"

It was excruciating to have to ask the question, but Sarann had looked high and low and was out of ideas.

Abby said "nope" automatically, as twelve-year-olds do, but Rodger was much more concerned.

"You took it out yesterday to check that you had your library card, remember? You thought you might have left it at the reference desk?"

"Yes. And it was in my wallet, so that was okay—Abby, don't wolf your cereal that way."

"Well, what am I supposed to do? The bus will be here any minute!"

"Then get downstairs earlier. You know how to tell time."

"You don't have to get sarcastic!" Abby cried, suddenly near tears.

She was obviously on edge; they all were.

"Did you leave it on your dresser?" Rodger asked.

"No, I've looked there."

"Run through everything that you did yesterday. Did you look on the hall table, your desk, the table next to your chair in the sitting room?"

"Yes," said Sarann, trying to seem calm though her stomach felt bound up in barbed wire. "I've looked everywhere."

"In the laundry room?"

"Why would it be there?"

He shrugged. "You were doing laundry." After a pause, he said, "You did look through your purse for it, didn't you?"

It was humiliating to be asked, and even more so to be

expected to answer. "Yes," she said with a glance at her daughter. "Of course I did."

"Well, a wallet doesn't just walk away," Rodger said tersely.

"This one must have," Sarann quipped. She was trying to keep it light, but she was becoming disoriented again, confused by her own confusion.

A horn beeped and Abby cried, "Oh, I *knew* it! That's the bus! I can't finish this, and it's all your fault!"

She pushed her bowl away so sharply that milk slopped over it, then grabbed her knapsack from the ladderback chair and took off in a sprint, her sneakers squeaking on the wide boards of the bare hall floor.

Barely acknowledging his stepdaughter's melodramatic exit, Rodger said to Sarann, "Think of all the places you've been around the house since yesterday afternoon. What did you do besides the laundry? You read; you wrote out some checks; you said hello to James—and little else—when he dropped off the book; you were on the phone—you cooked dinner. Ah." He rose from the table and methodically walked the perimeter of the kitchen, checking countertops and opening cupboards.

Sarann was amazed that he would even consider searching the cupboards. He was like a Jack Russell Terrier with his muzzle on her ankle; she wanted desperately to shake him off before he drew blood. "Rodger, I've recreated my entire day. I even walked through the garden, looking for the damn thing."

"That's right," he said, brightening. "You *were* in the garden." He got up from the massive oak table that once had seen service in the galley of a square-rigger and squinted through the French doors at the garden, ablaze with yellow daylilies, orange and red poppies, and deep-pink bleeding hearts, all dazzling in the morning sun.

She saw his shoulders slump. She saw him shake his head and mutter, "Oh, for—"

And she watched him as he went outside and approached a curved stone bench hidden behind a winterberry bush and tucked under an old, dying maple in a corner of the yard. The spot was cool and shady, and Sarann occasionally sat there; but she couldn't imagine why Rodger felt a sudden need to visit it. When he returned with her wallet and laid it, wet with morning dew, on the table in front of her cereal bowl, she was more frightened than relieved.

She could scarcely hear her voice over the wild thumping of her heart. "But . . . I didn't take it out there."

"Do you really believe that? My God, Sarann, you're beginning to seriously worry me. These lapses of yours aren't normal. They're coming too frequently; they're too bizarre. Why would you take your wallet into the garden?"

She tried to remember. "I . . . I don't know. I must have had it with me when I went out to look at the forget-me-nots. They looked so pretty, so blue from the kitchen; I just had to go out and see them up close."

She remembered the forget-me-nots; she did not remember the wallet. She remembered that the bench felt cool and hard and somehow comforting; she did not remember the wallet. She remembered that the flies were out in force and bothering her, and that's why she came inside.

She did not remember the wallet.

Nor did she expect the next blow; it caught her completely unprepared. Rodger said quietly, "Your wallet was lying in the copper birdbath next to the bench. Do you have any idea why you put it there?"

She sucked in her breath in shock and picked up the wallet, a slender, leather Liz Claiborne affair. It wasn't damp with dew at all; it was completely soaked. Her cash, her receipts, her photos—all were a soggy mess. Dazed, she looked from the wallet up to her husband. "But why would I put it in the birdbath?"

He was looking at her warily now. "I don't know. You tell me. Is there something that you're trying to hide—something more, I mean?"

"*Rodger.*"

But she had no right to be offended, so she added softly, "No, you know everything now."

"Then I'm running out of theories. You can't be this addled just because of Abby—we know she's adjusting to events remarkably well—and it can't be because of your shop, which you're obviously having a lot of fun with."

He took the wallet from her, then opened it and removed the soaking-wet twenties that were inside. She watched, mesmerized, as he laid them out before her, one by one like little drowned corpses, on the worn surface of the ship's table.

When he finished, he said quietly, "Do you resent my money, Sarann?"

Baffled, she looked from the twenties to him. "Resent it? No ... I owe you everything because of it. You've given me a chance to do something, to become something. You've given my daughter a chance at a real future. I wish I'd had money of my own to bring into this marriage, but ... resent your money? Why would I do that?"

He rubbed his square jaw in a lighthearted grimace and said, "I'm thinking of the, quote-unquote, stolen car ... of your refusal to unlock the front door ... and now of your misplacing your wallet filled with—well, obviously my—money. Even the missing stamp—that was on a payment envelope, wasn't it? Taken together, your actions seem symbolic."

"Of ... ?"

He gestured toward the money, then let his hand fall to his side. In a gentle but sad voice, he said, "You're a very proud woman, Sarann. Maybe you can't handle having some-

one take care of you—and Abby—after all those years of
struggling on your own. Maybe your recent behavior is a
way of acting out your rejection of me."

It was a new and startling explanation of the strange
things that had been happening, but it couldn't possibly be
the right one.

All Sarann could think to say was, "Huh." She tried to
stall before answering the charge by stacking Abby's breakfast bowl carefully inside of hers and then laying the two
bowls gently on top of Rodger's plate. (She'd chipped a bowl
in the set a few months earlier, and he had felt it keenly.)

"You have a degree in psychology, Rodger," she said,
carefully carrying the dishes to the sink. "You can't help
seeing patterns where there aren't any."

She turned around to face him. "But honestly, you're
wrong. I try not to think about your money one way or the
other."

That much was true. But she had gone from being part
of the Working Poor to being the wife of one of the wealth-
iest men in town, and it was hard not to notice the difference.
He knew it as well as she.

Obviously disappointed in her reaction, he said, "It was
just a thought." He snugged up his tie and picked up his
leather attaché, propped against a table leg. "In any case, you
might want to consider seeing an endocrinologist. Who
knows? It could be something as simple as a hormone imbalance. It doesn't have to be—well! Think about it, won't
you?"

He gave her a hurried, almost shy kiss, and he left.

Sarann immediately walked out into the garden and, ignoring the pesky greenflies buzzing around her, stayed sitting
on the curved stone bench for what later seemed like a long
time, trying to remember when and why she had dumped her
Liz Claiborne wallet into the new copper birdbath.

*   *   *

Ben McElwyn had one real passion in life: rowing. He'd got the bug when he was about ten and fishing from the muddy banks of the Thames River in Connecticut. It was pea-soup thick and the fishing was only so-so, but he was happy enough. He enjoyed being alone with his thoughts.

He was about to cast his line when out of the fog a preppy-looking guy in khakis and a dark blue windbreaker went gliding by in a long, sleek, beautifully varnished skiff, oblivious to the ragtag boy who watched, transfixed, as the skiff sliced quickly and silently through the river and disappeared again in the mist ahead.

It had been, for Ben, an unexpected and quite magical vision, as if he'd seen a unicorn, or a faerie, or a knight from Arthurian legend. If Lancelot had opted to chase the Grail by boat, surely this was the vessel he would have done it in.

Young Ben had waited an hour or more for the vision to return, and when it didn't, he ran home and in the course of the summer traded his fishing gear for a bike, the bike for a seized outboard, the busted outboard for a leaky little pram. The little rowboat wasn't much, but it got him off the riverbank and onto the water, which was a whole different ball game. It took him another ten years, but eventually he got himself an exact copy of the fast and beautiful rowing shell that had so awed him as a kid.

Unfortunately, the boat didn't come with a Grail to chase. Still, it provided him with a great workout and a place to be alone with his thoughts; so he couldn't complain. He liked his rowing shell enough to rent a garage so that he could work on it and store it there off-season. Over the years he lavished sweat and money and a certain amount of affection on it, and, stupidest of all, turned down a really good offer for it by one of his cop buddies. It was as near to a commitment as he'd ever made in his life.

On the evening that he received Abigail's stunning e-mail, Ben loaded his rowing shell onto the padded roof rack of his car and headed straight for the river. He needed to clear his head, big time. It was chilly and raw, but there wasn't any wind, and with any luck he'd be able to out-row the notion that he—Benjamin Lowell McElwyn, for chrissake—was somebody's father.

Nuh nuh nuh. The little girl was wrong, of that he was convinced. He slipped the glistening craft into the water and stepped into it with practiced ease, then slid the spoon oars into their locks and took a long, slow stroke, as satisfying as the first inhale of a cigarette.

Pleasure to follow, he promised himself. Don't think about anything else but the pleasure to follow. Focus. Feel good.

Forward and back he went with the oars, feathering them expertly, sliding them a mere inch or so above the water on the return stroke. His breathing deepened, his serenity returned, with every twist of his wrists and pull on the oars. Yes. This was more like it.

Forward, and back.

Forward, and back.

I think, your daughter.

I think, your daughter.

He tried to shake free of Abigail's terrifying words.

Forward, and back.

Forward, and *I think, your daughter I think, your daughter.*

The scary mantra became a drumbeat in his brain, a relentless reminder of why he'd fled to the river in the first place. He hated those four words, hated the little girl who wrote them, hated the woman who had put the lie in the little girl's head.

He wasn't her goddamned father!

I think, your daughter.

I think, your daughter.

He was hounded by the refrain with every stroke of his

oars as he plied the length of the river, chilled not by the raw, damp air, but by the conviction that his life—his cozy, sloppy, easy, noncommittal life—was about to be slammed on its ear.

The kid wasn't his, but someone was going to have to tell her that, and he wanted it it to be someone else than him. Who did you send on a mission like that? Priest? Rabbi? Lawyer? DNA expert?

He had to channel repeated surges of resentment at Sarann into his oars instead. She had a hell of a nerve, letting her kid go wandering off in search of a father. If anyone was going to do the searching, it should have been Sarann. Or would that have involved too many men to bother? God damn.

Poor kid. He wasn't blaming her, not at all. His own father had split when Ben was seven, and though he used to show up every once in a while, he hadn't been and still wasn't what Ben would call a father. He'd taught Ben to fish, true, and Ben had had his first cigarette, his first beer, and his first look at a dirty magazine in his father's pickup—but he wasn't what Ben would call a father. The beers, the fish, the guy talk—it had come in bits and pieces, just enough to tantalize a kid, to make him want to see his old man more. When Ben needed his dad for the big stuff, he was never there. Shit.

Shit!

He pulled up short and let his boat glide to a graceful, floating pause. A chop had come up; it lapped at the side of the skiff as it presented its beam to the wind. It was going to be a harder row back. The sun had set, and the pink-and-blue sky was pulling a blanket of gray up behind it, getting ready for the cold night ahead.

Ah, hell, ah, gee. Ben sat with his knees pulled up to his chest, his oars poised lightly over the water, as he tried to figure his next move. He sat that way for a long time, lost in thought, as his skiff drifted farther downriver.

When he finally shook himself free of Abigail Johnson Bonniface, it was dark and his limbs had locked up from inertia and cold. He didn't have a running light, of course, and the row back was going to be long and hard.

With any luck, he'd get run down by a passing freighter.

Chapter 9

CROTCHY MCELWYN WAS Ben's first cousin—a career cop and the reason that Ben had joined the force in the first place. Ben knew that things hadn't worked out in his life the way Crotchy had hoped, but Crotchy still kept tabs on his kid cousin, and he helped him whenever he could.

The two sat at the far end of the smoky bar at O'Brien's, a cop hangout, looking for all the world as if they were catching up on family gossip, which in a sense they were, only Crotchy didn't know it.

"The girl's from Farnham," Crotchy told Ben. "It's a little town in Massachusetts on the Essex River, not far from the coast. That's a nice area, Cape Ann. My wife's brother's a fisherman out of Gloucester. Tough times for those guys; they're running out of fish. One thing you've gotta say for cops—we never run out of crime. Here's the kid's address," he said, sliding a piece of scrap paper across the bar to his cousin.

He took a long slug of his draft beer, then filled in the rest of the blanks for Ben. "You were right. She's twelve. An only child; mother's name is Sarann, maiden name Johnson; stepfather is Rodger. He's headmaster of some fancy-dancy boarding school for rich kids called Faxton Academy. Tuition like you wouldn't believe; three times the size of my monthly mortgage."

"Thanks, Crotch. You make my job easy."

Crotchy let out a belch the size of his gut and said, "Yeah, well, you ask me again, I'm gonna say no. I mean it. You aren't on the force anymore. So what's with the girl? Child porn? Chat-room seduction? Buncha dirty bastards; I could kill 'em all, preying on kids that way. Jesus, if I could get my mitts on one of 'em for ten minutes."

"No, no, it's nothing like that," Ben muttered. "I'll fill you in when I'm a little further along in the investigation."

"Yeah, whatever. Hey! News. Hogarth's out on his ass without pay."

"No shit?"

"No shit. The asshole got caught stealing evidence again, only this time he didn't have time to plant it on his partner. He's toast."

"So there *is* a God."

"Haven't I always said? Still, that was an okay thing you did, not ratting out a rat. You're a good man, Charlie Brown. It cost you."

"Ah, bullshit."

A couple of cops walked past. Ben knew one but not the other. The one he knew said, "Heard about Hogarth?"

"You betcha."

They grinned and moved on and Crotchy slapped Ben on the back and said, "What goes around comes around, my friend. You say the word, you're back on the force. You never were convicted, anyhow."

"Not interested."

"Of course not," Crotch said, shaking his head. "You're having too much fun on your own. Ain't getting nowhere, won't ever see a pension, drive a rusty old Honda, not even an American clunker, but you're havin'—you *think* you're havin'—fun. Lemme buy you a beer."

"No, I owe you."

"That you do," Crotchy agreed. He held up two fingers to the barkeep, then said to his cousin, "You need to settle down. You ain't a kid no more, man. You're thirty, what, three? C'mon—you should be runnin' your own daughter over to soccer practice, not tryin' to rein in someone else's twelve-year-old brat."

Ben winced, then smiled politely. "Bullshit."

*   *   *

Crotchy was right: Cape Ann was a beautiful area. North of Boston, Ben hugged the ocean, opting for the scenic route instead of inland Route 95. He found a coastline that was very different from Connecticut, where on most days little nothing-waves from Long Island Sound lapped a flat and overdeveloped shore.

The wind was howling from the northeast through intermittent rain, creating huge rollers that slammed the rocky shore and ricocheted high in the air, sending a slick of salt spray over the roads that Ben drove. The scene was wild, majestic, romantic. Every cliché that Ben had ever heard about the North Atlantic applied to the Cape Ann section of its coast, and quite a few others as well. "Mean" came immediately to mind. Vindictive. Unrelenting. Punishing. And not to mention, fucking scary. Ben was at ease on the water, but all in all, he'd sooner go over Niagara in a barrel than venture out on that stretch of ocean today.

On the advice of a waitress, he detoured over to Marblehead just to watch the storm twist and pound the yachts moored there, and then, getting into the tourist spirit, he stopped in Salem to see what the witches were all about and ended up exploring its rich maritime history instead. He drove through Manchester-by-the-Sea just because he liked the name, and he wandered through Gloucester to see if the *Sally Jean*, Crotchy's wife's brother's fishing trawler, was tied up at the docks. (It was out and Ben was incredibly impressed.)

By the time he found out that the *Sally Jean* wasn't around, it was nearly dark and too late to proceed with his plan to look up his so-called kid, so he rented a room at a plain motel on a bluff overlooking the sea, and he dined on a huge platter of fish and chips, and he told himself, many, many times over, that he wasn't really being a coward, but simply a curious traveler.

Uh-huh.

His plan had been to call Sarann that morning . . . afternoon . . . evening. So far, he'd done everything but. As he
drifted off into fitful sleep, stirred by the roar of the sea, Ben
realized that he was going to do one of two things: either
just show up at her door, or turn tail and run like hell straight
back to Connecticut.

He'd know which one in the morning.

Sarann woke up happy to see that the nor'easter had blown
itself out. The sun was up and shining, and her mood had
risen right along with it. As she made the bed she found
herself humming, something she hadn't done in weeks.

Rodger noticed it. "You seem pretty chipper this morning," he remarked around the corner as he lathered up to
shave.

"I know," she agreed. "I feel as though I've just weathered an awful storm."

"You have. It was pretty wild all night. We lost another
good-sized limb off the maple."

"No, I didn't mean—" She abandoned the half-made bed
and went over to lean against the doorway to the bathroom,
where she watched her husband run a blade expertly from
ear to cheek to jaw, then up the length of his neck to his
chin, right side first, always the same routine.

"It's because of you, you know," she told him.

He looked surprised. Razor poised, he glanced at her
through the mirror and said, "Me? How me?"

"You've been so good about . . . you know. This thing.
And at least Abigail knows now. I'm not saying she's over
it—she's ridiculously jumpy and tense this past couple of
days—but at least everything's out in the open. That's the
first step to healing."

She wasn't sure if Rodger was grimacing or just working
his jaw into shaving position; in any event, he said nothing,

but only grunted noncommittally as he scraped away another swath of white foam.

"And . . . and I've been thinking about it, and I think you're right," she said. "I don't like it, but I guess we should have some kind of discreet investigation done, for a medical history, if nothing else."

Rodger tapped his razor gently on the bowl of the antique pedestal sink and rinsed the blade under a flow of water. "Exactly. I'll see to it."

"They will be discreet, won't they? Ben would never know?" Sarann said, hungry for reassurance.

"Of course he wouldn't. That's what private investigators do: investigate privately."

"True."

But if he ever found out, I'd die.

"And, Rodger . . . ?"

He was working on his left side now, drawing the blade in a smooth, easy arc from ear to jaw, waiting to hear what else she had to say.

She murmured, "I think your theory about me is right: subconsciously, I must resent your wealth—or, if not your wealth exactly, then having to share Abigail. That's an awful thing to say, I know," she admitted, looking away from his image in the mirror.

She fussed with a loose thread in the lace trim of her nightgown. "Kind of hypocritical, aren't I. After all my yammering that you get more involved with Abby . . ."

When Sarann looked up at her husband again, it was to see that he'd nicked himself. A thin, bright-red trickle of blood was finding its own path down his neck alongside a border of shaving cream.

"It's nothing," he muttered in answer to her look of pain. He tore off a piece of tissue and plastered it to the cut. "I should've switched blades. You were saying?"

She laughed self-consciously. "I was saying that I guess

I'd rather be considered possessive than unhinged."

He smiled. "I don't blame you."

She probably took less comfort from that than he intended. "Anyway, from here on in," she said in a brave new voice, "no more goofy behavior. I understand now why I did those things, so that should put an end to it." She had spent the night convincing herself, although, for the life of her, she still couldn't remember the wallet.

He smiled a second time. "I'm glad. Let's hope this does put an end to it."

"It will!"

She finished with a perky little lift of her shoulders and went back to making the bed, giving the ultralight comforter a couple of shakes before letting it settle like a summer cloud on their four-poster bed. After that she fluffed the pillows and squared their corners and stacked them up against the cherry headboard with absolute precision the way Rodger liked them, and by the time she was done, Rodger had finished with the bathroom and she had it to herself.

An hour later and still feeling optimistic, Sarann locked the front door behind her. Impulsively, she tried the key. Yes! Turned like a charm. Halfway to her car—still parked exactly where she had left it—she heard the phone ringing inside the house. She decided to let the machine answer; she was in a hurry to pick up her new sign.

ONBOARD ANTIQUES. Sarann did like the sound of it. She unloaded the heavy, gilt-lettered shingle from her car and lugged it into the shop, where her contractor Jimmy Sturgis and two of his helpers were doing their best to make sure that she missed the tourist season and opened in the dead of the following winter.

"I think we need to do something about these plain walls," Jimmy told her. "They could use crown moldings, something to dress 'em up a little. And the baseboards could use trimmin' out. Class the place up. And you should consider tiling the entryway; that always makes a good first impression."

"How much would all that cost me?"

"Not too much. It goes fast."

"Jimmy, I don't know . . . I think we need to hold a turn."

"It's cheaper to do it now than for me to come in later, Mrs. B."

"I know, I know. Just . . . let me think about it."

"You're the boss."

"Yeah, right," she said, grinning. "You've run this show from the start."

He shrugged. "I'm just saying, I'm here now. Once I pack up my tools and leave, you won't see me until next spring. I'm gonna be flat out."

"No problem," she answered, stepping back to admire her shingle. "By next spring I'll be out of business, and crown moldings won't be an issue."

"What kinda talk is that? You should do real good; this is a Broadway location."

"That's what the landlord keeps saying," she quipped.

"You'll see. A year from now you'll be having me back to put in a custom tin ceiling."

"God, I hope so," she said, giving herself a quick hug of hope. "I want this to work so much."

"Can't miss. If you want to sell pizza, what do you do? You set up shop next to a Domino's and a Pizza Hut, that's what. You know what they say—"

"Location, location, location. You're right. Farnham, a town of forty-five hundred, at present has only three dozen antique shops, most of them on this street," she said dryly. "They desperately need one more."

He ignored the sarcasm and said, "Farnham won't be your customers; tourists and dealers will. And let's not forget that you're only half an hour from Boston. Besides, you have an angle—nautical antiques."

She was thinking of her most expensive acquisition. "Yes, but how many people either need or want a thousand-dollar brass binnacle in their family room?"

"Maybe none; but they'll buy the glass fishing balls, the seamen's chests, the lobster buoys—and oars, make sure you have oars—anything that reminds them of the good time they had on vacation. Now that I'm on it, think about stocking some of those wood Gloucester fishermen incense burners— you know, just a little something so the customer don't go out empty-handed. They're cheap: four or five bucks. Tourists eat that kind of stuff up, trust me. Oh, and a rack of postcards. Those always sell."

When she looked iffy about selling souvenirs side-by-side with her painstakingly acquired antiques and collectibles, he shrugged and said, "But what do I know? Don't worry. You'll do fine."

He began to pack up his tools.

"You're leaving?"

"Got to; one of my regulars just had a tub overflow in his B-and-B. Job like that can't wait. The man's losing business."

"Oh." *He's losing business? What about me?*

Jimmy was crouched on the floor, snugging his drill into its carrying case. He looked up at Sarann and said, "You were planning on having me hang the shingle, right?"

She said, "It would be affordable advertising." Besides, seeing that shingle swinging from the building was bound to be one of the high points of her—until recently—quiet little life so far.

Jimmy shrugged and said, "I'll see if I can get back here tomorrow."

He and his help left, and Sarann thought how odd it was that someone as overcommitted as he was should still be drumming up business every chance he got. He was like a Depression survivor who stockpiled food.

In any case, she didn't dare go back to the well for any more funding. She was way over budget as it was. Crown moldings? In his dreams.

Sarann turned her attention back to her new shingle, pleased that it had turned out so well. She loved the anchor and chain, the gold-leafed lettering, the rich and dignified greenish black field. In her mind it typified Farnham: a small, charming New England town with an impressive history. How lucky that, out of all the small, charming towns in New England, this was the one where she'd dropped her own anchor. How lucky that in Farnham she'd found Rodger, the most forgiving husband in the world. If she could only coax the daughter she adored into doing the same, her life would surely be perfect.

A tapping on the store window behind her sent her jumping out of her daydream. It was her daughter, waiting to be let in.

"I saw you inside and I made the bus drop me off," Abby told her when she unlocked the door.

Sarann was all smiles. "What a nice surprise," she said. "I was just thinking about you."

"I didn't know you were going to be in the shop this afternoon," Abby said. She looked glum as she dropped her knapsack alongside a sorry-looking card table and slumped into one of the two rickety folding chairs drawn up to it.

"I had to pick up the sign," Sarann explained, "and I brought it here, hoping to get it hung today. See?" she said, pointing to the shingle that was propped up against an unpainted wall. "What do you think?" No doubt it was wrong to feel so pleased with something in front of her daughter, but Sarann couldn't hide her delight.

"Looks dark," Abby said, dismissing it. "Couldn't you have done it in turquoise or something?"

"Honey, this is New England, not Key West."

"Whatever." Somehow the girl managed to slump a little more deeply into the folding chair.

Rodger had made Sarann promise not to discuss Ben with Abby, and so far she'd managed to honor that wish. But looking at her daughter now . . . so hurt . . . so insecure . . . her own flesh and blood . . . so obviously another man's child, not Rodger's. . . .

He did not have the right to muzzle Sarann. It was a feeling that wouldn't go away. Despite everything, despite her guilt and shame and embarrassment and desire to atone, Sarann could not make herself believe that Rodger knew what was best where her daughter was concerned.

Sarann longed to hold her little girl, hold her and reassure her and convince that she was loved, despite all appearances to the contrary. But Sarann couldn't do that without crossing the huge divide that separated them.

She fell to one knee so that she could see her daughter's averted, sad face, and she stroked her cheek, and she said in an anguished voice, "Abby . . . honey . . . *please* forgive me. I made the biggest mistake of my life by not telling you, years ago, about your father. I had lots of reasons, some of them good, some of them not so good. I was so afraid of hurting you; I love you so much. That's the one true thing in every one of those motives: the fact that I love you so much. Nothing will change that. If you love me, if you hate me, if you forgive me, if you don't—I will always, always love you unconditionally."

She saw a tear roll out from the corner of Abby's eye as the girl sat with arms folded across her chest, staring resolutely past Sarann and down at her feet. Immediately, she saw Abby wipe away the tear—and that, she hated to see. It meant that her daughter wasn't yet ready to think about forgiveness.

So be it. Sarann would wait. Weeks, months, years, the rest of her life, if she had do. Wasn't that what mothers did anyway, held their breath and hoped that everything would turn out all right for their sons and their daughters?

"I think," Abby whispered, "that I might have screwed up."

Sarann blinked; the remark was so obviously not what she was expecting to hear. "*You* screwed up?"

Abby nodded. Still memorizing her shoes, she said, "I think I found him."

"Him? Who?"

"My father."

"You mean . . . who do you mean?"

"I mean, my father. Not my stepfather, not my grandfather, not Our Father in Heaven. My father. I only have one."

"How could you possibly do that?" Sarann said, dumbfounded. She stood up and looked down at her daughter, and her mind went absolutely blank. Blanker than when she saw her car in a different row, blanker than when Rodger handed her her soggy wallet. Those events were merely bizarre, but this one was impossible. Surely it was impossible.

"It was so easy, once you told me his real name," Abby said. "It took all of ten minutes. He's a private investigator."

"No, we haven't arranged yet for—who is?"

"My *father*!" said Abby, looking up with a flash of her old impatience. She had a quick temper—not from Sarann—which Sarann was completely not up to dealing with just then.

"It's all on the Internet," Abby added.

Sarann, who avoided the Internet the way some people avoided the Boston Marathon, had only a vague idea of what you could find on it. She'd made it her business to warn Abby about the dangers of chat rooms and starting up e-mail relationships, but she hadn't been terribly worried that Abby was going to research how to make a bomb or go surfing all the porn sites. E-mail relationships, those were Sarann's big fear. Compared to them, information Web sites didn't seem that dangerous.

Until now.

"How do you know," she asked after she caught her breath, "that this Ben McElwyn is your father?"

"I don't."

"Ah! In that case, I'm sure he's not. When I knew Ben, he was a computer-science major; he wanted to be a software engineer. I can't imagine how he'd end up a private investigator."

"But he dropped out of college and went into the army; who knows how he ended up?"

"I'm sure, not as a PI. He didn't have the personality for it."

"We'll see."

"How so?"

"I'm waiting to hear from him."

More stupefaction. "You *contacted* him?"

Now it was Abby's turn to look surprised. "Of course I did. What do you think I've been talking about?"

"You said that you found him, not that you *found* him!"

Wearily, Abby said, "It's like, you know, you never, ever listen to me."

"Abigail Johnson," Sarann whispered, dropping instinctively into a familiar form of address, "no one has ever listened harder to you than I am right now. No one."

She sat down with great deliberation in the folding chair opposite Abby's, pushed up the sleeves of her cardigan, and, resting her forearms on the dusty card table, leaned forward. "I'm begging you. Start from the beginning and tell me what you've done."

She was lightheaded from the realization that her daughter had blithely walked up to a big box marked PANDORA and, without a second thought, had thrown the lid wide open.

Maybe it was Sarann's deadly serious tone, maybe it was

her own newly desperate need, but either way, Abby seemed ready, finally, to talk. A tear slid out with her first few words, and by the time she was through, they were gushing.

"I know he's the right Ben McElwyn, I know it. There are only a couple, and the one I think is the right one is in Connecticut—"

Ben grew up in Connecticut.

"—and he could be a private investigator, he could, I don't see what's so weird about that. So I e-mailed him and I only asked him if he knew—you know—you. I told him mostly the facts that were in your letter, because those I *know* were true," she added with a sudden turn to the acidic.

"But he didn't answer, which could've meant just about anything, so I waited, and then I e-mailed again."

Sarann was making herself seem impassive, but inside she was experiencing a meltdown. E-mail! Her twelve-year-old daughter was e-mailing a man she didn't know! It was Sarann's worst nightmare come true, but with a cruelly ironic twist.

"He didn't answer that one, either, so I did like you always tell me to do: I gave someone the benefit of the doubt. I e-mailed him a third time, and I was still polite, but I wanted to give him some hints that he had a—you know—me."

"Dear God."

Despite her tears, Abby became hostile and defensive. "Well, who was gonna do it? You? Dad? Everyone around here is like, don't rock the boat and maybe it'll go away. Well, it *won't* go away. I won't let it go away! I deserve to know my father!" she cried.

She jumped up and wiped her eyes with her wrists in a gesture as heartrending as it was childish. Her dark lashes, thickened by tears, framed breathtakingly blue eyes that reminded Sarann of the reason that she and Abby were at such desperate odds in the first place.

"Don't you have anything to *say*?" Abby moaned. She broke into another spasm of tears.

Sarann was pinned between her promise to Rodger and her desire to make amends with the ill-used child who stood weeping before her. "You *will* know your father, I promise you," Sarann told her heartsick daughter. "Just . . . you have to let us go about this in a certain way," she pleaded, aware that it sounded inadequate. "You shouldn't have done that, Abby; that was a reckless thing to do! Don't contact him again. Don't. We'll take care of this in our own—"

"It's too late! Don't you get it? You waited too long!" Abby's voice was high and thin and very near to hysteria now.

"I know that, Abby, but I can't undo the past—"

"That's not what I mean!" Abby cried, slamming both hands on the table so hard that one of her silver rings flew off her finger and rolled to the floor. "He e-mailed me back, he asked who I was—and I told him! I told him I was his daughter and he knows and I'm glad and I don't care *what* you say now! I did it and I'm glad!"

"Abby, no—oh, don't say that," Sarann said, horrified. "Please tell me you didn't really do that! He's probably married, has children of his own . . . you could ruin his life!"

"So what?" she screamed. "He ruined mine!"

"Oh—stop it!" Sarann shouted, losing control at last. She took two steps across the divide between them and caught her daughter's arm. "Do you hear me? *Listen to me.* He didn't ruin your life. How could he? *He didn't know you exist!*"

Abby's blue eyes narrowed in furious resentment. "He does now! And he hasn't answered, which means he's just a shit like everyone else! He doesn't care! No one does! Dad's the only one, and even *he*—oh, what's the use?" she said, breaking down again. Crying hysterically, she grabbed her knapsack and stormed toward the door.

"Abby, where do you think you're going? Don't you dare go marching off into nowhere!"

Abby swung around and said through her tears, "Fine! I'll call Dad then, and he'll come get me. I hate you!" she cried. She turned to the gold-leafed shingle propped against the wall and gave it a good kick. "And I hate this shop!"

Chapter 10

LIKE A SUMMER squall that announces itself in a rumble of thunder and leaves everything in its path either cleansed or flattened, Abby had left her mark on Sarann: she felt as beaten down as a clump of phlox by the force of her daughter's emotions.

At various times all daughters assured their mothers that they hated them; Sarann understood that perfectly well. But this wasn't the kind of I-hate-you that came after being denied an R-rated video. This was a poisonous emotion, running as deep as it ran wide. Sarann began to fear that she would never be able to purge her child of it.

And now—on top of everything else—there was Ben himself, somewhere in Connecticut, being bombarded by Abby's e-mails. How long could *that* go on?

Sarann sagged onto the folding chair, unable to accept the unthinkable: Ben McElwyn knew. All those years, all those lies—wasted. And what would Rodger say? It was too much. She propped her elbows on the table and sank her head on her hands, heedless of the fact that she was sitting alone in an empty shop for all the world to see.

Sarann had been so dogged, so disciplined, so reasonably successful in shutting out thoughts of Ben all these years . . . until Abby got on the case. Since then, Ben had become an unavoidable part of Sarann's routine—she showered, ate, cleaned, shopped, drove, cooked, made love, phoned, pleaded, and argued, did it all with Ben hovering at the edge of her thoughts. Now it was bound to be even worse: after nearly a thirteen-year hiatus, Ben McElwyn would be front and center again in her life.

She replayed the awful scene she'd just gone through, picking it over for scraps of hope, and eventually she came up with one tiny bit: Abby had said that Ben hadn't answered her last e-mail after she'd identified herself as his daughter. That could mean only one of two things: either he was the wrong Ben McElwyn, or he didn't want to be the right one.

He hadn't answered her.

Emotionally adrift as she was, Sarann clung to that single piece of hopeful news the way she would to a Styrofoam cup afloat on the sea: simply because it was all that she had. She sat at the card table with her eyes closed, her face cradled by her hands, trying to keep from sinking under the weight of her compounded anxieties.

If Ben doesn't answer her, maybe we can somehow muddle through this. If only he doesn't answer her. Abby will survive it; Rodger will see that we get the facts that we need to know. Please ... please, don't let Ben answer her.

That hope was dashed, and she began to sink, when she heard the shop door open. Her latest visitor wasn't Abby returning, wasn't her husband wanting to know what was going on. It wasn't Gloria next door or any of her in-laws bearing good-luck plants or a customer eager to know when she'd be open for business. Her visitor was a mirage, a dream, a throwback to another Sarann in a different time.

"It can't be you," she whispered, aghast, staring up at him from her chair. "It can't."

He acknowledged her greeting, such as it was, with the slightest sideways dip of his head.

"Sarann."

Less than a day. She'd only been with him for less than a day in her life, but his voice was as much a part of her as the blood that was roaring through her veins.

"It *is* you."

His crooked smile was no friendly response, just a tight-lipped acknowledgment that they knew one another.

"Y-you haven't changed," she said, and it was close to the truth. His manner was tense and ultraguarded, but physically he looked the same: the same dark, shaggy hair; the same strong body; the same devastatingly blue eyes. After all that Sarann had been through, it really seemed nothing short of amazing that *he* could look the same.

She said again, "You haven't changed."

"You have."

She became instantly self-conscious about what she must look like. Although she was carefully dressed as a headmaster's wife in Eddie Bauer country casual, she'd just been through an emotional wringer. She couldn't possibly have any makeup left on, and she was clueless about the state of her hair. No point in sneaking off to the bathroom to put herself back together; Jimmy hadn't hung the mirror yet.

"I—it's been a long day," she said, disconcerted. She began jabbing at her hair, she had no idea why.

Ben looked confused by her explanation, and then he scowled. "I'm not talking about the way you look. I'm talking about the way you are."

Even worse. She had no answer for that.

"What the hell have you done, Sarann? How could you keep something like this from me?"

She smiled wanly. "Not without a huge amount of effort, I assure you."

"Jesus. You think it's a joke?"

His look was so filled with aversion that she wanted to hide from it. But in an empty shop with only a table and two chairs, that wasn't easy to do. She got up anyway and wandered over to a side window, as away from Ben as she could get. The view wasn't much—more shops—but it was the Alps in spring as far as Sarann was concerned. Anything, as long as it wasn't that look of aversion.

"I should have told you," she said with a pitiful shrug of her shoulders but without turning around. She couldn't look at him; she couldn't. It had been hard to tell Rodger, but this . . . ah, this. She could scarcely breathe from the effort of it. "I should have told you."

"Why didn't you?"

"Okay, that's—oh, God," she said, struggling for air. "That's a fair question. Because I didn't think you'd want to know."

"What're you, out of your mind?" he snapped. "What man wouldn't want to know? Sarann!"

It was an implicit command to turn around. She wouldn't do it. She needed that illusion of a confessional to get through this. She hugged herself, mostly to keep herself together, and said, "Some men *don't* want to know. You once insisted that you wanted to be free."

"And that was the reason?"

"It was one of them. There were others. When you called that time—you may remember—I told you that I was engaged . . . ?"

"Was I likely to fucking forget?"

Stung, she retorted over her shoulder, "That's hard to say. You were in your cups."

"The hell I was! I remember every word of that call!"

It took her aback, the depth of his vehemence. "Anyway, my night with you struck me as so completely out of character that . . . I don't know . . . I think I blotted it out. I'd never done anything like that before . . . I haven't done it since. I was engaged, I wanted to be married. What could I do?" she asked, in wonder still at her fierce attraction to him. "I blamed the brownies."

"Brownies? What brownies?"

"The ones that Gerry made?" she reminded him. "The ones laced with marijuana?"

"Laced with—! That's what you think was behind what happened between us? Brownies? Oh, lady."

She stole another glance at him. His face was flushed, his

voice husky with contempt. Something about him sent chills along the back of her neck, but she made herself go on, because he deserved an explanation, even if he thought it was a stupid one.

She said to the shops across the street, "When you called, I was focused on trying to get back on track with my fiancé, nothing else. We'd grown up together; our families were close. I was so horrified by what I'd done."

"How did you know that the baby wasn't his?"

"Mike was going to school at Berkeley. I guess I didn't mention that on the phone."

"I guess you didn't."

She winced. "Anyway, by the time you called me, I'd already missed a period, but I didn't think anything of it. I was working as a stock girl at Jobber's Warehouse; it was very physical, and I'd missed a period before. I actually went another two months before seeing a doctor," she admitted.

"But how could it have happened? You were protected. We discussed it! You went into the bathroom . . . you came out. So—what? What happened in there?"

She had relived the scene a thousand times in the last thirteen years, but never so vividly as now, with him standing just a few feet away. She was naked and in his tiny bathroom again; she could practically feel the diaphragm in her hand.

"I was too nervous to . . . to get it in right. I gave up." She felt her cheeks burn at that admission. "I wasn't very experienced," she said in self-defense. Of course, considering the way she'd behaved that night, he probably wasn't too convinced.

He muttered something under his breath; she was glad she couldn't hear what it was.

After a deadly pause he said, "And after your boyfriend found out, he dumped you."

She shook her head. "I broke it off myself. Mike didn't argue. I—I'm married now, though," she added.

"I know that, Mrs. Bonniface." The name sounded scathing on Ben's lips, an emotional lash across the back that she continued to present to him.

He added, "I guess that makes me a full-dress complication in your life, doesn't it?"

She sighed. "A little, yes."

"What was I supposed to be, as far as Abigail was concerned?"

"Dead. Run over by a bus. You were a lawyer."

"Perfect, just perfect," he muttered. After another pause he said, "Damn you, Sarann—will you turn around and *face* me?"

She did, but instantly her knees jellied. She recovered by sitting down on the newly tiled floor of the display window, set a foot or so off the shop's distressed pine floor. To any passerby, it looked as if they were old friends at ease with one another. But as intimate as they had been, as intimate as their connection now was, they were anything but friends.

"That howling teenager who ran screaming from here a little while ago—that was Abigail?"

Sarann nodded, then said, "But she's not a teenager yet."

"I know that. I've done the math. I only meant, she's at a melodramatic age."

Sarann said softly, "She's just gone through a melodramatic discovery."

Obviously at a loss, Ben planted his right fist squarely on his hip and rubbed his forehead with his other hand. "She *is* mine, isn't she? Jesus. Even I can see the resemblance."

He began to pace—a habit Sarann remembered from their brief time together—in order to shepherd his thoughts. She let him do it without interruption. God knew, she didn't have any brilliant ideas to throw out for discussion.

After a few traverses of the room he stopped abruptly. "What about *Mister* Bonniface? He knows?"

"Yes, he does."

"What did he say?"

"I think . . . that should stay between him and me," she said reluctantly.

Ben resumed pacing.

Sarann pulled her knees up and rested her chin on them while she watched him. He was as agitated as a tiger in a zoo half an hour before supper. His face was a study in tension: the muscles working in his jaw; the short breaths, quick on the intake, sharp going out; the sinews in his brow, pulling down in a fierce scowl every now and again.

Suddenly he leveled one of his scowls at her. "How could you not tell me this? What kind of woman does that?"

For whatever reason, Sarann hadn't expected to be knocked out of her revery at that particular moment. Startled, she raised her head and said, "I told you. One reason led to another until suddenly I was holding a baby in my arms, and it seemed perfectly reasonable—even desirable—to raise her myself. I bonded. Fiercely. But you wouldn't understand that," she said, unable to resist striking back. "I remember well. You prefer to be as free as a kite."

"How do you know what I prefer to be? You don't know squat about me."

"I know what you said."

"I was twenty-one years old!"

"Has anything changed since then? Do you have any other children of your own?"

"No—that I know of. But apparently you never can tell."

"Are you even married?"

He scowled.

"Ever been?"

"No. Since when is this about *me*?"

"I'm just trying to prove that my instincts were right in the first place. You were not, and never will be, a family man."

He snorted. "If by that you mean that I think children should come *after* love and marriage—"

"Is that right? I thought that's what they said about sex."

"Sex is different! Sex is sex. But babies, kids, that kind of stuff—you don't just jump into that."

Frustrated, she said, "So what did you expect me to *do*?"

"I don't know," he acknowledged gruffly. "That's a woman's issue."

"Well, I had the baby, and I'm glad of it."

"I could at least have contributed to her support," he argued.

Sarann dismissed the thought with a flick of her wrist. "I didn't need your support."

His look narrowed. "Oh? So that job at the warehouse worked out pretty good? You were able to put aside a nice little college fund for her?"

"Since when do you value college?" Sarann snapped. "You dropped out."

He did not like that at all. "Here we go, making this about me again. You're the one who's in the dock, missy. I didn't do shit!"

Her chin came up. "Boy, you've got that right."

"Again!" He threw his hands up in the air. "How could I help you if I didn't goddamned *know*?"

"How? I'll tell you how!" she said, suddenly losing it.

She dropped down from the window ledge and took a few steps closer to him. Pointing a finger at him like an outraged prosecutor, she said, "You went off to Germany! You didn't have to go off to Germany. How was anyone supposed to find you and talk to you quietly and ... and ... explain things if you were in *Germany*? Why not just join the Foreign Legion and call it a day? at least there'd be some romance to the thing!"

Stiffening from her burst of righteous fury, he said, "How *did* you know I was in Germany?"

Oh, damn. Instinctively she clamped her mouth shut, but it was no use. She was going to have to admit to that dark crisis of confidence in her life. "I called Gerry," she said, glancing out the window at a couple walking by who were looking in. "Gerry gave me an address. Obviously it was wrong," she added, mustering the courage to face him again. "Because . . . I wrote you, and the letter came back."

"You wrote me?" He looked stunned, as if some ordinary girl had landed a punch on the biggest, strongest, meanest, baddest jerk in class.

That would be him. And it felt good.

Immediately he went back to looking grim again, which brought them full circle to where they were when they'd started.

"You wrote me," he repeated, more to himself than to her. "You wrote me. And the letter came back." He couldn't seem to get over it. "Our lives have turned on a couple of lines scrawled on an envelope."

She was watching him warily. "I don't know what would have been different. It sounds like you've lived yours consistently enough."

His brow twitched—clearly he didn't take to being taunted—and he said, "So that's how you knew that I'd dropped out of school."

"Yep. Gerry."

"I never did like her. She had a big mouth."

"Not everyone is as tight-lipped as you—but then, I suppose it helps in your career."

He thought that was funny, she didn't know why. But his laugh, once she heard it, sent her cartwheeling back in time, and it frightened her. She had forgotten how much she loved his laugh.

She looked down—away from him—saw dust on her twill skirt, slapped it off, looked back up and there he was. Still there, still not a mirage. Still Ben McElwyn, father of their child. Still a full-dress complication in her life.

"How did you know I was even here?" she asked him. Her voice sounded shaky, reflecting her fear that he had known where to find her. He could have been a stalker, her dread was so great.

He answered easily enough, "A neighbor saw me whacking your doorknocker. I phoned you first, by the way, but I got the machine. You have a nice house. Nice neighborhood. You must have a great view of the river."

"No, not really. In the winter on a sunny day, you can see a glimmering. No more than that."

"Ah. That's a shame."

His mocking look was so like Abby's that Sarann wanted to smack it away. "That's all right," she answered in kind, just the way she did with Abby. "We somehow manage to get by."

"To be honest, I didn't come to talk about real estate," Ben said, pulling out a chair and dropping onto it. "I came to see Abigail for myself. And I have. So the issue of paternity, that's settled."

"Believe it or not, it was settled even before you laid eyes on her," Sarann said with a tight, wry smile. "But since we're now officially unanimous about it, I guess it can be put to rest once and for all."

A wild hope was forming in her mind. Trying not to seem eager, she began laying out a case before him. "You saw for yourself, Abby's lucky enough to live in a beautiful house in a wonderful neighborhood. You don't have to give another thought to her education, either. Her stepfather is headmaster of a prep school that his family owns and runs; he not only values an education, he can afford to pay for one. Next year Abby will be going to Faxton, and after that, to an Ivy League college. So—"

"So you really don't need me for a whole hell of a lot, is that it?"

"I just wanted to reassure you," she said with a shrug.

It was very hard just then to assess his mood. He looked thoughtful, but he sounded almost hurt. It wasn't until his next remark that it became clear exactly what he was feeling.

"If you're going to sell yourself," he said calmly, "I suppose it may as well be to the highest bidder."

She gasped and said, "How can you *dare* say something like that?"

"Oh, come on, Sarann! Your husband's people go back to the *Mayflower*, whereas you—granted, you may look the part in those clothes," he conceded, "and maybe you even sound the part, but let's face it: a Daughter of the American Revolution, you are not. You hail from my rung of the social ladder. So Mr. Bonniface must have married you for some other reason. Let's see. How many can there be? Offhand, I can come up with three."

He ticked them off the fingers of one hand with the index finger of the other. "Strength of character . . . warmth of heart . . . primordial sex appeal." With a steady look he said, "I'll leave it to you to decide which one I think was uppermost in his mind."

Her face was on fire. She didn't dare turn away, didn't dare give him the satisfaction of knowing how raw was the nerve that he'd touched. She forced herself to gaze serenely back into his fierce blue eyes. "Not everyone," she said lightly, "takes a bride based on the size of her breasts."

He laughed again, this time, harshly. "What planet were you raised on, Mrs. Bonniface? The man is forty-six—"

"Forty-two!"

"Forty-six, wealthy, established. He doesn't need status or pedigree or to merge dynasties. All he needs is a trophy wife, and by golly, I'd say he got himself one."

She was amazed at the characterization. In her wildest, weirdest, most deluded fantasy, she would not have thought of herself as a trophy for anyone.

She wanted so badly for her response to sound cool and ironic, but her eyes welled with tears, and she choked on her comeback. "What? You don't think he married me for the warmth of my heart?"

Ben stood up. "I've just had a glance into your heart, Sarann. The fire's gone out there. All I see are ashes."

The blow left her speechless. She bit her lip to keep the tears at bay and watched in silence as he walked out the door.

Chapter 11

SARANN ALLOWED HERSELF the luxury of a two-minute breakdown in the unfinished bathroom of her shop, and then—grateful that Jimmy had hooked up the new sink—washed her face, blindly dabbed on some color, and locked up.

She had no idea where Ben was. It seemed inconceivable to her that he was on his way to see Abby ahead of her; but it seemed just as inconceivable that he could be on his way back to wherever he had come from.

Sarann was reeling. She hadn't expected to care so much about what Ben thought of her; it was almost as big a shock as seeing him in the first place.

Oh, damn it, damn it.

If the years had somehow been crueler to him, or if he had somehow been kinder to her, then maybe she wouldn't be reeling as she stumbled into her car and headed for home.

Ben was in Farnham. Ben McElwyn was back in her life, big time, right where she had decided to put down stakes and take a husband and raise her—their—child. It was an all-consuming, completely unbearable thought: Ben—back! Oh, and he looked the same, he was the same. Ben. Her Ben. And yet not her Ben at all.

Because now there was Rodger. What would he say? What *could* he say? Abby had taken the ball and run with it, as only Abby could do. Twelve-year-olds didn't necessarily worry about tomorrow, or even an hour from now. With *this* twelve-year-old at least, it was damn the torpedoes and full speed ahead.

Damn it, damn it, damn it. Now what?

Wildly distracted, Sarann drove down winding roads lined with newly green trees and wrapped in the fragrance of spring, wondering how an evening so bright with promise could somehow be so black with foreboding.

The sense she had of being watched was acute. She glanced repeatedly at her rearview mirror. No car lurked behind, slowing when she did, turning when she did. Nonetheless, Sarann remained convinced that someone was behind her, following her every move.

It had to be Ben; who else could it be? He was behind every tree, in front of every mailbox. His ghostly image—looking shocked and bitter—was so vivid in front of her that she found herself slowing down, just to avoid running him over. He was somewhere near; she felt it in her bones.

Was she just being paranoid?

She remembered the old saying, *It ain't being paranoid if they really are after you.* But since there was no "they" in her life—it wasn't Ben who had been making her behave so oddly up until then—Sarann had to face the possibility that she was becoming, like her mother before her, scarily delusional. It made all too much sense. Put someone with Sarann's family history into a pressure cooker of family crises, and what did you get?

Crazy lady.

That's what the neighborhood kids used to call her mother as she paced the front porch or walked round and around the yard, talking to herself in distress. Sarann had never been able to get the kids to stop their taunts, just as she had never been able to convince her mother to stop her talk.

Crazy lady.

Sarann prayed that she herself wasn't headed down that road.

She's changed.

Ben tossed back a Jack Daniels and ordered another, won-

dering what had become of the naive, wide-eyed girl who
had brought such mind-bending joy to his bed. He remembered someone who laughed easily, spoke thoughtfully, and
loved with abandon.

Sarann Johnson was as beautiful as ever, there was absolutely no doubt in his mind about that. He felt her pull,
just as he had at Gerry's apartment all those years ago. But
that Sarann and this Sarann weren't the same woman at all.
This Sarann was an emotional wreck.

Jumpy, scared, anxious, desperate—where had all of those
traits come from? Ben could chalk them up to raising a kid
under false pretenses, he supposed; a lie as big as the one
she'd lived would certainly have taken its toll. And it
couldn't have helped matters to have him popping up un-
announced in front of her that way.

But there was something not . . . right . . . about her, and
he found it disconcerting in the extreme. She was a bundle
of nerves, with an anxiety level that seemed over the moon.
Twelve years ago, Sarann was independent and caring and
as optimistic as a miner in the Gold Rush. He had gravitated
instantly to that can-do quality in her; it was so unlike his
own why-bother one.

A dozen years. A lot of water had flowed under both their
bridges. Who knew what she'd been up to in all of that time?
Maybe she'd had a really rough go of it. Had she raised Abby
entirely alone? He hadn't thought to ask, for chrissake!

As for Abigail herself, he tried not to think of *her* at all.
The kid was obviously all set. She had the mother, the father,
the future assured. Sarann did not want Ben around mucking
things up for the girl; she'd just made that pretty damn clear
to him. Once upon a time, he had supplied the sperm, and
now maybe he could give the family a copy of his last physical. That seemed to be the extent of his role in this particular
fairy tale.

Pisser.

He stared at his refill and wondered whether he himself had changed as much as Sarann had. Had she looked at him and thought, *Christ, I once spent a whole night making mad, passionate love with you?*

On balance, he didn't think so. He'd been a bum then, he was a bum now. One thing anyone would have to admit, he thought wryly: unlike Sarann Johnson Bonniface, he had remained absolutely consistent during the last twelve years. Okay, there had been that one lapse of a phone call to Sarann a month after their night together, but other than that—absolutely consistent.

Ah, the hell with this.

He downed his shot and walked out of the bar, his throat still afire from the drink.

Sarann was relieved to see that the only cars parked in front of the house were ones she recognized: the elegant little BMW convertible that her husband so loved and, towering next to it, James's monster Range Rover in bully black. She was surprised to see her brother-in-law there so near to dinnertime.

Oh, damn. Rodger had arranged for Sarann and him to go with James and Glenys to an early lecture on geneology and the Internet, and after that, to dinner at The Wickford House. How could she have forgotten that?

Ben McElwyn, that's how. And before him, Abby. The day hadn't exactly been just another one at the beach.

Wondering how much Rodger knew by now, Sarann hurried into the house, apologies at the ready. She found her husband with his sister-in-law and his brother at the kitchen table, surely a sign of a friendly gathering.

Or not.

"Well! Here she is at last," Rodger said with deadly cheer. "We can still make it."

"If we sprout wings," said James. He was in a major snit.

They all stood up and there was a hurried shuffle of chairs and jackets and bags.

"Abby is—?"

"Upstairs," Rodger said briefly. Clearly he wasn't aware of his stepdaughter's bold adventures on the daddy front.

Sarann said quickly, "I'll run up and say good-bye."

"Oh, for God's sake. Just call up the stairs," her brother-in-law said, interrupting them. "We've got to leave now, or we may as well not go."

Glenys rolled her eyes at Sarann. Neither of the women was all that eager to sit through a lecture on using the Internet as a geneological research tool. It was James, the adopted son, who was obsessed with the topic, and it was James who began shepherding a reluctant Sarann down the hall and toward the door.

Before they made it there, Sarann spied half a dozen different-sized boxes, newly delivered and still unpacked, stacked neatly in the small front sitting room. She pulled up short.

"What're all those?" she asked her husband.

"Oh, yes—those. I took the liberty of checking one of the packing slips," Rodger said. "What a surprise to see that you've ordered me a new set of English gardening tools to replace the ones that have been in my family for years," he said dryly. "I guess I wasn't able to convince you that I neither wanted nor needed them, was I? Happy birthday to me."

Oh, no. No, no, no, not again. "That's not *true*, Rodger," Sarann said in a scandalized voice. "I *did* take you at your word! I admit I wrote out the order, but I never faxed—"

She clamped down tight on the rest of the denial. This was not the time—these were definitely not the people—to engage in a discussion of her collapsing mental condition.

Suddenly it all caught up with her: Abby's bombshell revelation; the appearance of the bombshell himself . . . the unnerving ride home . . . the forgotten dinner engagement . . . and now—tools! What next? Wandering through Farnham pushing a shopping cart and sleeping under the causeway?

"You know what?" she said, still frozen in her tracks. "I think I'll have to pass on this evening. I'm sorry to have made you all wait . . . but I have a truly splitting headache. Please . . . go on without me. You'll have a better time. Really," she insisted when everyone objected at the same time. "I can't go. I'm so sorry about this."

Rodger said grimly, "I suppose I'll stay home, then, too."

"No; bad idea!" Sarann insisted. She added quickly, "You and James will get so much enjoyment out of the lecture."

Her husband hesitated, then said, "All right. I may pass on dinner, though, and come home early."

"Yes, whatever."

James was about to tear out what was left of his hair. "For God's sake, man—can we go?"

Off they rushed, pulling away in the Rover and leaving Sarann behind with seven unordered boxes and a preteen who by now had shoved her chair up against her door again.

I'll take the boxes first, Sarann thought wearily. She called the gardening supply outfit, but customer service had stopped taking complaints for the day; the boxes would have to wait.

Just as well. What was she going to tell them? *I didn't order the gardening tools; I just wished I could?*

She sighed, because next on the list was Abby, still holed up in her room. Unsure of what she was going to tell her daughter, Sarann went up and knocked. Abby didn't answer. Sarann knocked again, heard nothing, became alarmed, and opened the door.

Old Molly, curled up at the foot of the bed, lifted her head, checked out Sarann, and lowered her chin back down on her paws.

But Abby lay utterly still, with her hands folded across a CD player on her breast. Her eyes stayed closed; she was wearing headphones. God only knew what kind of music soothed a misunderstood twelve-year-old. Whatever she was playing couldn't be doing a very good job.

How heartbreakingly sad and pretty she looked. With her pale cheeks still stained with tears and her black hair fanned across the pillow, she was the portrait of youth and betrayed innocence. For all her computer smarts and inventiveness, Abby Johnson was still a little girl. Sarann had been fierce in keeping her out of temptation's way: no provocative friends, clothes, movies, concerts, raves, video games. But those restrictions had their downside; Abby was much more naive than her peers. Naive children were easily disillusioned children, Sarann realized.

All you had to do was look at the one on the bed.

"Abby? Sweetie?"

Sarann wiggled her daughter's big toe gently.

Abby jumped.

Sitting up, the girl removed her headphones and left them dangling around her neck. "I thought we said you would knock," she said, staring at the violated toe.

Sarann smiled apologetically. "I did. Twice. I just wanted to check and make sure that you hadn't tripped and fallen into cyberspace."

"I'm done with all that," Abby said listlessly.

"Oh, don't be too sure. You know what they say: tomorrow is another day."

"I'm never checking my e-mail again. It hurts too much."

Was it possible? Abby seemed to be inviting sympathy. Sarann felt a quiet surge of maternal joy. She sat on the edge of the bed and made the decision to go through with her decision.

"You were right, you know," she said to her daughter softly.

Abby looked up. "About what? That grownups are all shits?"

Sarann smiled and let the little rebellion slide. "I mean, you got the right Ben McElwyn."

"I did?"

Abby looked as if her worst enemy had just told her that she'd got a hole in one. She wasn't quite willing to believe it.

Aware that her own heart was pounding at a runaway beat, Sarann said, "He's been in touch."

Amazement was followed instantly by outrage. "He got in touch with *you*? *Why*? It wasn't your idea! You don't even use e-mail!"

"He didn't e-mail me."

"He called?"

"Nope."

"He's . . . ohmigod. He's *here*? He's here *now*?" She threw down her earphones and went running for a comb.

"Wait, wait, honey, stop," Sarann commanded from her perch on the bed. "He's not in the house. I saw him at the shop where, unfortunately, things didn't go all that—"

Abby swung around, eyes narrowed. "All that what? All that *well*?"

Sarann smiled wanly. "He took me by surprise. I—what can I say? I was a shit. But—"

"Oh, *great*," said Abby, throwing up her hands.

"Wait, listen to me, Abby; don't get upset. I'll make it all right with him. I promise. You have to understand that I'm reversing almost thirteen years of habit. It's hard to let someone back in your life when he's . . . never really been part of it. But you said it best a little while ago: you deserve to know him. And you will. We'll make room for him in your life, if he's willing."

" '*If*?' He doesn't want to see me?" Abby was devastated. "Then why did he come to Farnham?"

How much truth could a twelve-year-old handle? At this point, Sarann decided, a fair amount. "Well, as I understand it, he came to Farnham to see for himself if you were his."

Abby sucked in her breath; her high, fine cheekbones turned a deep pink. "Like, what does he expect me to do? Stand in a lineup for him to pick me out?"

"Oh, no. He knows that you're his daughter, all right. He saw you when you left the shop."

Abby slapped her hands across her mouth. "I looked terrible!"

"That's all right; I didn't look any better."

"What difference does that make?" Abby said distractedly. "You're married to Dad, not to *him*."

Which certainly was true. It shouldn't have mattered at all. But Sarann had once been shockingly intimate with the man, and it made a difference to her how she looked, whether she wanted it to or not.

She said to Abby, "All women want to look good when they see someone; it's just the way we are." It was the truth, if not all of the truth.

Abby put down the comb and came back to sit in bed. Pulling a pillow into the nest of her crossed legs, she said eagerly, "What did *he* look like?"

It broke Sarann's heart; the child didn't even know something so basic as what her father looked like.

Sarann smiled and said, "Do you want the answer to be 'terrible' or 'not terrible'?"

Abby looked off into some middle distance of her imagination and sighed. "I guess I want, like, not too terrible."

"Okay, then—not too terrible," Sarann informed her gravely. "He hasn't got fat or bald, and he has all his teeth, as far as I was able to tell."

The fact was, he looked unbelievably terrific. Depressingly terrific. Sometime during their torturous meeting, Sarann understood why jumping into the sack with him had been such a no-brainer: Ben McElwyn was an irresistibly attractive male. Damn him.

"Is he married?"

Sarann shook her head. "And no children. No other children," she corrected.

"So I'm the only one," Abby said, weighing the fact. "Did he sound—you know—smart?"

Sarann laughed and said, "If you're wondering where you got all your brains from, rest assured. He sounded very, very smart."

"Oh, Mom. You know that's not what I meant. Well, maybe a little. But anyway, *you're* smart," she added magnanimously. "It's just that you never went to school."

Sarann gave her daughter a wry smile. "Well, when would I have had the time? Living in the forest, foraging for roots and berries all day, beating laundry against the rocks at the river—it was a hectic pace."

Abby gave her a sideways glance and said, "Cut it out, Mom. You know what I mean. College."

Is he smart? She may as well have asked, *Is he sane?* It occurred to Sarann that Abby, too, might be afraid that she had inherited a few faulty genes. Abby's earliest memories, after all, were of being awakened by her grandmother's night pacings, and early memories were the ones that stuck.

"When will we get to see him?" Abby asked, becoming more eager by the minute.

"When—? Ah. Well! That's a very good question. We haven't set a time yet."

"Where is he staying?"

"You know, I'm not sure? Somewhere around here." God in heaven, she was going to have to call every inn and hotel in Cape Ann.

"How long will he be around?"

"I didn't ask him, honey. You don't just pry like that."

"That's not prying; that's a perfectly innocent—wait a minute," Abby said suddenly. "You don't know where he's staying, or if he's staying, or for how long he's staying." The

joy and excitement in her eyes crashed and burned. "I should
have known."

After the warm and amazing tête-à-tête, Sarann couldn't
bear to see disappointment in her daughter's face. She got
up—reluctantly—and said, "You're right. I don't know. But
I will have that information for you shortly. That's a promise,
Abby. Tomorrow's Saturday; maybe we can all have breakfast together or something this weekend. If he's still in the
area."

The joy returned. "Oh, could we? Ohmigod, what will I
wear? But not in Farnham. Let's go to Gloucester somewhere
or at least Ipswich. I'll have to think. Would jeans be okay?
What was *he* wearing? Never mind, that doesn't help me any.
I don't have to wear a skirt or anything, do I? If I wore, like,
dress-up jeans and you know that top that Dad—?"

She became momentarily confused, then charged onward.
"That Dad said looked cool, the red one? Would that be
okay? No, I look like a dweeb in red. Maybe the lavender.
No, the one that's more bluish lavender. I think I look cooler
in that one, don't you? *Don't* tell Uncle James about this yet,
okay, Mom? He's going to have a cow when he finds out."

Out of the mouths of babes . . .

"I definitely am not going to say anything to anyone except your fa—dad, and neither should you. To anyone. We'll
take everything one step at a time. Not two steps or one and
a half steps or one and a quarter steps. *One.*"

"*I* know that," Abby said, looking offended.

But not very. She was simply too excited at the moment
to take anything personally. It was an amazing turnaround—
but then, twelve-year-olds were able to turn on a dime.

Sarann said, "All right; I'll see what I can find out."

"Here, wait; here's his Connecticut phone and address,"
Abby said, snatching a paper from one of her drawers.
"Leave a message on his machine; he probably checks it
when he's on the road." She ran the paper over to her mother

with such boundless hope in her eyes that it ripped through Sarann like a sawblade.

Her voice was low and loving and aching with remorse as she said, "Abby, honey, I'm going to do everything I can to make this happen, but we need to be prepared for the fact that he might not . . . might not want—"

Abby shot her a scandalized frown and said, "Of course he'll want to meet me. How could he not want to meet me? I'm his only child."

Sarann had no answer to that except a smile and a quick hug of reassurance. She went downstairs and did indeed leave a message on Ben's machine.

Ben, this is Sarann. It's, let's see, almost five-thirty. If you're still in the area but are checking your machine, can you call me, please?

She left him her number although she was certain he had it, and then she began the arduous task of calling every desk clerk in the area. Farnham had very few accommodations, but between Rockport and Gloucester, she had her fingers racing for the next forty-five minutes. It didn't help that Abby kept popping into the sitting room every other call to find out how the search was going.

Sarann had dropped as far south as Manchester-by-the-Sea when she got another call. She put the clerk on hold and took it; it was Ben.

She went back to the clerk and said, "Oops, never mind. Found him."

Found him found him found him.

Chapter 12

"BEN! THANKS FOR getting back to me," Sarann said when she had him on the phone again. Her voice sounded breathless to her, as if she'd run across the street to take his call.

Ben, on the other hand, was all business. "Sure. Look. Those things I said—"

"We both said things," she admitted, interrupting him. "They were things we needed to get out of the way." She added lightly, "Who knows? Maybe we would have had the same conversation thirteen years ago, if you hadn't been in Germany."

He answered with little more than a wry laugh, so she said, "Well, okay, maybe not *exactly* the same."

There was a pause—an exquisitely rich moment in which almost anything could have been said by either one of them. Sarann didn't want it to end, but end it did, when Ben said, "Abby knows?"

"Yes. She's very excited."

"That she tracked me down? She should be damn pleased with herself; she's a pretty smart kid."

"She assumes that she gets that from you."

This time his laugh was good-natured; Sarann wanted to bottle it and keep it in a dresser drawer for times of need. Instinctively she began moving out of the house and into the garden, where she could be safe from eavesdropping twelve-year-olds.

"I've seen firsthand the difference that knowing about you has made with her," she told Ben. "It's hard to believe. She's gone from being secretive and tense and just plain miserable to—well, you would have to see her to understand."

"I did see her."

"That was before. I mean after. She's a beautiful girl, Ben. Inside and out."

"I have no doubt you raised her well. I never asked: was it alone, the whole time?"

"The whole time," Sarann admitted.

She sat on a chair in a tucked-away corner of the property and kept an eye on the French doors of the house. Somewhere above her, a robin sang its poignant evening song; behind, she heard a crow calling down the night. Later she would remember the robin and the crow and their divergent songs; together they created the perfect metaphor for the turn her life was about to take.

"Almost thirteen years . . ." Ben mused. There was a melancholy in his voice that reminded Sarann of the robin. "When is Abby's birthday?" he asked, as if the thought had just occurred to him that young girls had such things.

"December nineteen," Sarann answered. She plucked a nearly spent blossom from a lilac tree behind her and rubbed it against her cheek, drinking in the last of its fragrance. "I was trying to hold out until Christmas, I can't imagine why. Abby would always have felt cheated for gifts."

Ben chuckled, and again Sarann heard a kind of robin-note of wistfulness in it. It gave her hope that he would say yes to her proposal. "Ben, she wants—she would love—to meet you. I told her that if you were still in the area, I would try to have us get together, maybe for brunch somewhere, this weekend."

His response to that was little more than an evasive guffaw. "Come on, Sarann—brunch?"

Clearly he didn't want to answer her request. "We . . . we don't have to call it brunch," she suggested, faltering. "We can call it a late breakfast."

There was another lengthy pause, and this one was not so much pregnant with possibilities as taut with apprehension.

It lasted so long that she finally said, "Beh-en?" She pronounced the word in two notes—the second one, of rising panic. He was so clearly going to say no.

"I . . . ah . . . don't want to sound like a cad or anything, Sarann, but . . . what exactly is in this for me? I can't outbid your husband for Abby's affections. I don't have the money, the access, the charisma to do it. Not to mention, I don't know diddle about kids. And even if I did have some overriding desire to get to know her, I'd never be able to bond with her in any meaningful way."

Sarann began to protest, but he talked right over her, as if he wanted to get it off his chest. "Who'll go to the father-daughter dances with her? Not me. Who'll show up on parents' day in college? Not me. Who gets to walk her down the aisle? Why do I think, not me?"

"*Ben*," Sarann said, aghast, though she knew the things he said were true. "That's defeatist thinking!"

She could practically hear his shrug over the phone. "She's going to be thirteen. It's too late."

"It's never too late! Children search for and find their parents after twenty, thirty, forty years! Don't you understand how deep their need is?"

His voice chilled a few degrees. "How, exactly, would I be expected to understand? *You* didn't, and you had Abby with you around the clock for almost thirteen years."

She shivered from the icy blast but went on. "That's just my point—I've learned from my mistake. I did a horrible thing, keeping her from knowing you. I can't undo that, no matter how hard I try. But I can do something now," she said in a voice wrung with pain. "And I am. I'm *begging* you, Ben. Don't turn your back on Abby. Please, please don't."

"This afternoon you couldn't get rid of me fast enough!" he argued.

"Yes, yes," she admitted. "But now I've seen my—our—

daughter's reaction. It's different now. She doesn't care about comfort and security at all; she wants you."

"Thanks! Thanks a lot."

Sarann ignored the sarcasm and went blindly on, convinced that she could convince him. "I thought I would be enough for her; I wasn't. I couldn't give her what I know she deserves. Then I thought, maybe a stepfather could—but my marriage seems to have had the opposite effect. All she wants now is to know her real father, and that's you, and no one else. You're the one, Ben," she finished softly. "The only one."

"Oh, *Jesus*, Sarann. I don't want to be the one. I don't have pets, plants, a home, a goldfish, I don't own my own *bed*, for God's sake, I rent! What am I going to do with a twelve-year-old?"

"You don't have to do much," said Sarann, amazed and exasperated at how hard it was to draw him in. "Spend a little time with her, let her ask you questions—and be willing to answer them. Let her see if her hands are shaped like yours, if you hold a fork the way she does, if you can carry a tune. Just simple things that would satisfy her curiosity." She added plaintively, "Is it so much to demand?"

"I didn't ask to have a daughter. I definitely didn't ask to have a twelve-year-old daughter," he said, digging in.

Aagghh. He reminded her so much of their night together a dozen years ago: edgy, noncommittal, almost irrationally determined to hold on to his independence. Still, Sarann had promised to deliver him to her daughter, and by God, if she had to sedate him and deliver him in handcuffs, she was going to do it.

"One meeting," she coaxed. "And then we'll both reassess. In fact, I have an idea. There's a carnival in Gloucester this weekend; we can meet you there. It'll be a pleasant, distracting environment in neutral territory. There'll be less pressure on everyone. How about it?"

"A carnival."

"Yes. Carnival. Not Kosovo. Carnival."

She heard the smile in his response. "I remember now. You had a mouth on you."

"And I loved using it on y—"

Oh, Gawd. That didn't come out right. "So?"

After his sigh came yet another question. "How much of a family affair will this be? Will your husband be there?"

"I . . . don't know. Obviously I'll have to ask him. I don't know what he'll say. He may want you and her to have time alone, with just me along. But . . . I don't know."

She hadn't thought that far ahead, but she could not imagine Abby at the carnival with two fathers—step, birth, or otherwise. She said, "Are you staying in the area? Can I call you somewhere?"

"I'll give you the number of my cell phone."

He did, and she said, "I think the carnival opens at noon on Saturday. Is that okay for you?"

"Fine with me. I'll be able to drive back to Connecticut afterward."

"Oh." Disappointed, she said, "Well, whatever's best for you."

He was the same as ever: ready to run. If she had him in the garden with her, she'd have tied him to the nearest tree until carnival time.

"Where should we meet?" he asked.

"How about—?"

The French doors opened and Rodger emerged onto the back patio.

"By the ticket booth," Sarann said, and she wrapped up the call with a hurried and guilty good-bye.

Looking more calm than concerned, Rodger came and sat in the chair beside hers. "Feeling better?" he asked.

"Yes. How was the lecture?"

"Kind of fascinating, actually," he said, stretching his

legs. "James was hypnotized, which is understandable for an adoptee. The twist is that he's so determined to find blue blood somewhere in his own veins. Personally, I think he ought to forget about bloodlines and pursue simple celebrity. Maybe his upcoming book tour will bring him the status he craves. His agent hasn't given up on the *Today Show*, did you know that?"

"Yes, Glenys said that there was still a chance. Do you suppose all this interest has something to do with that case in Boston? I mean, when someone as prominent as a congressman turns out to be a child abuser . . . it makes you wonder. How can someone who's so successful be so horrible? You want to hear what the experts have to say. The timing for James's new book is perfect."

Rodger nodded soberly and said, "The timing for James's new book will always be perfect, I'm afraid."

"You're right . . ." Sarann said, trailing off. She was pleased that Rodger wasn't still annoyed that she had bagged the lecture, but it made what she had to say to him that much harder.

"Speaking of computers—"

In for a penny, in for a pound, she decided. She swallowed hard and said, "Abby's had quite a lot of success with hers."

Rodger looked puzzled at the change of subject. "She should; she spends enough time in front of it."

"Uh-huh. Well, here's the thing," Sarann said in a nervous rush to get the truth out. "She's been—you know how we talked about getting a private investigator to look Ben up? It's the funniest thing, really. Abby's been doing the job for us, it turns out, and she's actually, you won't believe this, she's actually *located* him—Ben, I mean—and to top it all off, he's a private investigator himself!"

Poor Rodger. It was too much, too soon after Sarann's earlier revelation that Abby's father wasn't a dead lawyer.

He sat, stunned, trying to take it all in. At last he spoke.

"He's alive. And he's a private investigator. He himself."

"Yes; I don't know much more than that. Our meeting was a little—you can imagine—tense and emotional."

"You've already *met* with the man? For God's sake! Without telling me?"

"It's not as if it was some planned tryst, Rodger," said Sarann, startled by his tone. "He just showed up at the shop this afternoon. Even Abby didn't know."

"And you said nothing, just let me waltz off to a lecture."

Unhappy with how he was making it sound, she said, "I needed some time to think."

"And apparently to inform your daughter before telling me, isn't that what you implied you did?"

"I didn't say that, and I didn't mean that. With Abby, it just came out."

"This is unbelievable," he said angrily. He stood up and rounded on her. "Am I part of this family or not? How long will it take before I have your trust? Are you ever going to confide in me?"

"Who had time? You all rushed out of here—"

"You *pushed* me out!"

"Because I thought . . . because I felt . . . I don't know what I was thinking or feeling then," she admitted. "I was confused."

"Yes. You always are nowadays, aren't you, Sarann?" he said, looking down at her. "I suggested the other day that you might consider seeing a professional about your state of mind lately. Now I'm insisting on it. You're going to see Walter Irons."

They were words she dreaded to hear. "I don't think I need—"

But she did think. Something was obviously wrong with her, or she wouldn't be ordering garden tools after she'd been asked not to. Something was obviously desperately wrong.

She bit her lip, forcing back a flood of misgivings. "Maybe you're right," she conceded. "Maybe I should see someone."

He sat down beside her again and said more quietly, "I'm sure it's the best thing. If there's a problem, an imbalance, they have excellent drug therapy available . . ."

Her mind veered from the thought. It called up too vivid an image of her mother, facing each day's dose with loathing, having to be coaxed and scolded and pleaded with . . . and eventually giving up. Altogether.

With a simple, hapless shrug, she murmured, "You know about my mother, Rodger. That's why I dread—"

"I know, Sarann. I know. But we have to play the cards we're dealt."

He reached his hand out to her and she reared back.

"You have a lilac petal on your cheek," he said, brushing it away. "What? Did you think I was going to beat you?"

"I'm sorry, Rodger," she said, embarrassed. "I don't know why I did that."

"Another Freudian response, perhaps," he said, smiling.

"I . . . I don't know much about Freud. I'm sure that's not what it was."

"We'll let the clinical psychologists sort it all out," he said, reassuring her. "That's their job."

She knew that her husband had a Ph.D., not a medical degree, but she wished he weren't so convinced that she needed medicating. Anyway, whether she needed it or not, it wasn't tonight's problem. One thing at a time. She had to finish telling her husband about Ben.

"I've arranged for Ben to meet with Abby," she said straight out.

"*What*? When?"

"Tomorrow, at the carnival in Gloucester. It seemed like the easiest place."

"Out of the question. It's too soon. I refuse to go."

"Actually . . . I think it would be awkward—don't you?—if you were to be there with us the first time."

He didn't like hearing that at all. Through gritted teeth, he said, "I see. All right. I won't go. Abby won't go. And you won't go. It's too soon. We need to move slowly on this."

Suddenly his anger broke through the veneer of his calm, and his expression turned ugly. "Who the *hell* does he think he is, just showing up in our lives this way?"

"Oh, but Rodger, right or wrong, he's here now! Abby knows he's here now! It's too late to take our time. Besides, he might just—"

Up and fly away.

"We *have* to go," she said, dismayed that she was defying her own husband. "I can't turn back now."

She stole a look at Rodger and saw the muscles in his jaw working furiously. His mouth was clamped tight. His breathing was so labored that his nostrils flared with each intake of breath. He looked perfectly capable, at that moment, of the violence he claimed she feared in him.

But he was Rodger Bonniface, Headmaster of Faxton Academy, and he was nothing if not in control of his emotions. He stood up.

"I have meetings tomorrow afternoon at the school; I can't rearrange our fundraising drive around your needs," he said in a scathing voice. "I'm going to leave it to you to come to your senses—assuming that you can rally any. If I come back and you and Abby aren't here—then heaven help us all."

"Rodger, please!"

"That's my last word, Sarann. Don't bother with dinner. I'm going out."

He strode quickly from the yard, leaving Sarann in a state of shock. It was obvious to her that she was over her head about how to handle this. All she had to go on were her instincts and a really awful track record. So now what? Give in to his ultimatum? She couldn't—she wouldn't—do that, and yet Rodger was not the kind of man who backed down; ask anyone at the Academy.

What Sarann needed was some kind of manual to help her in calming and reconciling the odd triangle of people who currently made up her life, some pithy and soothing collection of thoughts that she could whip through before noon the next day. *Chicken Soup for Dummies*, something like that, she thought with a bitter smile.

Suddenly she had another, more practical idea: counseling. A family counselor would surely be able to help them. As soon as Rodger got back, that's what she would suggest. With any luck, she thought with mordant humor, she'd be able to get a volume discount for treatment of her psychosis as well.

She broke off a branch from the late-blooming lilac bush and went back into the house, feeling comforted by her plan and more pleased than she had any right to be. There were so many perils and twists and turns ahead in the road. Rodger was going to be furious; Sarann had never defied him before. She had a moment of fearful panic, then shrugged it off. For now, only one thing mattered: for the first time in Abby's life, Sarann was being completely honest with her. It was a wonderful, liberating, heady feeling. Sarann had never had it before.

She stuck her nose in a blossom and inhaled deeply. *I'm actually happy*, she decided. *Who knows why? It's ridiculous, but I am.*

She went straight to her daughter's room.

"You were very nice to stay clear while I worked things out," she said to Abby, whose bed had a dozen colorful tops scattered like tulip petals across it. Beaming with pride, she announced, "Mission accomplished. We meet tomorrow at the carnival."

"Oh, really!" said Abby with exaggerated surprise. "So

no brunch! Huh!" She didn't look directly at Sarann but slightly to the left of her.

"*Abigail*—you were listening in!"

Abby clutched a pair of painters pants to her small breasts and said in a comical plea, "I know I know I know I shouldn't have, but Mom, I couldn't help it. I had to hear his voice."

Sarann was appalled to think that Abby might have heard Ben backpedalling from their lives and Sarann dragging him back into them. "You heard . . . everything?" she asked, unconvinced that she could have.

"Yes, and it's not a problem, Mom. I'm cool with everything. *He* can go to the father-daughter dance with me, *he* can go to college on parents' day, *he* can walk me down the aisle! I mean—*duh*; he's my father!"

Chapter 13

ABIGAIL AND HER mother had their choice of parking spaces: they were almost an hour early for the carnival.

It was Abigail who had insisted that they leave the house by ten-thirty. Her reasoning was simple: "He might get there early, and then he'd have to just hang around."

"Oh, and that would be terrible," her mother agreed as she pulled into a space far from any other cars. "What could he possibly do to fill the time? Take a walk on the beach? Watch the boats coming and going in the outer harbor? Stroll through the park? Check out the carnival? You're right; he'd suffer so."

Abigail could tell that her mom was nervous. She always got sarcastic when she was nervous. It hadn't helped that Abigail's stepfather had totally freaked when her mother had told him about the plan to meet at the carnival. Abigail had been watching them from a window in the attic. She saw her stepfather gesture angrily, and she saw him storm out of the garden and then out of the house.

Still and all, at breakfast he had been extremely nice, at least to Abigail, so maybe he'd been able to think things over and cool off after a good night's sleep. Abigail wasn't worried. Her stepfather was always so busy with something or other at the Academy. Senior exams were coming up, and commencement, and before that the play, not to mention being in the middle of the annual fundraising drive. A headmaster didn't have much time to sulk.

Abigail was more worried about her mother. She had been as jumpy as a cat all morning. As far as Abigail could tell, it was going to be up to Abigail herself to stay cool, which wasn't easy to do when two hundred butterflies were zipping around in your stomach. More than anything, though, Abigail wanted to reassure her mother that she was doing the right thing in bringing everyone together—so she said soothingly, "The carnival was a really good idea, Mom. I know we're early, but I just don't want him getting worried that we might not show up."

"I do not think," her mother said in a really grim voice, "that Ben McElwyn is the worrying type. So *let it go*, Abby, would you?"

Whoa. Awesomely jumpy.

"Are we going to sit in the car while we wait for him?"

"No, let's get out and walk around," her mother said. She glanced in the rearview mirror and seemed surprised. "I didn't put on any lipstick?"

"You chewed it all off on the way over here," Abigail had to tell her. She was so totally absentminded today, even more so than lately. It was like she was stoned or something. "You look really nice," Abigail said reassuringly. "Even without lipstick."

Her mother seemed to calm down after that; she smiled at Abigail and said, "Thanks, sweetie. You look pretty swell yourself."

In a way, the compliment was annoying. Abigail had made a huge point of not dressing up, or at least of not seeming to dress up. But she had worked out every detail, from her crystal wrist bangles and prettiest bra (because it had the narrowest straps for under her tank) to her woven sisal Banana Republic belt (because they were in Gloucester, the fishermen's capital of the world, and a hint of something nautical—but not something gross like a belt embroidered with lighthouses or lobsters or anything—seemed like the right touch).

So, yes, she wanted to look swell, but no, she hadn't wanted her mother to notice that she did.

"Did you bring your camera?" her mother actually asked.

"Mom! Are you completely warped? I can't go taking *pictures* of him!"

Her mother said in a very casual way, "I only ask because you've been on my case for so long for not having any photographs of him. Now's your chance."

"Well I didn't and I wouldn't."

"Fine. Suit youself," her mother said.

She was, like, totally clueless about how to act cool. That was obvious in her next sentence.

"Maybe I'll be able to buy a disposable camera at the carnival."

Abigail groaned and said, "What are you *thinking*? You're going to turn *us* into a carnival!"

Her mother aimed the car key at the wagon and beeped it into locking itself, and they started to walk away, but she *still* wasn't done being a mother.

"Where's your pullover?" she asked Abigail.

"I'm not taking my pullover."

"It's cold by the water; it's still early in the season."

"It's going to be eighty-seven degrees today if you listened to the weather. I mean, like, a record?"

"Not by the water."

"But the wind's going to be from the west and not off the water," Abby had to tell her. "It'll stay hot."

"Since when are you a meteorologist?"

"Since we had to study weather in science."

"Fine. Don't take your pullover."

They walked basically without speaking and were almost out of the parking area and the carnival was right ahead and Abigail's heart was thundering with excitement when her mother amazed her, *totally* amazed her, by saying, "Let's go back for your pullover; I'll carry it if you won't."

"Mommm . . . ! No! I don't want it!"

"If you don't want it, I'll wear it; I'm freezing."

She spun on her heel and began marching back to the car without Abigail, who simply stared. The sun was shining and there was no wind, from the west or anywhere else. Her mother's knit top had sleeves on it, and her challis skirt went down almost to her ankles. It was hot out. How could she be cold?

She's stalling, that's all. Because she was afraid and maybe embarrassed to meet Ben McElwyn. Considering what their history was together, Abigail figured that it was perfectly natural for her mother to be filled with dread. Abigail, on the other hand, was excited and a little nervous, but not afraid. With her thumbs hooked in her front pockets, she made herself be calm as she waited for the next chapter in her life to begin.

The only problem was her shoes; she still didn't feel right about those. She had gone from sneakers to Mary Janes to sneakers to clogs to sneakers to espadrilles (gross!) and finally back to sneakers, because if she tripped and fell getting on or off a ride, she may as well cut both wrists right then and there.

"Abigail?"

"Yai!"

She whirled around, knocked out of her revery by, oh, God, by Ben McElwyn himself, standing in front of her.

"Hi," she mumbled, looking down. After all the rehearsing, that was all she could think of.

He stuck out his hand and said, "I'm Ben McElwyn. It's nice to meet you—I guess I should say, at last."

She nodded, but she didn't know how to take that. Was he being sarcastic, like her mother? Frowning at her stupid fat sneakers, she accepted his hand and, glancing up shyly, said, "Nice to meet you, too." What should she call him? She hadn't even decided! The whole thing was so totally awkward that she thought she'd die. "My mother—"

"Has walked off," he said, which was a completely accurate description. "I hope she's coming back?"

"Yeah, she went to get something in the car."

He nodded. "Gotcha."

He didn't look at *all* like the guy on the hassock, even though he was. His skin wasn't flour-white from being too close to the flash, but darkly tanned, and his eyes weren't rabbit-red at all, but a deep blue, deeper even than Abigail's. His hair, though, that was the same as in the photo and the same as hers: black and shiny and thick. She would have liked to say it was both their best feature, but didn't know him well enough yet.

"Have you been here for long?" she asked him instead.

"I just pulled in. I saw you two and was walking toward you when Sar—your mother turned and went off. That kinda left me standing in the parking lot with nothing much to do, so I figured, what the hey . . ."

Abigail nodded furiously in agreement. She wanted to shout, "I know, I know! She *does* that!" but that might sound disloyal to her mother, so she settled for: "Have you ever, you know, been to our carnival before?"

Which was about the dumbest thing she could have come up with. Of course he hadn't been. She was treating a dinky six-ride traveling show like a Six Flags Amusement Park.

He shook his head—naturally—and said, "But I'm looking forward to it."

Oh, no, he was being polite! "You don't have to say that," she told him quickly. "We only usually go because there's, like, *nothing* to do around here."

He laughed and waved his arm at the harbor. "With all this water around? You've got to be kidding."

Abigail shrugged off his enthusiasm, which was a mystery to her. "My mother won't let me have anything to do with the water. She tried to help a girl from drowning once a few years ago, but the girl drowned anyway. My mother never really got over it. She said it only takes a minute of panic and then you could be gone. It's a thing with her."

"Ah. That's too bad. Have you ever considered swimming lessons?"

Maybe he wasn't so smart, after all. "You could panic in a pool just as well," she explained with exceptional patience.

"But with an instructor nearby, you wouldn't—well! Some people don't like water, and that's a fact." He looked off at the harbor, which, it was true, was busy with boats and looked kind of refreshing.

"I used to go in when I was little," she volunteered. "You like the water?"

"*Oh*, yeah. It's a big deal with me," he said, squinting at the harbor in the late-morning sun. He turned back to Abigail and grinned. "But that's just me. I'm a water rat."

This wasn't good at all; Abigail must not have inherited that part. "You sail?"

"Nope; I row. I have a rowing shell."

Abigail knew what that was. "My mother would completely freak if I ever got into one of those tippy things."

He didn't say yes, he didn't say no; he just said, "Mmm."

Abigail wanted to like what he liked, so she made a decision on the spot. "I'm going to ask my mom again if I can take swimming lessons this summer. I mean, she gets nervous if I go in up to my suit!"

He didn't say boo, he didn't say ba. He just put his hands in the pockets of his pants and nodded and kind of smiled and rocked on his heels and said something like, "Yuh."

Abigail was hoping he'd say, "Let me talk to your mother; I'll see what I can do." Isn't that what a father ought to have done? *Mmm* and *yuh* didn't cut it with her. Stealing a page from her favorite teacher, she decided to take points off for lack of initiative. It was disappointing, but hardly the end of the world.

One thing she'd already decided: her father was a lot—a *lot*—handsomer than the guy on the couch. It was hard for

Abigail not to steal constant looks at him. She was genuinely thrilled. He was a to-die-for dad; all her friends would be so jealous. Plus, he was a private investigator! How cool was *that*?

Congratulating herself for a job well done, Abigail said, "Here she comes!" and waved a little wildly at her mother.

Abigail was very proud of her mother for standing up to her stepfather and making this happen. Her stepfather had a lot of authority and wasn't afraid to use it; it was hard sticking to your guns when he didn't want you to, but her mother had done it.

She waved again at her mom, who looked really pretty in her coral top and with her favorite floral skirt flowing around her legs. Just then, at that exact moment in time, Abigail could honestly say that she was the happiest she'd ever been.

If only it would last!

Sarann approached, and, as always, Ben McElwyn felt her pull. It was nearly as astonishing to him as the bemused interest he was feeling for the fresh-faced kid trying so hard to draw him out of his cave. He didn't see how she could succeed; it would be like getting a bear to come out for berries in January. Still, he thought Abby's efforts to make him feel at ease were touching and sweet.

But *Sarann*. Ben's feelings for her were neither bemused nor sweet. He was getting a hard-on just watching her breasts move in a gentle bounce under her top. The power she had over him was scary; it was going to take a whip and a prod just to keep his dick in line.

"Hey," he said by way of a hello.

She was a little breathless from her quickened pace. "Ben, hi," she said. "I can't believe I wasn't here to introduce you two."

"That's okay," he said with a wink at Abby. "We figured it out."

Now what the hell did he wink at her for? The one thing he did not want to do was seem to be Abigail's New Best Friend.

Abby beamed at him. "I *told* my mom that you might get here early."

Also pretty stupid, now that Ben thought about it. Why run the risk of seeming eager for this summit to happen? So much for succumbing to the lure of a harbor.

Sarann said, "Since we have time . . . do you want to get some coffee?"

What Ben wanted to get was a good stiff drink, but Sarann wasn't the type for elevenses—and then, of course, there was the kid. So they wandered onto the carnival grounds and found a stand that was open and got coffee and Diet Coke in paper cups that they carried around with them while they checked out the booths and rides.

It was a very small-town carnival, but damned if it didn't have a surprising amount of likeability to it.

"Chalk it up to nostalgia," Ben found himself admitting to Abby and Sarann. "My cousin Crotchy and I used to camp out at these things whenever they came through New Haven. He even got a job as a carousel operator for a year, before he came back home to settle down and get what my aunt called a 'real' job."

Abby wanted to know: "What kind of job could someone named Crotchy *do* without people making fun of his name?"

"He's a cop," said Ben. "But he could be an Avon lady; it wouldn't make any difference. No one's made fun of my cousin Crotchy since he turned sixteen."

"Dare I ask how he got the name?" Sarann said in an amused undertone when Abby got in line to buy a batch of tickets.

Ben grinned and said, "Sure—you can ask." He liked that in her, that she hadn't turned into some headmaster's prim wife. And he liked the way her skirt flowed over her hips.

"His name's not as bad as it sounds," he admitted. "When he was ten—I was six—he lost his nerve and got stranded in the crotch of a huge, high maple tree. Naturally the rest of the kids were relentless about taunting him into coming down. The name stuck. I think it's why he began weight-training, long before it was the rage."

When he looked at Sarann again, her cheeks were pink. "Hey, come on—the story wasn't *that* risqué," he quipped.

"No, no...I was thinking...I was somewhere else, that's all. Sorry. You were saying?"

"I was saying that the years have been good to you, Sarann," he said in softer, more serious tone.

"Mom, look! They have the Pooh Bear from last year. I'm going to try to win it. I bet I can, this time."

Abby's hundred-kilowatt grin snapped Ben out of his momentary lapse into insanity. What the freaking hell was he *doing*, coming on to Sarann like that? Thank God he hadn't actually gone and straight-out asked her to hop in the sack. *The years have been good to you, Sarann.* Well, that was patently obvious, and hopefully she'd accepted the compliment at face value and had ignored the spirit in which it was offered.

Hopefully.

Without looking at Sarann to see her reaction, he said to Abby, "So what's the deal with this—what's it called?" He reared back and read the sign that arched above their heads. "Rising Tides?"

Abby sat on one of the four stools at the low counter and plunked down a ticket, then waved away the kid who was running the booth with an imperious, "I know how."

She explained to Ben, "You have to aim the squirt gun at the target, and the water rises in the tube behind it for as long as you keep hitting the bull's-eye. If the water gets to the top of the tube, you win. A bell goes off to tell you."

"I see."

Abby gripped the nailed-down squirt gun with both hands and prepared to shoot. She had a keen eye and a steady hand; the water in the tube began rising rapidly. Ben got a little enthusiastic as it neared the top and said, "Hey, you're a pretty good shot."

Abby turned to him with a big grin and said, "Thanks!" and immediately lost her aim. The stream of water went off into space.

She broke into a peal of giggles as tinkling as any mountain brook. "My fault," she said, handing over another ticket. "This time I won't lose my concentration."

She didn't. The tube filled, the bell rang, and for her brilliant performance she was awarded a six-inch stuffed bear that was apparently named Pooh. "I don't have this size," she explained to Ben as they walked away.

Her mother smiled and said, "She does, however, have the two-foot and the four-foot versions."

Was that a reminder of how charmed a life the girl was living nowadays? Ben didn't want to think so, somehow. He said, "Good for you," which he was afraid came out like "Bully for you," so he changed the subject altogether. "How are you at darts?" he asked, eyeing one of several bust-the-balloon booths.

"Good! I'm good!"

"This is news," Sarann said, laughing.

Ben took a second to savor her laugh and then said to Abby, "One thing you always have to look for: the thinnest balloons. See those opaque-looking ones? Nice color, but too rubbery and harder to pierce. Let's go back to the booth by the sub stand."

Abby was dazzled by his expertise—which had the ridiculous effect of making Ben feel pleased—and the three of them headed for the dart booth that had the thinnest balloons.

Ben went first and humiliated himself. After using up three tickets, he'd only pierced one balloon. Abby, tossing alongside, did better, two balloons in three tries, but no prize. With a shrug, Ben said, "Not our fault; they weren't inflated enough."

"Children, children," said Sarann. "Forget your fancy theories; this is a game that requires practice. Step aside, please, and give me room."

She rolled up a pair of imaginary sleeves, a bit of whimsy that Ben found absolutely enchanting, and picked up her three darts. With a light and graceful arc, she let fly. *Pow. Pow. Pow.*

She let Abby choose a stuffed Kermit the Frog for herself. Another round. *Pow. Pow. Pow.*

Sarann presented Ben with a Miss Piggy, all for his very own.

"How the hell did you do that?" Ben asked, tucking the pig under his arm in a headlock as they moved on.

Sarann gave him an ironic and blazingly attractive smile. "I was a barmaid at D. J.'s Pool Hall for three years."

"Ah."

Hell. He didn't want her barmaiding in a pool hall or anywhere else. And where was Abby all that time?

"It was great—remember, Abby?"

"Yeah," her daughter agreed. "We played Barbie every night, almost."

Sarann tickled Miss Piggy's ear and explained to Ben, "D. J. was my mother's half brother, and he lived in a flat above the pool hall. I was able to have Abby stay with D. J.'s kids upstairs while I worked. D. J.'s wife was great about watching her; I never had to pay them a cent. Oh, which reminds me, Abigail, don't forget to send Aunty Peg a card for her birthday next week."

"I already bought one, Mom; you don't have to remind me."

"I'm not reminding you to buy one, honey, I'm just reminding you to send one. Two different concepts."

Abby rolled her eyes. Her cheeks flamed up a little. She stepped out ahead of them and then, apparently unable to decide whether to be embarrassed or not, broke into a run for nowhere in particular.

Ben smiled and said, "You keep on top of things."

"You have to; their heads are in the clouds at that age. They hear one percent of what you say."

"So I guess getting anything to sink in is related to how many times you say it."

Her head shot up. "You think I'm a nag?"

Uh-oh, danger. Back away.

"How would I know that?" he asked, opting for the truth.

Sarann let out a forlorn chuckle and said, "It doesn't take a rocket scientist. Of course I nag. I overprotect. I try to shield her from every rotten influence out there."

"All to the good, as far as I can see."

"Yes, but am I preparing Abby for what *is* out there? That's what I wonder, every single day."

If Sarann thought that he had an answer for her, then she was strolling in a parallel universe; Ben knew nada about parenting. "She seems like a great kid," he said, and he let it go at that.

Chapter 14

ABBY CAME BACK all sunshine and smiles again. She was ready to take on a ride. "Anyone want to go on the Twister?" she asked.

Ben looked to Sarann for guidance. She said, "Don't we always?" So, the "anyone"—that would be Ben. Not surprising. It wasn't as if Abby was going to say, "Hey, Dad, whaddya think?"

The two-tiered cars seated two in the back, stepping down to one in the front. Ben decided to let their young hostess handle the seating arrangement, which she was more than happy to do. "Mom, you'd better sit in front; your skirt might blow up if you take the high seat."

Ben let that one pass.

They arranged themselves as ordered (with Kermit, Miss Piggy, and Pooh Bear sharing the space between Ben and Abby) and waited while the operator loaded the rest of the cars. Abby chattered on about some amusement park out West where dozens or maybe it was three, she couldn't remember, people plunged to their deaths, while Ben tried mightily not to look down the front of Sarann's top. He failed. Sarann had cleavage, and what with her V-neck top and the car's two tiers working in blessed concert, Ben had a damn good view of it. He blew out air through puffed-up cheeks, letting off steam. What wouldn't he give to be able to lick the tips of those breasts until his tongue went numb.

Stop right there, he warned himself. He dragged out the whip and the prod. *Back in your cage.*

Sarann turned around and looked up at him. "Ben? Did

you know that 'carnival' originally meant 'forsaking of flesh'?"

What the hell was she asking him *that* for? What was she, psychic?

"No. I didn't."

"Giving up meat for Lent, in other words," she explained, setting him straight. "But I don't see the connection between a pre-Lent Mardi Gras blowout and an event that goes from place to place all year long."

Looking down at her, Ben got momentarily lost in the depths of her shimmering green eyes. Struggling to find his way clear again, he stammered and said, "Uhh . . . food, games, merriment, music—there are traits in common."

She laughed and said, "Fine, but you've just described the Super Bowl," and then she turned back around.

He wanted to scoop her in his arms from above and haul her away to be ravished somewhere. She was completely irresistible to him, just as she had been twelve-plus years ago. Then, now, later, it made no difference. She was Sarann, and she was imprinted in his brain. And, of course, in his groin.

This is ridiculous. What am I doing here, sitting in a Twister car with a bear and a pig and a frog, not to mention a twelve-year-old daughter I didn't know I had and a woman who's married to somebody else?

"Here we go!" cried Abby.

She was psyched, although Ben couldn't imagine why. Six cars spinning occasionally while one end of the platform rose and fell was fairly tame stuff. Abby must have thought so, too, because when they got close to the operator she hung over the side of their car and yelled, "Hey, c'mon, is this all you've got?"

It wasn't. The kid running the ride had a joystick that controlled the revolutions of each car, and he took Abby up on her dare, whipping their car around and around and around and around at a furious pace. Abby screamed in nonstop delight, drowning out any reactions that her mother was having below them. As for Ben, it was all he could do not to grab his head to keep it from flying off his neck. He didn't see how he'd get out of the ride with anything less than a lawsuit-sized whiplash.

But they survived. Laughing and thoroughly pumped, Abby jumped out of the car, eager now for the next, bigger, better thrill.

Okay, Ben decided, *this kid is scary*. She had the potential to be every father's worst nightmare. She was too willing by half for further adventure. Inevitably his thoughts went back to her mother on that fateful night: Sarann had been wide-eyed and willing as well. It was a great combination if you were the boyfriend, a horror story if you were the dad.

But he wasn't the dad, he was merely the biological father. He had to remind himself of that fact as he watched Abby scamper down the ramp and scope out the next ride. Abigail Bonniface was Headmaster Bonniface's concern, and Ben was there, literally, only for the ride.

"Gee, Ben, I didn't see you clamoring to go again," Sarann said with a wicked sideways look at him.

"You know the saying, 'I think my head is screwed on backwards'? I used to assume that was just an expression."

She laughed and again Ben took a moment simply to savor the sound of it before he said, "That's an amazing kid."

"Oh, you're only saying that because she's—"

Yours.

She veered away from the word. "Because you haven't been around twelve-year-olds," she amended awkwardly. "They're all alike, really."

"You don't believe that," he said, swinging Miss Piggy by one of her ears against his thigh as they walked.

"No," Sarann conceded, smiling. "She's bright, she's beautiful . . . she's everything to me."

Abby was making her way back to them through the

crowd; the grin on her face was infectious. Ben grinned back and said to Sarann, "Lord, the energy. Do they ever sleep?"

"Only in the morning, when they should be getting ready for school."

"She has a great smile," Ben said, aware that he was rowing down a whole new river without a chart.

"Yes . . . her teeth are perfect now. She had a slight overlap between two of the front ones, but Rodger had her in braces even before we were married. He said her smile was so nearly perfect, why stop short? They came off the day before our wedding. *I* never could have afforded it," Sarann added. "I was an assistant secretary—well, assistant to the administrative assistant—in his office, and the benefits didn't include dental."

She glanced at Ben and added almost wistfully, "I was probably rationalizing—but I used to think that the overlap was kind of endearing."

The surge of resentment that Ben felt toward Rodger Bonniface was sharp and unexpected. What right had he—not yet married, for chrissake—to play Pygmalion to someone else's daughter?

Whoa. Definitely, this was new territory. He'd never even seen those particular rapids coming. He pulled himself up short and mentally paddled into quieter, shallower water, where he resolved to stay until the day was done.

They watched while Abby detoured to a concession stand and then showed up with two cones of cotton candy. She handed one over to Ben, who didn't have much of a sweet tooth, and kept the other for herself.

"Mom won't eat these," Abby explained. "She gets cavities."

Ben himself did not. His teeth were strong, if not perfect. (Like Abby, he also had a slight overlap between two of his front teeth. He wondered whether Sarann even knew that.) In any case, Ben was willing to bet that the headmaster, he who insisted on perfection, was not the type to eat cotton candy, so he thanked Abby nicely, then pulled away a handful of the spun sugar and popped it, with feigned enthusiasm, into his mouth.

Yechhh. He smiled and said, "Great stuff, but there go our appetites."

"For?"

"Well, I figured, clams. I read that the Essex River has the best clams in the world."

What're you doing, what're you doing?

"Oh, ick, I don't like those things."

"What? You live on the banks of the Essex and you don't like clams? How is that possible?"

You're driving back to Connecticut in a little while, moron. You are not hanging around to eat clams.

Abby merely made an *ee-yew* face.

"How about you?" Ben said, turning to Sarann.

What're you doing, what're you doing?

Sarann had caught her lower lip with her teeth and was watching Abby and him with a half smile that had Ben wrapped up instantly in knots. If a Renaissance painter had wanted to paint something called *Doting Mother with Young Child*, all he'd have to do was capture that face on canvas.

The smile, wonderful as it was, faded into regret. "I can't. Rodger and I have to attend a fund-raising reception tonight. The Academy is in the middle of its annual drive. I *have* to be there," she added with almost desperate emphasis.

"We could get in and out early," Ben argued. "Someone recommended an eat-in-the-rough place called Woodman's."

No, really, man. What the hell are you doing?

"Oh, Woodman's!" said Abby, perking up. "I could get shrimp!"

"It's nice of you to offer, Ben, but no, I'm afraid not." Sarann glanced at Abby, who had suddenly turned into the third act of a Greek tragedy. "Unless maybe Abby is willing to leave the carnival early?"

"No! Why can't we do both?" cried Abby, slamming poor Kermit over her knee.

This was new. What happened to all-smiles-all-the-time? Suddenly twelve-year-olds didn't seem like such a great concept, after all. Ben shrugged warily and said, "It was just a thought."

And a lousy one at that.

So they returned to the business at hand, but with a little less gaiety. Ben wasn't sure who Abby was mad at; he was surprised to realize that he didn't want it to be him. They passed a hoop-shooting booth, and he quietly dumped what was left of his cotton candy and said, "Let's try our luck here."

"I like soccer," Abby said. "I'm not very good at basketball."

"I am," said Ben, taking a handful of her tickets from her.

"All those?" she said, scandalized.

"Trust me."

Five bucks' worth of tickets gave him a chance at the biggest prize: a huge stuffed animal. Why anyone would want a dust-collector like that was beyond Ben, but he'd seen Abby oohing and ahhing over them when they passed the booth earlier, and it had become surprisingly important to him that she be appeased. So: big stuffed animal it was. He took his two shots, got his two baskets, was awarded his prize. He handed over the three-foot dinosaur he won to Abby, then said to her mother, "And for m'lady?"

Sarann's lashes fluttered down in a most heart-stopping way, but when she lifted her gaze back to him, it was filled with pure sass. "The panda, then . . . if you can."

"I can and I will," he said with the cockiness of a kid who'd spent his entire youth shooting hoops at the corner playground and still kept up his game. "One, two, a panda for you," he intoned, and he took his two shots.

Down came the panda from the shelf. The operator was looking as if a professional gambler had just showed up at his craps table.

"More, more!" cried Abby, which very quickly netted her a giant pink something in the bear family.

"Abby, how are you going to carry those around?" her mother asked, laughing.

Abby hardly heard her; by now she was in what could only be called an animal frenzy. "That one next, that—that thing up there," she said, jabbing a finger at one of the shelves.

"The purple thing?"

"No! Not *Barney*," she said, completely horrified. "Next to it! Hurry, before someone else gets it!"

"The koala? Sure," Ben said, "but this will wipe out the last of our tickets. We'll have to go get—"

"*No*," Sarann said to them both. "Enough. This is crazy. We don't need these things. Abby, you're just being greedy. And we *all* seem to have forgotten that this carnival is for charity. They're going to lose their shirts because of us! Here you are," she said, handing her panda back to the startled operator. "Can I exchange this for the little version, please?"

She accepted a panda the size of Miss Piggy. Without being asked, Abby followed her mother's example. Granted, it was with more reluctance; but all in all, the girl acquitted herself very well. Ben found himself feeling another unexpected surge of emotion, this time, of—was it possible? Pride?

Get real, asshole. You didn't have anything to do with shaping her character.

And yet another unexpected surge: of regret that he hadn't.

Abby said, "Let's try the House of Mirrors. There's no line."

"Sure, go for it," Ben said. He couldn't seem any weirder to himself in there than he did out here.

There was no one inside except for the three of them and their various stuffed friends. It was a goofy interlude in an emotional afternoon; Ben wondered whether Sarann was as relieved as he was just to be able to look at himself and laugh.

She did seem merry. Standing in front of her distorted reflection, she said, "Aaggh, I never should have had that doughboy; will you look at my rear end?" She grabbed her outlandish hips with ham-sized hands that were attached to Popeye-sized forearms and Olive Oyl uppers and twirled in place, checking herself out from all possible angles.

Ben was checking her out, too, but not in the mirror version. Sarann was a delight, a vision of all he desired, and it was incredibly hard for him not to take her in his arms. A dozen years ago . . . if things had turned out differently . . . if her letter had found its way through the military labyrinth and had reached him overseas . . . who knows?

Don't go there, boy; that way madness lies.

Abby squeezed in front of her mother and began hogging the mirror, moving her hips in a Hula-Hoop motion and scaring everyone. They all laughed and moved on—a typical American family to anyone who happened to be looking. But there was no one to notice except a pig and a panda and a few of their pals.

House of Mirrors was right. It was all an illusion.

They emerged in the bright light of the carnival grounds and Abby said, "Okay, what next?"

Sarann answered, "The Ferris wheel."

"Mom, I wasn't actually asking you for your choice," Abby explained gently. "I was more like talking out loud to myself."

"Whatever. I want to go on the Ferris wheel; the view is always so pretty from it."

"But there's a line; we'll waste time!"

"You have your whole life, Abby," Sarann said, almost sharply. "You *have* the time."

Abby thought about it and said, "Okay, but *you* wait in line. I want to get a balloon."

Off she went, leaving Ben with the unexpected gift of her mother. He stood just a little behind Sarann, relishing the nearness of her, studying the glints of sunlight sliding through her honey-colored hair, trying to catch the scent of her perfume over the smell of popcorn and suntan lotion around them. Did she still use Charlie, he wondered?

"Oh, my God—you remember that?" she said, looking up over her shoulder at him.

Had he actually asked her that out loud? He couldn't believe it. He tried to cover his embarrassment by muttering something about noses having long memories, and then he changed the subject altogether.

"When do you open for business?" he asked. "Your shop, I mean," he added, God only knew why.

"Next Friday the movers empty my storage shed into the store, ready or not. I'm excited but scared to death. I don't want to blow this.".

"Yeah, being self-employed can be just a little on the terrifying side—but you have a safety net," he couldn't help observing.

"That makes it worse. If I fail myself, that's one thing. But to fail Rodger after all he's done . . . Well, I'm not going to, that's all," she said with a lift of her chin.

He was curious, so he said, "You don't need a job, obviously; why are you going into business?"

She grinned. "Funny you should ask. That's what Rodger wanted to know. I told him that I need to do something, be something, make something of myself. Farnham is the antiques capital of the Northeast, and I've always had an interest in objects with a history. I never could afford anything, but that didn't stop me from looking. To me, antique shops were like museums—except that you had to go to a library afterward to try to figure out what you'd seen."

"And now you live in a home that's probably a museum itself."

She nodded. "I was so naive; I used to think that people liked antiques for the stories behind them, and because they wouldn't have to worry about dings and scratches. But they're incredible investments. Rodger always shutters whatever rooms the sun streams through."

Life in a cave; what could be more fun? Just the environment for a twelve-year-old, too. "So your husband is an expert; that should help."

"Oh, yes. Rodger's very supportive—even though every day he thanks God that I want to run an antique shop and not something that might actually make money, because this way there won't be any question that he's not cutting it as a breadwinner."

Chuckling, Ben said, "He sounds like a great guy."

Prick.

"Oh, he *is* a great guy," she said, a little too earnestly. She looked away.

Ben's nose came up. Was he catching a whiff of trouble in paradise?

Chapter 15

"SARANN?" Ben touched her shoulder and she turned, finally, to look at him. He said, "Rodger's all right with this, right? With the three of us getting together?"

Or why else would she be there?

"He's not real, real all right with it," she admitted after a sigh. "I mean, he understands that Abby has every right to know her father, but he was hoping that she could know you some other way."

"Yeah? How? Via hologram?"

"Okay, I phrased that wrong. He was hoping that she could know *about* you," Sarann said. "You know, where you were born and where you went to school, the places you worked, the churches you attended—if you went to church. That kind of thing."

She was starting to squirm, which Ben hated to see, but he wanted to know what the hell he was up against. "What did he expect me to do? Put together a photo album of myself for her?"

"Oh, no, not at all." She looked around, apparently to be sure that they were among strangers and that no daughters were lurking, and said, "He would have . . . paid someone. Someone like you. He talked about having all the information gathered by Christmas, as a present for Abby. He sounded almost enthusiastic about it," she added in pathetic defense of him, "so it's not as if he didn't want Abby to know you exist."

Ben was flabbergasted. "Jesus Christ, now I've heard it all."

It sickened him to think that someone had been about to

go around to check out the hole he was renting and the broads he was seeing and the bars he hung out at. The plan was fucking intrusive, and enough to make him want to quit his so-called career on the spot. Shit!

"So much for honesty is the best policy," said Sarann, looking pained at the scowl on his face. She bowed her head a little and said softly, "You asked me a question; I didn't want to lie. I'm done with that."

He pulled himself up short. "Look . . . Sarann . . . Jesus . . . I'm not dumping on you; I'm not. But you have to understand where I'm coming from here. It offends me that you and your husband didn't just pick up the phone and ask me straight out what you wanted to know."

Her comeback was quick. "Really? What about your own clients? Do they offend you because they don't just pick up the phones themselves when they want to know something, and instead pay you to find it out for them?"

"You know something? I think they do piss me off!" he admitted. "I'm a big believer in either figuring it out or letting it go. I don't think much of having someone else do my dirty work for me."

"Oh, *you* picked a good line of work."

He had to agree with the absurdity of it: a private eye who didn't like to pry.

"Hey, maybe that's the reason I'm not making any money at this."

She laughed at that, and the squall squeaked past to the south of them.

Or so he thought. But he was too intensely curious not to ask, "How exactly is your husband planning to handle my showing up out of nowhere? Anyone looking at me will guess immediately that I'm not a dead lawyer."

That was good for a woeful chuckle, but Ben could tell that Sarann was going to be facing some music when she returned home with Abby after the carnival. He could also tell that the couple standing in front of them had begun to eavesdrop, so he nudged Sarann to tip her off about it, and then he said, "Did I tell you that I had that eleventh toe removed?"

Immediately Sarann began to play along. "Really!" she said in a perky tone. "I thought you planned to just stop with the twelfth."

He wanted to kiss her on the spot but settled for a grin. "Yeah, well, it bothered me that my feet still weren't symmetric."

"In retrospect, I think you did the right thing," she said gravely.

In retrospect, Ben realized that he'd never got over her. "Sarann—"

"Oh, look, we'll make it onto this ride," she said, seeing that two gondolas were still free. "Now where did Abby get lost?"

She looked around for her daughter while the eavesdroppers were loaded into a gondola with two others, and then it was their turn. With Ben urging her to keep moving, they climbed aboard and the operator motioned for the next two in line to join them.

Ben hurled a mental curse at the operator, and it worked. The next party was a group of four who didn't want to be split up; the operator decided to let Ben and Sarann have their very own gondola.

The rush of pleasure was so strong that Ben felt the hairs on his forearms stand on end. He decided to forget all that stuff about life's cruel turns; God was good. He started out demurely enough by taking a seat opposite Sarann on the nearly circular bench and immediately began plotting how to get nearer her.

In the meantime, Sarann wasn't paying any attention to him but was looking all over for Abby. They were halfway to the top when she spotted her with three other girls her age, all waving at them. Abby was the only one with a helium balloon tied around her wrist; it had a pink heart on it that sailed back and forth as she waved.

"I'll wait here," she yelled up, and she gestured to the spot in which she was standing.

Sarann nodded and then, still smiling, looked over at Ben. "What are you sitting over there for? You can't see the harbor, facing that direction."

She patted the space next to her and Ben, no fool, kicked Miss Piggy out of the way and scooted right over. He watched Sarann and not the landmarks that she was taking such pains to point out to him as they made a slow arc through the sky, floated down to ground level, and then began another ascent. He was ecstatic; it was like having sex, only longer. He studied the freckles scattered across her nose as he would a constellation in the sky, and he hung on the sound of her voice as if it were a brand-new symphony by Beethoven. Up they went, arcing across, floating down, her thigh searing his through the thin fabric of her skirt, her arm brushing his as she waved to her daughter on the ground.

Once or twice she pointed out something with her left hand. The sight of her wedding band, holding down a substantial diamond that looked entirely wrong on a creature of such simple beauty, made his blood boil; he wanted to pull both rings off her finger and hurl them into the sea.

She couldn't be taken—she couldn't.

The thought that Sarann Johnson had been free up until mere months ago was even more painful to Ben than it was astonishing. The thought that he hadn't done a damn thing about finding that out was most painful of all. Twelve years ago, Sarann had kept him at bay—had driven him off—by appealing to his sense of honor. He'd had no sense of honor back then, but he thought, back then, that it might be nice to have one.

Today he couldn't care less.

The wheel began to slow and, despite Ben's silent prayer and muttered curse, it stopped and began emptying its passengers.

Sarann said softly, "What goes around comes around, I guess."

Something in her voice made him look out at the water and say quietly, "Sarann, where do we go from here? What do you want me to do?"

He turned to watch her face, because he was convinced that although her answer would be exceedingly proper, the look in her eyes might not.

He was disappointed. She, too, looked at the water while she considered her response. When she turned to him, the look she gave him was damnably forthright.

"I think we'll have to be guided by Abby. If she wants and needs to have you in her life, then I would be incredibly grateful to you if you could make room for her, Ben. I'm not sure how we would work it out. We live in such a small town; there will be gossip."

Raw with disappointment, Ben said, "Ah, yes, a headmaster's fear of scandal."

Sarann's defense of her husband was staunch. "Well, can you blame him? Rodger bought into my lie completely, and now his only choices are to look like either a naive fool or a petty conspirator—as he's pointed out to me."

"I'll bet he has."

"Why do you say that?"

"I don't know," Ben groused. "I don't like him."

"You don't even know him!"

"But I know *about* him; that should be enough," he said, unable to keep a sneer out of his voice. "After all, weren't you going to introduce my daughter to me that way? By word of mouth?"

My daughter. He'd never called Abby that before now.

The word sounded shocking to him, like the first time he used the F-word when he was a kid.

Sarann, on the other hand, didn't seem shocked at all, maybe because she'd lived with the concept all those years. She said, "This can only work if we all stay civil. I think that Rodger will rise to the occasion and put the best face on things. He's been wonderful about forgiving me; he's that kind of man. Abby—well, it's pretty obvious how Abby feels about you. As for me, I want what she wants. And . . . and what you want, of course; I want that."

Oh, sweet Jesus, if only you knew what I want right now.

And maybe she did. It had to be obvious in his face; he wasn't really able to disguise the attraction he was feeling for her. Nor did he particularly want to. She was big on truth? Okay, she was getting a good dose of truth.

"It's a lot to ask, I know," she went on. "There would be driving back and forth—chunks of your time, wasted."

"Oh, yeah," Ben said dryly. "I might have to give up the bridge club and most of my macramé projects."

She got a kind of exasperated smile on her face. "Well, you could be a master chef at a fancy restaurant in your off hours; how would I know?"

"Come have supper with me and find out," he said with a burning look.

She seemed taken aback, and Ben realized that it wasn't what he said so much as how he said it that had her looking around in distress for Abby. Damn it! He had to do it; he had to push it too far.

"Here she comes," Sarann said, waving at her daughter just a tad too desperately for Ben's taste.

Abby and three of her friends—all in stretch tops, pedal pushers, clunky shoes, and crazy shades of lipstick—approached with tentative looks on their faces while Ben wondered how Abby had accounted for him as she waved up to them in the Ferris wheel: See that guy; that's my pop? My mom's one-night stand? Just this guy I tracked down on the Net?

Sarann said, "Hi, girls, having fun? Deirdre . . . Morgan . . . Lisa, this is Ben McElwyn." Straight and to the point.

Ben flapped his fingers onto his palm and said, "Hullo, ladies; nice to meech'all," which sent them into a sudden fit of baffling giggles. Abby, looking the youngest, acted the calmest.

"I told them that you were a private eye, I hope that was okay," she explained, still without addressing him as anything. "Everyone wants to know if you're packing heat."

Yikes.

"Uh, no. No heat," he said, glancing at Sarann. *At least not today.* He could understand the fascination of little boys with weapons—but little girls?

"Do you even know how to use a gun?" asked the shortest one with the tallest shoes. Definitely, she had an attitude.

"Sure. More or less."

The girls exchanged a look, then giggled nervously. The short one, Morgan, said, "Then show us. There's a shooting booth here. We'll pay for your ticket."

Little snot. Taking his cue from the frown on Sarann's face, Ben said, "If it's all the same to you, I'll pass."

Morgan muttered to the others, "Told you."

The one called Lisa shrugged and said, "They probably have to have a gun to get their license or something. That doesn't mean they know how to use it."

Abby felt obliged to defend him. "Of course he knows how to use a gun. He's an expert shooter."

With her back to her mother and her friends, Abby gave him a heartfelt, pleading look and mouthed the words, "Dad. *Please.*"

The "please" wouldn't necessarily have cut it with Ben; but oh, the "Dad." He was knocked for a loop by it. Granted, it wasn't out loud and it was aimed only at him, but Abby might as well have shouted it from the rooftops. Dad. Ben was a dad. He was her dad. Dads did what their daughters wanted them to, wasn't that how it went? Daughters wrapped their dads around their little fingers. Daughters with big blue eyes and jet-black hair and their mother's winning ways didn't even have to half try. Dad he was, and Dad he would always be, to this precocious, moody, vulnerable sprite of a twelve-year-old. Nothing could alter that fact.

Dazed by the realization and profoundly moved, Ben said, "Okay, young ladies, since you're all so fascinated. Lead the way."

The four little wenches looked pleased with themselves as they took off—giggling, of course—ahead of Ben and Sarann.

Sarann said in a surprisingly grim voice, "Are you sure this is a good idea?"

Was she kidding? Ben didn't have a clue if it was a good idea or not. He said uncertainly, "It's no big deal."

"It is to me. Don't you read the papers? We don't need to encourage an interest in guns."

Ah, shit. Now what? He'd already said yes; they were nearly at the booth. "Sarann, it'll take half a minute."

"You're missing the point, Ben!"

This was not the time to have their first quarrel over how to raise the kids. "I promise not to inflict permanent psychological damage," he said, trying but failing to make it sound light.

The girls were gathered in front of the shooting booth. They seemed to be jumping up and down without moving; it was the damndest thing.

Morgan, who was obviously the instigator, said, "We already gave the guy the tickets. You have three tries. You get to shoot a hundred BBs into the target; you have to completely wipe out the red star in the middle, and then you get a prize."

Of—what else? A stuffed animal.

Caught in the middle, Ben said, "Understand, it's been a while since I've used one of these things," and picked up the BB gun.

Sarann was not happy. That was evident in the way she folded her arms across her chest and looked away, waiting for him to be done. Anyone would think he was putting down the family pet. He took aim at the little red star and let loose, shooting out maybe a third of it.

"Well, he has to warm up," Abby explained earnestly to the rest of the gang. "Try again," she said to Ben. "Concentrate."

He made a big deal of doing so, and shot out half of the star this time.

Abby looked shocked. "Come *on*," she urged. "You can do better than *that*." She sounded almost angry in her disappointment. The kid was going to be a hell of a mother.

"It's nothing I have an interest in," Ben said, looking past Abby at Sarann. He was doing his part, she had to see that. No one could accuse him of glamorizing guns.

He thought he'd done pretty well and wasn't prepared for the scene to play out the way it did.

Sarann turned to Abby in what appeared to be a maternal fury and said, "Abigail Johnson, you are being positively—!"

But then she checked herself, probably more for Abby's friends' sakes than for Ben's, and she said with almost serene calm, "It's much later than I thought. We're going to have to go home right now."

Exactly what kind of deadly threat Sarann had managed to convey to Abby, Ben couldn't say; but somehow she got it across that she meant business. Ben had been watching the two of them closely, but he never saw it happen. Maybe they were witches and communicated in some superhuman way; but whatever the case, Abby didn't waste time howling. She

turned quickly to Ben and said to him in a voice too low for
the others to hear, "This has been so cool. It was like, really
cool. It was the best carnival I've ever been to. The *best*!
Here—I want you to have this," she said, thrusting the balloon string into his hand.

She was looking at him with such complete—Ben
couldn't think of another word—*adoration*, that he felt his
face heat up with pleasure. The kid really liked him, even
though he'd botched the target shoot. He'd passed the test;
his daughter liked him!

He smiled at the balloon and said, "Y'know, I had a great
time, too? I'd have to say in all honesty that this was the
best carnival *I've* ever been to, as well."

He turned to Sarann. She had one hand balled into a fist
and up against her mouth; all that was missing was the blow-
gun and poisonous dart.

"Thanks for inviting me," he said with a look that was
rich with intent. Did she get it at all, what he was feeling for
her?

Maybe so. "I'm glad you were able to stop by on your
way through Cape Ann," she said in a voice that sounded
killingly casual. "It was good to see you again." She held
out her hand while managing to look right through him,
which was another thing that everyone knew witches could
do.

Ben said, "Yeah. It was good." God damn it, it *was* good.
Couldn't she see that?

He was convinced that she could. Which would explain
why she was so busy shooting BBs through his heart. She
was trying her damndest to kill whatever there had been between them on the Ferris wheel.

He was paralyzed with pain, so he let her go. She and
Abby went off in one direction, the gang of three in another.

That left Ben to mull the lessons he'd just learned. They
were threefold. Number one: Do not accept double-dares

from twelve-year-olds; they know more than you do. Number two: If you do accept the dare, play to win; don't wimp out and make the whole thing pointless. And number three: When a woman says, "Are you sure this is a good idea?" she means, "Try it and you die."

"You gonna take your last try?" asked the guy in charge of the booth.

"Hold these," said Ben, handing the operator his balloon and Miss Piggy. He picked up the gun again.

This time he shot to kill, obliterating the red star before he was halfway through his alloted BBs.

Chapter 16

ABBY DECIDED THAT the most important thing was not to hurt her stepfather's feelings.

Her mother had told her many times how lucky they were to have someone as generous and respected as Rodger Bonniface willing to accept a ready-made family, especially when they came from such an ordinary background. (When her mother said "ordinary," she really meant "poor.")

Personally, Abby didn't see it. She figured she was as smart as anyone she knew, and not horrible looking, and her manners were *definitely* better than the eighth-graders she knew from Faxton Academy—so why should she have to fall on her knees in thanks when the Academy kids got to take everything they had for granted? It's not as though her stepfather was risking his life by bringing in a couple of zoo animals to live in his house with him.

Still, he was bound to feel hurt that Abby was going to be seeing so much of her real father in the future. "So I'm really going to make an effort to make Dad feel still important," she announced to her mother as they drove home from the carnival. "It's only fair."

But she added, "Mom, I don't want to call him 'Dad' anymore. It doesn't feel right. It never felt right. Why can't I call him Rodger?"

Her mother seemed down about things, including this latest request. "Oh, honey, you'll make everything so complicated if you try to change now," she said. "Can't you just go on doing what you're doing and call him Dad? At least for a while longer?"

"Well . . . I'll see." It was a point she could negotiate later,

Abby decided. In the meantime, she was still flying high over her real father.

"Even though he's not a very good shot, isn't everything else about him, like, beyond cool? He's so cute, and he's funny, but in, like, a quiet way? Sometimes Dad—oh, this is going to be so confusing!—sometimes Rodger-Dad seems to force it, you know? He tries too hard to be funny."

"That's a good thing, not a bad thing, Abby," said her mother. "It means that your stepfather wants you to like him."

"Don't I know that? But that still doesn't make him funny." She added in a mutter, "I don't see why I can't just call him Rodger."

They passed Gloucester's famous memorial to fishermen, and Abby let out a moan of dismay. "We should've showed him—Dad, I mean; my *real* dad, I mean—the Man at the Wheel! It's our most famous thing! Oh, well. Next time," she said, and she sat back happily to dream.

But her mother was staying really, really quiet, and eventually it bothered Abby too much for her to keep on enjoying her plans and speculations.

"Mom? Are you going to be in serious trouble with Rodger-Dad about this? Would he possibly give you an ultimatum? Would he, like, divorce you and leave us because we're going to be seeing my real father?"

Her mother sighed and said, "You shouldn't call Ben your 'real' father, Abby; Ben is your birth father. Your real father is the man who kept an eye on you for five years and paid for your braces even before he married me, and who loves you and clothes you and feeds you."

"Yeah, yeah. But, Mom? Would he? Divorce you, I mean?"

"No. It's not going to be an issue. We'll work something out. Stop jabbering, Abby; you're distracting me from my driving. I just drove through a stop sign, if you didn't notice."

Abby didn't say anything after that. She had things to think about, too. On the one hand, she really did believe that Rodger-Dad was a good father. He'd already promised her a used car on the day she got her driver's license, and a brand-new one to replace it if she graduated with honors. And he always tried to watch her play soccer, even if he had to rearrange a meeting. But . . . on the other hand . . . what if he *did* divorce her mother? Would that be so terrible? Would they be back to living in a three-room apartment and thriftshop clothes again? And would *that* be so terrible? At least her mother would be able to have anyone she wanted over.

Abby chewed on her thumbnail. She just didn't know how she felt about all that.

After a round of meetings, Rodger Bonniface returned home to an empty house. He changed immediately from a shirt and slacks to jeans and a black Polo shirt, then went downstairs and fixed himself a snack to go with the sherry he took from the sideboard. He slipped a classical CD into the player mounted under one of the kitchen cupboards, then took a seat at the table overlooking his garden and tried to force himself to eat.

The cheese and crackers sat untouched, but he was pouring himself another sherry when he heard the sound of tires on the cobbled drive. His wife and stepdaughter were back.

The sober expressions on their faces were at odds with the menagerie of stuffed animals in their arms. Rodger said to Abby, "Lookit that haul! So you had a pretty good time, huh, pumpkin?"

"Pretty good," said Abby, dumping the creatures on the hall table.

Rodger looked at his wife but said nothing.

Sarann murmured, "I have to get a couple of aspirin," and headed upstairs.

Rodger pointed to the jumble of animals and said, "Looks like someone got lucky. Who won at what?"

Abby shrugged and said, "Oh . . . the usual. Darts, hoops. More darts. BBs."

"So . . . you won all those yourself?"

She waved an arm at the creatures on the table. "They're all my prizes."

He said in a wistful voice, "I wish I'd been able to go."

Abby squinted at her stepfather in disbelief. "You said that carnivals are dirty, filthy places where everything sticks to your clothes!"

Rodger grinned and said, "That was yesterday. I didn't know they were giving out such good stuff."

"Anyway, you had meetings," said Abby with a sympathetic shrug, "which I guess was too bad."

"I don't have any meetings tomorrow, pumpkin. Whaddya say—want to go to the carnival with me tomorrow?"

"The—tomorrow? Um . . . I don't think Mom will let me go twice. Plus, I know she has to work at the shop getting it ready for the movers."

He said, "No problem. Just you and me. I'm sure your mother won't object."

"Oh. Well . . . if you really want to, then I guess . . . okay."

"Great! We'll go on every ride, and we won't come home until we win whatever's left in the booths. It'll be fun, just you and me. We don't do that enough."

Abby smiled briefly and headed for the refrigerator. "What do we have to eat?" she said, passing right over the plate of cheese and crackers. "I'm starved."

"You haven't eaten yet?"

Abby shook her head. "Mom made us come home."

"Oh? How come?"

"Because of your reception, I guess. That's what she said."

"That's hours away."

"That's what she said."

As her stepfather watched, Abby pulled out a box of Cheerios and poured half of it into a deep cereal bowl on the counter, then filled the bowl with so much milk that some Cheerios floated up and over the sides. She picked up most of the runaways and tossed them back into the bowl, then picked up the bowl and hesitated, uncertain where to go with it next.

"I think a sandwich would have been more filling," her stepfather said from his seat at the table. ·

Abby shrugged. "If Cheerios are good enough for Seinfeld. . . ."

"Seinfeld?"

"Yeah, he's—oh, well, never mind." She glanced at the back stairs and said, "Guess I'll eat this in my room."

Sarann propped the little stuffed panda on her bureau, then decided that it was too conspicuous there. She tucked it among the bedpillows (terrible location), sat it in the corner of the wing chair (not much better), and tried nestling it in the folds of a chenille throw draped over the Windsor rocking chair. Besides reminding her once again that very few places in the house were her own, the endearing creature fairly glowed with another man's presence. It may as well have been Ben that she was trying to tuck inconspicuously somewhere in the room.

Oh, God, why did I accept this?

More to the point, what would she do with it? She couldn't just dump it in the garbage; it would be like throwing out the Flag, or tossing a rosary. It shocked her even to be making such grave comparisons. The panda was nothing, a small stuffed toy that she'd be embarrassed to donate to anyone.

But she hugged it anyway, and inhaled its vaguely carnival smell, and tried to figure out how to keep it separate from the rest of her life and yet an integral part of it.

Damn it! She had to get downstairs and feed her family; she couldn't just stand there, paralyzed over a panda. She ran to the closet and crammed it on the same shelf where she used to keep her returned letter to Ben.

And when she turned around to go downstairs, there was Rodger.

"*Oh,* my God; you startled me," she said, clutching one hand to her chest.

"I can't imagine why; this is my bedroom, too," said Rodger with a wounded smile. He glanced at the panda but did not comment on it.

"I guess I'm used to Abby clomping around in her sneakers."

"We've been married nine months. You're still not used to me?"

"You know that's not how I meant it, Rodger. Why do you twist what I say?"

His eyes narrowed an infinitesimal amount. "Are we going to argue? Because if we are, I think I ought to take myself off to my study and do some work. I don't want us walking into the reception looking like a Hatfield who brought a Mc-Coy by mistake."

Abby was right; his humor *was* forced. But at least he was trying; it was more than Sarann could say for herself. She made herself smile. "I'm sorry; it's this headache."

"Again? You have them so often. The next time you're at the doctor's, you ought to ask for something stronger than aspirin."

She shook her head. "I feel cobwebby enough as it is. I've never handled medicine very well. Look how I stagger around when I take something for a cold."

"Because you try too hard to stay in control. You should allow yourself to let go, let the medication do what it has to do. Is that why you're not seeing a doctor about—well, this other thing? Your chronic confusion? Because you're afraid of the treatment?"

"I don't know; I suppose it could be. Rodger, do we have to talk about all of this now?" she asked.

"Of course not. I came upstairs—since you didn't seem to be coming downstairs—to find out how the afternoon went."

"Abby didn't tell you?"

"I didn't ask. From the looks on your faces when you came in, I assumed, not well."

Both mother and daughter had been trying instinctively not to seem too happy; how did you explain something like that to a husband and stepfather?

Sarann did her best. "It wasn't that it didn't go well so much as that no one's sure what's next. It's my fault, I know that," she said, anticipating his next remark. "The thing is, you're the one who stands to lose the most, as you've told me. So I guess I'm wondering—we're all wondering—how you mean to handle this," she asked humbly.

He glanced at his watch. She wondered how much time he needed to give her a simple response . . . unless maybe it wasn't so simple.

His answer confirmed her fears. He turned and sat down in his exquisite George II needlepoint wing chair—which luckily no longer had a panda sitting in it—and tapped his fingertips thoughtfully together. Even in jeans, he looked Ivy League. Maybe it was the wire-rimmed glasses, or the embroidered polo player on his Ralph Lauren shirt. Maybe it was the Harvard in his soul. He looked good in black, she thought inconsequentially as she waited for his answer. Judicial. Once again she felt like one of his students, about to be handed detention. Or a prisoner in the dock, about to be handed a sentence.

He said, "We're going to have to lie."

"Oh, Rodger, no, I don't—!"

"Let me finish. I've thought about this—thought about nothing else—since yesterday. The only way I can see out of this mess, the only way that we can let Abby have access to her biological father and still preserve a smidgeon of honor for me and thereby spare the Academy, is for us to present a modified version of what actually happened in your past."

"But I'm done with lying; I wouldn't even be able to keep a new lie straight. It's exhausting, Rodger, believe me. Sooner or later you get tripped up; look how *I* got tripped up!"

"This won't be that big a stretch," he said, looking determined. "People have to be told that you've lied about McElwyn; that's fairly obvious, isn't it? I'm sorry, Sarann, I wish it could be done some other way. But you've made your bed—"

"I know; I know," she said, looking anywhere but at him. She had no regrets about her night with Ben, but she was deeply ashamed about the fraud. Would the feeling ever end? Her glance around the room ended on the shelf of the open closet, where an exiled panda sat in button-eyed reproach.

How could you do this to me?

She looked back at her husband. "What do you want me to say?"

That must have been what Rodger wanted to hear from her. He seemed to relax, and his manner became friendlier. It was as if the judge had come around to the front of the bench and offered Sarann a beer while they discussed which prison she thought she'd like the best.

"All right," he said with a warm and reassuring smile, "we know that you have to come clean about McElwyn. That's a given. Now, you don't want to give everyone the idea that you're a slut, which, good grief, you certainly are not. But having made up a far-fetched story about Abby's father being a lawyer who died young—well, it was an implicit admission of guilt and shame, wasn't it?"

"I made that up so Abby would be proud, growing up, that's all," Sarann said softly. "Not to cover any sense of shame."

"Be that as it may, that's how it will strike people once they find out that McElwyn is alive and well and not exactly attorney material."

He got out of the chair and began pacing the room as he worked through his plan for her. "On the other hand, what if people found out that you lied because you had suffered— well, let's call it a nervous breakdown, something like that? Once they realize that the story you fabricated was really nothing more than a fantasy to ease you in your understandable pain of being abandoned by McElwyn . . ."

He laid the mental photograph of a jilted, despondent woman before Sarann and let her stare at it for a while before he said, "Once people realize that, they'll feel genuine sympathy for you. It's night and day different from regarding you as—"

"A slut." Beaten down, Sarann shook her head and whispered, "But it wasn't that way at all."

His face creased in sympathy. He stopped pacing and came over to her and took her in his arms and held her close. "Darling . . . sweetheart . . . don't you think I know that? Nowadays most people wouldn't think twice about your choice of single motherhood. The problem is, you complicated everything with that lie . . . and now I'm afraid we're stuck with it, you and I. Sarann, I'm desperate," he admitted softly. "As God is my witness, I cannot figure another way out of this. Can you?"

She murmured into his chest, "If we just tell the truth—?"

"It will be the end of my position as headmaster of Faxton Academy, and it may be the end of the Academy itself."

She sighed. "Because trust is everything in a small boarding school. Everyone has to be above reproach."

"Exactly. You've heard me say it many times. When the teachers live with their students in the dorm houses . . . Reputation is everything at a small school like Faxton."

He held her at arm's length. His face, usually serenely handsome, was haggard with worry and anguish. He had so many responsibilities—to the school, the faculty, the students. To her and to Abby and to his family who had put their lives into making the Academy the success story that it was.

And then there was Sarann, able with one good lie to tear it all down. She had an obligation to him, them, everyone, to do the right thing. And just then, definitely, her judgment about what constituted the right thing was as murky as the tidewater that surrounded them.

"Tell me what you want me to say, and I'll do it," she said with a catch in her throat.

"Shh, shh, you won't have to say anything. No one we know would be boorish enough to ask you directly about your past, and if someone does, you should cut them dead; they'd deserve it."

Sarann had read many columns by Miss Manners over the years; she knew that her husband was right. It was comforting to know that she wouldn't have to make up any more lies. But it was depressing to think that poor Rodger was going to have to do it for her.

"Will we get through this?" she asked him.

His answer was husky with emotion. "We definitely will. I love you, Sarann, and I love Abby. We'll get through this. Don't worry; leave this to me. I'll take care of you."

After that he kissed her with a fiery passion that she hadn't felt from him in weeks. It was startling, even electrifying—nothing at all like the perfunctory lovemaking that they'd shared recently.

Sarann wondered, as she let herself be kissed by him, whether he wasn't just jealous of Ben.

Chapter 17

BEN GOT HOME tired, pissed, hungry, and grimy. The last thing he needed was a torn bag of smelly garbage strewn across the hall in front of his door.

"*Fuck.*"

The door across the hall cracked open. "Benny, is that you, dear?"

Ouch.

"Yes, Mrs. Calliston," he said in a hushed voice, "Sorry I woke you up."

"No, I've been waiting for you to come home."

"You should go back to sleep," he scolded softly. "It's late." He wrapped his balloon string around his doorknob and began stuffing the torn bag with chicken bones, coffee grounds, banana peels, empty Ensure cans and used-up Depends—the daily dreck of a feisty little white-haired lady who was trying her damnedest to live on her own.

Behind him he heard the widow fumble with the chain and then open her door wider. There she hovered, five feet of frailty bent over a walker. In an apologetic voice she said, "I put the bag of garbage by the door because I forgot you said you were going away. It must have been the dog from the boys upstairs that got into it, Benny. I started to pick it all up, but—"

"Don't even think about it," he said over his shoulder. "I'll have it cleaned up in no time."

"I think there might be an apartment coming up soon on the first floor, if I can afford it," she said as she watched. "I could take out my own garbage then."

"Nope, absolutely not," he said. He stood and shook his

finger at her the way she was always doing at him. "Now will you go back to bed and leave this to me?"

"Here," she said, fooling with something on her side of the door. She handed him a partly filled trash bag. "I started to pick it all up . . ." she repeated.

"Hey, thanks!" he said, as if it were a six-pack of Coors. "Now good *night* to you." He began pulling her door gently shut on her.

"Wait, one other thing," she said, pulling it open again. She clutched her robe lapels modestly at the neck. "There was a man here asking questions about you yesterday."

"A man? What kind of man? What kind of questions?"

"Well, I didn't actually open my door when he knocked. But I did peek when I heard him knocking down the hall. You know what a gossip Mrs. O'Neil is. *Well*. From what I could tell, they had a fine old conversation about you."

God damn. It wasn't surprising. They were even entitled. But still. God damn. So she'd gone and done it, hired someone to check him out, and then she'd lied to his face about it. He was sickened by the thought.

Hold it, hold it. It could be the headmaster's work and she didn't know squat.

"Were you able to hear anything specific?"

His elderly neighbor nodded. "He asked if you were married; what kind of work did you do. If you have any children. Oh! And what kind of car you drove. He made it sound like you were taking out a loan or something. I couldn't hear any of Mrs. O'Neil's answers, though; she's one of those whispery types. Everything is *pss-pss-pss* when she talks. You know what I mean? I'm always adjusting my hearing aid with her."

"Did he give you his name?"

"Yes; I think it was something like Lozario, something like that." She added, "You won't tell Helen that I said anything, will you, Benny? Because I know sometimes you help her out, like that window you replaced."

"Only because the landlord couldn't get to it and it was forty degrees out." Ben did not want to be regarded as some kind of Samaritan; he did not. He tied the bag's open end around itself in a knot and said, "Anyway, mum's the word, don't worry. I'll sweep up those corn niblets tomorrow morning first thing."

"Oh . . . but . . . the mice . . ."

"The mice. Yes. Okay," he said wearily, "I'll do it right now."

"I'm so sorry, Benny. I don't know how I could have forgot you weren't going to be home. My memory's going, it really is."

"Nonsense. You're ten times sharper than anyone else I know," he said, poking through his pocket for his keys.

Mrs. Callistan beamed like a debutante with a full dance card. "I don't believe you for a minute, Ben McElwyn. I've seen how you charm the women."

"Ah, if only I could charm you as easily," he said, flashing her a good-night grin.

She waved him a girlish response and closed and locked her door after her.

The inside of Ben's apartment didn't look—or smell—a whole lot better than the outside. He discovered that he'd left a quart of milk on the counter because he thought it might be going bad. Now he knew for sure.

As for the rest of the place: after he rinsed out the carton, he looked around with a newcomer's eyes and decided that he was one visit away from being shut down by the Department of Health. It wasn't just the stacks of newspapers and unopened mail, or the newsprint-stained Formica counters. It wasn't the recycle bin on the chair, or the groceries—hopefully not perishable—still in their bag on the kitchen table. It wasn't the dirty dishes in the sink, the dirty laundry on the floor, or the dirty sneakers that he'd managed to get on, but not in, the dishwasher for a serious cleaning.

It was all of it. All of it, taken together, pointed to a man who had raised not caring to an art form. It had been very important to Ben, not getting involved, and it was still important to him. But something inside him was stabbing at his gut like a staple dropped and lost during surgery. Why did he suddenly *care* that he lived in a pigpen?

Sarann. Sarann and Abby—two prongs of a staple—had suddenly dropped into his life, and there wasn't much he could do to get them back out of it, short of major surgery.

Sarann's words on that magical, wretched night came back one more time to haunt him:

You live in this pit because it's easier to leave a pit. If you fixed it up—bought a rug or some dishes from Kmart or a philodendron from Stop and Shop—you might begin to care. And pretty soon you'd start having people over, because you wouldn't be ashamed.

He couldn't have Abby seeing how he lived, he just couldn't. Not that he'd ever invite her to do it—but what if the kid hopped on a bus to see for herself? Runaway twelve-year-olds were not exactly a phenomenon, and Abby was more resourceful than most. Hell, she probably had her own Visa card; she could charter the whole damn bus if she wanted to.

Sarann? Would she ever bring Abby to see him there? Ben laughed softly at the notion. Fat chance. Still, his mind had been obsessed with the game of "what if" all the way back from the carnival, and as tired as he was, as despairing as he felt, Ben couldn't help playing one last round.

What if Sarann were here right now?

The answer to that was stupidly easy. He would blindfold her and put a clothespin on her nose, and then he'd take her to his bed.

Except, of course, she was married.

Married. Jesus. How could she *do* that to him?

Still in a state of denial over it, he began picking at the mess in the kitchen, moving stuff from here to there and back again. But it was two in the morning and he was whipped and all of it was just going to have to wait. Maybe Martha Stewart knew how to put a home together in three easy steps; Ben McElwyn possessed no such skills.

He checked the grocery bag—cans and boxes, thank God—and decided to go to bed and call a cleaning service in the morning.

An hour later he awoke with a start from a troubled sleep. He'd forgotten to sweep up the niblets.

Sarann bounced her niece on one shin and laughed as the baby cackled with joy. "Oh, ow, Maggie! You're getting too heavy to do this, fat stuff. You're going to break my leg."

"Do you really think she's too fat?" asked Glenys, instantly on the alert.

Still grinning, Sarann said to her sister-in-law, "Are you kidding? She's the most perfect baby I've ever seen—aren't you, sweetiecake?" She lifted Maggie in her arms and blew bubbles into her stomach, sending her on another round of cackles and shrieks.

"You're going to be sorry, Sarann," warned Glenys. "She'll be so riled up that you'll never get her to sleep."

Sarann didn't care; she loved playing with her niece. The child had a sunny disposition, rarely cried, and brightened every room she occupied. She had given Sarann some of the few moments of pure joy that Sarann had known in the past few months, and for that Sarann owed her big time. She whisked Maggie in her arms and whirled her around the room until she felt her own tension melt away like ice cubes in August.

"I love you and I could just squeeze you squeeze you

squeeze you!" she said to her niece, hugging her cheek-to-cheek as she rocked her in her arms.

Glenys was watching them with an indulgent smile on her face as she clipped on her second gold earring. "Your hair looks nice," she told Sarann. "Are you highlighting it?"

"No; it's the sun, I guess. I've been out in the garden."

"Rodger lets you mess with his plants? I'm impressed. Shocked, if you want the truth."

"He let me have a little patch behind the big clump of lilacs. I like it there. It's my own little world."

Sarann put Maggie down on the carpet; the child made a fat-legged dash to hide behind a big wooden toybox at one end of the room. Sarann dropped down to all fours and said in her growly monster voice, "I . . . munna . . . find you!"

A loud shriek, and out ran Maggie, showing herself before who knew *what* horrible fate befell her. Sarann acted astonished at Maggie's miraculous reappearance, and they hugged and tickled, and then Maggie said, "Find me, find me!" and ran right back behind the toybox.

"Thanks for pinch-hitting, Sarann," said Glenys. "I couldn't find a sitter anywhere in the state. I don't where they are; they can't *all* be going to semiformals tonight."

Sarann wouldn't know; by the time she was old enough to attend a semiformal, she was pretty much taking care of her mother full-time.

"I don't mind this at all. Anytime you need a sitter, just call; I'll make the time."

"You're so good with children," Glenys said. She added out of the blue, "So what's holding up the show?"

Sarann answered with an awkward shrug, "We're trying."

"Hmmm. Is either of you considering getting checked over?"

Again Sarann shrugged; she was intensely uncomfortable with the subject. "It hasn't been that long yet; not even a year."

With a tentative grimace, Glenys said, "This is none of my business, but—since you so obviously love children and they love you back—you ought to consider seeing an ob-gyn, Sarann. You haven't had a baby in a while."

"I haven't been married in a while," Sarann said instantly.

Why had she said it that way? It implied that she'd been married in the first place. She was still doing it! How was Rodger ever going to get the new version of Sarann's past out there if Sarann kept pushing the old version?

"I've offended you," Glenys said. "I'm sorry."

"Not at all. It's just that I'm not that worried yet—"

James entered the nursery with a scowl on his face. "Are you coming or not?"

"Of course I am, although not if you take that tone with me. So what do you think?" she asked, jiggling an earlobe at him. "These, or the diamond studs?"

"Definitely those. It's an author's reception in Boston, not a New Year's gala in New York."

"Oh, but, darling," Glenys said innocently, "how would I know? You're the only one I've ever met who's written a book." She made it sound a little like robbing a a 7-Eleven.

James muttered something as his wife left the room in search of her watch, and then he turned to his daughter. "Maggie, come over here, baby."

The child stayed crouched behind the toybox.

"Maggie—I said come here. Hurry up!"

"She's playing hide and seek with me," Sarann explained.

"I hide, I hide." Two big blue eyes under a mop of flaxen hair peeked over the top of the toybox at her father.

"No more hiding," said her father. "Bedtime now."

"No. I hide." She crouched down in an air-raid position and waited with glee for someone to find her.

"Maggie, I'm in a hurry!"

James marched over to the child and brought her out from

behind the toybox and lifted her in his arms. "Say good night to Daddy," he said sternly.

She looked abashed. " 'Night."

"Now give Daddy a kiss."

She wasn't so sure about that.

"Come on. Good-night kiss." He gave her a single jiggle on his arm to nudge her into compliance, and she planted a light if sulky peck on his cheek.

"You be a good girl, okay?"

Still pouting, Maggie nodded obediently.

He put her back down and she bolted instantly to Sarann.

"God, I'm going to be late for my own reception," James said. "What is it with this family?"

He walked out without a word to Sarann, but that was understandable; he was completely distracted. His book was about to be released, and the evening in Boston was a private reception before the official kickoff in New York of a nationwide, multimedia book tour. Hopes were high that the book would do well: the scandalous congressman had the topic of child abuse once again front and center in the news.

Sarann had a deep revulsion for the very concept of abusing children; it was incredibly painful for her to read or tune into a story about it. On the other hand, someone obviously had to be the expert, and James may have had the best reason of all to study child abuse: Sarann strongly suspected that before his adoption, he'd been removed from an abusive home.

She couldn't be certain of that, because Rodger didn't confide much to her. But he did once remark, almost with annoyance, that the book which was taking so much of James's time away from Faxton was as much a form of therapy as it was an attempt at distinction. If it was true, then Sarann should have been more sympathetic toward her brother-in-law. She felt guilty that she was not.

In any case, it didn't make the subject of child abuse any

less painful to dwell on. Sarann's own father had doted on her and her mother, and Sarann remained convinced that if he hadn't died young of heart disease, he would not only have raised her to be a world-class scientist, but he would have prevented her mother's slide into mental disease as well. In Sarann's mind, fathers ranked just a rung below the Almighty.

And their daughters were supposed to adore them. It was nature's way. Just look at Abby . . .

"Come on, sweetie, let's warm up some milk, and then Aunty Sarann will read you a story and sing you a song, okay?"

She held the child close as they went downstairs, but her mind was on another daughter now, and other fathers than James.

Contrary to her mother's prediction, Maggie allowed herself to be put to bed as easy as pie.

After snugging the child in her crib, Sarann went down to the kitchen and sliced a monster apple into a dozen wedges, then took down a book from among the thousand on the shelves of the cozy library and curled up with it on the leather loveseat, determined to read it through.

The book was *The Perfect Storm*. A dinner guest had recently pointed out to Sarann that she was the only human being in Cape Ann and perhaps in the country who hadn't yet read the harrowing bestseller that had put their Gloucester on the map. Everyone at the table had smiled in disbelief, and, although her husband had fully understood Sarann's reason for that, Sarann herself had felt like an unread ignoramus.

The reason that Sarann hadn't been able to read the book (and despite all the local hoopla had skipped the movie altogether) was that four years earlier, she had not been able to keep a little girl from drowning. It was as simple as that. Despite many agonized replays of the traumatic event with

her husband, Sarann still had not been able to put it behind
her. The sight of children laughing and splashing at the water's edge sent chills through her; the idea that children actually sailed in boats on oceans took her breath away.

Always, the sight of children in or near water brought
back images that Sarann would give anything to be able to
forget. A young girl, in water barely over her head, flailing
and screaming for help. Sarann, swimming out to her in what
seemed like agonizingly slow motion. More screaming, more
flailing, more panic. Sarann's wind kicked out of her as she
tried to help. A tangle of other arms, trying to save, failing
to save. The girl, laid out on the sand, her face gray, her wet
ponytails still bound in pink rubber bands. Sarann, breathing
into the body, trying to force life back to where life had
flown.

A school outing, gone from happy to horrific in a few
short minutes.

She had an odd, wistful hope that reading *The Perfect
Storm* would be a form of therapy. And although she had
expected to be too wary to let herself get fully involved in
the book, she was wrong. Before long she was caught up in
the ominous tale, knowing full well that the fishing boat was
going to sink and yet praying with all her heart that the sun
would come out or that the *Andrea Gail* would head back to
port.

She was five hundred miles at sea and thoroughly terrified
when she heard a soft gurgle of laughter coming from the
monitor: Maggie, at least, wasn't caught up in the nightmar-
ish hell of the crew but was enjoying a baby's sweet dreams.

In a downward spiral of apprehension, Sarann turned the
page . . . read it with dread . . . turned another page.

The crew was going to drown. They would struggle with
the imminent horror of it—they would flail, they would cry
out—and then they were going to drown. Away from their

loved ones, alone and in terror, they were all going to die in
the deep blue clutch of the sea.

Sarann could scarcely breathe. Her anxiety level had become so high, her tension so extreme, that she had to put the
book down. She might not get through the story after all,
and certainly not tonight. She got up from the loveseat; she
couldn't sit still. She had to do something, anything.

I have to check on Maggie, she realized. For what was a
crib if not a baby's small boat?

Hurrying barefoot across gleaming floors sectioned off by
precious oriental rugs, Sarann pivoted at the newel post to
race up the stairs. She looked up, not really focused, and
that's when her heart came to a screeching stop.

On the landing, baby Maggie was standing on fat, wobbly
legs, about to descend the steep colonial stairs.

Sarann gasped and began a cautious ascent, at the same
time gently waving the child back. "No, no, no, honey," she
cajoled. "Go back to bed. Back to bed, honey. No, no; no
stairs."

With neither hand supporting her tippy little body, Maggie
teetered perilously in place. "An-An," she said, addressing
Sarann with a sleepy smile. She reached through air for a
wall that wasn't quite there.

No please no.

Sarann had an inspiration. "Maggie, go hide. Go hide
from An-An."

It was a thought. Maggie's eyes snapped into better focus
and her mouth opened in interest, then shaped itself into a
grin.

"I hide."

Around she whirled, so decisively that she lost her balance, falling mercifully forward on the landing with Saran
just two steps behind her. She scooped up the baby as if she
were a freed hostage and held her in a vise-grip until she
reached the nursery.

But Sarann pulled up short, with Maggie still in her arms, after she stepped over the threshold. In the soft glow of the nightlight, she stared at the crib.

The cribrail was in the lowered position.

But that wasn't possible.

The cribrail was in the lowered position.

"Oh, nooo," Sarann moaned, as devastated now as she had been at the scene of the drowning. *I must have forgot . . . I couldn't have forgot . . . I did; I forgot. Oh, dear God; please don't do this to me.*

She was going mad; like her mother, and day by day, she was slowly losing her grip. Only now she wasn't merely an embarrassment to others, but a danger to them.

Shaking from the realization, she tried to force herself to carry on in some rational way. With paranoid caution, she laid Maggie on the changing table and began unsnapping her blanket sleeper.

"Maggie has a wet diaper, hasn't she?" she said in a soft, singsong voice to the baby. "Who's such a pee-pee, hmm? Maggie is, isn't she?" she cooed.

But her mind was racing in a thousand directions at once, all of them ending in the same circle of hell.

No more babysitting; I can't be trusted. Not with Maggie, not with anyone.

Not with Abby. How could she drive her daughter around in a car when she couldn't remember filling it and ran through lights and stop signs? How could she be entrusted with valuable property when she couldn't remember where she'd left the car and couldn't figure out how to use a house key?

"What a good, little, pretty baby you are, snuggle-buggle," she said, her voice choking in anguish.

How could she possibly, possibly be entrusted with the life of a twenty-one-month-old baby when she couldn't be counted on to do something as automatic as raising the crib bar?

"Maggie, Maggie, I won't hurt you," Sarann insisted. "I really won't."

A flurry of tears dropped on the baby's exposed belly; Sarann wiped them away.

She wrapped Maggie in a clean diaper and blanket sleeper and laid her with infinite care on her back. In a soft, stricken voice, Sarann sang Raffi lullabies as she hovered over the crib and stroked the child's hair. At least half a dozen times she checked to be sure that the cribrail was up and locked in.

In minutes, Maggie was asleep. So peaceful, so trusting . . . so untroubled by perfect storms and imperfect aunts. In a state of near-despair, Sarann arranged a straight-backed chair to face the crib, and that's where she sat until she heard James and Glenys coming through the door downstairs.

Chapter 18

WHEN SARANN RETURNED home the lights were out, which wasn't surprising; Rodger was an early riser.

She tiptoed up the stairs and instead of going straight to her bedroom, detoured into Abigail's. Sarann could not go to bed without seeing her daughter.

She opened the door to the darkened room and called her name softly.

Abby rolled over from a sound sleep and mumbled, "N-uh?"

Sarann smiled in relief. Abby was fine; she hadn't drowned at the carnival or been abducted by aliens. It was silly, stupid, to have such improbable fears, but Sarann sat down on the side of her daughter's bed anyway, just to reassure herself. "How was the carnival?" she asked in a nighttime voice.

"Mommm," Abby groaned. "I have school."

"I know, I know, but . . . did everything go okay?"

"Mmm-hmm . . ."

"And did you win lots of stuff again?" Sarann asked, although she already knew the answer to that one.

"Mmm-mmm."

"And did you go out to eat afterward at Woodman's?"

"Mmm."

"And your—Rodger? Did he have a good time?"

"Mmm."

"Did you actually get him to go on any rides?"

Abby pulled the woven blanket over her shoulder and burrowed more deeply into her pillows, disturbing the cat, who jumped down from the bed and left.

"Zuh klutz," Abby mumbled.

Sarann laughed softly and said, "Come again?"

"He's a klutz," Abby said, yawning. "He was always fall-ing out've his seat or something inta me." She flopped over onto her other side, presenting her back to Sarann. "I wanna go to *sleep*, Mom. Stop talkin'."

"Okay, okay," Sarann said, relieved that no disaster had befallen either of them. No ride collapsed, no BBs went wild. It was almost hard to believe—but then, Sarann hadn't been part of their equation that afternoon. She bent over her daughter and kissed her long, silky hair. "I love you, Abs," she whispered. "I hope you know that."

"Then why are you keeping me *up*," Abby moaned.

"Good night, grouchy," Sarann said with an indulgent smile.

On her way back to her own bedroom, Sarann felt a rush of gratitude to Rodger. It couldn't have been easy to carve out a block of time for his stepdaughter at this point in the school year. Probably he did it because he was a little jealous of Ben, but that was understandable; Sarann could hardly begrudge him the feeling.

After undressing quietly, she slipped into bed alongside her husband without waking him. She tried to lie still, but she was restless. She was frightened of what lay ahead for her—an evaluation and drug therapy, with who knew what success—and she was desperate for reassurance. She wanted someone's arms around her. She wanted someone to con-vince her that she was okay, she wasn't losing it, she'd be all right, she *was* all right.

She wasn't able to convince herself on her own; before very long she was shaking with panic. She listened to Rodger's light, even breathing, trying to decide whether to wake him or not. Despite her fears, something in her hesi-tated. She wanted her husband around her but not in her, and you didn't wake a man out of a sound sleep just to beg for a hug.

If she did wake him and they did end up making love—would that be so bad? As she lay there, feeling lost and afraid and alone, Sarann had to admit that it would. Sex with Rodger wasn't what she wanted now; it didn't begin to answer her need.

Far worse was the sudden realization that sex with Rodger might never answer her need.

Something is missing. I can't make myself love him. Not in that way.

It was the first time she'd ever admitted it to herself, and the shock from having done it kept her awake until morning.

Ben woke up with a hard-on that wouldn't go away. It was vastly annoying, this ongoing, dragged-out state of arousal, and it was new. Generally he was quick to relieve himself, one way or another, but for the past few days Ben felt vaguely . . . guilty about doing anything at all.

Because why? That was the question he asked himself as he lay in bed in a state of wretched longing.

Maybe because he was expecting Sarann to walk out of the bathroom and up to his bed again?

Married, fool. Get it through your thick skull.

He had a vivid flashback of her sitting thigh-to-thigh with him in the gondola of the Ferris wheel, talking about, of all things, men, fish, and the sea, and he realized that he'd never seen or heard anything so enchanting in his life. Sarann was all that he had remembered, and more besides: a caring mother, a feisty survivor, a hopeful idealist, a funny and winsome grownup (much more grown up than he was).

And the mother of his child. And the wife, God damn it, of another man.

Ben understood, in his misery, that he was going to have to deal with the last two facts head-on. There was no time like the present, so he made two phone calls. The first was to Crotchy's wife Dolores, who had been itching for years to get her hands on Ben and knead him into yeasty husband material. Dolores carried a long list of single women in the pocket of her apron, and she was thrilled to hear that Ben had plans at last to become presentable.

Ben declined to inform her that the list in her apron pocket could just stay put. All he said was, "I need someone to clean up this place, say, once a week." He didn't say why.

"Done! I know just the service," said Dolores, unable to keep the joy from her voice. "Reliable, and very good rates."

"And I'm thinking, new sheets; fix the blinds; a couch wouldn't hurt," he threw out, piling on the treats for her. "Maybe you could give me some help with that stuff, too."

"Oh, Ben, you've made me so *happy*," she gushed.

"Yeah, well, think cleaning service first. I wouldn't open the door to my oven right now for all the lottery tickets in Connecticut."

"It's a cute apartment in a nice old building," Dolores said, obviously to convince him that he was Doing the Right Thing. "It just needs some TLC. And furniture."

"Don't get carried away, Dodi; all I said was a couch. I think maybe, though, it should be a hide-a-bed."

"Guests! My God, you're planning on having guests. Ben, I'm going to cry."

"Knock it off, Doe," he said gruffly. "Just let me know where to leave the key."

Dolores hung up to get things going before he changed his mind, and Ben sighed and made that second call, punching in a number he wasn't quite sure he'd committed to memory.

She answered on the second ring. He'd got the number right; there was no mistaking that airhead voice.

"Cherie, darlin'," he murmured. "I'm callin' to 'pologize for being such a pig the other day . . ."

* * *

Sarann was dressed in jeans and a tee-shirt, ready to leave for her shop, when Rodger pulled in behind her car in the driveway, effectively blocking her way. She was surprised at his return, but not nearly as surprised as when James pulled in alongside him. It was exam week; obviously they had other places to be.

She met them at the door. "Is everything all right?" she asked unnecessarily. Obviously everything wasn't.

"Let's go into the sitting room, shall we?" said Rodger in his headmaster's voice.

In a rush of dread, Sarann rephrased. "Is it Maggie? Is Maggie all right?"

"Yes."

"Is Glenys—?"

"Yes," James cut in curtly. "Everyone's all right."

Chastised by his tone, Sarann let the two men lead the way. They brushed off her suggestion of coffee and in fact avoided looking at her altogether as Sarann sat down in her usual chair and James sat down in Rodger's. Rodger himself remained standing, his right arm straddling his ribcage, the elbow of his other arm perched in the palm of his right hand. His chin was inclined slightly on his thumb and index finger; his eyebrows were knitted in concentration. He was the picture of a headmaster all over.

Suddenly his head shot up. "Sarann . . ." he began, as if he'd made a decision to do something brave. "James has come to me with a very disturbing discovery."

They knew about the cribrail?

For one irrational second, Sarann was convinced that James and Glenys had a videocamera in the nursery that had secretly taped her neglect.

"What is it?" she whispered.

It was James's turn to speak. He opened his schoolbagstyle attache, lifted a gleaming kitchen knife from it, and held it out to her blade first.

Completely unprepared for the sight of a knife in his briefcase, Sarann recoiled from his offer. "What're you *doing*?" she asked her brother-in-law. Her voice said plainly that he was the one behaving bizarrely, not she.

"Do you recognize this?" James asked in the tone of a prosecuting attorney.

She looked at it again and nodded. "It's one of yours," she said.

"Right. Did you take it from the knife block last night?"

"Well . . . yes. Wasn't I supposed to?" she asked, confused.

"Why did you do that?"

"To cut an apple. Glenys told me that I could help myself."

"What did you do with the knife after you'd cut the apple?"

"I put it in the sink. I'm sorry; I guess I should have washed it and put it away. But Maggie couldn't possibly have reached it, if that's what you're thinking."

"She damn well could have!" said James, exploding. "You left this knife behind the toybox, exactly where she likes to hide."

"I did not. I did *not*!" cried Sarann, jumping up from the edge of her chair. But even as she shouted the denial, she felt overtaken by the the all-too-familiar maelstrom of confusion and panic.

Her brother-in-law was wagging the knife at her like an accusing finger. "Glenys found this knife on the floor behind the toybox when she was picking up the room this morning. My God, Sarann, if she hadn't happened to glance there . . . my *God*, Sarann. What were you thinking? What could possibly have been going through your mind?"

Wide-eyed with shock, Sarann cried, "No, I didn't do it,

James, honestly . . . I didn't . . . I wouldn't do something like
that. I love Maggie as if she was my own. I love her. I know
that knives are dangerous . . . really, I do. Especially yours;
they're like razor blades. I'm very careful when I use them.
Please don't think . . . you can't really think . . . oh, my
God . . . oh, my God."

By now she was panting like a fox run down in a hunt.
She had no recollection of taking the knife into Maggie's
room; but neither did she have a recollection of leaving the
cribrail down. She didn't recollect anything, anymore. She
knew it, and looking at Rodger, she knew that he knew it,
too.

"Oh, Rodger," she said in a broken wail, *"help me."* Sob-
bing, she held out her arms to him, her hands hanging limply
at the wrists as surely as if someone had snapped them in
punishment for her misdeeds.

After exchanging a single look with his brother-in-law,
Rodger came to her and held her close. "Shh, shh," her husband said, patting her back. "You've taken the first step;
you've admitted that you need help. It wasn't easy for you,
we both know that. You've been fighting reality for a pain-
fully long time . . . I've tried to cover for you, Sarann, and
that's my fault. It was a mistake. We should have got this
thing out in the open right away . . . so you could get help.
Shh, shh, shh . . ."

He took out a monogrammed handkerchief from his
pocket and handed it to Sarann, but she felt oddly reluctant
to blow her nose in something so exquisite, so she waved it
away and tried to manage on her own, wiping her nose, like
a child, with the back of her knuckles. It was the wrong thing
to do before two such fastidious men; she saw the look of
distaste on both their faces.

"Excuse me," she murmured, and she fled to the box of
tissues in the powder room.

When she returned, James was studying the rug and shaking his head as Rodger whispered to him in an urgent way. They stopped immediately when Sarann got within earshot, and her brother-in-law said awkwardly, "Well, I've got to get back to the Academy. I'm, uh, sorry I had to do this, Sarann, but Maggie comes first. You understand."

"Of course I do," she said, braving a smile. "I would do the same if it were my own Abby."

Rodger turned sharply when she said it, which puzzled her. "Well, I would," she told him with flagging resolve. It was so hard to stand up to him, now more than ever.

"I have to get back as well," he said. "We'll talk about the next step later this afternoon. You'll be home all day?"

"No, I had plans to paint the walls of the shop—"

"*You*?" He looked amazed. "Why do you think I'm paying a contractor?"

"The painters won't be able to come for another week and a half, Jimmy told me. They're all backed up. Everyone is. The movers are scheduled to bring in the inventory on Friday, Rodger; I can't reschedule them. I don't mind doing the painting. Anything to get the job done."

"Sarann, really," her brother-in-law chimed in. "Everyone appreciates that you're spunky—but *really.* . . ."

For whatever reason, Sarann decided to draw a line in the sand, daring either man to cross it. "I have the time; I have the experience. Why shouldn't I?"

I might not be able to be entrusted with the care of a child, but I damn well can paint a wall red. If that embarrasses you, too damn bad.

Her smile for them was thin and brittle, but it was the only one she could find.

James picked up his briefcase—presumably containing his kitchen knife—and said, "Whatever. I've got to go."

"I'll walk you to your car," said Rodger.

The two men went out together. Sarann heard James mutter something about a day laborer, and then he got into his car and Rodger came back inside the house.

Sarann had her handbag slung over her shoulder; she was ready to go.

"Are you sure you're going to be all right?" he asked solicitously.

"Yes. I'll feel better doing something."

"All right. I'll put in a call to Walter Irons. He'll do a thorough evaluation; I'm sure he'll be able to accommodate you quickly." He hesitated, then said, "Are you *sure* you're going to be all right?"

"Rodger—!"

"It's just that I'd feel better if you stayed home. I don't like to see you out on your own right now."

"You mean, without a guardian?" she said, bristling. "I'm not a ward of the state quite yet."

"You know what I mean. You're upset; distracted. God knows, anything could—"

"Stop. Rodger, stop," she said tiredly. She added, "Does James know about Ben?"

Rodger nodded. "I had to tell him, of course."

Suddenly the whole series of bizarre events seemed particularly unreal. Sarann felt in her bones that there was nothing wrong with her. She felt fine—if anything, annoyed.

"I can drive myself to the shop," she told her husband. "I can open a can of paint. I can use a roller—even a brush—without hurting myself."

His face fell. "Ah, no, Sarann, no . . . don't slip into denial. Please . . . not when you've come this far."

Sarann recognized that look. It exactly expressed the way she felt when her own mother tried to shake off Sarann's pleas that she take her medication.

Instantly chastened, Sarann said, "I'm not denying anything. I'm not. I just want to get something accomplished without *screwing* it all up." Her frustration and anger erupted despite her attempt at self-control, which didn't do much to reassure Rodger.

He looked at her gravely. "Okay. Well . . . as long as you're all right."

Was he being sarcastic? It was always so hard to tell with him. How much easier if he would just . . . *emote*, once in a while. Laugh, scream, shout—if he could just be more like Ben.

She clapped her hand over her mouth as if she'd said it out loud. Rodger, looking alarmed, said, "What? What is it? Do you feel an episode coming on?"

Episode? Is that what they were? Sarann shook her head and said in confusion, "Maybe I'll sit with a cup of tea before I go."

"Yes, that's an excellent idea. I'll make you a pot of our family brew," he said, guiding her back into the sitting room. "You just have a seat . . . put your feet up . . . rest."

She protested feebly. "No, Rodger, you have things to attend to at the Academy."

"Nothing more important than you."

Not wishing to seem like an ungrateful harpy, Sarann let him make her the tea. It was very sweet, really; everyone in his family thought that their odd-tasting brew was a cure for whatever ailed you.

But could it cure schizophrenia, that was the question, she thought wryly.

Rodger came back with a tray that held one of his favorite teapots and two slices of toast spread thick with marmalade. Sarann felt more guilty than ever for taking up his time.

"You shouldn't be fussing over me, Rodger. Please, I'll feel awful if you don't leave for school right away."

"And I'll feel awful if I do," he said with a hapless smile. "But . . . I'm afraid I have to. I left my development coordinator sitting with a bagel and a cup of coffee in my office."

"Rodger, you didn't!" Sarann was mortified. Did the

whole school know that she was a head case now?

"Don't worry about Christa," he said, reading her thoughts. "She was tallying reunion class fund totals and working up the countdown newsletter for our Web site. She probably doesn't even realize that I've gone. Now you drink your tea, and if you don't want to go to the shop, don't. Heck, I'll paint the walls myself for you," he said, charming her with a grin.

She laughed at the notion; little Maggie knew more about painting walls than Rodger did. "Thanks for the offer, anyway," she told him, almost shyly. "And for . . . everything," she added, lifting her cup.

"My pleasure, darling. What are husbands for?"

He kissed her lightly and went off at last to his meeting, and Sarann made herself sit for a while and finish what she and Abby secretly called the Awful Ambrosia, a combination of teas blended especially for the family by a Boston herbalist.

The tea didn't do much to lift her spirits, but it did fortify her enough to call her sister-in-law.

Glenys listened without interruption to Sarann's somewhat garbled apology, which included mention of the knife but not of the cribrail.

"I've been more distracted than I realize," Sarann finished up.

"Because of Ben McElwyn, you mean."

So Glenys had been told as well. "Mostly that," Sarann admitted.

"Well, I don't know what to say," Glenys answered. "I know you have your reasons for behaving the way you are, Sarann—and really, I do sympathize; it must have been devastating having a man run out on you. But . . . all I can see is the knife. Why would you leave it someplace like that? I'm no psychologist, but it seems to me that you must have some issues with other women having babies—"

"No, Glenys, that's not true! The thought never even occurred to me!"

"Not consciously, maybe, James thinks." Glenys sighed and said, "Try to see it from my side. You know how Maggie likes to bring me everything she finds. If she had fallen carrying that knife . . . My God, I shudder every time I think of it. What's the point of my putting safety latches on all the cupboards and padding the corners and moving things out of her reach if *you* yourself are going to be a da—"

She ended the harangue as abruptly as she got into it. "Under the circumstances . . ."

It wasn't necessary to spell it out for Sarann. There would be no babysitting for the foreseeable future, and maybe not ever again. It broke Sarann's heart to be denied the joy of watching Maggie, but if their positions were reversed, Sarann would have reacted exactly the same as her sister-in-law. That was the worst of it: that everyone was responding perfectly reasonably to Sarann's descent into an abyss of unreason.

She shook off the thought vigorously, because she knew there was hope. Dr. Irons had been reassuring during her initial consultation with him; Sarann just hadn't been willing at the time to hear what he had to say.

All that was changed now. Maybe it was the tea, but Sarann persuaded herself that once she allowed herself to be placed on a regimen of medication, she would be welcome again at her in-laws' house. Mental illness was a disease, just like any other. One in ten Americans had some form of it. It wasn't so rare, and there was an army of expertise available to help her through it.

She drove to the shop, beating back dire thoughts with positive ones, determined not to let events roll over her and leave her a passive, whimpering victim. Sarann had managed to meet every challenge thrown at her in life so far. This was just another one to take in stride.

One step at a time, she told herself. One step at a time.

Dear Dad,
Is it okay if I call you that? I just wanted to e-mail
you to let you know what a great time I had on Sat-
urday. I know it was great, because I went again on
Sunday and it wasn't anything the same. So you must
be the one who made the difference. I hope you got
back okay. It's not that long a drive, is it? On a map
you don't look far.

I wanted to ask, are you going to be busy next
Thursday? Because I graduate from sixth grade then,
and mom is going to have a party for me. Mostly fam-
ily will be there, stepfamily, I mean. So it would really
mean a lot to me if you could be there. But if you can't,
I would understand. But I know you said you don't do
much on weekends unless you're working. And you did
say that things were a little slow, I remember that.
Actually, I remember everything you said <grin>.

Thanks again for coming up here. It meant more to
me than you could ever guess. I can hardly wait to be
able to tell Deirdre and Lisa who you really are. It'll
be awesome.

                              Love,
                         Your daughter Abigail
P.S. Please, presents are totally not necessary or at
least optional <grin>.

Dear Abigail,
I had a good time at the carnival, too. You're an im-
pressive young woman, and your mother has done a
great job of raising you on her own. Though you never
mentioned it, I know you're graduating first in your
class, and now that I've seen you, I'm not surprised.
You have a wonderful future ahead of you.

As far as the graduation get-together is concerned,

that date may be iffy for me. I have another commit-
ment which I may not be able to get out of. (Or should
that be, "out of which I may not be able to get"?) I'm
sure I'll be talking with your mother soon, though, and
I'll have a better idea by then. Incidentally, I'm as-
suming that you ran this idea past her?

Warmly,
B. M.

P.S. Where do you like to shop?

After carefully laying dropcloths around the perimeter
of the newly varnished floor of her store, Sarann got to
work. The first swath of Chinese red that she brushed on
was just the jolt she needed. Positive and optimistic, red
had attitude. Red had confidence. Sarann loved it.

She'd finished trimming out the door and windows and
was about to begin rolling the walls when Gloria Dijon
popped in on the way to her own shop, took a peek, and
gave Sarann two thumbs-up.

"That red is gonna do wonderful things for the blue-
and-white porcelain you picked up at Brimley's," she said.

"Oh, yes—my China Trade porcelain. One teapot,
three cups, and four saucers; that's the extent of my antique export ware," Sarann said as she crisscrossed the
walls with red. "The question is, what will the color red
do for my wood Gloucester fishermen incense burners
selling for three-ninety-eight apiece?"

"It'll make them look worth at least four-ninety-eight
apiece."

They had a laugh over that, and Gloria wandered
across the street with her coffee to open up Glorious Stuff
for a couple of hours. Sarann settled into a Zenlike calm
as she transformed one wall and then another into a completely different experience. With every painted wall, her
mood improved. It amazed her how much better she felt

whenever she was in her shop. It was more than just therapeutic to be there; it was like a rebirth.

The phone rang. Sarann answered with an upbeat, "Onboard Antiques." (She did love saying that.)

"Sarann?"

"Ben?"

Ben. Ben! *Ben*. Thoughts of incense burners, broken teacups, and misplaced knives flew out the papered-up window. All Sarann heard, all she knew, was the sound of Ben McElwyn's voice. Her own voice turned instantly low and intimate. "Ben. Hello."

Chapter 19

"HI YOURSELF," BEN said softly.

He listened to his answer in horror. *Hi yourself*? It was the single most inane thing he'd ever said to a woman on the phone.

He cut to the chase. "I, ah, called to see how you and Abby were doing. You left a little abruptly on Saturday. Was it the BBs?"

"The—? Oh. No," Sarann admitted, "not entirely. Abby tends to get fixated at times, that's all. Believe me, you didn't want that to be one of them. *Do* you carry a gun?" she added, as if she'd been thinking about it a lot.

Ah, hell. "Sarann, I'm a PI. Of course I carry a gun. Sometimes two."

He heard the wince on the other end of the line, so he added, "But only when I'm on the job."

"Are you on the job now?" she asked—a little wistfully, he thought.

"No. Though God knows I should be."

He was anywhere but. In fact, he'd just got back from a quick visit to Cherie which had ended with his throwing up his hands and saying, "I can't do this," and running away like a freaked-out virgin in a whorehouse.

And that had brought him, of course, right back to Sarann.

He said with what he felt was alarming candor, "It's just that Saturday was a pretty heavy-duty day, and you've both been on my mind constantly since then."

He could hear the pleasure in her voice wrap itself around her response: "You made a great impression, you know."

She didn't say on whom.

"Abby did have a pretty good time," he said, thinking of her e-mail.

Sarann laughed and said, "That, she did."

"Did you?" he said point-blank.

"Well . . . sure! My collection was missing a panda; now it's complete."

He said nothing. Silence was a weapon, too.

Sounding almost distressed about it, she said, "Of course I had a good time. You're an easy person to have a good time with."

"Putting aside my unbeatable charm," he said wryly, "I meant—"

"I know what you meant, Ben," she said in an intimate murmur that sent a pleasurable chill up his spine. "And the answer is, Yes, but so what?"

Yeah. So what. Ben had been asking himself the same thing repeatedly from the moment they'd stepped off the Ferris wheel. So they'd clicked. So he hadn't been able to take his eyes off her. So she'd given off vibrations as seductive as they were down-home friendly.

So what.

"So what?" he said lightly, afraid to press her too soon. "So . . . it's good to know that Abby's parents don't hate one another's guts, no?"

It wasn't an honest answer and Sarann knew it, but she seized on it with relief. "Yes, that does make some things easier."

"And some things harder," he quipped. If only she'd allow him, he'd tell her exactly which things they were.

If she got the pun, she wasn't letting on. She sounded oddly, suddenly frightened as she said, "Ben, some things have happened since I saw you."

The tone of her voice put him instantly on high alert. "Oh? Like what?"

"They're not exactly new things. I mean, they've been

going on for a while. But they've just got worse. I don't know why," she said in something like agony. "I don't know if they're related to my seeing you or not."

Ben waited, none too patiently. When she didn't elaborate, he prompted her. "I need more than that to go on, Sarann. I'm a good PI, but not that good."

"This isn't easy for me to admit," she said, faltering still more. "I don't know why I even brought the subject up. We've barely become reaquainted—"

He snorted. "I know you don't believe that," he said, trying not to sound scathing, "so why even say it? Jesus, Sarann, just tell me. What is it? Does it have something to do with Abby?"

"No, no—nothing with Abby. Oh, God, I feel so humiliated. Ben, I can't go into this. Not now. I never should have brought it up. It isn't something you can talk about over the phone."

"Fine; we'll do it face-to-face, then," he said promptly. "When do you want me up there?"

Her reaction to his offer was one of reserve, but Ben was convinced that he heard a note of longing in it. She said, "You can't just be shuttling back and forth all the time. You have a job to do, guns to wield."

She hadn't lost her sense of humor. Ben was relieved; whatever it was, it couldn't be life-and-death serious.

"This may or may not be the right time to mention that Abby and I exchanged e-mails today," he said, hoping to finagle some kind of visit out of the coming weekend. "She's invited me to her graduation party Thursday; did you know that?"

"She *did*?"

Crestfallen, he said, "Well, I guess that answers my question. I figured it might be hellishly awkward—putting it mildly—if I accepted, so I made up something about a prior commitment in my e-mail back to her."

Sarann sounded disgustingly relieved. "That was very considerate, Ben. Thanks."

Shit.

Well, what had he expected? To be welcomed with open arms?

"Ben, I should warn you," Sarann said. "The Bonniface family—all of Rodger's circle, in fact—are probably going to be very . . . well, hostile . . . to you."

Something in the way she said it made Ben hazard a not-so-wild guess. "Hostile, huh? Could it be they're now under the impression that I seduced and then abandoned you?"

"It's my fault," she admitted sheepishly. "I put Rodger in an untenable position with my lies. I'm so sorry. I screwed up big time. God, did I ever."

"No, you didn't," he found himself insisting. "You did what you had to do to get through life. You used some bad judgment and you had some bad luck," he said, wishing he were there to hold her close and comfort her. He felt utterly tender toward her just then.

"Don't beat yourself up over this, Sarann," he went on. "Sometimes decisions aren't made; they just kind of evolve. My guess is that the way you handled Abby's story was of the second kind."

"Ben! That's exactly what it was; how can you know these things?"

He laughed. "Gee, it musta been all those courses I took in grad school."

"I wish you were here," she said suddenly.

The simple admission sent Ben's heart rocketing through his throat. She wanted him—or at least, she wanted him there. It was his fantasy, the one thing he had wanted to hear.

"I'll drive up tomorrow. What time?"

"I—oh, tomorrow, no. Faxton has its graduation cere-mony tomorrow. Afterward there'll be an afternoon tea, followed by a round of receptions; it's a big day. Wednesday? Could you come then?"

"Of course."

"I could meet you in town for lunch; or we could meet at my shop. I'll be finished painting the walls today, and tomorrow when I'm at Faxton, Jimmy's going to bring in a display cabinet for me. Wednesday I load it with vintage jewelry and smalls and then have to do the window treatments; Thursday is Abby's graduation and party, Friday's moving day—aaghh, what am I *doing*, boring you with my schedule?—and Saturday, believe it or not, is my grand opening. Refreshments," she added wryly, "will be served."

He said in soft bemusement, "Are you what they call a soccer mom?"

She laughed self-consciously and said, "What I wanted to say was that Wednesday would be the best day for me. Is it for you?"

No, he wanted to say. *Wednesday, Thursday, Friday, Saturday, Sunday, Monday, Tuesday, and every week from there on in—that would be the best day for me.*

He said, "I'll take what I can get."

"Ben? I wish you *could* come to Abby's graduation," Sarann confessed. "She'd be so thrilled to have you there."

"Maybe the next one."

"Yes . . . the next one," she said, but she didn't sound all that optimistic.

He said lightly, "Families tolerate just about anyone these days, you know. They have to; otherwise there'd be no such thing as Thanksgiving."

Her laugh was wistful. "It's so strange; when I'm talking with you, I feel as if the last dozen years have never been. And so many other things besides. So many other . . . awful . . . things. But I'll leave all that for Wednesday," she added, making an obvious effort not to end on a downbeat note.

They hung up, and Ben went to bed with an assortment

of possible Awful Things floating in and then out of his dreams. They ranged from jealous husbands and snobby relations to an intolerant country club; it wasn't until Wednesday that Ben realized he was a lot more naive than his twelve-year-old daughter.

At eight-thirty on Wednesday, Ben was hotfooting through Rhode Island on his way to Massachusetts, his spirits soaring at the thought that he would be seeing Sarann before noon. The day was bright, breezy, and about as perfect as a June day got. Ben took it as a sign of good things to come.

He was almost reluctant to answer his cell phone when it rang in his car, afraid that it might be Sarann getting cold feet. As it turned out, that would have been a wildly positive scenario. Instead, he was connected to a hysterical preteen who made no sense and who scared the living bejesus out of him.

Crying and wailing, Abby stammered an incomprehensible explanation of her tears: "All over the floor . . . red feet, oh, my God, I know it wasn't Mom . . . she wouldn't . . . she *couldn't* . . . oh, my God oh my *God* . . . and now she's gone I don't even know why and . . . I can't see her to even talk to her and even though it's just not yet when *will* it be? Oh my God, oh my God—this isn't *happening* . . . be-because I don't know what to do, I don't know what to *do*," she moaned. "I was up all night, I thought she was coming back, I didn't go to school even, but she can't come back yet—"

She broke down in wrenching sobs that sent Ben into a cold sweat.

For two reasons. One, Sarann was apparently gone. Two, Ben didn't know how to calm down the only one who could tell him where.

"Abby, just . . . calm down. You have to calm down. You're not making any sense. Abby, you have to calm down. Calm down." He kept throwing out the words "calm down" like grains before a chicken until eventually, tentatively, Abigail did calm down and he was able to turn a small part of his attention back to the road he'd been ignoring.

"Now. *Where* is your mother?"

"At a place ff-for recovering. I wrote d-down the name. But it's too far for me to take a cab, it's near Pearl Pond."

"Okay. Now. Take a deep breath and start at the beginning. What happened, exactly—exactly what happened—that made your mother have to go to this recovery place near Pearl Pond?"

He heard the child take a huge swallow of air and then let it out before she continued. "Okay. The day before yesterday, my mom was painting her shop. She finished and got home just before suppertime. I was already home from school. She was in a funny mood—happy and scared at the same time is how I would describe it. She brought my . . . my . . . my—"

"Calm . . . calm," Ben said, throwing down two more grains of corn. "She brought your what?"

Another big swallow of air. "My favorite supper, deep-dish pizza. My stepfather was at the Academy, so we had like a girls' night out. Mom said the walls turned out perfect. She was glad about that because she was nervous about the red. And she said that I could help her at the shop this summer when I wasn't at French lessons or soccer camp. She had red paint on her nose, and her fingers had red on them. Mom laughed about it and said how now no one could notice the pizza sauce on her fingers. It was like the old days, when she used to paint our apartments, but the landlord sometimes paid for the paint. One landlord even bought us a pizza once because my mom was saving him so much money. So we had like, a really nice time, it really was like before," Abby said, near tears again. "We ate almost the whole pizza. I wish I *could* have helped her with painting the shop, because then I would have seen for myself."

"Seen—?"

"The floor of the shop. No way would she have walked all over it after stepping in paint. No *way!*" Abby said angrily. "My mom is the neatest painter you ever saw. One landlady told us she was better than any of the professionals they hired. You have to take my word. Or, no, you could check, couldn't you? If I could remember her name. Her first name was Mary."

"That's okay, Abby, we'll figure something out. Now, when did she go? How did she get there?"

Ben never got to find out the when or the how because his cell phone rolled over and died. Just like that. Not even a fade-in, fade-out, lingering sort of death; just a sudden and infuriating demise.

Ben was apoplectic. He didn't even know where Abby was, much less where Sarann was, and he still had a long way to drive. Unable to deal with the delay, he pulled over at the first phone he could find and punched in the number to the Bonniface house.

Let her be there, he prayed. *Let her be able to hear my voice.* What good was a father if he couldn't reassure his panicky child?

The phone rang once . . . twice . . . three times.

Abigail couldn't bear it. "I'll get it," she said, wiping her nose on the back of her hand.

"No—let the machine pick up, honey," said her stepfather. He caught her by her shoulder. "It's nothing that can't wait."

He turned her around to face him and looked into her eyes with a sad smile. "I've never seen you this upset," he said, "and you shouldn't be." He took out a crisp handkerchief and handed it to her and said, "Here, love, blow your nose."

Abigail used it to dab gingerly at her nose, then didn't

know what to do with it and laid it furtively behind her on the pillow of her bed. Still smiling, her stepfather picked up the handkerchief and rubbed it slowly against his own nose, which wasn't even running, and then stuck it in his jacket pocket.

He sat on Abigail's bed, which also confused her; he never sat on her bed. But then, she hadn't been at her desk in front of her computer, which is where she usually could be found when he came in to see her. She had been lying on her bed and crying her eyes out, and he had heard her when he returned home, but she hadn't heard him. She hadn't even heard him knock on her bedroom door.

He patted the unmade bed beside him. "Come sit. Let's talk about what's happened."

Abigail hung back. "Shouldn't we be checking the message? It could be the place where Mom is." She finally remembered the name, too late to tell her father. *Why* did he hang up on her like that? When she called him back on his cell phone, all she got was a recorded message.

"Laurel Place," she said aloud, committing the name to memory. She realized that her mother would like that name. Her lip began to quiver again. "What if it was Mom?"

Her father shook his head, still with that same sad smile.

"This is her first day there. She'll be very preoccupied with evaluations . . . testing . . . learning the routine. Then, too, she may even feel a need to sleep, or at least to nap. She'll have taken something to calm herself, and that may make her sleepy."

"Mom doesn't even take aspirin, hardly," Abigail said in sullen defense of her.

"Yes, but this is different. You heard her yesterday afternoon, honey; you couldn't help but hear her. I'm sure the neighbors for miles around heard her. She desperately needed something to soothe her then, and she wasn't much better on the drive out to Laurel Place. It wasn't an easy drive. You would have been very upset if you had been in the car; *she* would have been upset if you had been in the car. You know that."

Abigail bowed her head and nodded.

"But she'll get better, and then this will all be just a bad memory. So the next thing is for us to decide what kind of present would really cheer her up when we visit her on Sunday." He patted the bed again.

Reluctantly, Abigail sat down next to him. "I don't know why we have to wait until Sunday," she argued.

"We've been through all that, Abby," said her stepfather.

He sounded disappointed that she was so totally stupid, so Abigail said, "I know: because tomorrow is my graduation and Saturday is my party. But, like, who wants a party now? Not me. I specifically *don't* want a party."

She couldn't be clearer than that.

He began to rub her back in a slow circle. "The invitations have been sent and the caterers hired. Don't you think your mother would want you to have the celebration?"

Reluctantly, Abigail had to nod in agreement.

"And don't you think that people will think things are worse than you and I know they are if we just upped and canceled the party? Don't you think that that would really look bad?"

She hadn't thought of it that way. She nodded, once again reluctantly.

"Remember, you have to seem very happy and cheerful on Saturday," he advised her. "It's the best thing you can do for your mother."

He slowed the circles and seemed to press harder, the way her mom had done using Ben-Gay after Abigail had hurt her shoulder. Only there was no Ben-Gay.

She began to feel awkward and kind of tried to lean forward, as if she was going to rest her arms on her thighs, to get away from the rubbing. Just then he slipped his hand under the left shoulder strap of her tank top and she whipped her head around and stared at his hand.

"Your bra strap was showing," her stepfather said, adjusting the shoulder of her tank and patting it when he was done.

Abigail was mortified. A hot flush of emotion washed over her, and her heart began to thunder in her chest. Her bra strap! It was the most a man had ever touched her, which was why she was acting like such a child. Plus, her mind had been on her mother; he had caught her by surprise.

"I'm sorry," she mumbled in confusion. But she wasn't sure what for. For letting her stepfather see her bra strap in her bedroom, she supposed. She stood up quickly and said breathlessly, "Can we check the answering machine now? Deirdre was supposed to call me to say what she decided to wear to graduation tomorrow."

His eyebrows twitched just a little, the way they did when someone tried to argue with him. Abigail knew at once that she had made a mistake.

"I didn't realize that your outfits were so important," he said with one of those chuckles of his. "What are you planning to wear? Will you show it to me?"

"Um . . . I guess so," Abigail answered, sidling away from her bed and toward the closet.

"I guess I'll have to get used to taking over things like this for your mother—until she gets back, I mean."

"I buy my own clothes a lot," Abigail said in the most grown-up way she knew how. "I know what to wear."

She swung her paneled doors open and unhooked a hanger that had a pale blue dress with tiny embroidered flowers circling the bodice. She and her mother had picked the dress out the week before. It was expensive—maybe too expensive, her mother had said—so when Abigail got home, she went out of her way to thank her stepfather.

"This is the one," she said.

"*Very* nice," her stepfather said, smiling in approval. "You have excellent taste. Will you try it on for me?"

As he said it, his cheeks got red, which made Abigail's cheeks turn hot and red in reaction. She looked away and stared at the iron footboard of her bed as she said, "Why? You'll see it tomorrow."

He made a sound in his throat that she didn't know if it was good or bad, and said, "You're right. I will. Well! When you're right, you're right."

If he would just get out of her room!

"So what are your plans for the rest of the day?" he asked, and then he said, "I guess I'm the one who'll need to keep tabs on your comings and goings now. At least my schedule will be lighter, now that school is done. And, I'll be making a point to work from home as much as I can."

It was bad news all around for Abigail.

"I'm going over to Lisa's house; I'm supposed to be there about now," she said, lying about both the place and the time.

"Ah. Well, I've got to run back to the Academy for just a little while," he said in answer to her prayer. "I just came home to check on how you were doing. What time would you like me to pick you up from Lisa's?"

Abigail said quickly, "That's okay, you don't have to. I'm taking my bike."

He didn't look very pleased about that. "You know, until things get a little more sorted out with your mother, maybe you'll want to stay closer to home. You can always have one or two of your friends come over here."

But her friends didn't want to come to a headmaster's house. For that matter, Abigail didn't think it was such a great place to be in herself. You always had to be so careful, like the time she put her knapsack on the little half-moon table in the hall. Anyone would think the knapsack was a flaming torch, the way he gasped when he saw it sitting there.

"You don't have to worry about my friends coming over,"

she said evenly, thinking about the knapsack. "Because Mom will be back soon."

"Yes. Soon!" he said with a big smile on his face.

That smile. There was absolutely no doubt in Abigail's mind that Rodger Bonniface was the biggest class geek of all time back when he was a boy in school.

"Could we check to see if there's a message on the machine now?" she asked him again. *Why* did he put the machine in their bedroom? It was so exasperating.

"I'll do it right now, before I leave," he said with that smile. "And if there's a message for you, you'll be the first to know."

Chapter 20

BEN PULLED UP to an empty house.

There were no cars in the drive, and no one answered his knock. Now what? He stood on the sandstone stoop, at a loss over his next move. He had the right to be concerned about Sarann, but obviously not to be informed about her. The fact that he hadn't yet met Rodger Bonniface made any inquiries even more awkward. And since all of Sarann's friends and relatives now believed that Ben was a shit to boot . . .

Well, tough. He had to find out where Sarann was, and for that he needed Abby. And if Rodger, friends, and family didn't like it, Rodger, friends, and family could take a flying leap.

On a hunch, no more than that, Ben drove into Farnham to check out Onboard Antiques. He was hoping to get a peek through the windows at the paint-slobbered floor, but he did a whole lot better than that: he discovered his daughter crawling over it with a Sherlock-Holmes-sized magnifying glass.

Joyous at the sight of her, and more than a little amused by her detective-wannabe spunk, Ben tapped on the window, watched her jump sky-high, and waved through the opening where the brown paper had peeled away from its tape. When Abby recognized him, her face lit up like a sparkler on the Fourth of July, and Ben had to admit, it made him feel good.

She ran to get the door for him, then hauled him inside and locked it quickly behind them.

"You're *here*! So soon! It's, like, a *miracle*!" she cried, and she threw her arms around him and gave him a bear hug that turned his emotions inside out and upside down.

He held his arms out warily, as if he were being frisked.

"Heyyy, kiddo, what did I do to deserve *this* kind of welcome?" Whatever it was, he'd do it again.

"You're here, that's all," she said, rushing to the window to tape up the drooping brown paper. "You'll straighten everything out. The problem with my stepfather is that he's clueless, and he doesn't believe in my mother enough. You do."

She turned to him and planted her fists on her hips. "But first: why did you hang *up* on me?"

"My cell phone conked out. When you called, I was in the car, on my way here. I pulled over and tried phoning your house, but your machine kicked in; you must have already left."

She shook her head slowly and said, "We were home. My stepfather wouldn't answer."

"Because he knew you'd been in contact with me?"

She shook her head again. "He just said it was nothing that couldn't wait. He was upset because he walked in and saw me—well, crying."

"I'm sorry, Abby. Truly. It was the cell phone."

"That's okay," she said with a breezy shrug. "Shit happens."

He lifted one eyebrow at that, and immediately she became a little girl again, rolling her eyes in disillusionment over the fact that he was an old fart, after all.

Which was fine with Ben. "So now let's take it from the top. Where has your mother gone off to?"

"Laurel Place. It's a recovery center."

"Recovery from what?"

"Lots of things. Drugs, alcohol." The girl made a face and added, "Mental illness."

Obviously no one could suspect either of the first two disorders. But a cold and clammy hand reached around Ben's throat when he considered the third.

Awful things.

"So why is your mother there?" he asked as innocently as he knew how. He had no idea how much Abby knew about her grandmother's history of mental disturbance. He wished now that he knew more about it himself.

Abby was indignant. "My mom's there because of *those*," she said with disdain. She pointed to the trail of footprints that crisscrossed through a pool of spilled red paint lying like congealed blood on the glistening, newly varnished floor.

Ben had been studying the floor himself as they talked. The red imprints were obviously from sneakers. Each print was a morse code of dots and dashes, ridge-marks from a deeply carved sole and heel. The prints went up to and apparently under a display case that was pushed up against one wall of the room.

Ben dropped down into a catcher's position for a closer look. "And you don't think these are your mother's?"

Some of the contempt dropped away from Abby's voice as she said, "Well, just because they're the same style and size shoe that Mom wears . . ."

She reached into her knapsack and came up with a well-worn Rockport walking-type shoe that she handed to him. "This is one of Mom's."

He turned it over, saw that it was free of paint, and placed it over one of the prints. A perfect fit.

"Obviously you didn't clean any paint off this," he said.

"It never had any. I never saw *any* shoes with paint, and I looked through Mom's shoe rack and the laundry basket where she keeps all her old pairs that she refuses to throw out because they might come in handy for gardening or who knows what. My mom's like, *so* cheap that way. I think she has every pair she's ever owned. She always buys the exact same ones, and she walks so much that she wears them out fast."

"You don't think your stepfather might have thrown the paint-covered ones out?"

"I didn't ask," Abby admitted. "I was too upset."

She jammed her hands in the pockets of her baggy pants and stood, Watson-like, over Ben as he examined the prints.

"How did you get here?" he asked without looking up.

"I biked."

"All that way?"

"It's not *that* far. But I have to get back soon, because my stepfather will have a cat if he finds out I've come here. He thinks I'm at Lisa's house, and he didn't even like the idea of that."

"I'll drive you home," Ben announced, laying the sneaker on one print, then another. He handed the shoe to his daughter. "Put this on, would you?"

Abby didn't ask why, but took it eagerly and chucked her own right shoe for it.

"Now walk around more or less where you see the trail go. Try to land on the footprints."

She did, but ended up taking longer strides than were natural to her. Abby was shorter than her mother, but would that make the difference? Ben wasn't sure. He went back to studying the prints.

"You know what?" he said at last. "I'm with you. I don't think your mother made these footprints, either."

"I knew it, I *knew* it!" cried Abby, jubilant. She dropped down to her knees and squinted at the prints again. "Why?"

"Well, look at them. They're too evenly spaced, too neatly done. It's as if someone was trying extra hard to make sure that each one came out clearly. Have you ever seen a fingerprint being taken?"

"Yes, I had it done once in third grade when a classmate was kidnapped. We all had them taken at the police station. But the kidnapper turned out to be Jason's father. Jason eventually got back with his mother, though," she added. "He wasn't killed or anything."

Heaven help today's children, thought Ben. God, the way

their minds were forced to work. "Well . . . good," he said softly. He himself knew about too many Jasons who hadn't got back with their mothers; who would never be able to get back with their mothers.

After a minute he shook off the pall and said, "What kind of business was here before your mother? Do you know?"

"It was a hobbyshop—trains and model planes and stuff."

"Do you know why it closed?"

"Yes; the owner gave up. I think he tried to sell the business, but nobody wanted it."

"Did your mother ever say whether the hobbyshop owner resented her moving into his storefront?"

"Him? I saw him once. He was too old to resent anybody; he was sixty-two."

"Ooh, a real Methuselah," Ben said dryly.

Sixty-two was about how old Ben felt when he finally stood up; his left knee, damaged in a chase after a suspect, was and would forever be a creaky, painful mess. He gave the defiled floor a last, sweeping look and said, "This is a deliberate act, pure and simple. The question is, by whom?"

He turned his attention back to his daughter, who had an uneasy look on her face. He said, "I hate to ask you something so personal, but is anyone who's close to your mother acting hostile toward her, as far as you know?"

Abby surprised him by nodding solemnly. She went up to the window, climbed onto a chair, and peeked up and down the street before turning to Ben and saying quickly, "I think you'd better take me home now. But oh! My bike; can you fit it in your car?"

Ben said, "I carry a rack in the trunk; no problem."

They locked up the shop and as Ben loaded her mountain bike, Abby told him what she knew.

"After Jimmy—he's my mom's contractor—came in yesterday and discovered the footprints, he called my mom on her cell phone. She was at graduation at Faxton. She, like, totally freaked over it when she heard. She stayed for the ceremony, but right after that she went straight to the shop to check it out. She was totally shocked. Totally. That's what my stepfather told me this morning. She couldn't figure out how she could have done it and not noticed it."

"That makes two of us," Ben said as he double-checked the bungee cord. Abby's bike was state of the art, much better than the one he himself owned.

"My stepfather told me that shows how stressed my mom is. She keeps doing things and she doesn't even know it."

Ben looked at her sharply. "Like what things?"

Awful things.

Abby got the same look of confused unease on her face as she had in the shop. It was uncharacteristic, as if she were trying to read a crystal ball that was filled with spit.

"My stepfather didn't say. He said we'd sit down soon and have a long talk about all the things that have been happening that I didn't even know about, but not this morning; there was too much that he had to wrap up at school.

"But I heard them last night, my mom and him, after they got home from the receptions. The receptions are after the tea," Abby explained as she waited for Ben to clear off the mess from the front seat of his car. "Parents and students can go from dorm house to dorm house and talk to the teachers and stuff who live in each dorm with the five or six students. The dorms aren't really dorms but just old houses, like Tidewater where I live, but not as nice, naturally. No antiques."

Ben didn't care about antiques. He threw himself into the driver's seat and began moving out of the small parking lot tucked behind the shop. "Your mother and stepfather came home—when?"

"Early," Abby said. "They weren't supposed to be home until nine, but they were home by seven-thirty. They went straight to their room—my mom's bedroom—my stepfather's bedroom," the child said in an excruciating bid for accuracy, "and at first they were just talking in normal voices. Actually, my stepfather was doing most of the talking; my mom was just listening.

"I could tell that my mom was upset, but I didn't know why. I didn't know about the paint then. I couldn't hear what she was saying, but every once in a while I heard her say *no*. Her voice always went up when she said no, and then she would drop it down again. I think because she didn't want me to hear."

Abby's voice was dropping low, too, as she became obviously more emotional. Ben didn't want to add to her agony, but he had to get the information, and she was his one and only source. He said, "Inside the shop, I asked you if anyone seemed hostile toward your mother. Was it your stepfather that you were thinking of?"

She scrunched her face and said with a puzzled frown, "No . . . I wouldn't say that. You can tell that he's worried about my mom, but . . . no. Not hostile. But my Uncle James, I'm not so sure about him."

"How so?"

"I think he knows about you; that you're, you know—"

"Alive?" Ben asked with a smile.

"Yeah. That. Plus I think something happened when my mom was babysitting there the other night. She came home kind of wired. She wouldn't let me go to sleep, just kept wanting to hug me and things. It was weird. Anyway, when I called my aunt yesterday morning, my Uncle James answered and I heard him say, 'It's her kid' when he handed Aunt Glenys the phone. Why would he say it like that? 'Her kid'? It makes it sound like he's disgusted with both of us."

"He probably didn't mean it the way it sounded," Ben said, but he wanted to smack Uncle James upside the head. "Do you like your uncle?" he asked casually.

"He's really my stepuncle," she corrected. "And the answer is no. Not really. He's, like, a total snob. One time, my friend Lisa and I gave our hair a henna rinse just for fun? My mom said it was okay as long as it washed out. It turned out kind of bright, actually; but my uncle totally freaked when he saw it. He said, what will everyone think? We look like trash. Plus, when he comes over, all he talks about is this book he wrote and this tour he's going on in a couple of weeks and how he's going to be rich and famous—well, he doesn't come out and *say* that, but you can tell that's what he's hoping. Is this really your car?" she asked, looking around curiously.

"Yeah, yeah, it's a little messy, I know," Ben admitted, trying to convince himself that the jumble of papers, files, surveillance equipment, and dirty shirts on the back seat constituted merely a little mess and not a health hazard. "I didn't have a chance to clean it out before I came. But I'm getting a maid service," he added. "Do they do cars?"

With a wry look, Abby said, "I don't think so. Is this where you keep your gun?" she asked, reaching for the glove compartment.

"Hey! Hands off."

"It's locked, anyway," she said, sitting back. "Have you ever shot anyone?"

Ben glanced at her in wonder. From hysteric to sleuth to impertinent snot, all in the space of a couple of hours. He wasn't sure he could keep up with her, so he didn't even try. "Why don't we stick to the subject, okay? Tell me about your aunt. What's she like?"

"Aunt Glenys? She's all right. Mom likes her. She's a snob, too, but not as bad as Uncle James. He's the worst. Sometimes I get to babysit Maggie. That's their daughter; she's not even two yet, and she talks in sentences. Wait, turn here! There's a shortcut through the woods and it comes out right by our house."

She said it in such a do-or-die way that Ben found himself whipping his Honda into a sudden hard right. They bounced

over a potholed dirt lane that cut through scrub oak and pine
trees and emerged at last on the winding country road on
which she lived. Abby waved to a neighbor who was pruning
some lilacs alongside the gully in front of her house; the
neighbor waved back. Ben glanced in his rearview mirror.
She was watching them—no doubt taking down his license
number. He wasn't driving a Volvo or a Lexus, after all, just
a quiet old Honda, so he must be up to no good.

"Oh, good, he's not home yet," Abby said, and she really
did sound relieved.

Ben pulled into the drive and unloaded her bike for her.
She said, "You're not going to tell anyone where I was, are
you?"

"Not if you don't want me to." He wasn't sure if that was
the right answer and resolved to get a manual to tell him
what the hell was.

"Are you going to Laurel Place now?" she asked him
wistfully after she took the bike from him.

He hoped she wasn't going to beg to come along; he
didn't need any manual to tell him that that would be asking
for trouble.

"First I want to do a little checking up," he said, hedging
his answer. "Then we'll see."

"My mom doesn't belong there. Even you said she
doesn't belong there." Carbon-copy blue eyes stared at him
as she bit her lip to keep it from trembling. "Can't you bring
her back?"

Ah, jeez. "Abby, I don't know what I can or cannot do.
But I don't think I can just pick your mother up like . . . like
a panda bear and bring her home."

Abby's mouth shaped itself into a tremulous smile at the
mention of the carnival prize. "She had the panda on the
shelf of her closet, but—you probably didn't notice—now
it's in a box at the shop. And not because it's for sale."

Ben swallowed and said, "When I said 'panda,' that was

just a simile I used. You know what a simile is."

"Yes." Her look turned oddly luminous. "And I also know what the panda is."

"Well . . . I'm glad," he said, more confused than he'd ever seen *her* so far. His heart was knocking around his chest like a billiard ball on a pool table. What the hell was she trying to do? Play matchmaker?

"Listen, I'd better take off. I'll get my cell phone fixed; call me on it anytime, Abby. Anytime."

"Okay. And, Dad?"

He still wasn't used to that "Dad"; it did take his breath away. "Uh . . . huh?"

"I can't see my mom until Sunday. When you go, will you—?" She thought about it and slid one of the neon-pink barrettes from her shining, straight hair. "Give her this from me, okay?"

"Can do," Ben said gruffly, accepting the humble token. Jesus. What was wrong with this picture? Who kept a mother separated from her only kid that way? Ben knew that treatment centers isolated their patients from family and friends as a matter of policy; but he couldn't have shipped off Sarann somewhere like that in a million years. Call him soft, call him stupid, but the Sarann he knew belonged with the Abigail he knew.

In an emotional good-bye, Abby threw her arms around him again in one of her bear hugs, and this time Ben let himself hug her back. "You watch out for yourself, kiddo," he said; he didn't know why. Maybe because he thought that with Sarann at Laurel Place, no one else was going to be around to do it.

He drove away weighed down by misgivings so deep that it made getting kicked off the force seem like a free trip to Hawaii.

* * *

Abigail stored her bike in the garage out back, then went inside to execute Plan B. She would call Laurel Place herself and see if she could talk her way into her mother's room. The number was listed, which was good; but she couldn't get past the receptionist, which was bad.

"But this is an emergency," she begged.

She was handed over to the assistant to someone who was very nice and explained that her mother was undergoing a comprehensive assessment and that she had a very busy regimen but that she would be happy to take calls or visits on Sunday.

"It's like she's in prison!" Abby said in dismay.

"No; recovery," the assistant said, but she didn't sound quite so nice now. "You want your mother to get well soon, don't you?"

"Yes, but—"

"Abby! Abby, where are you?"

"Oh, no," Abby whispered, and she slammed down the phone.

Her stepfather knocked and came right in.

"You *scared* me," Abby said, but she was more angry than scared. It was like she was in prison, too.

Her stepfather walked over to the phone and slid his hand along the handset as if it was made of silk. "*You* got off in a hurry," he said, and he added with a chuckle, "A secret love, maybe? You look so guilty."

"I do not," she said without smiling. Her love for her mother was no secret.

"I was just pulling your leg, honey," her stepfather said, looking as if she'd insulted him. "You're still upset. I can tell."

It was so totally true. She was upset and mad and frustrated, and that made her suddenly reckless.

Out of the blue, she said, "I hope Mom didn't go to Laurel Place because she thought she made those footprints, because she didn't. Somebody did those on *purpose* and tried to throw the blame on Mom, I don't know why. Yet."

"What on earth put all that into your head?" asked her stepfather, amazed.

Abby realized how completely she had spilled her hand. She couldn't very well explain Ben McElwyn's theory about the footprints, so she simply said, "Because—because I looked at all Mom's shoes, even the ones in the basement, and none of them had paint on them." Which was true, as far as it went.

Her stepfather got a really unhappy look on his face. "Sweetheart, I know I said I'd sit down with you to explain, and maybe I should have done it right away, but things have been hectic at school. We had a fire today at River House, did you know that?"

"No! When?"

"It happened when I came home earlier to check on you. It wasn't a big deal—a small electrical fire—but it could have been worse. Thank goodness the students have gone for the summer. Still, as you can imagine," he said with a forlorn smile, "I'm not having a very good day."

"Sorry about that," Abby mumbled, though she didn't think it was her fault that he was having a bad day.

He sighed and closed his eyes and pressed his lips together as if he was praying to God for help, and then he opened his eyes and said, "Wait here."

He went downstairs, and when he came back he was holding a pair of sneakers in his hand. They were slopped all over with red paint. He handed them to her. "Are these what you were looking for?"

"No!" Abby said, thrusting her hands behind her back and shaking her head. "I mean, n—I guess so." *Oh, no, oh, no, oh, no*.

He laid them on the rug, next to her desk. "I think," he said in a depressing voice, "we need to have that talk now."

Chapter 21

LAUREL PLACE WAS a converted estate deep in horse country, and Abby was right; it was much too far to come by cab. It wasn't easy to find, either, tucked as it was in the woods on one of those winding country roads that seemed to crisscross the country beyond Metrowest Boston. Remote and oppressive: those were Ben's initial impressions as he drove down an expansive drive, lined with mountain laurel, that led to the main house of the campus.

The lodge was a Victorian stick-style mansion with a steeply pitched, cross-gabled roof. The sides were banded, the peaks trussed, the porch deck all but hidden behind wide, ornate wooden balusters. All that was missing was a dark and imposing tower, but the house, half hidden by massive oaks on either side, was forbidding enough without it.

Suppressing a chill, Ben pulled into the macadam-surfaced parking lot and assessed his next move. Courtesy of his cousin Crotchy, he knew that Laurel Place was an exclusive enclave where the wealthy routinely dropped off and then forgot their more inconvenient members. Spa, retreat, recovery center—call it what you will, it was a dumping ground, pure and simple, for undesirable human beings.

In one of the cabins sprinkled around the main lodge, Sarann was lodged and was being treated—the staff would say, of her own free will. Ben didn't think for a minute that Sarann was there because she deserved to be. *She* might think so; she had done awful things, she'd told him. Awful things.

Bullshit. Maybe if the footprints hadn't been faked, Ben could see it. There was a family history, after all, and he wasn't fool enough to believe that psychoses and neuroses could not be inherited. But if there had been one fraud, who's to say that there hadn't been others? He was trying his damndest to withhold judgment, but in his gut he was thinking: bullshit.

He ascended the wide steps, flanked by pots of blood-red flowers that were the only splashes of color in a sea of gray paint. On the veranda, a young woman and several older ones sat in a circle of wicker chairs, each of the women looking eerily uninvolved in a halfhearted conversation that stopped altogether when Ben passed by on his way into the heavily paneled, darkly varnished, altogether gloomy lobby.

In the lobby he was brought up short by a sharp-eyed receptionist with a ready smile who asked how she could be of service.

He gave her his name and said, "I have an appointment to see Sarann Bonniface."

She flashed him an oh-dear look and said, "I'm so sorry, but the residents have a busy schedule that doesn't allow visiting time until Sunday."

"Oh?" he said cooly. "Doctor Irons assured me that Mrs. Bonniface would be available for a brief interview. He suggested four thirty would be convenient, and it's now—" Ben looked at his watch and then, with an intimidating smile, at the receptionist. "Four thirty-two."

She looked a little less sure of herself. "That would be very unusual—"

"I'm aware of that. Perhaps you could call Doctor Irons to verify the arrangement," Ben suggested.

"I can't do that; Doctor Irons is on a flight out of the country," she said, clearly unhappy that a predicament was forming.

Ben had found out about the medical director's flight when he called and chatted up an assistant in the director's office. It was no accident that Ben had waited until the man was out of cell phone range and his assistant, on her way home for the day.

"Ah, a flight. That explains it, then," he said sympathetically. "Doctor Irons did sound harried when I spoke with him."

"Can you tell me what the visit is about?" the receptionist asked, rather than moving down the chain of command and referring Ben to someone there.

Her mistake; Ben gave a silent cheer and said, "Absolutely. I'm a private investigator, here at the request of the parents of Jerry Koshewksi, who was arrested last night for allegedly vandalizing the floor of Mrs. Bonniface's antique shop. The parents naturally are distraught. Their son's never been in trouble before, and they have reason to believe that Mrs. Bonniface herself might have done the damage accidentally."

"They hired a private investigator for that?"

Ben tried a disarming smile on her. "Hired, no. They're close friends of mine. The boy's my godson. I really think this thing can be cleared up quickly," he urged her, "if only I can see Mrs. Bonniface for just a few minutes."

She looked unsure, but in the end she relented, putting a call through to an attendant to go fetch Mrs. Bonniface and haul her over. After that she called Sarann on a house line and advised her that someone would be coming for her.

The receptionist hung up without having to explain who that someone would be. Ben found the fact depressing; it meant that Sarann was already used to being summoned and then sent back at whim. After thanking the receptionist, he faded into a background of palm trees and snake plants and studied the lay of the land while he waited.

Besides offices, the main lodge housed therapy and recreation rooms, so Ben was able to see a certain number of inmates—he couldn't possibly regard them as voluntary residents—exiting through the lobby on their way, apparently, to their cabins. What he saw on all of their faces was an eerily similar expression: uninvolved, placid, and vaguely sweet.

Crotchy was right; the people there were being dumped and sedated. Laurel Place was nothing more than a high-class babysitting service, and it was completely unnerving for Ben to imagine Sarann as one of its charges.

A discreetly dressed—matron?—arrived with Sarann in tow. Because Sarann wasn't prepared to see him, Ben almost hated to come out from behind the plants; if she let on that she knew him, the jig would be up.

Sarann didn't let on. The flicker of recognition that he saw in her green eyes died out almost immediately. Ben was dismayed to see that she didn't look angry, she didn't look afraid. She didn't look anything.

"Good afternoon, Mrs. Bonniface," he said, cutting the receptionist out of introducing him. *Sarann, Sarann, play along.* "My name is Ben McElwyn and I'm here to ask you just a very few questions."

She looked puzzled, but then, what else would she look in the circumstances? So far, so good.

"Would you mind walking out with me?" he asked courteously. "I saw a bench with a view of the garden; we can sit there while we chat."

"A garden—?"

The receptionist interrupted and said, "We have an empty conference room right here that you can use, Mr. McElwyn."

Ben quelled her objection with a look of barely repressed fury. "I think Mrs. Bonniface will be more comfortable near the garden, don't you?"

"I . . . suppose that would be all right."

She nodded to the matron, who turned and left, probably to take up a perch in a nearby tree.

With a stiff smile, the receptionist said to Ben, "Mrs. Bonniface will want to freshen up for supper, which is served at five-fifteen. Please be brief."

"Of course." He turned to Sarann with a tender smile that only she could see. "Shall we?" he said softly, beckoning toward the massive double-doored entry.

With Ben doing the talking, all of it small, they walked over carefully groomed grass toward a circular rose garden where two gardeners, if they were gardeners, were busy clipping spent blooms. The concentration of colors in the ring was spectacular, but Ben was struck by the absence of fragrance. All those roses, all for show. They might as well be plastic.

They sat on a bench and immediately one of the gardeners picked up his bushel and began moving closer to them.

Well, fuck this, Ben thought, and he said loudly, "Why don't we move? It's too hot in the sun."

Sarann, poor Sarann, smiled wanly. She wanted only to please. Her smile ripped through Ben's heart like a paring knife, leaving him short of breath. He wanted to go back to the main lodge and burn down the pharmaceutical cabinet, then go from cabin to cabin and free all the inmates. Maybe he was being naive, but he knew in his bones that they couldn't all be psychotic. He knew that one in particular was a normal, well-adjusted, eminently desirable member of society.

He knew, quite suddenly, that he loved her deeply, that he had always loved her, that he would always love her.

He stood up and held out his hand to her—in the circumstances, a stupidly reckless act. He didn't care. If he didn't touch her, didn't reassure her, didn't reassure *himself* that she was whole and genuine and in the wrong place, then he might as well throw himself down the nearest well, because life without her, now that he'd found her, would definitely not be worth living.

And if that made him just another nutcase, so be it.

She took his hand, which thrilled him, but after she stood up she let it go, which crushed him. They strolled over to another bench, this one under a weeping willow alongside a small pond. It couldn't be Pearl Pond; it was too insignificant to rate a name.

"Is it deep?" Sarann asked after he sat down next to her.

"I doubt it," Ben said. "It looks man-made."

Still, it was pond enough to be home to the usual suspects: water lilies and cattails and half a dozen ducks. And there were frogs; Ben could hear them.

"I don't like it when it's deep," Sarann murmured.

She didn't sound distressed, but you'd never say that if you were looking into her eyes. Too late, Ben remembered her hangup about drowning. He said, "It's not deep at all. You could walk across it and not even get your knees wet."

"Good," she said with the same sweet, heartbreaking smile.

How was he going to get her out of there? He had to get her out of there.

"Sarann . . . darling . . . why are you here?"

She smiled that heartbreaking smile, but he didn't think it had anything to do with his use of the endearment.

"I don't know."

"Do you want to be here?"

Another, even sadder smile. "I don't know."

"Did you tell Rodger that you wanted to come here?"

She looked unsure; his spirits soared.

"I don't know," she whispered.

"Did Rodger tell you that you should be here?"

She sighed. "Yes. Oh, yes."

"Did he say *why* you should be here?"

She nodded, then looked down at her jumper and began pulling a loose thread from a pocket. "I did some awful things."

"What were they? Do you remember?"

"Not exactly. I remember what they were, but I don't . . . remember . . . when I did them."

He could see that she was struggling to clear her mind enough to contemplate them, and that she was failing in the attempt.

"What were they, Sarann?" he coaxed. "Tell me some of them."

Her brows drew down in concentration. "Well . . . there was the wallet."

"What about the wallet? Tell me about it."

"I ruined it. On purpose."

"Are you sure it was on purpose?"

"I guess so. That's what Rodger said. Because it had money in it."

Ben said gently, "Is that all? That's not so awful."

"Ohhh, but the knife," she said with a shudder. "It was so sharp, like a razor blade. You would cut yourself . . . you would bleed. She could have died. She could have fallen and died. Are you sure it's not deep?"

"I—what? Yes, it's not deep. It's very shallow," he said, straining to make sense of her words. "Do you want me to walk through the pond to show you?" he added with a re-assuring smile.

"No, no!" she cried, gripping his thigh to restrain him. "You could drown, and then what would I do? Don't, Ben . . . please, please don't!"

Whatever she was on, it was powerful stuff.

Ben took her hand and smiled and said, "It's all right, Sarann; I can swim."

"That's what we thought about Kelly! But she couldn't! She said she could, but she couldn't! We couldn't save her, either one of us. I tried and I tried. I heard her screaming . . . I swam to her . . . tried to hold her up . . . but it was too late. It doesn't take long. And then . . . it was too late! Ohhh . . . she looked so, so. . . . Her face was so gray, so gray. She was still a little girl. They covered her with a beach towel . . . it was red and purple, but her face . . . her face was gray."

Sarann bowed her head and sighed heavily, then said in a soft whisper, "She had pink rubber bands on her ponytails. I'll always remember the pink rubber bands."

Sweet Jesus, Ben thought. Was the drowning trauma enough to unhinge Sarann? His conviction that she was being manipulated for reasons that he had yet to fathom faltered a little. He bent down and turned to see her eyes and said, "You did your best to save her, Sarann. It wasn't your fault. None of it is your fault."

"No; you're right," she said, lifting her head and surprising him. "That *wasn't* my fault. But the other things. . . ."

"What other things, darling? What other things besides the wallet?"

She sighed and said, "Rodger told them all the things. You could ask them, maybe. In there. They would know better than me. Than I. Rodger doesn't like me making mistakes in grammar," she explained poignantly. "It embarrasses him."

"Your English is excellent, Sarann," said Ben, fiercely indignant for her sake. "Anyone would be proud to know you."

God damn it, what kind of husband was this asshole?

"There are a lot of things I don't know how to do," she said, drifting away on another tangent. "We don't have dinners and parties with Academy people; not enough, anyway," she said, shaking her head. "Because of me. I don't know enough about Faxton, you know? Rodger never talks about the school. So I don't know what to say. But . . . it's my fault anyway," she insisted gently. "I should have made a bigger effort."

She was playing absently with her hands. Ben took them in his and said, "Listen to me. Rodger is extremely lucky to have you for his wife. I mean that, Sarann. You're a warm and beautiful woman and a wonderful mother, and any man—*any* man," he added, his voice husky with longing, "would consider himself blessed to have you as his wife."

Something in what he said or the way he said it penetrated the haze she was in. The lethargy and vagueness fell away, leaving in their stead a look of sudden understanding. A soft, entirely different smile hovered on her full, bare lips, and her gaze, green and deep and breathtaking in its beauty, settled on him in a look of trust and gratitude.

Gently freeing one of her hands from his, Sarann lifted it to his face and skimmed her fingertips over his upper lip.

"I wish Rodger were you," she said simply.

It was all that Ben wanted to hear.

"Sarann, you don't belong here," he said with passion. "You never should have been brought here. You haven't done any awful things, okay? Now tell me what you *think* you did to make you have to come here. Take your time," he added, though he was afraid that the matron was going to swoop down on them any minute.

"Everything?" she said, squinting in concentration. She stared off at some faraway place in her mind. "All right . . . I'll try."

She began, haltingly at first and then with more assurance, to tell him about what Ben thought was dumb little stuff that anyone with a lot on his mind might do: forgetting to stamp an envelope or two, putting the wrong check with the wrong statement, writing down the incorrect date for a function. The fact that she had repeatedly forgotten that she'd filled her gas tank, that was more problematical; most busy people just forgot to fill them, period.

She was methodical, which might explain why she had reported her car stolen when she couldn't find it in the parking lot. And she was impatient, which might explain why the key to her house wouldn't work when she tried it a couple of times.

But somehow, after sitting through her halting litany of so-called sins, Ben didn't think so.

She was sounding more and more lucid as they went along, so he took a chance and threw out his theory to her. "Sarann," he said, interrupting her, "don't you see? Someone's playing games with your head, that's all. Someone's got it in for you and is trying to bend your mind. Someone is gaslighting you, Sarann. You know—like in the movie?"

She let out a little sad laugh and said, "That's what I tried to tell myself—until Maggie."

"Maggie's your niece? The one who's already talking in sentences?"

Sarann's smile was quick and fond. "Yes, that's Maggie. She's so sweet. I would never hurt her . . . never. And yet . . ."

Sarann drew a murky, agitated picture of the baby tottering at the top of the stairs, and then recounted the horror she felt the next day when her brother-in-law apparently tried to force some knife on her. She began to cry, leaving Ben trying to fill in the considerable gaps himself.

"Sarann," he said, trying to reassure her, "I don't know what's going on—but I sure as hell am going to find out. I promise you, I'll find out. But I'll need a little time to prove it. In the meantime, don't take any more medication. Don't. I know they'll say it's to calm you down, but you don't need it. Do you see what I'm saying? There's nothing wrong with you—nothing. So you don't need any medication."

She looked as if he'd just told her she could fly. Hopeful but wary, she said, "But—how can I do that, not take the medication?"

He smiled and said, "Old trick. Hold the capsule under your tongue and then spit it out later. If it's liquid—"

She shook her head, pathetically eager to do her part. "It's a pill."

"No problem, then," he said, squeezing her hand. "All

right. I'll be back for you as quickly as I can. By Sunday you'll be with Abby where you belong."

At the mention of her daughter's name, Sarann began to cry again. By now the matron was bearing down on them from out of nowhere, and Ben had to spend his last precious seconds urging Sarann not to say anything to anyone about their talk. He remembered Abby's barrette in time to fish it out of his pocket and hand it to Sarann. "Abby wants you to have this."

"Ab-bee," Sarann said in a low moan, but she had enough presence of mind to jam the thing into her jumper pocket before the prison matron arrived and said to Ben with a right-eous scowl, "I think that's about enough. Don't forget to sign out at reception before you leave."

After that, she turned to Sarann. "You're upset, dear," she said, helping her up despite Sarann's protests. "Come along, and we'll freshen up before supper. That's a good girl."

Chapter 22

AT THE LAST minute, Abigail changed her mind. She would not wear the blue dress with embroidered flowers that she and her mother had picked out and that her stepfather liked so much. Just looking at the dress made Abigail feel incredibly depressed and nervous. She would wear the plainest thing she owned, a brownish sack that she really couldn't stand. It was only a sixth-grade graduation, after all.

She took the brown dress out of the closet and then, she didn't know why, she propped a chair against her door. After slipping the dress over her head, she checked herself out in the full-length tilting mirror that her stepfather had moved into her room especially for her. She looked awful, which was just how she felt. Tommy wouldn't even notice her.

What did it matter? What did anything matter? Her mother hadn't called. Her father hadn't called. The only human voice she'd heard since yesterday was her stepfather's, and the things he'd had to say to her were too depressing to think about.

Like a brownish sack. That's just how she felt.

When the phone rang, Abigail almost didn't answer it; her stepfather had told her that whenever he was in the house, he would take every call, because he had a lot of important business going on. But then she saw that he was out back, cutting roses for her graduation dinner, and she jumped to get it before he heard it ring.

It was the call she had been praying for, which made it that much harder for her to believe.

"Dad! Where are you? Did you see Mom? Is she okay? What did she say? Is she . . . okay?"

Her father's voice was so relaxed and reassuring that Abigail was almost suspicious.

"I saw your mother and she's fine," he told her. "She can hardly wait to see you."

"Did you give her my barrette, though?" Abigail wanted to know.

"Yup. She was very touched by that. It was an excellent idea."

"Yeah, because she can wear it in her hair and think of me. But, Dad," said Abigail, dropping to a whisper, "I've got news—but first, did Mom *really* seem okay to you?"

"Why?"

"The sneakers! My stepfather showed them to me. I don't know where they were in the house, but he showed them to me, all full of red paint."

"*What?*"

"That's more or less what *I* said. So what does that mean? We thought we had it all figured out, that it was someone who had it in for Mom, when all along . . . Dad? What does that mean? I'm *so* depressed."

"Don't be depressed, Abby. We'll get to the bottom of this. There's a pattern here. Shit," he said, but that was more to himself than to her. Then he said, "Your mother mentioned something about Maggie almost falling down the stairs, something about a knife. I don't suppose you'd know anything about that?"

"I know about the knife," Abigail said, speaking quickly now because she was on borrowed time. "My stepfather told me that Mom left a sharp knife on the floor right by Maggie's toybox and Maggie could have picked it up and hurt herself. That didn't make any sense to me, leaving a knife on the floor. Who does that? But Aunt Glenys found it there after Mom babysat the other night, so it must have happened. But I can't believe it."

Her father was so quiet for so long that Abigail finally said, "Dad? Did we get disconnected again?"

"No . . . no," he said, "but while I think of it, here's my new cell phone number. They weren't able to get the other one fixed fast enough."

She took it down and said, "My stepfather called off most of the graduation party. Only people close are coming. I'm cool with that, but then why did he tell me I had to have the party in the first place and had to act like I'm not upset about Mom being in Laurel Place?"

"I can't answer that . . . yet," her father said. "Look, Abby, I've got to get going. I'll see you soon. Stay cool, stay calm. Have a great graduation. I wish I could be there for it."

"Do you, Dad? Really? Even though it's only sixth grade?"

"You bet; you only graduate once from sixth."

She was about to ask him if he went to junior high or regular high when she saw the doorknob turning on the door to her room!

"Hafta go," she whispered, and she laid the handset in its cradle as quietly as she could.

Oh, but he would feel if it was warm! She began to blow on the handset to cool it off.

"Abby? Abigail," came the voice from behind the door. "Please move whatever is against this door. Right now."

She didn't know what to do: blow on the handset or move the chair. She kept blowing frantically on the handset.

The door began to open, pushing the chair in front of it. The chair didn't work at all! In a panic, Abigail picked up the phone again and tried to look natural as the door opened wide.

"I was *just* going to call Deirdre," she said with a look that she hoped said, "Can't I have any privacy in this house?"

Her stepfather glanced at the chair caught in the doorknob

and smiled. He said, "Is that why you got off the phone so quickly with Mr. McElwyn?"

Instead of denying it, she said the dumbest thing possible. "How do you know?"

"I picked up the phone to make a call," her stepfather calmly explained, "and I heard you talking to a man." He added, "I assume it was Mr. McElwyn, anyway; I'm not really sure how many others you call Dad."

Abigail's mind went suddenly blank. She couldn't remember what she'd said on the phone. She stood there, racking her brain.

Her stepfather waited.

"Well . . . he *is* my father."

"And you seem to want him not to forget it, judging from the number of times you called him 'Dad,' " her stepfather said, still smiling. "I admit I'm hurt."

"I'm sorry," she mumbled, staring at a dustbunny under her desk.

"I've noticed that lately you haven't been calling me Dad. Would you rather just call me Rodger now?" he asked.

She looked up at him in surprise. "Yes."

"All right, Abby. Do that, then." He looked at her kind of oddly. "You're not wearing the pretty dress?" he asked with a sideways dip of his head. He always did that sideways dip; he reminded her of Howdy Doody.

"No, I'd rather wear this."

Her stepfather stuck out his lower lip and made a sad-clown face. "Awww . . . wear the pretty blue one. For me. Please?"

She looked at her new Swiss watch, a graduation present that her stepfather had given her the night before, right after he gave her all the bad news about her mother. "I don't have time to change."

"Sure you do," he said, going over to her closet and taking the blue dress down from the rack. "Just hurry up. I'll start the car. You'll be the most beautiful girl at graduation if you wear the blue dress. What girl with raven hair and sapphire eyes wears brown?" He made a sudden face like he just stepped in dog poop. "That doesn't make any sense."

His last few words jogged Abigail's memory. She remembered telling her father about the knife, and her stepfather must have heard her! Why else would he use the same expression, doesn't make any sense? Oh, God . . . he could have heard everything she said. What if she'd got her father in trouble?

She tried to make up for it with an extra-friendly smile. "Okay," she told her stepfather, "if you really want me to, I'll wear the blue one instead."

"Oh, honey . . . yes," her stepfather said in a croaky sort of voice. He handed her the dress, still on its satin-covered hanger. She could see that his hand was shaky as he lifted it toward her face. He stroked her cheek, then leaned down and kissed it, a wet kiss that she had to force herself not to wipe off.

Suddenly he said, "But not the pink barrette," and slid it out of her hair. "It doesn't go."

He tossed it on the dresser on his way out.

Ben McElwyn stood in the lobby of Laurel Place for the second time in two days, and his mood this time was a lot more hostile.

The receptionist was a lot more hostile, too. "I've spoken to Dr. Irons; he's never heard of you," she said bluntly. "Please leave before I call security."

Ben gave her a tight little smile. "This is an old mansion, isn't it? Very, very nice. Did I mention I used to be a building inspector before I turned PI? Yesterday I counted at least nine code violations. Please let me see Mrs. Bonniface. It can be right here, or in that conference room you suggested. It makes no difference to me. The meeting will take less than a minute. All I need is a simple yes or no from Mrs. Bonniface. Did I mention," he said with a particularly malevolent smile, "that I used to be a building inspector?"

The receptionist sputtered for a second or two and then said, "Wait here." She went down a hall and disappeared, and when she came back she was grim.

"You get one question. Here. At the desk. Then you go," she said in a deadly tone.

Ben gave her a businesslike smile. "You bet."

He took up his position behind the snake plants again, wondering what the hell code violations they were all so worried about, and waited until Sarann came through the double entry doors.

This time, it was with a duffel bag. Ben went wild with glee. Grinning broadly, he walked up to Sarann and said, "Ready to go?"

"Yessir," she said.

Ben swung around and said to the flabbergasted receptionist, "Okey-dokey, that answers the question."

Sarann handed him her bag and said to the woman behind the desk, "I'll be checking myself out now. Is there somewhere I have to sign?"

Just like that. Ben wanted to thumb his nose at the witch behind the desk.

Still, despite Sarann's impressive composure and resolve, it took them well over an hour to get out of Laurel Place. It was like a prison break made in slow motion, a ridiculously surreal affair; but at the end of that time Sarann was seated in the front seat of Ben's car, no one else's, and Ben was beside himself with joy. He had no idea that a thirty-three-year-old male with no money, no house, a used car, and a lousy job could be so happy.

He had no idea he could be so much in love.

*   *   *

Sarann was struggling with the effects of the medication. Her mind would be clear one minute, and the next minute she would drift off into confusion again.

"I hope you're right that this feeling will pass," she said to Ben as he drove down Route 1, headed for Farnham. "Because I don't exactly feel on top of my game."

She sighed and looked at her watch, then looked at her watch again because she'd forgotten why she was looking at it in the first place. She was more convinced than ever that they were being followed and couldn't stop looking in her sideview mirror. Her heart was racing, her throat was dry, she couldn't sit still; and even though she understood that those were perfectly reasonable responses to the situation she'd just escaped, she couldn't get away from the fear that she was having what Rodger liked to call an "episode."

"Oh, Ben, it's no use!" she said with rising panic. "My mother was schizophrenic and so am I!"

"Is that what the bastards told you?" he asked.

"No," she admitted. She slumped back in her seat. "Before I checked in to Laurel Place, I was diagnosed by Dr. Irons as having a 'schizotypal personality.' It's what they call a premorbid state," she said.

"Based on sticking the wrong check with the wrong bill?"

Her smile was glum. "Based on my hypersensitivity, my paranoid attitude, and my difficulty—you'll vote for this one—in forming good personal relationships. The omitted stamps and all the rest of it gets clumped, I think, under odd behavior.

"Of course, all that was before the knife," she added wryly. "The knife probably bumped me up into full-blown schizophrenia. The only question left for them was, would my condition respond to drug therapy or not?"

Ben snorted. "What a crock. According to those criteria, I'm a schizophrenic. Every cop I know is a schizophrenic."

She shrugged and said, "Maybe you all are." After a moment she asked, "How is it you know so many cops?"

"Because I used to be one," said Ben, adjusting his rear-view mirror. "This is probably not the optimal time to con-fess that I was asked politely to leave the force."

He threw her a quick look, but not so quick that he couldn't have seen the shock she felt.

"*Ben*. Why?"

"Long story short: I wuz framed," he said simply. "You may believe that or not, as you like."

"Of course I believe it. But . . ."

She sat back again. Smiling ruefully, she shook her head. "Boy, we're a pair."

"How so?"

"We wuz *both* framed," she said with the same rueful smile.

Ben reached over and took her hand, and instantly she felt better. No other man had ever had that kind of power over her, and, she now realized, no other man ever would.

He surprised her by silently lifting her hand to his lips and kissing the back of it—once, twice . . . the third time undid her. She felt a slow wave of delicious, building, and wildly inappropriate pleasure wash over her, the same sen-sation that once had led to wildly inappropriate sex.

Sarann parted her lips to say something to him but ended up simply drawing in breath. Anything else was beyond her.

"I shouldn't have done that," he murmured, releasing her with a sigh of his own. "It makes it seem as if I have an agenda."

"Don't you?" she asked faintly. She was suddenly afraid that he might not.

"I want you for myself, that's absolutely true," he said, throwing her a look so burning that she was forced to look away. "It's also true that I'd like to see that miserable excuse of a husband of yours hurled into the deepest pit of hell for what he tried to do to you. But those two desires, believe it or not, are unrelated."

"I still can't believe it. *Rodger*." She thought of the knife, and stared out the window at the countryside as it rolled by, reluctant to face the crisis she knew was ahead.

The first words out of Ben's mouth after they'd pulled away from Laurel Place had been: "Your husband's behind all the mind games, Sarann. Your husband is gaslighting you."

Ben had then proceeded to explain to Sarann exactly how Rodger could have been behind all the bizarre events, but Sarann hadn't registered a thing after, "Your husband is gaslighting you." Maybe it was the medication, maybe it was the shock, but either way, Ben was going to have to explain everything to her all over again.

"But if he moved my car on me at the mall, that meant he must have followed me around all day. That's just creepy," she said, shuddering. "A sophisticated man like him."

Ben said, "The only sophistication I see was in his adept use of phone features."

"And the tea . . . I always felt so weird after the tea. Could it have been spiked?"

"He has access to the school's medical locker. What do *you* think?"

"I still can't believe it," she said again. She began to run her hand through her hair in a distracted gesture but ran into Abby's barrette. Immediately her thoughts shifted to her daughter, graduating with honors without her mother there to see and applaud her.

She absolutely despised Rodger for that.

"Why would he do it, Ben? Men don't go around gaslighting their wives in this day and age. They just divorce them if they're tired of them. If they're homicidal, okay, maybe they chop them up and bury the pieces. But this! It's so . . . vague, so indirect."

"You said yourself that a headmaster's reputation is everything," Ben mused. "Presumably it wouldn't be good for business if Rodger wanted a divorce and you got nasty about it."

"But I wouldn't do that," she argued.

"So hey. Maybe *he's* the one who's paranoid." After a moment, Ben said, "Did you sign a prenuptial agreement?"

"Well . . . yes. Was that wrong?"

Ben shrugged and said, "Depends. If you hadn't signed and he wanted to be rid of you, it might well have been cheaper for him to put you somewhere like Laurel Place than to risk losing half his assets. But since you did sign a prenup—I'm assuming the terms were brutal to you—he could assume that you wouldn't be going anywhere."

"Being the gold digger that I am," Sarann said dryly.

"I only meant, since you'd be likely to stay put, he'd have to figure out what to do with you once he decided he wanted out of the marriage. But you signed. So never mind. Why *did* you marry him?" Ben added.

"Because . . . because I'm a gold digger, obviously," Sarann said, abashed by the question. In a more humble tone she said, "Because I *am* a gold digger, in a way. I wanted the best life I could find for Abby. I wanted her to have everything that I never had. She's so bright, so willing— she's getting the Girl of the Year Award, did you know that?—and I wanted her to go to the best schools on the planet."

Sarann slid the barrette from her hair and absently stroked its smooth plastic surface. "As it turned out, I couldn't quite afford to do that on my salary as an office assistant," she said with a soft, ironic laugh.

"What a disaster this marriage has been," she added in a mournful whisper. "We have absolutely . . . *nothing* . . . in common. And worse, neither of us respects the other. It was a disaster from the start, Ben." She bowed her head and stared at the pink barrette. "I never loved him."

It should have been an easy confession; Sarann wanted Ben to know how she felt about him, and that meant, first, that he had to know how she felt about Rodger. Still, the words caught in her throat like snippets of barbed wire; it was incredibly painful to admit that she'd climbed into the bed of a man she didn't love. Or even, when she came right down to it, *like* very much.

"What a fool I was," she summed up sadly.

"We've all made bad choices for good reasons."

"You're just being kind; you don't mean that."

"You're right," he said without looking at her. "God damn it; I can't *believe* that you sent me packing and waited instead for an asshole like Rodger."

"Because I was a fool, Ben."

"I love you, fool. Are we clear on that, at least?"

He shot her a glance so on fire, so completely frustrated and ardent at the same time, that she quailed. "I . . . think so."

"Oh, what the hell . . ." he muttered, and he pulled over onto the shoulder in a cloud of dust. He snapped off her seatbelt and yanked her toward him in a deep, hard kiss that seared the edges of her soul, leaving her both stunned and wanting more. She met his tongue with a hunger that easily matched his. She had waited so many, many years for his kiss, and by now she was famished.

"I love you, Sarann, I love you," he said in husky groans against her mouth. He battered her with his kisses, with his protests of love. "I've loved you since the day I saw you . . . Sarann . . . Sarann, I love you," he said, over and over again.

The warmth of his lips on hers melted away the last of her scruples. She had forgotten the taste of him, the scent of him, the scratch of his chin, the sound of his voice in passion.

When she saw him in her shop, she knew that she loved him. Now she remembered how much.

"Ah, Ben . . ." she said, arching her neck to savor his fiery caresses. "You must know . . . you *have* to know . . ."

"Say it, then," he said hoarsely. He dragged a trail of hot contact along the curve of her neck, returning to her mouth to beat down her resistance with nothing more than his tongue. "Say it for the first time. I want to hear it, I need to hear it. *Say* it, Sarann."

"I do, I do love you," she said in a soft wail. "God help me, I do."

They kissed again, an altogether different kiss this time that was a pledge of their fealty to one another, made on a blissful plane where neither psychiatrists, husbands, traffic, nor trauma could intrude. A sense of Abby was with them, to be sure: in a way, they were finalizing the commitment that they had made almost thirteen years earlier.

Sarann floated out of the kiss half dazed but joyful. She whispered against his cheek, "Oh, Ben—we've *found* each other."

The only problem was, a state trooper had found them, too.

Chapter 23

THE TROOPER, A hulking stereotype with a square jaw and a grim look, walked from his vehicle back to their car, sending Sarann's heart racing even more than it had in Ben's arms.

"Oh, no, oh, no," she said in a low wail. "They're going to take me back. Ben, don't let them. Please don't let them." A sharp-edged rock seemed to lodge in her throat as she watched Ben dig out his registration and then roll down his window. "What should I say?" she asked in a panic. "What should I do?"

"Nothing at all; everything's going to be fine," Ben told her calmly, and immediately she felt better.

I have a friend, now; I have an ally. She had time for only a short prayer of thanks before the trooper said to Ben, "Can I see your license and registration, please?"

"Here you go," said Ben easily.

The trooper looked them over and handed them back. "The shoulder is not a lover's lane," he informed them. "There are better places for that."

He didn't smile—but he didn't arrest them, either. Sarann felt a ridiculous surge of relief roar through her, testimony to the frazzled state of her nerves.

"I don't know how that could have happened," Ben said with a wry grin once they were on their way again. "Whenever I drove the getaway car, I always kept a sharp eye on the mirror."

Sarann burst into nervous giggles. "I feel like a teenager caught by the lake. Don't you *dare* tell Abby about this."

Ben stroked her cheek with the back of his fingers. "I'll

wait until we're old and gray and she has a twelve-year-old of her own. I love you. Don't ever leave me again."

Sarann caught his hand in hers and kissed his knuckles softly. "How could I? How *did* I?"

He turned his hand so that his fingers pressed against her lips. "Shhh. No more apologies, no more regrets. It's all water under the bridge now."

Ben wasn't the kind of man who forgave easily, but when he did, Sarann decided, it was without reservation. What a contrast with Rodger. She leaned back in her seat and closed her eyes, and suddenly there he was: Rodger P. Bonniface III, a man she had known only as an employer. A man she had married partly because she'd been so flattered that he had asked her. A man who was everything that she was not, well-connected and well-educated, and completely used to having his way. A man who was a stranger still.

She shuddered and opened her eyes again. They were passing the golf course now, about to drop through Farnham. Before long she would be face-to-face with Rodger; she couldn't begin to imagine how it would go.

"He must know by now that we're on our way," Sarann said uneasily. "What do you suppose he's thinking?"

Ben said, "A man like that? Anyone's guess."

They became lost in their own thoughts. Sarann gave two or three brief directions to skirt around summer tourist traffic—bypassing Onboard Antiques, which clearly was never going to become a reality for her—and suddenly they were on the winding country road that would take them to Tidewater, where a party was being thrown for their little girl by people who were not her parents. By strangers.

"Rodger was afraid of being blackmailed by you because of me, you know," she said as his exquisite house came into view.

"What, are you defending him now?" Ben said, a little sharply.

"No . . . not at all; I'm just trying to understand. Maybe it was his dread of being blackmailed that was behind the gaslighting. Maybe he thought you'd be less likely to shake him down if I was holed away somewhere."

"Doesn't make sense. He didn't know I existed when he started his campaign."

"Damn it; you're right. Then why—?"

"With any luck, we'll soon find out."

The wine-colored house loomed ahead, its driveway filled with three cars—and a silver van.

Sarann took one look at the van and said, "I don't believe it; Rodger's mother is here! That's her wheelchair transport. Why would she come to Tidewater *now*?"

"How do you stand with her?"

"She came to the wedding, she came to the shop. That's pretty much it," said Sarann, drawing a quick sketch for Ben. "I'm sure she didn't approve of the marriage, although Rodger has never said that. Mrs. Bonniface has Parkinson's, and lately it's become worse. She and her husband ran the school with equal authority; after he died, Rodger stepped in and filled his father's shoes. She's still obsessed with Faxton, despite her condition; the disease hasn't changed that at all."

Ben muttered, "This is not gonna be pretty."

He pulled in alongside the van, giving it plenty of room to leave if it needed to. Before he got out of the Honda, he reached behind his seat and came up with a painstakingly wrapped small box, tied in narrow pink ribbon. The present was awkwardly taped to a giant card.

"Oh, Ben—for Abby," Sarann said, touched despite her nervousness. "And my gift for her is still sitting in a dresser drawer."

Ben winked and said, "I signed this from both of us."

It was a gesture as endearing as it was confrontational— Ben all over, Sarann thought. She gave him a determined smile, and they got out of the car together to take on Rodger and his campaign to make her drive herself crazy.

There was no need to ring the bell; Abby swung the door open and nearly knocked Sarann down in her rush to repossess her. Sarann wrapped her arms around her daughter, whispering her name and rocking her with a fierceness so intense, so personal, that Ben's eyes began to smart and he had to look away. He'd never seen a bond like that before.

In the shadow of the hall he spied a man who had at least ten years on him and who stood like some general at the top of a hill, surveying the savages mustering in the valley below.

Ben hated him on sight.

Bonniface came out of the shadows and approached them in silence, a silence that mother and daughter rushed to fill at the same time.

"Rodger, this is—"

"Rodger, this is—"

Sarann and Abby both stopped and looked at one another. Abby blinked and looked off to the side.

Ben decided to step into the sudden void, saying simply, "Ben McElwyn." He couldn't bring himself to offer his hand.

Rodger didn't bother to introduce himself—generals never did—and instead got straight to the point. "We got a call from the director of Laurel Place. We've been expecting you."

"I thought Irons was at a conference in Sweden," Ben said before he could stop himself.

"He is."

Whoa. Bonniface, one; McElwyn, zip.

"May we come in?" Ben asked. No way was he going to barge through the door and subject himself to an arrest.

Rodger nodded and they trooped in behind him, with Abigail still clinging to her mother. They passed through a hall hung with framed vintage photographs and went into a dining room occupied by several grownups and one blond and photogenic toddler, all gathered around a formal table and having cake and ice cream. Behind them, several discreetly wrapped presents were arranged on a sideboard that even Ben, an antique ignoramus, knew had to be worth a very considerable amount.

Ben was still holding on to his own offering. He turned to Abby and said, "For you. Happy graduation."

She'd had her eye on it all along, but she accepted it with a spontaneous-sounding, "For *me*?" and added it to the pile while Sarann did the introductions.

Ben was presented first to the mother-in-law, a once-grand but now stooped woman with eyes as blue as Abby's, a small nose just made for looking down over, and a head of silver hair, every one of them shellacked into place. After that he was introduced to Glenys and James and little Maggie—a perfect Polo family lifted from a Ralph Lauren ad. Their acknowledgments of him were frigid but polite.

How impressively civil they were all being. Ben decided to lob the goddamned grenade and get it over with. "I wonder if I could have a word in private," he said to Rodger. "I know the timing stinks."

"Whatever you have to say," Rodger said grimly, "you can say it here. We're all family around this table."

All except for Sarann, who was standing off to one side, since no one had bothered to get a chair for her. Ben shrugged and said, "Hokay, if that's how you'd like it."

Suddenly Sarann said in a particularly gentle voice, "Abby, would you mind going to your room for just a little while?"

Abby glanced from her mother to Ben, then scanned the company, then clamped her lips tightly shut. She left without a word. Smart kid.

The elder Mrs. Bonniface spoke first in a voice that was

weak and high-pitched, out of character for a matriarch. "I hope that you're not going to create a scene." She wheeled her chair back from the table, presumably getting ready to roll if Ben should start shooting.

Ben's response was a tight smile. "All the scenes have already been created, and not by me."

Little Maggie cut through the ensuing silence with her spoon, banging it on the tray of her highchair. "More 'scream!" she said, holding up her empty bowl.

Comin' right up, Ben thought.

Aloud he said, "For a while now, Sarann has been afraid that she was going bonkers. I'm sure there's a more politically correct way to say that, but, being professionals, undoubtedly you get my drift."

No one smiled, and he went on.

"I'm here to tell you that, in fact, the events were staged. Sarann was being gaslighted."

He'd lobbed the grenade. Nothing happened.

So he pulled the pin.

"By one of you."

"What? That's *outrageous*!"

The protest came from James; Rodger was silent and simply looked puzzled. Mrs. Bonniface had no expression at all for Ben to try to read—an unfortunate effect, presumably, of her disease. Glenys looked afraid.

Sarann was watching them just as carefully as Ben; he wondered whether she was getting the same readings.

He went on to expound his theory. "It's not a challenge to throw a few extra gallons of gas into a fuel tank every once in a while, especially if the car's sometimes parked where Sarann can't see it. And it's even easier to remove the mail left in a roadside box for pickup by the mail carrier and then to play havoc with it. Unwanted garden tools? Anyone with someone's Visa number can order a set and have them sent to someone's address. As I say, none of that's hard."

"This is ridiculous," James said, his voice rising. "We don't have to listen to this. Get out."

"No." It was Rodger, listening intently to what Ben had to say. "Let him continue."

"Upping the ante without being caught—now that's hard," Ben went on. "It takes determination, maybe desperation. Sarann complained—you all heard her—that when she tried several times to put her key in the front door, it didn't work. It's an old trick. But Sarann had no reason to suspect sabotage; she was among people she trusted."

He glanced at Mrs. Bonniface for some clue as to how much she knew about the so-called episodes, but her face remained as rigid as the artfully draped fabric above the multipaned windows in the room. Once in a while she would blink; it was hard to read much into a blink.

Rodger, on the other hand, was looking as mesmerized as Glenys looked nervous. Ben began to get an uneasy feeling about it all. No one asked him how one would go about screwing up a lock, but he told them anyway. "Breaking off a toothpick in a key slot will make it unworkable; taking out the fragment with a long tweezers later is easily done."

Glenys flushed all pink under her straight blond hair. "How would anyone possibly be able to predict that Sarann would use her key, and that later they'd be able to pull out the fragment without being discovered? That's just silly."

"Oh, the person we're talking about is an opportunist, no question," Ben agreed. "If the buggered lock business had turned out differently . . . well, no great loss. He—or she—would simply have moved on to the next dirty trick. All *we* actually know about are the ones that Sarann got caught up in; who knows how many other attempts never made it onto the scoreboard?"

James was drumming his fingers on the tablecloth, which for some reason made Ben wonder: who set the table? Had

Glenys stepped in for Sarann, or had Rodger, control freak that he was, done it himself?

Rodger said, "So the wallet, that—"

"Was dumped in the birdbath by someone other than Sarann. That's a no-brainer. Anyone who knows Sarann knows that she's too mindful of a hard-earned buck to destroy a designer wallet."

Dead silence.

These rich families, they did hang tight. Ben couldn't understand why everyone wasn't looking at Rodger, the obvious suspect, with horrified glances. What the hell was the matter with them?

Glenys spoke up. "I suppose you think that one of us planted a knife in my daughter's room?" she asked, her voice rising to a pitch just this side of hysterical. "I suppose you think one of us would risk Maggie's life?"

Hearing her name, Maggie cried, "More *ice* cream! More more more!" She banged loudly on her tray with the spoon.

"Oh, please," Ben said to Glenys over the thwacks of the pounding spoon. "Laying a knife on the floor just in time for someone else to see and pick it up isn't exactly akin to striking a match in a refinery. The knife was strictly to scare the bejesus out of Sarann. Let me tell you folks," he said, anger rising in his throat, "it damn near worked."

Sarann was blinking back tears; he threw her a look of pure sympathy and hoped that for the moment it was enough.

In the meantime, Maggie began to seriously fidget, trying her best to squirm Houdini-like out of her highchair. Her chocolate-covered hands were grabbing at the tablecloth, and her chocolate-covered face had a look on it that was anything but Polo-like. "Mom-mee-*ee*," she whined, suddenly tired of being denied seconds. She began banging her feet back and forth on the high chair. The whine dissolved into a loud wail. *"Mahhhhhh-meeeee!"*

Rodger said quietly, "Glenys. Please."

Glenys unstrapped the sticky kid and hauled her out of the chair, presumably to clean her up before she did something bad to the tablecloth, which looked like it came off the captain's table on the *Titanic*.

They left the room with Maggie in a full-fledged tantrum, kicking and screaming. Ben had never taken the old jingle, "I scream, you scream, we all scream for ice cream" quite so literally before.

Sarann turned to Rodger and over Maggie's howls, said, "What about the lowered bar on the crib? I don't understand how anyone could *do* something like that; how anyone could take that kind of chance."

That got Mrs. Bonniface's attention. "What are you talking about?" she said sharply. "Answer me now!"

Matriarch, hell; she looked like the Queen of Hearts just then. Even Ben cringed a little.

James jumped up and said, "This is absurd, letting some stranger come into our house and throw out idiotic interpretations of obvious events. Sarann has major issues about not being accepted into wealth and status, it's as simple as that. She hates us all because she thinks we've spurned her. Which isn't true. It's in her mind. That's the whole problem! It's all in her *mind*."

His face was flushed a deep, ugly red; he wasn't looking at Ben or his adoptive mother or anyone else in the room. As far as Ben could tell, he was talking to the pile of presents.

"James, you're not going anywhere. Sit back down," Rodger said, sounding like the headmaster he was. "I want to get to the bottom of this."

He turned to Ben with a troubled look on his face. "But what about the red paint? I found the shoes myself under the laundry tub. They were sticky with laundry soap, as if someone had tried scrubbing off the paint without success. Are you saying that those were planted there? Like the knife in Maggie's room?"

"That's exactly what I'm saying," said Ben, but he felt a little less sure about who it was he was saying it to.

"I did not track the paint, Rodger," Sarann told him emphatically. "I really did want to open that shop. I was devastated when I saw the ruined floor."

Her eyes were glittering with contempt as she added, "And all of you know that I'd never waste a good pair of sneakers."

I love you, Sarann. Give 'em hell.

Rodger slumped back in his chair. He looked dazed. He said softly, "My God." He stared at his younger brother, who immediately began to sputter again. "God damn it, this is an outrage! Why the *hell* are we sitting here listening to this? I will *not* subject myself to this farce any longer."

"James, shut *up*," his mother said. "Peter's outside and will hear you."

James said, "The hell with your driver!" and slammed the table with the flat of his hand. He stood up again, brushing aside Rodger's objections.

He said to Ben with a furious look, "Do you have any idea who I am? Who're *you*? Some has-been of a cop who'd stoop to dealing the drugs he's confiscated, the lowest of the low, a two-bit PI spouting nonsense out of both nostrils, defending Sarann because you have the hots for her and for no other reason."

He turned to his mother, whose blue eyes were wide with shock, and said, "If you want to stay here and be insulted, go right ahead. I'm leaving. Glenys," he bellowed, "get Maggie's things. We're leaving. Move it!"

Ben had just one thing to say to that.

"Y'all have keys to one another's houses, isn't that right?"

"Good grief," said Rodger hoarsely. "We do." He didn't seem able to come out of his daze.

Ah, shit.

That, in a nutshell, was Ben's reaction.

In the middle of the uproar, Abby decided to come back downstairs. With a smile that had to be either warped or feigned, she said brightly, "Would it be okay if I opened my presents now?"

No one paid any attention to her; everyone was on the move. Mrs. Bonniface was wheeling her chair and calling for her attendant, James was herding his wife and their howling daughter toward the front door, Rodger was urging Sarann by the elbow into the next room, telling her something that had her looking confused, and Ben—Ben was thinking, what the fuck just happened here?

"Dad! Oh, Dad, I love this!" cried Abby, holding up a little gold heart with a diamond chip in the middle.

Ben smiled lamely. It looked so much more dazzling at Kmart.

Abigail sat next to her father on the garden bench, looking down at her chest every five seconds. The late-evening sun glimmered on the diamond of her necklace in a magical way, the most beautiful thing she had ever seen. It was her very first present from her father, and she would treasure it always.

"Dad?"

"Hmm?"

He hardly heard her. He was sitting with his elbows on his thighs and with his chin on his knuckles and he was staring at the French doors at the back of the house. Abigail, too, was waiting for her mother to get done talking with her stepfather and come out; but this was nice in the meantime.

"Dad, Mom isn't ever going back to Laurel Place, is she?"

He shook his head slowly. "Never."

"So why was she sounding so upset talking to Rodger when I went inside to get us the Cokes?"

"I don't know, Abby. I wish I did."

"Then why don't you just go inside and ask her?"

"She asked me not to interfere."

"Would that be interfering, really? I'd call it just getting an update. They've been in there for almost an hour."

"I know, Abby. I know."

He was so tense. Abigail personally couldn't understand why. From what she'd been able to overhear of the big fight, her father had more or less accused someone in the family of playing dirty tricks on her mother. It *obviously* had to be her stepfather; who else could it be? In which case, she and her mother would be moving out and starting over in their own apartment again, which was fine with Abigail. She didn't want to go to Faxton, anyway. She was sick of hearing the very word Faxton.

"Dad?"

"Hmm?"

"What did you study in college?"

"Software engineering."

"I like math."

"Maybe you'll be a programmer."

"But I like English better."

"Maybe you'll be poor."

"Not if I write Harry Potter stories."

"Maybe you'll rule the universe."

She laughed and said, "I don't want to *be* Harry Potter; I just want to write about kids *like* Harry Potter."

"It's great that you've got ambition," he said, but really, he was just staring at the French doors.

Abigail began to get nervous. She said, "Everything's going to be all right, isn't it, Dad? You said that it would."

"And I meant it, Abby." He looked at her and not the doors as he said with a smile, "I made it to your graduation party, after all."

"Is that what it was? I'd call it a demolition derby."

"Hey, snot," he said, lightly elbowing her in the ribs.

She giggled and said, "Well, it's true." She loved that he called her snot, loved it so much more than being called love and sweetheart and darling by her stepfather. An amazing amount more.

He was about to say something when he suddenly stared back at the French doors. Abigail knew without turning that her mother had finally appeared. The look on her father's face made her whip around to see if it matched the look on her mother's.

It did.

Chapter 24

SARANN, PUFFY-EYED AND bearing a sickly smile, waved Abby over to the back porch while Ben stayed on the bench and waited his turn. His chest was too constricted to allow easy breathing, so he abandoned the effort altogether, like a man going down for the third time in the rapids of a river. He was about to die, it was as simple as that. It was his death sentence that he saw in Sarann's face.

After a brief exchange with her mother, Abby went inside. Ben stood as Sarann approached.

Pointing to a hedge of spent lilacs farther down the property, she said, "I know a better place."

So did he: anywhere that wasn't Tidewater.

But he followed Sarann in silence through an opening in the thicket and emerged with her in some kind of secret garden, scaring up some big-winged moths in the process. It was a tidy, simple place, a small clearing with a few heady rosebushes, some pink-flowered low things that smelled good, and some white-flowered low things that smelled even better. Ivy had got a toehold in one corner, and in another, there was a pile of square-shaped iron pigs waiting for a second chance to be useful. Ship's ballast in a garden: in a town of shipbuilders, it didn't seem strange, merely whimsical.

Sarann said softly, "This is my private place. We can talk here."

There were two rickety twig chairs whose sides had been shredded by claw-sharpening creatures, probably cats, but who could be sure? The enclosure was well away from the house.

Sarann began to brush away fallen leaves and seed pods from the second, clearly unused chair. "I haven't been here much lately; the shop has filled most of my time," she said over her shoulder. "The mosquitoes can get pretty bad, but I have repellent in that little covered basket, so if you want—"

"*Sarann*," he said in a desperate groan. He caught her by the arm, turned her around and kissed her hard, trying to draw life from her, trying to survive. His emotions were reeling, his panic, severe; he knew that if he lost her now, he would never find her again.

For a sensational moment she was his, returning his hot, wet, wild kiss with equal fervor, meeting the thrust of his tongue, clinging to him as fiercely as he clung to her. But the moment ended as quickly as it had begun, and she wrenched herself free.

"Wait . . . stop," she said, breathless from his terrifying need for her. "Ben . . . oh, please . . . don't make this any harder."

God, he did not want to hear those words. They were so at odds with the desperation in her kiss, and yet so perfectly in sync with it.

"*What*," he said, holding her fast by the shoulders. He fixed her with a look as bitter as it was imploring. "What are you going to say that's going to be so damn hard? I dare you to be that insane."

She put her hands over her face and said in a muffled voice, "I can't think when you hold me. Let me go, Ben. *Please*."

There was something so abject in her manner that he felt abusive. He was the one who was going insane. He couldn't let her go; he couldn't keep hanging on. Finally, in a burst of frustration he threw up his hands as if her shoulders were lava and said, "Fine! Say whatever it is that's so goddamned hard to say."

She bowed her head. "It wasn't Rodger."

They were the words Ben most dreaded to hear. He had seen them coming; he had *seen* them, as clearly as if they had been marching down the lawn in big neon letters.

It. Wasn't. Rodger.

"The hell it wasn't," he said, but the words came out flat and without conviction.

She heard it, too. She turned in a little semicircle of confusion, and then she sat on the edge of the twig chair and clasped her hands over her long skirt like a genteel virgin at a garden party. In the dying light he could make out that her lips were wet and swollen from his kisses; he prayed to God that they would be that way when she went back into the house.

Because she was going to go back into the house, the hated house called Tidewater; he could see it in her eyes.

"It was James." She let out a long, shuddering sigh. "I don't know why I never figured that out. In retrospect, it seems so obvious."

"You must be joking," he said. But in the back of his mind he was thinking, Fuck, it *was* James, that fuckhead.

"You know yourself that he has a key to the house," she said, reaching for a half-broken twig hanging from the chair and idly snapping it free. "But it turns out that he's had keys to our cars as well. I didn't know that. Now I do."

"Because Rodger considerately informed you."

She said patiently, as if Ben were a particularly slow student she wanted to encourage, "James was there for the key episode. James was there for the wallet episode. If he got hold of my wallet, then he was able to get my Visa number, which is how he pulled off the garden-tool episode. Don't you see? James was there, every time."

Ben could feel himself going down, down, down, but he tried with everything he had to claw his way back to the surface. Savagely, he said, "And I suppose he hid his car in the bushes across the road just on the offhand chance that you might go out of town, and then he followed you *all* the way to the mall in Beverly, just so that he could move your car and confuse you."

She said with a mournful smile, "He didn't have to hide in the bushes. I had forgotten, until tonight, that I'd called his house at the last minute and asked if Glenys wanted to come shopping with me. He knew exactly where I was going. I guess he didn't want to try a stunt like that locally; he might have been recognized." She sighed and said, "Rodger, on the other hand, had no idea where I'd been that day until I called him to say the car was stolen."

Down, down, down.

Sarann had to see him sinking, had to see that he was fighting for his life—but, like the foreman of a jury, she kept working her way down the counts of the verdict.

"The knife—well; you said yourself about the knife. And as for the crib bar, I can't believe I left it down, but I must have. No human being could have been so deliberately reckless with a child's life; only accidentally so. But everything else . . ." She shrugged. "James."

Ben held his hands palms up in a gesture of incredulity. "Why? Why James? Why Rodger was hard enough, Sarann; why James is a hell of a lot harder to answer." He drove the point home with a fire-breathing sneer; it was his last, best hope for turning her around, for making her leave Tidewater forever with him.

"James wants to oust Rodger from the position of headmaster," she said simply. "He wants Faxton Academy for himself. He's had ideas for years about reforming the curriculum. Even I knew that; he used to get into heated discussions with Rodger, but I always thought they were philosophical ones."

She tried to cheer Ben up with a smile—slow kid, flunked the test, how sad, try again—as she said, "Rodger pointed out, and I've seen for myself, that James is finally making some headway with their mother about putting his ideas in place: orienting the school toward a more computer-heavy curriculum, for example."

"Who the hell would want control of a boarding school enough to gaslight you?"

"James. He's an adopted son, remember. And a younger son. All of his life he's been a junior rival to Rodger. Rodger told me that James has a history of sabotaging his successes going back to when they were kids."

"James."

"Mm. You know that book about child abuse that he's written? It's raised him a lot in Mrs. Bonniface's esteem. She likes his ambition, his drive, and she's very impressed by the media blitz that's coming up. She thinks it's a great opportunity to promote Faxton. You can't buy that kind of advertising, you know," Sarann added with an almost pathetic smile. "I guess James figured that now was his best chance to become the heir apparent."

"By getting you put away? Give me a break."

Sarann shook her head. "By making it look as if Rodger had to put me away. By embarrassing Rodger. It was bad enough that Rodger married someone beneath him; to have it be an unbalanced someone would have thrown his judgment completely into question. His mother would have lost all confidence in him. After all, she has a dynasty to keep up. When James found out I had an illegitimate child, it was frosting on the cake."

"That's a completely idiotic theory," Ben snapped.

One that was so plausible it was scary. He had to turn Sarann around about it, to convince her that it was a lie. He didn't even *care* if it was a lie or the truth anymore; he just wanted her to leave with him.

Almost without hope, he said, "Call Rodger's bluff, then. Confront the old lady. Ask her point-blank if it's possible that James is trying to knock out his brother."

Sarann gave him that same, sweet, oh-you-dope smile. "Mrs. Bonniface would never admit something like that; she can't. Rodger and I talked about it in the house. She won't do anything to jeopardize the upcoming tour. The Bonniface name is on a book that's expected to be a national bestseller. Right now, James is more critical to her interests than poor Rodger is."

"No!" Ben said harshly, sick of the tennis match they were playing. "Just . . . don't believe him, that's all. Don't believe him and come away with me!"

His explosive response had her up from the twig chair and walking away from him. It made him sick to see it.

She stopped at the far end of the enclosure and turned back to face him.

"Rodger doesn't want me to leave. He begged me. He pleaded with me."

"*I'm* begging you. *I'm* pleading with you!"

She shook her head. "You didn't see him. He—it was embarrassing to see. He's so proud, and he was actually weeping . . . he fell to his knees, and then he . . . oh, God. I can't. I can't just walk out on him if he's telling the truth. You can't kick a man when he's down. I owe it to him at least to step away gradually."

"You don't owe him shit! This is nuts! You *are* nuts!"

It didn't even get a rise out of her. "It was my lie that started his downhill slide," she said with infuriating nobility.

Ben was close to tearing his hair out, and she saw it. "It's just for a little while, Ben, until he comes to terms with everything," she pleaded. "He and I will have separate rooms. I can never be his wife again, you know that."

"No! I *don't* know that!" Ben shouted. "You don't belong there, you can't stay with him! The bastard is lying!"

"You have absolutely no proof of that!" she said, fiery at

last but for all the wrong reasons. "A man is innocent until proven guilty; that's how the system works!"

Ben cornered her with a few long strides. "This isn't about the law, God damn it," he said, seething. "This is about your *heart*."

He wrapped one arm around her and gripped her jaw with his hand, kissing her roughly, practically lifting her from the ground with the force of his hold. He knew full well that what he was doing was less a kiss than it was a branding. He was marking Sarann for his own because she belonged to him as surely as he belonged to her, and no one else.

Let her go back to Tidewater, then, with her swollen lips and her tearful eyes and her mournful voice. Let Rodger Bonniface see what he was getting: another man's woman. And God help the bastard's soul if he took her.

Sarann's kiss never tasted sweeter, her body never felt softer, than it did during that searing last embrace in her secret garden. Ben was all the more flabbergasted that she was able to break herself free of him and cry, "Don't *do* this to me!" before fleeing without another word through the arched opening in the wall of lilacs.

Stunned, Ben sat on the twig chair that she had cleared off for him, and in a state of disbelief, he waited: because Sarann obviously had to tell Rodger that she was leaving before she came back.

The evening star rose bright in the sky, and still Ben waited: because Sarann had to explain to Abby all that had happened before she came back.

The Big Dipper came out, pointing the way, and still Ben waited: because Sarann had to add a few things for Abby to that duffel bag of hers before she came back.

The Milky Way began to shine in a ghostly, diaphanous arc across the velvet-blue sky, and still Ben waited: because Sarann had to gather any number of papers and documents before she came back.

When his joints were stiff, and his neck ached, and his clothes were clammy with nighttime dew, Ben stepped out haltingly from Sarann's secret garden and stood on the wet grass of the rolling lawn behind Tidewater. It was only then that he understood that Sarann, his Sarann, was not coming back.

The house to which she had chosen to return was completely, appallingly dark.

Chapter 25

THE APARTMENT TO which Ben had no choice but to return was amazingly, cheerfully bright.

And clean.

Despite his black mood, Ben had to smile: Crotchy's wife had grabbed the ball and run it all the way in for a touchdown. It was possible that Dolores had had a maid service in to do the work, but somehow Ben didn't think so. What he was looking at went way beyond the average use of elbow grease.

Every surface of his kitchen—floor, counters, cupboards, switchplates, trim, sink, stove, fridge—sparkled in a way that made Ben want to walk out and walk in again, just to make sure he was in his own apartment.

The apartment looked bigger as well, maybe because every loose item had been in its place. Someplace, anyway; Ben had no idea where everything had been stowed. He knew where the beer should be, though, so he opened the fridge, only it wasn't his fridge but some ad for GE. The stuff with green mold, that was gone, and so was whatever had been lying in a sticky orange pool under the crispers. The Heineken was where he kept it, in a door shelf, but even there, all of the labels had been lined up to face the same direction.

Dear, compulsive Dodi; he wondered whether *she'd* accept his hand in marriage. He popped the cap on one of the greenies and wandered through the bedroom, living room, and kitchen that he called home. Dodi's loving touch was everywhere, from the new miniblinds on the bedroom windows to the three red geraniums lined up with precision on the windowsill above his sink. New sponge, new dishrack, new blue-and-white-checked flouncy thing across the top of the window—it made Ben positively ache to have a woman there to share it all with.

To have Sarann.

If you fixed it up—bought a rug or some dishes from Kmart or a philodendron from Stop and Shop—you might begin to care. And pretty soon you'd start having people over, because you wouldn't be ashamed. And you'd begin to care about them, too; they'd become your friends.

"Sarann," he murmured, just to have the sound of her name drifting around his kitchen. "Look. Better than a philodendron. Three geraniums."

He smiled bitterly. What the hell good was caring?

He set the empty Heineken down and headed for the john to pee. When he came back, the green bottle was still there, glaring at him from Dodi's spotless counter. Ben sighed and rinsed it out and put it in the cardboard box clearly marked RECYCLE that Dodi had stuck under the sink.

One thing he knew: no one would be able to accuse him of not caring.

"Why didn't someone wake me *up*?"

Abigail was in her nightgown, staring with dismay out the window at the driveway where her mother's car had been parked just two seconds ago. Abigail had jumped out of bed and had run downstairs when she heard the car start, but she had been too late. She could still see a dry rectangle of stones where the car had been—although that wouldn't last long; it was starting to rain again.

Things were going from bad to worse. First Abigail learned from her mother, after all the uproar the other day, that nothing was going to be very different, at least for now, except that her mother was going to be sleeping in the small spare room on the third floor. Then Abigail was asked, again by her mother, that she not call Ben McElwyn until things settled down a little.

Abigail loved her mother totally—she found out just how totally when her mother went off to Laurel Place—but she couldn't stand living in Tidewater anymore. It wasn't where they wanted to be, so why were they staying?

And then to top top it off, the rain. It was the third day in a row of wet, gloomy weather, and she couldn't stand much more of it. The house was too dark and too dreary when it rained; it made her mood even more restless and depressed. And camp wasn't until August. August was a million years away.

"I was *supposed* to help Mom with the movers, you know," she said, lifting Molly out of her nap and stroking the sleepy cat. She glanced over her shoulder to see her stepfather staring at her hard. Something was wrong; he wasn't smiling his dorky sad-clown smile.

"I know that," he said. "I told your mother that I'd take you to the shop as soon as you eat and get dressed. But there's no rush; the movers aren't going to be there to take everything away again for another couple of hours."

But he didn't exactly look relaxed as he added, "All I'm asking for is just a little bit of your time, and then I'll drive you over." He held up a big brown envelope while he waited for her answer.

Still hugging Molly, Abigail sank with a sulky "Okay" into the deep cushion of her mother's chair, then tucked her bare legs under her nightgown and made a nest for Molly to curl up in.

Abigail had absolutely no desire to give her stepfather even a little bit of her time. She liked him less each day, and basically she just didn't get it. Everyone she knew had divorced parents. Why couldn't *she* have divorced parents? It wasn't fair. She couldn't even really call her mother and stepfather separated yet, despite what her mother had told her. How could you be separated from someone when you lived under the same roof with him?

Her stepfather laid the big brown envelope on the butler's table by his chair and then moved the table in front of Abby and Molly. Molly didn't even look up. She was old, older than Abby by a year and two months, and she always slept hard on dark, rainy mornings.

"I wanted to show you something, Abby. It may upset you," he warned her, "but you're grown-up enough to know the truth about people. And you're important—you're *everything*—to me," he said in a weird, strained voice. "Please . . . try to understand why I'm showing you these, all right? Just try to understand."

Abigail didn't like the sound of that at all. She uncurled poor sleepy Molly and put her on the floor to find another napping place, and then she leaned forward to see what was in the envelope.

Photographs. Her stepfather was taking out large black-and-white photographs as he said, "I don't know if your mother told you, but she and I agreed to have someone investigate Mr. McElwyn after we found out about him; we wanted to make sure that he didn't have any dark secrets in his closet after we learned about him."

Abigail was amazed to hear her mother had done that, but she didn't say anything, only nodded.

Her stepfather laid out the first three photographs in front of her. "This is where Ben McElwyn lives," he said, pointing to a photo of a hall door with garbage strewn all over in front of it. "This is where he goes to drink—almost every night," he said, tapping the photo of a dark-looking bar crowded with ordinary-looking people. "And this is the kind of woman he dates," he said, pointing to the third photo, of a blond woman in a short tight skirt with a low-cut, tight midriff top. Abigail could see her stomach, and it was perfectly flat.

Abigail looked at all three photos, but she looked at the third one the longest.

"This woman sees a *lot* of men; I have other photos of her with them," her stepfather explained.

"So what?" Abigail said stiffly. "Maybe she likes men."

Her stepfather made an impatient sound. "Look at her, Abby; she's obviously a prostitute."

"Just because she wears cool clothes?" Abby looked away from the photo. The woman was as pretty as a model; it was depressing. "I really don't think so."

"You just don't want to think so."

Why was her stepfather doing this? It was so embarrassing to be alone with him and with these photographs spread out. Abigail just wanted to hide in her room away from him. She got up, before he had the chance to lay out the next batch of photographs.

"Does my mother know about these?" she asked, convinced that she didn't.

"No," he admitted. "I got the report yesterday, and I was reluctant to look at it before now, partly because I knew what the gist of it would be. I knew the report would be disgusting."

"It's *not* disgusting!" she said angrily. She wanted to add, "You're disgusting!" but she was afraid to. She realized, out of the blue, that she was afraid of her stepfather. He was just too creepy at times like this. She began to back out of the room.

Her stepfather understood what she was up to, that she was trying to sneak away from him. He got a kind of look in his face. He said coldly, "Your father's a drug dealer, you know."

"He is *not*!" Abigail cried, scandalized by his accusation. "How can you *say* that?"

"He got kicked off the police force because he was dealing cocaine. I have the documentation right here. He and his partner would break up a deal and then confiscate the drugs and sell them later. Did you know that your father used to be a cop?"

"I—no."

"Why do you suppose he's working, if you can call it that, as a private eye? Because he was a crooked cop and that's all he could do. That's the man you're calling dad. He lives in squalor and he dates hookers. That's the man your mother wants to cart you off to. She wants to leave Tidewater—Tidewater!—and go back to a life like this," he said, tapping the garbage picture. "She wants to live with a drug dealer who sees hookers. She wants—"

"Shut up shut up shut up!" Abigail shrieked, slapping her hands over her ears. "Everything you say is a lie!"

She turned and began to escape up the stairs, but her stepfather was right behind her. He caught her arm over the banister and held her so hard that she wanted to scream at him to stop, but she was afraid to.

"I'm telling the truth and you *know* it, Abigail," he said, looking up at her through slanted eyes.

He seemed more like a werewolf than a stepfather to her. Panicking now, she wrenched her arm out of his grip and took off for her bedroom.

"Abby, listen to me!" he yelled from the bottom of the stairs. "Don't run away . . . don't go, Abby! I'm only thinking of you!"

Abigail slammed the door to her room and pulled the chair up to it, even though she knew the chair wouldn't work. Her heart was slamming against her chest like a tennis ball after her best serve as she picked up her phone and hit the speed dial for Onboard Antiques.

No answer. No answer. Her mother must have stopped for coffee somewhere. She ran to her chest of drawers and pulled out all six drawers, then pushed the empty chest up against the door and put all the drawers back in. Not even Superman could push the door open now.

She waited.

After five or ten minutes, her heart slowed down to normal. She tried her mother's number again, but no one answered. But there were no sounds outside her door, either.

She wondered if maybe she was overreacting.

And then a knock, just when she wasn't expecting it! *Bam* went her heart against her chest again.

"Abby, how much longer before you're ready to go? I've got to get to the office for a meeting."

"Five more minutes?" she said faintly from the other side of the door.

"Okey-doke. Hurry up. I'll put out some cereal."

Dear Dad,
I promised Mom that I wouldn't call you, but I didn't say anything about e-mail, and this is kind of an emergency. My stepfather just showed me pictures of where you live and of a lady that you're seeing (she has long blond hair and she wears really, really short skirts) and he told me that you were kicked off the force because you got caught selling coke. The drug, I mean. I told him he was a liar. I was right, wasn't I? He's a liar? Mom said that for a while she was sure that my stepfather played some dirty tricks on her, but it turned out she was wrong and it was really Uncle James, which is totally weird. But anyway, I'm pretty sure I'm right about my stepfather, even if Mom wasn't. Please tell me you weren't kicked off the force for dealing drugs, at least. (I can understand about the blond lady.)

Love, Abigail

After rejection, humiliation. That was Ben's reaction to the e-mail his daughter had sent him half an hour earlier. Even so, the humiliation he felt was nothing compared to the searing hatred he had for the man who was trying to drive a wedge between Ben and her.

Ben picked up the phone to defend himself to Abby but got the damn answering machine. He called Onboard Antiques, but struck out there, too. And meanwhile, he was holed up with his laptop computer in a motel in southern New York outside of Binghamton, about to leave for an interview with Kelly Laringa's mother. Ben's intention, admittedly a long shot, was to find out more about the drowning that had so traumatized Sarann.

He didn't know how, he didn't know why, but the death of Kelly Laringa was tied to the campaign against Sarann. His first inkling of it had come in the rose garden of Laurel Place, when Sarann had rambled on in horror about the drowning during her drug-induced haze. Since then, Ben had made the same connection several times, always when he wasn't focused on it: falling asleep . . . shaving . . . driving between Mass and Connecticut.

He had decided to call the inkling a hunch, and even though his hunches generally didn't pan out (which is why he was getting out of the business of private investigating and back into computers), he had decided to follow up on this one. After tracking down Jeannie Laringa's whereabouts, he had packed a bag and driven out to Binghamton on the offhand chance that she would tell him in person what she wouldn't on the phone: the facts about her daughter's death and her subsequent move to another state.

But first things first. Ben hit the "reply" button above Abby's e-mail and began a mad hunt-and-peck.

Abby,
I tried calling but I got the machine, so this will have
to do. I'll try to answer your questions.

One: I live in an old but pretty nice apartment building, and I have a cousin with a wife you'll love who has boxed my ears good in an effort to make me learn housekeeping. It's working. Two: the long-haired blond woman is someone I saw one and a half times. She's a lot of laughs but no one I ever want to see again. Three: Yes, I was asked to leave the force, but for a crime I didn't do. I was never convicted of it.

And four: I've never lied to you—at first because I didn't care enough to do it, and now because I care too much to do it. I hope that answers your questions. I'm on the road. The new cell phone has turned out to be a dud as well, but I'll keep in touch.

> *Much love,*
> *Your father*

Filled with new outrage, he sent off the e-mail before driving out to Jeannie Laringa.

"You want us to load the sign, too?"

Sarann folded her arms across her tee shirt and considered her beautiful shop shingle, still propped up against the wall where she had set it down. Jimmy never did get around to hanging it outside, which turned out to be just as well; he would've had to take it right back down again. She could still see the scuffmark where Abby had kicked the sign in fury before running out of the shop.

"Take it," Sarann told the movers, turning her back on it. "I don't want it."

Maybe the dealer in New Hampshire who had bought her inventory lock, stock, and incense burners would be able to distress it a little and sell it as a piece of Americana. If not, he could use the thing for kindling; it made no difference to Sarann. When she opened her next shop—and she was absolutely determined to do that—it would not be called Onboard Antiques.

The first thing I'll do is I'll pay Rodger back. Then I'll get another job, and I'll use whatever little I have left from this sale to start over. On my days off I'll go to every yard sale and flea market in New England, and then I'll haul my stuff to the middle of Iowa, as far from water as I can get, and I'll call my shop Heartland Antiques or Far From the Sea or something.

It was a balm of fantasy that made the sting of watching half a year's work being carted out the door seem somehow more bearable. If only it would do the same for the raw, burning pain in her heart.

Ben hadn't called.

Which wasn't surprising. Why would he? This was the second time she'd jerked him around, the second time she'd fled from him into the night. By now he must be finding her tendency to cut and run just a little bit old.

Sarann knew she had handled the encounter in her garden badly; no matter how many times she replayed the scene in her mind, it never came out any better. Ben had to have walked away from there thinking that she'd chosen Rodger over him, but the truth of the matter was that she had chosen her self-respect over either of them.

She wanted to leave her marriage with that intact. God knew she was leaving it with little else. Besides Abby, her self-respect was the only thing that she *could* take with her.

Would Ben understand? Sarann wouldn't know that until she paid off the money that Rodger had fronted, sublet the shop, and found another job. (She'd torn up her prenuptial agreement and handed it back to her husband. A document based on a fraud, she reasoned, had to be fraudulent itself.)

Ben, please, please don't give up on me.

The burliest of the four movers interrupted her reverie. "Okay, now . . . that cement statue," he said, nodding to a five-foot-tall angel. "We can't guarantee delivery in one piece if it ain't crated."

"But I thought *you* were going to do that. The man who came here to do the quote said—"

"No crate, it stays."

"No, honestly—he told me—"

"Mom!"

It was Abby, just dropped off and already yanking the back of Sarann's tee shirt. "I hafta tell you what happened—"

"Honey, I'm *really* busy now," said Sarann, focusing purely on the movers. "No, please! Don't take that box out yet," she called, running after one of them. "I need to go through it first. I didn't expect you guys so early," she explained as the mover dropped the box with a loud thunk.

And a sharp tinkle. She sighed and said, "Because I wanted to make sure that the stemware was well packed."

All the national carriers had laughed when Sarann had called and requested almost instant service; Eezee-Duzit was the only outfit available, and now she knew why.

Abby was still standing, still waiting.

"Is it important?" Sarann asked her daughter, distracted by the thought of having to renegotiate the value of the broken contents. "Can't it wait?"

"Well . . . I guess so," Abby said.

"Good, because—no, no, the card table and chairs aren't going. Those are my husband's," she explained unnecessarily to the kid who was about to haul them off to the truck. "Abby, why don't you run across the street and ask Gloria if she has any crating material? As soon as the movers are done, we'll go out and grab a bite to eat and we'll talk, okay? And then we'll come back here and see if we can clean the paint off the floor."

"What? Why do *we* have to clean it up?" Abby said, her mouth agape at the injustice of it. "*We're* not the ones who messed up the floor."

"Hush," Sarann said with a meaningful glance at the movers. "We're doing it because—because—because I said so. So *don't* give me any long faces."

She turned around and saw a cardboard box sitting on the pavement in the pouring rain. "Aggh! That box is full of silk flowers!"

Chapter 26

FOR THE WIDOW of a groundskeeper, Jeannie Laringa lived in a very nice house indeed: a big, white, multigabled Victorian with fish-scale shingles, a wraparound porch, and one, two, three fireplaces, judging from the brick chimneys towering over the steeply pitched slate roof. Granted, Binghamton, New York, wasn't Bridgehampton, Long Island—but still. The wrongful death suit that the Laringas had brought against Faxton Academy, sponsor of the picnic at which their daughter had drowned, had apparently resulted in a fairly decent settlement.

As he walked from the dirt and gravel drive across a flagstone path that led to the bright blue front door, Ben saw that the paint was beginning to peel in spots and the expansive lawn needed cutting. Mr. Laringa would probably not approve.

He lifted the brass lionhead door knocker and let it come down hard twice, but it was just a formality; a moving curtain in the big bay window had tipped him off that he was being observed. The door opened and Ben faced a woman in her midfifties who once had been a beauty. The years hadn't been kind to her, but there was plenty left to admire: great cheekbones; shadowy gray echoes of thick black hair; eyes of riveting blue under a sweep of long lashes.

Those eyes were wary as she said, "I could have saved you the trip, Mr. McElwyn. I really don't have nothin' new to say. I hardly knew Sarann Johnson. But . . . come in if you want," she said, stepping aside to let him pass.

Ben followed her through a long hall improbably carpeted in brown shag, and into the main parlor, improbably furnished in French Provincial, all of it pretty new. He was willing to bet that the settlement had got the Laringas not only a house, but lots of new stuff to put in it.

But Ben, the new Ben, thought: small comfort.

The widow sat at the doilied end of the sofa and pointed to a brown vinyl recliner arranged at a ninety-degree angle to it. "You can drop it there if you want; that's where my Raymond sat."

Ben dropped it there and said, "I appreciate your seeing me, Mrs. Laringa. I know it must be hard to revisit the past."

She surprised him by saying, "In some ways, it's not. If we talk about Kelly, it's almost like she's still here—you know?"

Ben didn't know. He used to try to talk about his runaway father all the time with his mother, and her answer was always the same: "Suppose we talk about something else."

But he nodded to Kelly's mother anyway, and he smiled, and she sighed and seemed to feel better somehow that he understood.

"She was a good, good kid, my little Kelly," she began without prompting. "My youngest, my only girl, and by far the quietest. Never said boo. She was always off in her own little dream world, maybe because all she had was much older brothers; she didn't know any of 'em all that good. She used to like to dress up and pretend that she was older than she was, trying to get them to notice her as an equal and not just treat her like a kid. Never worked. They'd shoo her away when she tried to hang around them. That was too bad. Plus, I think, myself, that them rich kids at Faxton had no use for her, either, and she felt kind of hurt about that. She never talked about it, but that's what I think."

"She was a student there?" Ben asked, surprised.

"Yeah, can you believe it? And we didn't have to pay a cent of tuition. Not to mention, we had a small house to live in on the edge of the campus. It was a good job that way.

Not much pay, but benefits. Still, we were never going to afford college for Kelly, so what was the use of her learning French?"

She smiled to herself. "Ray did love to brag that his little Kelly was taking a foreign language, though," she said.

"He was proud of her," Ben said sympathetically.

"That he was. Would you like something to drink?" she asked, warming a little. "Lemonade, or coffee?"

Ben declined in a friendly way and brought the conversation back around to Faxton Academy. "You must have been so pleased when your husband found a job there," he suggested, leading her gently along.

"Actually, the job found Ray. He was raking someone's yard and Kelly was helping him bag the leaves, when the headmaster stopped his car in the street and walked right up to Ray and offered him the job. Just like that. At the time, we were living in a real bad place in Gloucester near the docks—the rats!—so Ray jumped at the chance. We didn't even know about the tuition then; just the little house would have been enough. So that was a real surprise, especially since they only gave free tuition on a case-by-case basis, I believe. It was hardly ever done, although maybe that's changed."

The knot in Ben's stomach wrapped itself a little tighter. "And the school had an annual picnic, unfortunately," he said softly.

She nodded in sad agreement. "There were grownups everywhere, but for some reason, Kelly went off on her own. There was a little boat over in the weeds on the other side of the lake. I call it a lake, but it's really just a big pond. Anyway, she untied it and shoved off in it, no one knows why. There were no oars. The boat was old, it was rotted, but she got into it and took off. I've never understood that. Kelly was no boater. She didn't even know how to swim, really. A little, but not really."

Ben didn't have to guess. "The bottom of the boat fell through," he said.

She nodded. "From her weight. It sank and Kelly panicked. Who wouldn't? She started to scream . . . everyone rushed to save her . . . but she was nowhere near the picnic area. It took a long time. Sarann Johnson was the best swimmer; she got there before some of the others, but it was too late. I know she tried; Mr. Bonniface tried; but—"

"The . . . headmaster?"

"Oh, yes, he came from another direction, closer than Sarann, but it didn't matter. Kelly was in a panic, screaming and thrashing . . . they couldn't save her. Almost," she added with a heavy sigh. "But in the end, they couldn't."

It was as if the widow had yanked away mosquito netting that had been hanging in thick folds over the tragic event. After straining to see through it for so long, Ben was almost blinded by the clarity of the picture he had in front of him. Blinded, and stunned.

Breathless from the horrific vision, he said, "They were all three in the water together?"

Rubbing her upper arms as if she were cold, the widow said, "I think so; there was so much confusion. Parts of it seemed to happen so fast; other parts, in slow motion. I do remember this: afterward, Sarann Johnson was as distraught as I was. When they brought my poor baby ashore and . . . and they laid her on the beach . . ."

She was looking, but not looking, at the coffee table in front of her. "I don't know, I took one look at my Kelly and I knew right off . . . she was gone, my baby was gone . . . and I cried and carried on, I know I did. But Sarann Johnson, she and a math teacher kept giving Kelly CPR, she wouldn't give up until the paramedics took over. You know? She wouldn't give up."

"Some people are like that," Ben said. The knot in his

stomach gravitated to his throat. "But it was the right thing
to do."

Mrs. Laringa nodded. "I know that now. They say sometimes the young ones recover. Just . . . not my Kelly."

"So the boat belonged to the Academy, I take it?"

"Yes, and the funny thing was, we didn't even think about
suing. To us it was an accident, pure and simple. But a lawyer read about it in the paper and contacted us and explained
that the boat was what they call an attractive nuisance. And
even though it didn't feel right—well, we sued. But Faxton
didn't hold it against us. They understood. That's what their
insurance was for, Mr. Bonniface told us. They were so good
about it. That's why when the offer to settle come in, we
took it. It was a good offer, my lawyer said. We trusted him.
He was a good lawyer. He moved things along."

"And you ended up in Binghamton—far from Farnham."

"Because I had family here. As soon as Mr. Bonniface
found that out, the first thing he did was look up a real good
agent to find us a house. You know, one that looks out for
the buyer, not the seller. Like I said, he was good about
everything. I can't complain."

"It's a beautiful house," Ben said, searching for something
upbeat to say.

She nodded and said, "Didn't know I'd be spending my
old age in it alone, though. It's too much for me to keep up;
I'm thinking of selling. My husband's gone, my mother who
lived with us for a little while—she's gone. My kids are
spread out all over . . . I didn't even put up a tree last Christmas; I was in Indiana."

She was sad and lonely and she wanted to talk, so Ben
made himself sit still and listen, though he was desperate to
get to a phone.

"My oldest son's in Maryland," she was saying. "He
wants me to move there. I don't know . . . the summers are
so hot down there. Have you been?" she asked politely.

Ben shook his head.

Rodger Bonniface had been in the water. With Kelly.

"But . . . I suppose a person gets used to the heat," she said with a sigh. "You just don't go out in the hot months, that's all."

Kelly had been screaming and thrashing. In the water. With Bonniface—doing what? Trying to hold her. Up? Under? Jesus.

"—lonely. I'm too young to stop living; too old to start, if you know what I mean. Thank God I have my boys. They're good boys. Even Scott. He was the one who came back and lived here a bit. No job, for a pretty long while."

Sarann had been distraught, as much as Kelly's mother. She and a math teacher . . . CPR. Where was Rodger? Off to one side, no doubt coughing and hacking from his efforts to save a little girl from drowning. A heroic attempt; too bad, too bad it failed. That's life; what can you do? Accidents happen.

"—a real rough patch. But they're hopeful that they got it all, and she's already back at her job. She's a nurse, and has a real good attitude. It's my son who couldn't handle her cancer."

She lived in her own little dream world . . . she used to like to dress up and pretend she was older than she was, trying to get her brothers to treat her like an equal.

"I framed the cutest picture of Kelly and her—"

"Really? I'd love to see it," Ben said. He could hardly hear his voice over the pounding of his heart.

"It's on the mantel in the other room. I'll fetch it," said the widow, getting up from the sofa with an eager step and a grateful smile.

Ben stared at the ceiling while he waited, rubbing his hands across the stubble of his beard, trying to convince himself that if he'd been wrong about Rodger the first time, then he could be wrong about Rodger this time. Except that he

was right. Right the first time. Right, now. James was nothing, a noisy niblet that Rodger had dropped in their path to
distract them. Ben had zeroed in on Rodger Bonniface
strictly on instinct—but he'd missed the motive completely.

The motive was Abby. Jesus Christ, the motive was Abby.
Just thinking about it sent chills down his spine. He jumped
up, in a cold sweat to get out of there, get back to Farnham.
He had to get back to Farnham *now*.

"It was taken at Niagara Falls; my one son and his wife
live in Buffalo," said Mrs. Laringa as she came back into the
parlor clutching a silver-framed photograph. She handed Ben
a shot of a young girl posing with an older woman in front
of the roaring falls.

Ben could have been staring at his own daughter. It wasn't
just that the two girls shared black hair and blue eyes and
wristloads of bangles. There was something more than those
superficial similarities that made Ben's heart ache in sympathy and pound in panic: an aura of innocence and naivete
that beamed from the child's face.

Innocent. Naive.

Abby.

"She's very pretty," Ben said softly. He felt a burning
need to have his hands around Rodger's neck. "How old was
she when this was taken?"

"She'd just turned thirteen the week before. It's the last
one I have of her."

Another photograph popped into Ben's head with sudden,
exceptional clarity: a studio portrait of a girl of about the
same age, taken back in the 1940s. He remembered black
hair, beautiful eyes, a tailored dress—but no aura of naivete.
He'd been struck by the arrogance in the child's face when
he saw the vintage photograph hanging among a collection
in the hall of Rodger Bonniface's elegant house, but not until
that moment had he connected the youthful face with the
one, now gelled by Parkinson's disease, that had glared at

him from a wheelchair at the dining room table.

"I'm sorry, Mrs. Laringa. Truly," he said, handing back the photo.

Her smile wobbled a little. "Thank you. I miss her. She'd be graduating from high school now."

"I'm grateful that you were able to see me. I know you didn't have to," he said as they began making their way toward the door.

"It was no bother. I just wish I could've been more help. It's a shame that Sarann is still taking the accident so personally after all this time. I hope you can help her get past it. She did her best. Tell her that for me. Tell her I said hello, okay?"

"You bet," Ben promised.

The widow seemed to want to end on a less melancholy note. "How's your weather out east? It's been real nice here," she said as she got the door for him.

Ben smiled; anyone would think she lived in Texas. "Still pouring cats and dogs when I left."

"Imagine that."

She stood on the porch until he pulled out of the drive, then waved as if he were kin. Ben waved back, feeling another surge of rage toward Rodger Bonniface. He hated him for so many different reasons that he was beginning to lose track of them all. He called Sarann from the first phone he could find and wasn't surprised when the machine kicked in. He called the shop. No answer.

He calculated the distance to Farnham and was overwhelmed by the time involved. Up to Albany . . . then across Massachusetts . . . in rain. Six, seven hours, anyway. Anything could happen in that many hours.

If he touches either of them in any way, I will kill that fuck with my bare hands.

He wondered whether he might not kill him, anyway, just to square up history.

*   *   *

"Abby, for God's sake!" cried Sarann. "Why didn't you tell me this before?"

Abby looked around the other tables in alarm before turning back to her mother in wide-eyed admonition. "Shhh! Everyone can hear!" In a low, exasperated voice she said, "You *told* me to wait until *lunch*!"

"Not for something like this! God! I can't believe he did that," Sarann said, reaching for her bag.

She took out her wallet and pulled out a ten and a five, then threw them on the checkered cloth next to their untouched burgers. "Let's get out of here; we can talk in the car."

Abby whispered, "Mom, nooo, that's even worse; everyone will notice we left without eating."

"You know what? I don't give a shit what people think anymore. We're going. Now."

They breezed past a couple who were dorm parents at one of the Faxton student houses and then almost knocked down Gloria Dijon, in the process of collapsing her huge polka-dotted umbrella before coming into the cafe.

"I saw the movers pulling out as I arrived," Gloria acknowledged with a mournful sigh. "So it's over, I guess."

"Ohhh, no, it's not," Sarann said cryptically as she popped her own umbrella open. "Trust me, it's only just begun."

Sarann was furious that Rodger would try to work on Abby behind her back. She'd been trying so hard to do the right thing, to act with a level of civility that would spare Rodger's reputation—for what? So that he could do something low and slimy like drag out photographs of women Ben had been dating? It was appalling. It was *sick*.

Once in the car, Sarann said to her daughter, "All right. Start at the beginning."

Abby seemed abashed by the depth of her mother's feeling; her answer was measured and brief, too brief to satisfy Sarann. She said, "I want to know *exactly* what he said."

"Well . . . for one thing, he said that hiring a private eye was also your idea," Abby ventured.

"If I agreed to that at all—and I remember feeling queasy about the idea—it was before the carnival. I would never have agreed to it after we saw your father. What else did he say?"

"That I was old enough to know the truth about people."

"Which is true. Except that he's telling you lies."

"And that I was important to him."

"Yeah, right. He acts like it. So . . . you only let him show you the three photos? Good for you, Abby."

"Yeah. But, Mom, he said that Dad was a drug dealer!"

"I've *told* you, Abigail. The cop that your dad worked with was crooked and your father got implicated. And you know why I think that happened? Because your dad would never rat on a partner if he suspected him, no matter how much it cost him personally."

"Was that the right thing to do?"

"Oh, Abby . . . that's such a complicated question. There are times when maybe . . . I don't know . . . but I don't think that letting your partner get away with a crime is right. On the other hand, I'm not a cop. I know they're fiercely loyal to one another."

Abby said quietly, "When *should* you tell on someone?"

"When you know absolutely that something is wrong. At least then."

"Oh."

She sounded as though she'd been given a tough piece of meat to chew on, so Sarann let her chew. Sarann had plenty to chew on herself.

Her mind was made up. She would not stay another night. Not in the attic, not in the basement, not in the house. Rodger could cry and beg and plead and kiss her shoes on the soles for all she cared. She would not, she could not, stay with a man who was mean-spirited, manipulative, and vindictive, no matter how much standing he had in the community. She and Abby were leaving, and the community could think what it damn well pleased.

"Abby, you know how I said we were sticking around until Rodger and I had a chance to work out an arrangement?"

"Uh-huh?"

Sarann switched the window wipers to their highest speed to try to throw off the never-ending rain. "Well, things have changed. This morning changed everything. We don't owe anything to him, not after what he did. We're going back to pack our bags," she announced.

"All riiight!" Abby said in a rousing cheer, pumping the air with her fist.

"Stop that; this is serious, Abigail," Sarann snapped. "Don't think we're leaving Tidewater for any lap of luxury, because that's not going to be the case. You won't be driving around in a Mercedes and going to summer camp and telling time by a thousand-dollar watch—that watch stays behind, by the way."

Her daughter instantly pulled it off her wrist and said, "Here. Take it. I don't even wear a watch."

"You'll need one to keep up with the bus schedule," Sarann said dryly. "I'll get you a Timex."

Abby laughed and said, "At least I won't have to sit on a towel all the way home from soccer practice."

Her joy and relief were infectious. Sarann knew that there would be tough times ahead, times when every nickel mattered, but all she felt now was relief. Relief, and hope. For the first time in nine months, she felt confident that she was doing the right thing.

Abby picked up on her mother's smile.

"We'll be living with Dad, right?"

Sarann felt her cheeks burn hot. "That's all to be determined."

"But you want to, right?"

"Why do you always have to push it?" Sarann said, sighing. She slowed her driving and leaned forward to see the road better. The rain was coming down harder than ever; people were talking about flash-flood warnings.

"Your father and I have . . . powerful feelings for one another," she finally admitted, feeling ridiculously guilty about it.

"How powerful? You love Dad, don't you? *I* do," Abby added serenely.

Sarann said quietly, "Yes, I love him."

"Then what's the problem?"

"For one, I happen to be married to someone else."

"But not for long."

"True. But it makes things a little complicated right now."

Abby pondered for a while, then said, "How long does it take to get a divorce in Massachusetts?"

"Oh, Abby. That is not today's problem," Sarann said. "Today's problem is just to pack some things and get out."

"Where will we go?" her daughter asked in a voice less breezy than before. Presumably the cold reality of imminent homelessness was beginning to sink in.

"We'll stay at an inn, for tonight."

"Will they take pets?"

"We'll find one that does. We'll have to take a cab there. After tonight, I don't know."

"We don't have any furniture."

"That's right."

"Do we have any money?"

"Not a whole lot."

Abby sat back and considered.

After a moment, she said simply, "I was right. We'll be moving in with Dad. Um . . . speaking of Dad, there's one other thing."

They were nearly at the house and Sarann didn't see

Rodger's car in front of it. He wasn't due home until five, but you never knew. With a sigh of relief, she said, "What other thing?"

"I e-mailed Dad this morning—no, before you yell at me, wait. Because of what *happened*. I told him about the photographs and I . . . might have said something to him, like, is it true or not."

"Abby, I *asked* you not to—"

"Call. Not to call. Nothing about e-mail."

Incredible. How could a kid be so smart and yet so clueless?

Because there were times when it suited her, that's how. Sarann said, "I suppose you'd better check your e-mail as soon as you get inside, then."

"Like—"

"Don't say it, Abby. Don't say 'duh' or I will have to remove your tongue."

Abby giggled and was out of the car before it came to a stop. She didn't bother putting up the hood to her rain gear but took off at a gallop for the front door, trying to outrun the downpour. By the time she let herself in, her hair was hanging in wet wiggly snakes around her face. She didn't care; she was on an adventure.

Sarann, on the other hand, was in a state of turmoil. She had had a plan, a reasonable plan: liquidate her inventory, pay off Rodger, find a job, get an apartment. Everything in due course. Instead she was going to grab whatever she could, pile a few bags and boxes into a cab, and never look back.

She had a couple of hours to do it in. Tops.

Chapter 27

BY THE TIME Sarann got inside, Abby had cranked up her computer and was screaming excitedly down the stairs, "I have e-mail, Mom! He answered already!"

They read it together. Standing next to her daughter, reading as eagerly as she, Sarann was hard-pressed not to stroke the screen. She wanted badly to feel Ben's reassuring touch, but that wasn't possible; his reassuring words would have to do.

"Did you see how he signed it, Mom?" Abby asked shyly.

"Yes, honey. I did," said Sarann. She pulled her daughter close in a squeeze.

" 'Much love, Dad.' "

"Yes, honey. I see."

Abby looked up, blue eyes shining. "Aren't you glad I found him?"

"I suppose you want a medal?" Sarann asked with a wry smile.

"Not a medal. Just a new last name."

But that reminded both of them of the one they had, and the exquisite moment that they were sharing popped and disappeared like a bubble of soap.

"We'll have to pack quickly," Sarann said, returning to the crisis at hand. "I'd rather avoid a scene. Take the clothes you absolutely can't live without; go heavy on the summer stuff. Pack a couple of your good sweaters. Don't take any shoes that don't fit. Don't take any jeans that you *might* someday wear. Don't take anything if you don't absolutely love it."

Abby listened open-mouthed. "Aren't we gonna get the rest of our *clothes* back, even?"

"We might. We might not. Abby, you have to understand: this is not a good situation. It could get very ugly very fast, so stop wasting time chatterboxing."

"*You're* the one who's chatterboxing," Abby said, jumping up from her desk chair. "I know exactly what to pack."

"Good. Don't use the rolling luggage that you got from Mrs. Bonniface for graduation. That stays behind."

Abby's face fell. "Oh, but—"

"No. Use duffel bags. Shopping bags. Garbage bags, if you have to."

Abby indulged in a single sigh of protest, and then she got to work.

As for Sarann, she was like a homeowner who's been told to evacuate before a flood—and the relentless, drumming rain that drowned out every sound but the sound of itself simply deepened that illusion.

Tidewater might be safe and on high ground; but Sarann felt anything but. There was something cowardly about fleeing before Rodger got home, but if she stayed until then, it would end in a knockdown, drag-out argument, and she wanted to spare Abby and herself the trauma.

So she went through one drawer after another, making decisions which—after the one to leave—didn't seem hard at all. The sexy nighties stayed; she despised the associations. The lacy bras and the high-cut panties, same deal. The fancy blouses, silk dresses, double-strand pearls and Italian shoes— why? What use had she for any of them anymore? She had probably gone to her last faculty reception for a while. She packed her Little Black Dress, though, because every woman needed a little black dress. There was such a thing as New Year's Eve, even for the working poor.

She went into the bathroom and began emptying her cabinet of cosmetics, hair dryer, curling iron—simple things, easily replaced; but the same impulse that made her cling to the little black dress made her want to be able to look nice tomorrow for . . . whoever. She picked up her pointy tweezers and saw that the tips were bent, and then she remembered Ben's explanation for getting a broken piece of toothpick out of a lock.

She dropped the tweezers, with loathing, into the garbage can.

Before long, the front hall was piled with half a dozen duffel and shopping bags filled with sweaters and clothing. A huge T. J. Maxx bag held a menagerie of new stuffed animals, among them a small panda. In exchange for their booty, they left four house keys sitting on the hall table.

"That's all we can handle," Sarann told her daughter. "Go through your computer discs and take any that you want, and I guess any musical CDs. We'll try to pick up a player for you somewhere."

Abby was aghast. "I'm not leaving my *computer* behind, am I?"

"Have you been listening to anything I've said?" Sarann snapped, becoming more tense with every sweep of the minute hand. "We're leaving the way we came in."

"But we had more than *this*," said Abby, pointing to the pathetic mound in the hall. "We had furniture, a TV, a stereo, blankets and pillows, phones—we had stuff!"

"All donated. Stop whining. We'll get more *stuff*," Sarann said caustically. "You may not realize this, but there are kids in Africa who don't have e-mail accounts."

"Right, and neither do their friends. It all works out!"

"Abigail, I am not going to stand here arguing with you," Sarann said. She scanned the gallery of photos on the wall and unhooked one of a younger Abby in a petting zoo, ignoring the wedding photo next to it.

She packed the zoo shot, then said to her daughter, "If you're going to howl every time you feel a little pinch, then heaven help you in the future. Make up your mind right now. Do you want to stay here, or do you want to start over?"

It was, of course, a rhetorical question. Abby was going to start over if Sarann had to shoot her out of a cannon.

Out came the lower lip, down went her gaze. "Start over," she muttered.

"Fine. Get your discs. I just have to grab some files and then I'll call a—"

Sarann never got the chance to call a cab or anyone else. The door opened and Rodger walked in. He dumped his dripping black umbrella with a thunk into the copper stand, smiled, and said, "Wow, it's really coming down out there."

Abby, still standing on the third step, turned and made a break for her room. Sarann, shocked, said, "It's only four; why are you here?"

They were like some twisted sitcom, where father-knows-best arrives and says, "Honey, I'm home!" in a cheerful, loving voice and all the women run away screaming.

Rodger said calmly, "I was concerned about the basement taking on water; the ground's so soaked."

But he was looking at the bags piled up in the hall, and it was obvious from the way his chin lifted ever so slightly and his brows twitched, ever so slightly, that he knew exactly why they were there.

In a strained voice, Sarann said, "Rodger, you know it's not working out. I told you that the other night, I explained it all to you . . ."

"Yes, you did," he said with a thoughtful nod. "I remember your words exactly: 'I don't want to put you in an awkward position, or embarrass you in the community.' "

"I did say that," she acknowledged. "And I meant it."

He took off his glasses and took out a handkerchief from the inside pocket of his linen jacket, then began wiping the lenses dry. "And you think that running off with him three days later won't be awkward? Won't be embarrassing?"

"I'm not running off with him," Sarann said, defending herself. Which was ridiculous; she wasn't the one who had to defend herself. How did she always end up that way?

"You'll forgive me if I don't believe you," he said. He slid his glasses back over his ears and refocused his look of contempt on her. "You've been with him alone. Abby's been with him—alone. The odds are good that I'm right and you're lying."

It was that word "lying" that cut the last thin thread binding Sarann to him. She had tried her best to atone for her initial deception when she married him. But the only lies she'd seen lately were the ones being hurled at her from over the Bonniface fence.

"Think what you like, Rodger," she said wearily. "It doesn't matter anymore to me." She began heading for the sitting room, where she'd left her address book.

"You won't get away with this," Rodger threw out behind her. "You won't get Abby."

Where had she left the book? Not by her chair? Now she remembered: by the kitchen phone. She turned to walk out again, but he was standing in the door, blocking her way.

The sight of him brought back the sound of him. "What . . . did you say?" she asked, recalling his last words as if they'd been whispered from some shore across the Atlantic.

"I'll fight for her custody," he said with eerie calm.

She was confused. Whose custody? *Abby's*? "You can't be serious," she said, brushing the thought aside. "Please move. You're in my way."

"Get used to it, Sarann. I plan to be there from now on." He closed the door behind them and threw the bolt.

"You're *not* serious. Rodger, you're not," she insisted. "This is insane. I'm her mother. No one would give you custody of Abby. Who would do that?"

"Any rational judge. Ask yourself: who has standing in the community? Who's the more stable element? Who has

vast experience with children—and can offer superb educa-
tional opportunities? Who has the resources to give a bright,
motivated child everything she needs? Who has an extended
family in the area, all of them preeminent in the field of child
care? Who, in other words, has the child's best interests at
heart? That's what a judge will ask."

"Me," Sarann whispered, stunned. "I do."

His chuckle sounded genuinely amused, which made it all
the more chilling. "Let me put this another way. Who told
everyone the whopper about Abby's birth father? Who tried
to block her own daughter's discovery of him? Who's been
acting very erratically, so much so that she felt obliged to
check herself into a treatment center for counseling and therapy—just last week? As for the suitability of the father—if
he is the father—I have a thick file, with photographs, that
suggests there are better choices."

Sarann took three steps back from him, as if she'd wandered too close to an open sewer. "You miserable pig," she
said, choking back a wave of fear and revulsion. "Abby
would never choose to stay with you."

"Are you sure? Her allowance right now isn't that much
less than what you'll be able to take home from whatever
low-paying job you manage to land—assuming that you can
find a job, with your history of mental health. After you lose
whatever low-paying job you have—and you will—because
you've had to go to court one too many times, Abby may
well become disenchanted. No kid who's reached spending
age likes to be poor."

Sarann's once-rising spirits crashed and burned. She
stared at the floor between them as if it held the smoldering
debris of her hopes. "Don't do this, Rodger. I'm begging you.
Don't. You can't hate me that much."

"I don't hate you. I love Abby."

She lifted her gaze in anguish. "Why do you *care*? We
were only with you for nine months!"

"True. That's a problem. We may have to share custody—unless something happens to you."

She reared back. "Are you *threatening* me?"

"Do you think I'm threatening you?" he asked blandly.

"I'll have you arrested!"

"With your record of instability and paranoia? I don't think so."

Reduced almost to speechlessness, she sputtered, "That—that isn't how our laws work!"

He smiled. "Now, that's where you people are so amusing: in your ability to believe in equal justice for all. Really, it's charming. Just delightful."

The coil that had been winding itself more and more tightly inside of Sarann for months suddenly snapped; with a cry of frustration she lunged at him. She intended to pummel but, like a bobcat protecting her kit, she scratched him instead, bloodying his cheek. The sight of the wound was more familiar than shocking; she stepped back, breathing heavily, waiting to see how she could best hurt him again. What would it take to stop him? A knife? A gun? What would it take?

He favored her with a grimly pleasant smile and then walked over to a carved giltwood mirror that she knew had cost him over twelve thousand dollars, and he studied his cheek the way he might have done if he'd nicked himself shaving.

"Thank you," he said, stretching his face to reveal three long grooves, each of them dripping red onto his jacket and shirt. "This will do nicely."

Sarann blinked at his response. What kind of man was he? He wasn't human. She was being outmaneuvered and outwitted by something out of her nightmares. She watched as he pressed his hand to his cheek, then appraised the blood-marks on his palm and fingers. He walked toward her. She stepped back again and bumped into the closed door behind her.

Smiling, he held out his bloodied hand and reached for her face. She tried to avert his touch, but he made contact with her cheek, smearing her with his blood. Her revulsion was intense; she felt an urge to throw up. Her eyes were closed against the horror of him, and she was unprepared for what happened next: he caught her wrists and pinned them against the door behind her, then drew close and licked his blood from her cheek.

"Oh, God, Rodger . . . don't," she whispered. She was dizzy with nausea.

"Ah, Sarann . . . this is loveplay between mates, no? You don't find this erotic?"

"Don't."

"One more lick. You taste so good."

"I said—*don't!*" she screamed, suddenly yanking free of his grip and pushing him away from her, catching him off balance.

He stumbled backward and fell, but nothing in him broke, nothing died. In a flash he was on his feet again, coming at her, catching her by the arms, this time more securely.

She tried to whirl out of his grip but he held her fast. Her heart was leaping against her ribs, her head was on fire; but her revulsion was easily as great as her fear. She had *married* this thing!

"Get *away* from me!" she cried, but she needed garlic, she needed crossed sticks. He wasn't human.

"Think about it, Sarann, think about the money," he kept muttering. He was like a crazed and drooling brute, and he absolutely terrified her.

Behind her, the door to the sitting room suddenly exploded inward, sending yet another shock wave through her. She turned to see someone lunging at Rodger, pulling him away from her. It happened so fast, so definitively, that it

was a second or two before she realized that it wasn't the
vanguard of a SWAT team, but Ben McElwyn, appearing
from nowhere. He caught Rodger by the neck with one hand
and slammed him backward into the carved giltwood mirror,
which got dislodged from its hook and dropped to the floor
and shattered before falling face forward, sending gilded bits
of wood flying.

Whether it was from the force of the blow or the sound
of money breaking, Rodger sobered instantly. Sarann
watched in amazement as he metamorphosed from demon to
human, all in one easy smile.

"I'm sorry if you took offense when I asked you to stay,
Sarann," he said, looking wounded, which of course he was.
"There was no need to draw blood."

She turned away from him. "Ben, please, let's go."

Ben stepped between Rodger and her like a bodyguard
and followed her out to the hall.

Abby was there waiting, looking aghast. "What did he do
to your *face*, Mom?" she said, and she burst into tears.

"Nothing; he didn't do anything, honey. He didn't hurt
me," Sarann said, trying to ward off an attack of hysterics.
"Help your Dad pack the car while I wash my face clean."

"Are you sure you're all right?" Ben asked Sarann, ignoring Rodger behind them.

"I'm all right."

"I'll wait out here."

Sarann went into the powder room and slapped water on
her face, then rubbed her cheek fiercely with a handtowel.
She refused to look in the mirror, afraid of what she might
see there: horror and stupidity and disillusionment.

But at least it's over, she thought. *The worst is over.*

Ben was still standing guard with one arm around Abby,
but Rodger was nowhere to be seen. Sarann felt a rush of
panic. What if he was calling someone—child and family

services, Laurel Place, the police, his mother? She didn't know. He had money. She didn't know.

"Leave everything; let's just get out of here," she said anxiously to Ben; she was thinking like a fugitive again.

"We're taking your bags," Ben said calmly, and suddenly Sarann remembered. He wasn't afraid of the same things that she was—of Rodger and of all those different authorities. Ben was afraid of commitment.

And apparently not even of that.

"Moll-leee . . . Moll-leee . . . here, Molly Molly Molly . . ."

Looking worried and bedraggled under the hood of her yellow rain gear, Abigail came up to Ben and said, "She could be anywhere, Dad. She gets really upset when there's a commotion."

Ben wished he had an umbrella, he wanted to wring out his socks. He wanted to book a room, he wanted meat and a cup of coffee. He wanted, desperately, to tell Sarann what he'd learned about the tragic end of Kelly Laringa. He wanted to do a hundred things, but searching for a runaway cat in the pouring rain was not one of them.

Sarann came up to them and held her umbrella over Ben's head and hers as they talked about what to do next. It seemed anticlimactic, after their grand exit, to park the car a little down the road and go back looking for a cat, but that's what they'd done. Sarann had told Abby that they would come back tomorrow, but Abby had been inconsolable. She blamed herself for leaving the front door open after she let Ben in.

So here they were: three soggy people, one umbrella, and no cat.

"I think we need to get settled somewhere for the night, Abby," Sarann told her. "Molly won't go far in this rain."

"Then why isn't she coming when I call?" Abby argued. "I've been all up and down."

"I'll drive back tonight and look some more," Ben offered.

"She won't come if a stranger calls. She doesn't even come for Mom, just me."

"It's true, Ben."

"Okay, we'll be here at the crack of dawn, then," he told Abby. "Y'know," he added, "I feed a stray who comes through my window from the fire escape; that cat would be downright embarrassed if we made this kind of fuss over him."

That got a very tentative smile out of her.

"She'll be fine," Sarann said soothingly. "Cats are more resourceful than dogs; everyone knows that."

Ben wasn't quite sure how Sarann's argument turned the tide, but it did; Abby felt reassured enough to give her parents permission to leave the scene. They drove away with all of them keeping their eyes peeled for an orange-and-white prima donna who could use, Ben suspected, a little attitude adjustment.

After being turned away from a couple of bed-and-breakfasts near Gloucester, they lucked out and found one with two rooms that shared a bath between. The Steppe Inn was a gray-shingled, rambling structure girdled in roses and daylilies, all of them droopy and flattened by the nonstop rain.

The inn was small and out of the way and, even in the present circumstances, Ben thought, charming and romantic.

"I wouldn't mind living in a place like this," he said as the innkeeper led them up creaky stairs to their rooms.

"The Steppes are retiring soon," the innkeeper told them. "Make 'em an offer."

Abby gasped and said, "Dad—*could* we?"

"Uhh . . ."

"Abigail, for Pete's sake."

"Maybe let's hold a turn for the moment," Ben said.

Yikes. He was going to have to watch what he wished for around this kid.

The rooms were fine. This was no designer version of old-fashionedness, but the real thing: wallpaper a little on the timid side, furniture that could have come out of his grandmother's house, braided rugs whose colors had blended together after years of wear. Through the sheer curtains he could see a blinking light in the dark, off in the distance. They'd have a water view, come daylight.

Abby and Sarann took the room with the queen-sized bed; he took the one with the double. Sarann sat on the edge of the chenille bedspread in the women's room, and Ben could see that the events of the day were catching up with her. Abby, on the other hand, was busy opening drawers and checking out the complimentary soap.

"Why don't you two shower and clean up while I find us some food," he suggested. "You'll feel a lot better. I'll take my shower after we eat."

It was starting to hit him where they were and why. It felt oddly, wonderfully intimate to be on neutral ground with Sarann, never mind the circumstances. Ben felt an unexpected surge of entirely, *entirely* inappropriate lust—until Abby popped back out of the bathroom and said, "Look what I found!" and held up a foil-wrapped condom.

Ben looked one way.

Sarann looked the other.

Abby said with a straight face, "How come the Hilton didn't put these in our room when we were in New York, Mom?"

"Someone left that behind. Throw it out. And wash your hands."

Abby walked back into the bathroom murmuring, "This place is so cool."

So much for the surge. Ben cleared his throat.

"Chicken or burgers?" he asked.

Chapter 28

WHEN BEN GOT back with his supplies, he saw that the doors on both sides of the shared bathroom were wide open, making the two bedrooms a suite.

He liked that.

"Soup's on," he called over, dumping four different bags on the small round table in a corner of his room.

Sarann walked in, grinning at the haul. "When I said I could eat a horse, I didn't think you were actually going to bring one back."

"I got wine," Ben said. "For the Quarter Pounders, a full-bodied, complex, and if I may say so, exceptionally balanced Cabernet. For the McChicken, a Chardonnay: full-bodied as well, but also—it says—buttery and smooth."

He took out the two bottles of wine, a corkscrew, a six-pack of Classic Coke and a six-pack of Diet. In the shopping bag were a bag of Ruffles, a can of Cheese Balls, a bag of pretzels, and two cans of Pringles, because he liked Pringles and it was a long drive back to Connecticut, which is where he assumed but could not swear that they'd be going the next day.

"Pringles!" said Abby, rifling through the bag.

Good thing he got two.

"I also got a *New York Times*, a *Newsweek* and a *People*. And a *Seventeen*; is that too old for you, Abby?"

"No," she said politely, "but they have all the Harry Potters in the library downstairs."

"Oh, *well*. In *that* case—" he said, and he tossed the magazine over his shoulder, making Abby laugh, which he found that he loved doing.

Sarann, on the other hand . . .

"For you," he said, pulling out a cellophane-wrapped bunch of flowers that he'd bought at the market with the Pringles. "Because some days are better than others."

"Thank you," she said softly. Her lashes fluttered down and then came back up, and Ben thought, *yes*; that's what he loved doing for Sarann.

Sarann replaced artificial flowers in a vase with his real ones, while Abby passed out the food. Ben got another armchair from the other bedroom, and he and Sarann sat in those while Abby ate on the rug with the copy of *People*, which happened to feature a teenaged hunk on its cover, spread out in front of her. The talk at dinner was easy and neutral—nothing a twelve-year-old couldn't handle.

But Ben knew things that had to be said, and soon. How did parents handle the X-rated stuff? The answer was pretty obvious: they talked about it in bed. But bed for Ben and Sarann clearly wasn't an option. He began to get restless, waiting for Abby to become bored and leave.

Sarann picked up on his edginess. "Abby, it's late and your dad looks wiped—"

"No, he doesn't," said Abby, glancing up at her father.

"I think it's time we moved over to the other room," Sarann said quietly.

Abby seemed to do a quick assessment of the new social configuration. She looked confused, but not as confused as Ben felt. All Ben knew was that Sarann was calling the shots, at least for tonight.

Still, things had to be said.

"Sarann, I'd like to talk to you for a couple of minutes before you turn in," he said. There was nothing lighthearted in the request.

She picked up on that, as well. "Sure. Abby? Scram."

Abby pulled a comically long face and, scooping up the discarded *Seventeen*, came up to Ben and threw one arm around his shoulder. " 'Night, Dad," she said, kissing him on the cheek.

"Good night, honey. Don't let the bedbugs bite."

For some reason, Abby thought that was hysterical; she left laughing, closing both bathroom doors behind her.

Ben said to Sarann, "I guess I'm going to have to get some newer material."

"She adores you," Sarann said simply. She locked her hands and stretched her arms out before her. "So. Wassup?"

She smiled at him over the unopened Cabernet and the barely touched Chardonnay and Ben thought, I can't do this. I can't.

"Sarann, you know how we've been playing Ping-Pong over the gaslighting—it was James, it was Rodger, it was James?"

The smile faded. She nodded.

"It was Rodger."

"After today, I'm inclined to agree," she said in wry understatement.

"That's not how I know." He got up and sat on the bed nearer the chair she was in, so that he could lower his voice even more. She watched him with obvious, mounting alarm. He hated, *hated* what he had to say to her.

"I saw Jeannie Laringa today."

She sucked in her breath through parted lips and held it. Her eyes got a blank look to them; clearly she was frightened. When she exhaled again, it was in a series of distressed pants. She bit her lip, trying to keep herself in control.

"How is she?" she asked, her eyes welling with tears.

Ben was putting her through it again. Sarann, the woman he loved—he was hurting her so that he could try to get Rodger put away, despite the fact that the odds were long. But Sarann was key; no one else.

He tried to smile; he failed. "She's sad. Lonely. Her husband's gone, now, too."

"Oh, no . . ." The first tear fell, followed by a thin stream of others.

"We talked about the drowning . . ."

Sarann nodded, not even trying to wipe away the tears.

He had to take her back to that place, and instinctively he knew that the best way to do it was to speak in a voice that was soft and low and soothing. All that was missing was a swinging watch on a chain.

"She told me how hard you tried to save Kelly . . . how you wouldn't give up on her . . . she was very grateful . . . she wanted me to tell you that, Sarann . . . how grateful she was."

Tears were streaming freely now. Sarann didn't see Ben, didn't see anything around her. She was somewhere else, in that terrible place, and Ben was encouraging her to stay there. His own pain from watching her was acute, but he kept his voice low and loving and utterly sympathetic as he said, "Jeannie Laringa showed me a photograph of Kelly, with her aunt. At Niagara Falls."

Sarann said in a trancelike whisper, "The water was splashing . . . I couldn't even see her . . . she kept going under . . . we couldn't seem to get hold of her . . ."

No turning back. Ben forced himself to go on. "Rodger was in the water with you . . . ?"

Sarann nodded violently and began panting again, hiccuping her response. Her eyes darted from left to right, as if there was too much to view on the screen of her memory. "He wasn't with the rest of us . . . he was at Holden House, he said. But I saw him as I was swimming out . . . he came from the direction of the Laringas' cottage, not from Holden House."

She frowned and shook her head in one last, obvious effort to turn off the screen. But she was too far into it; she kept watching.

"He got to Kelly before I did . . . he got to her and he was grabbing her . . . and she was screaming and . . . and, oh, no, no, she was trying to hit him, lashing out at him . . . *now* I remember, now I understand . . . she scratched his face . . . oh, dear God, poor Kelly, poor Kelly . . . she scratched his face and later he had the marks from it. He kicked me . . . and I got sick and dizzy and I almost went under . . . he kicked me in the stomach, in my ribs . . . I had a bruise, I was all bruised . . . and later I thought, I thought it was because he was trying so hard to save Kelly . . . oh, my God," she said, clearly shocked.

She bowed her head. In a flat, heart-wrenching whisper, she said, "He was drowning her."

And she broke down in muted, shuddering sobs.

Ben slid to his knees and put his arms around her. He held her. He stroked her hair. He said, "It's all right, it's all right. He'll pay, Sarann. He'll pay."

She looked up at Ben in agony and confusion. "How? *How*? Kelly is dead."

"I know," he said. "I know. Here, sit by me. Let me hold you."

She left the armchair for the bed and buried her head in his shoulder as he held her close, rubbing her shoulder, whispering words of comfort. They stayed that way a long time, each of them aware that Kelly was gone and that Abby was in the next room.

After a while, Sarann said in a low, dull voice, "It was Rodger, not me, who lowered the crib bar . . . I heard a sound . . . but I was reading a book, *The Perfect Storm*, and I was on the boat—you know? I was in the storm; the sound was on the boat, not in the nursery." She sighed and murmured, "I'll never read a book like that again."

Ben smiled and held her more closely and said, "Sure you will."

"He was willing to risk his own niece," she said after another long silence. "To make me think I was crazy."

Another silence. And then: "He didn't want to put me away, not for the long run. He wanted me to kill myself. I know they thought about that possibility at Laurel Place; it was obvious from their questions."

And finally, the ultimate realization. "He wanted Abby. He wanted our daughter. But she would have resisted him. She would have ended up like . . . Kelly."

"It's not going to happen, Sarann. I promise," Ben said.

She nodded into his shoulder. "Ironic, isn't it?" she murmured. "I was so busy monitoring my own so-called madness . . . that I wasn't paying attention to his." She shuddered. "I only hope that Molly stays out all night; I don't want him getting his hands on her."

Ben tried to reassure her. "He knows that he overplayed his hand. He'll tread carefully now."

Sarann sat up suddenly. "But—he won't!" she whispered with new urgency. "He's going to fight for Abby, he said that!"

In a low and frightened tone Sarann repeated the arguments, the threats, the twisted reasoning that Rodger had presented earlier. When she was done, Ben said, "Maybe we should be grateful to him for handing us the game plan."

"*If* that's his plan. He probably has another plan altogether!"

Ben smiled and said, "Sarann, you're giving him too much credit."

"Because he's evil! Evil people are smarter than good ones!"

"No, they're not," he argued. "They're just more evil."

It was almost impossible to convince her that they were safe, and that was Ben's fault, he knew. Eventually—after the last check to be sure that Abby was in bed and asleep—Sarann came back into Ben's room and said exhaustedly, "We should get some sleep. I'm more and more worried about Molly."

Ben took Sarann in his arms and held her one last time. "We'll go before breakfast. We'll find her. And after that, we'll put Rodger away. You can bet on it."

He tilted her face toward him and kissed her softly. "Good night. I love you. And Abby. I won't let anything happen to either of you." He smiled and added, "I can't believe my luck. Thank God for the Internet."

Sarann laughed and kissed him back, just as wistfully. When she left him for the other room, she seemed reasonably comforted.

Dog-tired and ready for sleep, Ben finally showered, pulled back the covers, and collapsed into bed. And that's where he lay, tossing and turning and wide awake for the next couple of hours. His thoughts and emotions were all over the map, but the place they came back to most often was Tidewater. It was aptly named, he thought: beautiful on the surface, oozing slime beneath. The old-timers had a name for the water that ebbed from the shore with every tide: garbage water. That about summed up the situation.

Ben was not a religious man. He'd never been very confident about divine retribution, but he had a real good feel for the man-made kind. All he had to do was get Rodger Bonniface sent off to prison, and the inmates there would take care of the rest: the worst one among them spat on a child molester.

He stared at the ceiling, trying to will away the steady flow of anger and vile thoughts that flowed in and out of his consciousness. He had to sleep . . . had to be there for the woman and the child he loved . . . he had to sleep.

He heard the door on their side of the bathroom open and close and then, in a flashback to a time long ago and far away, he heard the one on his side of the bathroom open and close.

He reached over and switched on a lamp.

"No," Sarann said, mouthing the word.

He turned it back off, but not before noting that she was wearing nothing but a thin short gown with two thin straps. It was the most he'd seen of her in nearly thirteen years, and it made him instantly want to see more.

But that was not to be. The room was pitch-black, and silent except for the steady drone of the rain. He stayed propped on his elbow, ready for anything, hoping for one thing.

She sat on the edge of the bed and leaned close to his ear, giving him the blissful chance to inhale the scent of Sarann nearly naked as she whispered, "Move over."

Done. He slid a little, but only a little, to the far side and held up the blanket for her. With a little shiver, she got in bed and lay along the length of him, face-to-face. He dropped the blanket down, coccooning them in their own sweet warmth, and he let his arm enfold her.

"Sarann . . ." he whispered.

She pressed her fingers to his lips and in the faintest possible voice said, "Shhh. No talk."

Because of Abby, possibly; but there seemed to be more to it than that. There had been so much talking, so much theorizing, and what was the point? How could you second-guess the devil?

Sarann leaned close to Ben's ear and whispered simply, "Erase him from me."

True to her wishes and to his desire, he stayed absolutely silent as he guided her gently onto her back and, with a slow, tender determination, rolled her nightgown up over her breasts. With his mouth and his tongue, he caressed her nipples in turn, lightheaded from the pure bliss of it, aware, despite Sarann's silence, that he was driving her up and up with hunger; and then he decided, and she did, too, that the nightgown would have to go. Even one thin and crumpled layer between them was too much. He wanted all of her; he wanted to give all of himself.

She slipped off her nightgown and he got rid of his boxers, and then they were right: skin to skin and heart to heart, the steady beat of the rain cleansing the world around them, at least for tonight.

Erase him from me, she had whispered. Ben could easily have implored her to do the same for him. He had fought against evil for most of his life; with fists and guns and with the law at his side, and sometimes without. But the way of love was new to him, and he was astounded by its potential. He loved Sarann with his whole heart, and he loved his little girl. If they, in turn, loved others, could it work like an emotional chain letter? He didn't know. He was cynical enough to doubt it, in love enough to try it.

Without a word, he kissed Sarann, a long, deep kiss as humble as it was erotic, because it was she who had taught him the way out of the wilderness. He had wandered around in it for more years than he cared to count, wanting to do the right thing without knowing how. Now he knew, and it was because of her example. And her love. And their child.

Sarann, Sarann, I will love you forever, he thought, telegraphing his pledge with his touch, his kiss, and finally, his wet slide into depths, all kinds of depths, that he had never known before.

He heard and felt her shuddering exhale against his throat; it was sweet music to him, and it left him aching to hear the rest of her song. With a slow slide out, a slower slide in, he played her, lifting to a higher and higher plane on the sound of her sighs. In absolute quiet, they were achieving perfect harmony. It was an erotic high unlike anything he'd ever known before.

He felt every ripple and squeeze around him, every lift and fall beneath him, the tips of her breasts . . . the strands of her hair against his cheek as she turned from his kiss, thirsty for air, and then came back for more. He inhaled every aspect of her scent: the inn's plain soap, the trace of her perfume, the sultry richness of her skin in the humid air. He tasted her mouth, so much more complex, full-bodied, and smooth than any Cabernet could ever claim to be.

And all in mind-bending, erotic silence. He was wild with love for her, wild to have her, and as much as he wanted to drag it out, he couldn't. The slow slides became a regular rhythm and then a hard, pumping scramble to climax. His own shuddering sigh came just after hers—as deep, as intense. And a dozen years overdue.

Their collapse was complete, their silence, almost stunning. After a long, long moment, he propped himself on his elbows and tried to make out the features of her face, but the room was truly pitch-black. Was she satisfied? He thought she must be, but . . . was she satisfied?

Balancing on his elbow, he skimmed the features of her face lightly with his fingertips, trying to read it as a blind man would. Her cheeks were high, her lips taut: She was smiling. He felt her kiss on his fingers, and then a playful nip.

He grinned. Satisfied.

He was reluctant to move because he knew she would leave, but even he understood that Sarann couldn't plausibly be in the bathroom all night. So he rolled onto his side and sure enough, she stood up. Before she left, she bent down for one last, wonderfully silent kiss, and then she was gone. Ben wondered whether he had dreamed the whole thing. But then he heard water running, and the other door open and close, and after that, only the sound of the rain.

In ten more seconds he was asleep, and he stayed that way until dawn.

Chapter 29

"IT JUST WON'T *quit*," Abby said in awe. She sounded like Ben the time he visited an ex-cop in Seattle and didn't see the sun for twelve straight days.

Ben wasn't happy about the weather, either. There had been flash flooding in some of the river creeks—swollen by rain and a series of high tides on Essex Bay—and he didn't have a clue whether Molly was one of those cats who never wandered far from the hearth. Nor did he dare ask. All he could do was hope.

Sarann was working her spin. "If Molly's not inside the house, she's probably curled up in the garage."

"If the doors are open. Mom, if Molly wanted to come inside and if she was meowing, do you think he'd still make her stay outside all night?" Abby asked. She sounded as if she might prefer the number-two option.

Sarann said over her shoulder, "I honestly don't know, honey."

They were about to find out. Bonniface's BMW was still parked behind Sarann's ex-Mercedes on the graveled area in front of the house. Sarann and Abby saw his car, too; the tension level rose perceptibly.

"The doors are open!" Abby said, pointing to a restored carriage house set to the side and the back of Tidewater. "I'll bet she's in there."

"Sarann, I think it would be better if you stayed here," Ben suggested.

"You're right," she said. "I'm a red flag to him now."

So she stayed in the car with the engine running and the car parked on the road, while Ben and Abby checked the carriage house before coming up empty and having to back-track to the main house.

They knocked and the door opened almost immediately. Bonniface was on his way out, umbrella in hand. The look he gave them was neither friendly nor hostile, merely polite, as if he were confronted with two strangers who had lost their way and were asking directions.

"No, I haven't seen her," he said in answer to Abby's question. "Have you looked in back?"

"Yes; she's not there."

"I'm really sorry, Abby; it's a shame that she ran off." He added sympathetically, "Pretty rotten timing, wasn't it?" and even Ben was ready to swear that he meant it. Christ, the guy was good.

He turned to Ben and said, "Is there somewhere I should call if Molly does show up?"

"I'm pretty sure you have my number somewhere," Ben said grimly.

Bonniface let it pass. "Well, I'm off to the Academy. Good luck in your search."

It was seven A.M.—pretty damn early for a summer work-day.

Bonniface locked the door behind them, stepped around them, got in his car and drove away. Ben said, "Well, let's keep looking."

Sarann waited until Rodger drove off before joining them, and then they spread out across the grounds, calling the elusive cat. The river was presumably still off limits to Abby, so Ben offered to check out the shore himself. The ground went from wet to soggy to muddy to swamped, all well before Ben reached the dock on the riverbank; a cat would have to be half tadpole to get around comfortably in these conditions. Ben's slacks were already wet halfway up to his knees.

The dock was in a lot worse shape than the spiffy runa-

bout floating next to it. Ben was surprised that something
Bonniface owned would be in disrepair, but then he remembered the bureaucratic red tape involved in touching anything
on a shoreline; permits could have been in the works for
years.

Ben made his way back up the slope to the house, calling
"Here, kitty-kitty, here, kitty-kitty," and wondering what the
hell people, including him, saw in cats anyway. They were
nothing but aloof, perverse, picky, choosy, overly coy and
unjustifiably arrogant carnivores—and if Bonniface did anything to this one, Ben fully intended to cut off his nuts.

They hooked up in front of the house and Ben said, "I'd
better move the car somewhere else; no one will be able to
see it as they round that curve."

Abby had a thought. "Sometimes Molly goes over by that
shortcut we took that time? She likes to chase birds in one
of the people's yards. They have a potting shed; once I found
her curled up there when Mrs. Dickerson called to say she
had an orange-and-white cat and was it ours. And you can
park next to the shortcut in a space where hunters and fishermen sometimes leave their cars."

So that was the plan. They drove a little way down the
road to the shortcut, Ben parked his car, and they checked
with Mrs. Dickerson. The news was good; Ben was amazed
at how relieved he was to learn that the cat had been there
not long before, but took off into the woods across the way
when Mrs. Dickerson, a bona fide bird nut, dashed through
the rain to get to the shed for seed to top off her feeders.

Off they went, hunting for Molly. In what had become a
routine, they fanned out again, with Ben checking the houses
that backed on the shortcut and Abby and Sarann calling for
Molly at the edge of the woods. They were all soaked
through; and Ben, a believer in big breakfasts, was famished.
All because of a cat. Was it possible to feel any more miserable?

The answer to that, he learned, was yes.

*   *   *

Abigail flipped her hood back, even though the rain was still coming down. She was all wet, anyway, and the hood prevented her from seeing to the side when she turned her head. Her mother was searching her way to the left, and Abigail to the right, of Mrs. Dickerson's house in the middle of the shortcut. If only Molly would just show up! Then they could all go back to the Steppe Inn and get dry and get some food.

She felt better, knowing that Molly was near. But where? Abigail was almost at the road her house was on; she was running out of places to look. When she reached the road, she tried to see up and down it, but the rain made it hard to see; it kept getting in her eyes. Besides that, there was a curve right ahead.

She decided to go just past the curve; from there she could see a fair distance until the next curve, before her stepfather's house. When she got to the first one, she climbed a high embankment above it, slipping and sliding as she clawed at the weeds and grass growing on it. From her vantage point at the top she could see pretty well, except for the rain.

No Molly in sight, but Abigail called her name over and over, anyway. Discouraged, she was about to turn and rejoin her parents when she saw her stepfather's car coming in her direction. It confused her; he was supposed to be on his way to the Academy, in the other direction. She crouched down, afraid that he might have seen her in her yellow rain gear, but the car stopped, right in the road. She watched as the driver's door opened and her stepfather got out and walked to the back of the car and then stooped down. She saw him stand up slowly, his back to her. He turned; he was holding her Molly! At least, it looked like Molly; Abigail only saw dark orange, no white; but the cat was all wet, and she was limp.

Was she hurt? She couldn't be—dead! Abigail didn't know what to do. She looked back toward the shortcut, but didn't see her mother or father. By the time she ran back to them and then they all went to the house . . . no, she had to be with Molly. Molly needed her.

She made the decision to scramble down the embankment and run toward the car, waving her arms at her stepfather as he was throwing a U-turn. She knew that he was angry at her mother. But he wasn't angry at her, and *nobody* could be angry at Molly.

Sarann knew that it was never one thing that created a crisis, but always two or three. They were all in the woods and looking for Molly because of a snowballing chain of events: Abby had left the front door open; Ben had kicked the sitting room door open; Sarann had been in a state of high alarm; and—the final straw that had sent Molly bolting—the mirror had fallen with a thunderous crash and shattered.

Cats did *not* like noise and chaos. The woods were quiet. If Molly was there, they might not find her for a while. She was a great mouser; there was good shelter; it was summer and, despite the rain, fairly mild. What more did she need? Sarann was calling in her most soothing voice, but no cat was responding. She ventured farther and farther into the pines, following a couple of the paths that crisscrossed the area.

"Moll-leee . . ." Please, she thought. *Come to me.*

Molly was on the back seat. She wasn't dead, Abby's stepfather said. But Abby could see that she was definitely hurt. There was blood on her hind paw.

"Her eyes were open when I picked her up," her stepfather said as he pulled into the carriage house. "How does she look now?"

"Her eyes are closed," Abigail said. "They're closed!"

"I think she's all right, Abby, just scared. Her paw didn't look too bad. We'll take her inside and look her over."

"How will we know if she's okay? How can we tell?"

"I can tell, Abby. Have you forgotten I'm a doctor?" he joked. "I'll carry her in; you get the doors."

Inside the house they laid Molly right on the kitchen table. Her eyes were open now, but she did look scared. Abigail's stepfather looked Molly over very, very gently, lifting first one paw and then another. Then he felt along her stomach.

"Pet her gently, Abby; scratch her under her chin," he said soothingly. "So she'll know everything's going to be fine."

"Can I?" she asked, surprised and more than happy to do it. The vet never let Abigail handle Molly while he was examining her.

"She's purring!"

"Well, why not? She's back home, where it's safe and where she belongs. I don't think she was hit by a car, though; she might just have tangled with another animal. I'm glad I noticed her. She must have been lying in the ditch and started creeping out of it when she heard you calling her from on top of the berm."

"You saw me there?" Abigail asked, surprised.

"Abby. Of *course* I did. You were high up, wearing a yellow slicker. Kind of hard to miss, wouldn't you say?"

"Yeah . . . I guess so."

But then why didn't he stop and wait for her? She didn't like that at all.

Her stepfather must have been able to tell that from her face, because he said, "You don't seem very grateful that I found your cat. Don't I get a thank-you?"

Abigail kept petting Molly, reassuring her that nothing was wrong, that she was with people who loved her. It bothered her that Molly was so limp.

"Thank you," she murmured to her stepfather.

"Not much enthusiasm there, Abby," he said in a soft and different voice. "Can't you do a little better than that?"

She looked up at her stepfather in confusion. "Better? You mean, like, thank you very much?"

"Oh, Abby," he said with a disappointed sigh. "That's what you'd say if someone held a door open for you at the post office. I've done more for you than that; you know I have."

Abigail looked down at her cat again and said nervously, "It's okay, Molly, really." To her stepfather she acknowledged in a mumble, "You've given me lots of things."

"With many more to come," he said. He turned away from Molly, which didn't seem right, and he said to Abigail, "All I ask is a hug in return."

He held his arms out to Abigail, who had no choice but to step inside the circle he made with them. He caught her very tightly and pressed her cheek against his chest with one hand. "Oh, Abby, Abby," he said in almost a moan. "Oh, my darling Abby . . ."

With one eye open, Abigail was watching Molly so that she wouldn't fall off the table if she got dizzy or something. Abigail tried not to think of how scared she was, because she knew that Molly was scared, too, and someone had to stay calm between them.

It was up to Abigail to stay calm. For Molly's sake.

"She's not with you?"

Ben's heart shot up to his throat. "I thought you two were together."

"We went in separate directions along the shortcut," Sarann said. "We were supposed to meet back in the middle."

"Oh, Jesus. All right, retrace her direction. I'll drive back to the house, just in case she wandered off that way."

"I'll go with you."

"Sarann, no; if she's here, we don't want her wondering where we've gone. I'll come right back if I don't find her."

Sarann said, "Hurry," and immediately began to jog in the direction that Abby had gone.

The road that Tidewater was on was as picturesque as all get out, but it was all curves and knolls; Ben knew that it would be the easiest thing in the world to run someone over if he took a curve at all carelessly. He slowed to a crawl as he passed by Tidewater. He knew that Sarann had forfeited their keys, so Abby couldn't be inside, checking to see if her stepfather had been lying about Molly; but he rolled down the window, anyway, to get a better look. No Abby; no Molly.

Aware that his heart was still stuck in his throat and realizing that that was the price of fatherhood, he continued a little farther down the road for no other reason than that they hadn't yet canvassed that area.

And then, when he was half a block away from Tidewater, his world turned upside down and inside out with dread: he remembered that the doors to the carriage house were now closed.

They'd been open when Rodger Bonniface left that morning, and now they were closed. Closed. To hide his car, which was inside. Or maybe not, maybe not; maybe Bonniface had just gone out for bagels, driven back, and parked his car in the garage and out of the weather, just as any normal person might do.

Well, I'm off to the Academy.

Oh, hell. Oh, Jesus. Ben slammed on the brakes, backed into a drive, and took off for Tidewater, his tires spinning on the wet, leaf-strewn surface of the road. If Bonniface was there, then Abby was, too. Every instinct Ben had was now locked on that inevitability. Bonniface had her. He had Ben's and Sarann's little girl.

"You know what goes really well with a hug?" Abigail's stepfather asked her. "A kiss."

Abigail's face was fire-hot and her heart was pounding all over the place. She had never had someone press his parts up against her before, least of all a grownup, and even if it *was* through her shorts, it felt totally shocking. She shook her head and without looking up at her stepfather, said, "No. No kiss."

"One. One kiss. And then I'll let you go."

"No, please, no kiss," she said, trying to back out of his arms.

He held her tight. "Abby, *one*. That's all. One."

Her eyes were filling with tears. She looked up at him and could hardly make out his features as she begged, "Please don't," because she knew the kiss would not be on the cheek.

"One."

It was hard to breathe. Abigail closed her eyes as if she were about to be slapped and waited to be done with the ordeal. One kiss, that's all he wanted, and then she could take Molly and go.

She felt his lips, which seemed huge and mushy-soft, on top of hers and then, completely unexpectedly, she felt his tongue stick deep into her mouth and slither around like a snake.

She wrenched away from him in shock; no one had ever kissed her like that before, not even her boyfriend Tommy.

"Why did you *do* that?" she said, wiping her lips with the back of her arm. It was so totally gross.

"It was nice, Abby, come on, wasn't it? It was sexy . . . different . . . wasn't it?"

He kept asking her that, and he wasn't even hearing her when she kept shaking her head and saying, no, no, no every time.

"Abby, I've loved you so long . . . since the first day I saw you. You were so young then, but now you're not, you're a young woman now . . ."

She was so scared. He was scaring her so much. She wanted her mother, her father, where were they? Molly was sick, Abigail had to stay with her. Why wasn't someone coming for them?

"Abby, sweetheart . . . I'll give you everything," her stepfather said, getting closer and closer. "Everything you ever wanted, if only you'll stay with me . . . please, please stay . . ."

He was like in a trance.

"No! You're creepy," she blurted. "You're disgusting! You give me the creeps!"

His face turned dark and ugly. He lunged at her, but she turned and escaped through the French doors into the yard and ran as fast as she could away from the house, down to the river in the pouring rain, away from him as fast as she could, thinking about Molly, would she be all right. She wanted to wipe her tongue with her shirt, but she couldn't stop to do it. She had to run, had to run away. She was wearing plastic clogs; she lost one, then the other. Barefoot now, she slipped and fell on the grass, got up, ran even faster, hysterical that he was going to catch up to her. The grass got wetter, muddier. The mud oozed between her toes.

She had promised her mother that she would never, ever go down to the dock alone but here she was, she could see it in front of her, with her stepfather's boat tied to the float that was level with it, that's how high the river was. Her heart was pounding and her side hurt, but she didn't stop; she kept going until she was on the dock. The river was up to it, slopping over the boards. She hadn't been in a boat since she was a little girl, but it was her only chance; she untied one of the lines with shaking hands and dropped it in the boat so that it wouldn't get caught on the propellor, just like she'd seen in the movies. She didn't know how to run a boat, but she'd seen movies. You turned the key and then it was like a car, like bumper cars, it was all the same. You just steered it.

She looked up the slope toward Tidewater and there was her stepfather, sprawled on the ground. He had fallen too! If only he couldn't get up, if only he'd broken an ankle! She ran to untie the second line but the rope was wet, it was hard to undo. She struggled and struggled and then at last it was free. But the boat was pointed downstream already, and the river was pulling it hard. The river pulled the second line right out of her hands; the boat took off with no one in it!

She watched it with horror, trying to decide if she should jump in after it, try to catch up with it . . . but she was afraid. The river was moving too fast, the boat was like someone had turned on the motor and was escaping—only it wasn't her.

She was still staring at the boat in disbelief when she felt her stepfather's arms wrap around her chest tightly from behind. And then she knew: she should have taken her chances in the river.

Ben saw Abby struggling in Bonniface's arms, and something in him snapped. With a howl of fury he took a leap onto the dock and in three or four strides was nearly on top of them—until a rotted plank gave way and his right leg plunged up to his thigh in the river below. The pain was searing, the shock, acute; but he pulled himself free and hobbled to his feet, confronting them.

Abby said, "*Dad*," in a wail of terror and reached out to him with her one free arm.

It was the wrong thing to say, to do. It infuriated Bonniface. He yelled, "You little bitch!" and, still holding her by the shoulders, hurled her off the dock and into the raging river.

In a flash Ben was diving into the river after her, but not before knocking Bonniface down in reflexive fury. He saw

Abby's yellow jacket appear, disappear, appear again as he fought to keep up with her, fought to keep track of her. She didn't struggle, she wasn't Kelly, she had no devil to engage. He saw her trying to keep her head up, almost going with the flow, just there for the ride. Ben began fighting his way into deeper water to the left of her, trying to catch a faster current, going for the passing lane. He was a good swimmer, never better or faster than he was then; he caught her, lost her, caught her again.

She saw who he was and she didn't struggle. Her eyes were huge, but she let him take charge. He got his arm around her and they rolled down the river together, Ben holding on to her, Abby paddling like a cocker spaniel and keeping her head above water. But he was getting tired; the river was moving too fast, and with his burden he couldn't just hang a right and head for shore. For the first time, the thought occurred to him that they might not make it—but if not, it would be together. He wasn't going to let go.

Maybe it was his mental yelp of despair that got the attention of Divine Providence and made Him sit up and do something: because Ben saw, coming up at a bend, the spiffy runabout that had been tied to the dock at Tidewater. It was caught in the upper branches of a huge maple tree that had been dislodged by the rain and had fallen parallel to and a little in the river, its roots upended and pointing to heaven and to hell.

"Grab the boat," Ben just had time to say to Abby, and then they were approaching it as a whizzing speed, one shot only, do or die.

Ben reached for the tow ring, missed, died a small death, and grabbed at the stern line that was trailing downstream.

He caught it. Caught it, and held onto it for both of their lives, with Abby doing a backup number on it. With a prayer of thanks, Ben said, "Hold on; we're going to try to get in the boat."

Easier said than done. Their extra weight dislodged the boat from its tenuous hold on the tree and suddenly they were all three on the road again, on the road down the river of hell. Ben couldn't believe it: just when he'd begun to believe.

The boat slid downstream, first athwartships to the current's flow, then straightening out a little so that the bow was nosing downriver. Behind it Ben and Abby trailed like waterskiers, except without the skis. Ben had one arm around Abby; his other arm was killing him. Hold on, hold on, just hold on, he kept telling her over and over.

Their river odyssey came to an end at the next big bend, where another tree, this one with many bare branches, had lodged in the middle of the river. The runabout rolled into the trunk bow first, then snugged up alongside it as neatly as if it had docked itself.

"Okay! Let's try this again!"

Ben hovered below his daughter, ready to catch her if she fell in her scramble aboard; but she was a nimble kid, especially for a waterlogged one, and after some scrapes, slips, and bruises, they were both safely aboard and catching their breath.

Since they didn't have a key for the engine, that's where they stayed, safe and sound, until Sarann showed up with three firefighters in an emergency rescue boat. Her joy at seeing them was the biggest high that Ben had ever known. It was something to be that loved; he couldn't imagine how he'd ever survived without it.

After a reunion in the rescue boat and emotional hugs all around, Ben said, "How did you know where to find us?"

"I went around to the back of the house and saw you dive in after Abby," Sarann said. "As soon as I saw you latch on to her, it was the oddest thing . . . I knew it would be okay. I ran back to the house and I called the police, and they coordinated with the rescue boat."

"Was Molly on the kitchen table, Mom?"

Sarann looked puzzled by the question. "On the table? No, on one of the chairs, cleaning herself. She has a cut on her paw; we'll have to get it tended to."

Ben turned Sarann aside and said in a low undertone, "Did the bastard cut and run, then?"

Sarann was even more puzzled by his question than by Abby's. She said, "You didn't see him? He got back to his feet after you knocked him down and then—I don't know how it happened, because he was standing there and looking downriver as I was running toward the dock—his knee suddenly just . . . buckled. He lost his balance and fell off the edge of the dock; another boat is looking for him now."

Abby, eavesdropping shamelessly, said, "Mom! He fell when he was chasing me. I'll bet he twisted something!" She looked delighted with her own deductive powers.

Rodger in the river: how profoundly fitting.

It would have been an exaggeration to say that Ben felt thigh-slapping joy; but he did feel a surge of hope that maybe there was a God in heaven, after all. He was quiet after that, and so was Abby, looking bedraggled in a gray blanket. Aftershock, he supposed. He wondered how many years of therapy Abby was going to have to go through before she got past all of this.

But then he took heart; he thought, maybe none. As the crew was scanning the shore, he was watching Sarann murmuring soothing nothings to Abby, and Abby obviously responding to the comforting sound of her mother's voice alone. And he couldn't help thinking that somehow, in some way that no male could ever know or understand, the healing had already begun.

The rain had all but stopped by the time the rescue boat let them off at the first sturdy dock they passed so that the firefighters could join the search for Rodger Bonniface. He was no ordinary citizen, after all.

They weren't that far from Ben's car, still parked behind

the Mercedes. There would be inquiries, there would be allegations, there would be a long, hard road ahead . . . but for now, there was only a short walk through someone's riverfront property to get to the road that would take them, for the last time, to Tidewater.

Ben and Sarann, and Abby still wrapped in her blanket, began the short trek back. Sarann said to their daughter, "So I guess you've officially got your sea legs now, huh?"

Abby nodded. "The boat *was* kind of fun, Mom." She added with a smile at her father, "Even though we weren't actually in it for most of the time."

"I think," said Ben, "that our next boat ride is gonna be on a Disney cruise ship."

"Is that a promise?" Abby asked instantly.

"In stone."

Ben took her hand in his, and he threw his arm around Sarann and pulled her closer for a kiss, and the three of them walked through the rain-soaked grass, headed for high ground.

Epilogue

"SO—WHAT DO you think?" Ben asked, propping a half-broken, weathered picket back into an upright position. "We should be safe from a yuppie invasion for a few years, no?"

Sarann was unhooking the Century 21 sign from a post that was standing at a lopsided angle after being in the ground through the long, wet summer. She said, "If they come, we'll sell and move on. I think we can keep one step ahead of them."

She slapped the sign idly against her jeans as she and her husband stood gazing at her first home, his first home, their first home ever. It was a sweet little Cape, surrounded by other Capes and ranches and just-plain-shacks in the entirely unfashionable but safe and friendly town of Fairhaven, Massachusetts. They lived on a peninsula now, not quite on shorefront but close enough for Sarann: they could see the ocean from one of the bedroom dormers.

Which is where Abby was right now, with Molly, both of them looking down at Ben and Sarann from the deep windowsill in the so-called master bedroom (it was a little less tiny than the tiny bedroom). "Mom, Dad, this is so cool. I see a fishing boat heading back to New Bedford. It's like being in Gloucester."

"Except without the emotional baggage," Ben murmured to Sarann as he slipped his arm around her and pulled her close.

Sarann loved the way Ben couldn't seem to be near her without touching her, holding her, drawing her near, because she felt the same way about him. It was her idea of what a husband and wife should be.

"I'm definitely thinking, plain black shutters," she said.

He grinned. "What? Instead of that cheery pink?"

"And I'm thinking, pale gray shingles."

"You want to paint out that interesting shade of—what would you call that, anyway?"

"Puce?"

"That's a good word for it; are you making it up?"

"No. There really is a puce, and that really is it. I'm thinking—"

"You know what *I'm* thinking?" he said with a sideways look at her.

Actually, Sarann had a pretty good idea, but she said demurely, "That it won't be any work at all to make me flower boxes for all the front windows?"

He turned and encircled her and, heedless of whatever new neighbors were peeking through their front windows, gave her a long, slow kiss in their tiny front yard.

He tipped his forehead onto hers. "Ah, Sarann, Sarann, what you do to me," he murmured.

"Can our neighbors tell?" she said, raising the Century 21 sign over his groin. "That's all I'm worried about."

He laughed and said, "Wicked woman, come to bed with me," then nibbled her lower lip to try to clinch the deal.

Abby yelled down, "Hey, you two—get a room."

"Hey, yourself; you're *in* it," Ben shot back.

"Okay, okay; I know when I'm not wanted. I'm going to go unpack *my* room—the one *without* the view. C'mon, Molly."

Sighing happily, Sarann said, "Let's get to work," except that she wouldn't consider it work at all, but one of the real moments of joy in her life.

Along with the morning she had given birth to Abigail.

Along with the afternoon she had married Ben McElwyn.

Along with the evening, three weeks ago, that two lines had shown up in her pregnancy kit.

They walked inside to freshly painted rooms filled with cardboard boxes and crammed with a charming assortment of pine and oak vintage pieces that Sarann had been steadily acquiring over the past few months. Iron lamps, rag rugs, hooked rugs, a sewing table and even a weathervane—all sat in confusion, waiting for their assigned places.

"Let's hear it for EMC stock," said Sarann, surveying their booty. "Weren't you clever to buy into it, all those years ago."

"Yeah. Too bad I didn't have more money to do it with, though," Ben said. "You deserve a great big house on the shore."

"Bite your tongue," she said. "Do you want someone mistaking us for yuppies?"

"Fat chance," Ben said. He plugged in a floor lamp and turned it on, and the dining room walls glowed a friendly, sociable yellow. "Listen, I don't want you going overboard with the unpacking," he warned Sarann. "You just point and I'll do the lifting."

"Fine with me," she agreed.

After a special arrangement with the seller, they had worked night and day for two weeks making the inside shine. New paint, refinished floors, new tile in the bathroom, even new fronts on the kitchen cabinets—looking back, Sarann could honestly say that every minute of it had been fun. Now it was going to be even more fun.

But not as long as a particular box remained piled on top of some others in the dining room.

She pointed to it and said, "You can start by lifting that one and taking it down to the basement. I wish we could set it on fire instead," she confessed.

On the box was scrawled a single word: TIDEWATER.

In the box, in multiple files, was a mounting record of a class-action suit against the estate of Rodger Bonniface and

Faxton Academy, including a newspaper with a headline that Sarann would never be able to forget:

HEADMASTER OF FAXTON ACADEMY DROWNS; FOUND TRAPPED UNDER FALLEN TREE IN ESSEX RIVER.

Sarann had not wanted to have any part of a suit against Rodger's estate; but after the inquiry into the circumstances immediately before his death, several past students of Faxton Academy had come forward to say that Rodger had molested them as well. After that, Sarann had no choice. It wouldn't have been fair to the others not to lend their support.

"*Do* you think his family knew?" she asked Ben for the thousandth time.

For the thousandth time, Ben said, "Yes. James, so-called expert on child abuse, would have looked like a moron if anyone had found out about Rodger. His book would have bombed; that's what bought his silence. Okay, maybe he couldn't swear to it. But he suspected. As for their mother? Yes, again. She's a cunning old woman. She knew."

"But we'll never be able to prove it."

"We'll see what happens at the trial," Ben said, dismissing the subject for the thousandth time. He had that ability: not to dwell.

He slipped a sweatband over his black hair and said, "So, lady—where d'ya want da box?"

"In a corner somewhere," Sarann said. "And would you face the label to the wall, please?"

"Your wish, yadda yadda," he said, grinning, and he lifted it up and walked out with it.

He made her smile. He always made her smile. When he came back up the stairs, she was waiting for him at the landing; she threw her arms around him and kissed him.

He savored it and stole one or two more before murmuring, "And to what do I owe this pleasure?"

"To the fact that you give it so well. I do love you, Ben McElwyn," she said, pulling him back down to her for another kiss. "I do love you."

SAFE HARBOR

Antoinette Stockenberg

USA TODAY BESTSELLING AUTHOR OF
A CHARMED PLACE AND KEEPSAKE

A BEAUTIFUL CON WOMAN has brought her latest scheme to the quiet charm of Martha's Vineyard, thereby wreaking havoc with several lives. Talented local artist Holly Anderson has a vested interest in exposing this conniving vixen who brazenly seduced her father into a scandalous affair and a reckless game of theft, blackmail and possible murder. Then there's Sam Steadman, a man with a few secrets of his own. The darkly handsome photographer has come to the island to track down the thief who stole the only worthwhile possession his parents owned. Soon it's clear that Sam and Holly are after the same woman. And as lives and hearts collide, they've got to decide if they're enemies or allies, strangers . . . or something much, much more.

"Antoinette Stockenberg is pure magic."
—Susan Elizabeth Phillips

"Stockenberg is a fresh, exciting voice. Her writing is delicious!"—Jayne Ann Krentz

"Stockenberg takes her place alongside LaVyrle Spencer as a writer of depth and perception."
—*Under the Covers Book Reviews*

AVAILABLE WHEREVER BOOKS ARE SOLD
FROM ST. MARTIN'S PAPERBACKS

SH 3/01

KEEPSAKE

Antoinette Stockenberg

USA TODAY BESTSELLING AUTHOR OF *A CHARMED PLACE*

KEEPSAKE, Connecticut, is a quaint, peaceful town—a cozy haven for families, friends, and old memories. Then Quinn Leary returns, reopening a scandal the town would rather forget—the murder of a popular high school girl fifteen years ago. Quinn has come back to clear his father's name and right the wrongs of the past. Olivia Bennett doesn't realize it but she has been waiting for this moment . . . for the return of the only man she has ever loved. Soon family secrets, shattered dreams, and fierce rivalries come together in powerful and unexpected ways, offering a once-in-a-lifetime chance for new beginnings . . .

"Stockenberg takes her place alongside LaVyrle Spencer as a writer of depth and perception."
—*Under the Covers Book Reviews*

"Stockenberg [is destined to become] a major voice in women's fiction." —*Publishers Weekly*

AVAILABLE WHEREVER BOOKS ARE SOLD
FROM ST. MARTIN'S PAPERBACKS

K 3/01